Maverick

DAVID GLEDHILL

Copyright © 2015 David Gledhill

Published by DeeGee Media Ltd

All rights reserved.

ISBN-13: 978-1507801895

ISBN-10: 1507801890

This book is dedicated to all those who gave their lives to secure the right of the people of the Falkland Islands to choose their own way of life.

CONTENTS

	Prologue. 21 May 1982, Rio Gallegos Airbase, Argentina.	5
1	Two Years Later in the Officers' Mess Bar, RAF Brize Norton.	13
2	Villa Reynolds Airbase, Argentina, 1984.	21
3	Aboard an RAF C-130 Hercules Freighter in the South Atlantic.	23
4	Rio Gallegos Airbase, Argentina.	37
5	RAF Stanley, the next day.	41
6	Mount Alice, West Falklands.	51
7	Rio Gallegos Airbase.	55
8	Government House, Port Stanley.	61
9	The Upland Goose Hotel, Port Stanley.	65
10	Mount Alice, West Falklands.	71
11	Runway 26, RAF Stanley.	75
12	Near Villa Reynolds Airbase, Argentina.	81
13	Operations Wing, RAF Stanley.	83
14	Villa Reynolds Airbase, Argentina.	121
15	The Upland Goose Hotel, Port Stanley.	125
16	The Intelligence Section, Villa Reynolds Airbase.	131
17	No. 751 Signals Unit, Mount Alice, West Falkland.	139

18	Quick Reaction Alert, RAF Stanley.	143
19	Government House, Port Stanley.	147
20	Rio Gallegos Airbase.	151
21	Government House, Port Stanley.	155
22	The Argentinian Naval Base, Trelew.	159
23	Government House, Port Stanley.	163
24	The Globe Hotel, Port Stanley.	167
25	Over the Bahia Grande off the Argentinian coastline.	169
26	The Air Defence Operations Centre, Buenos Aries.	175
27	Over the Bahia Grande off the Argentinian coastline.	179
28	On the High Seas, West of the Falkland Islands.	183
29	Over East Falkland.	191
30	Operations Wing, RAF Stanley.	199
31	No. 23 Squadron Crewroom, RAF Stanley.	203
32	Government House, Port Stanley.	207
33	Headquarters British Forces Falkland Islands, East Falkland.	211
34	Overhead Mount Pleasant Airfield.	213
35	The Argentinian Military Cemetery, East Falkland.	217
36	Government House, Port Stanley.	221
37	MI6 Headquarters, Century House, London.	223
38	Government House, Port Stanley.	229
39	Over East Falkland.	231

40	Approaching Falkland Sound.	235
41	Black Eagle Camp outside RAF Stanley.	255
42	Approaching the Falkland Islands Protection Zone.	259
43	Mount Tumbledown, East Falkland.	263
44	Over East Falkland.	267
45	Heritage Hall, Port Stanley.	281
46	Black Eagle Camp outside RAF Stanley.	287
47	The Hospital, Port Stanley.	295
48	Mount Pleasant Airfield, East Falkland.	297
49	Port Stanley Jail.	301
50	MI6 Headquarters, London.	303
51	The Magistrate's Court, Port Stanley.	305
52	Port Stanley Jail.	309
53	The Coastel Accommodation Barge, Port Stanley Harbour.	317
54	Government House, Port Stanley.	321
	Author's Note.	325
	Glossary.	327
	About the Author.	332
	Other Books by the Author.	333
	Map of the Falkland Islands.	334
	Stanley Airfield.	335

DAVID GLEDHILL

PROLOGUE

RIO GALLEGOS AIRBASE, ARGENTINA, 21 MAY 1982

The Skyhawk fighter-bombers of Gruppo 5 led by Captain Pablo Carmendez rolled down the main runway at Rio Gallegos. Deployed forward from Villa Reynolds to be closer to their targets in the Falkland Islands, the pilots had been flying constantly since operations began on 1st May. They were now only 400 miles away across the cold waters of the South Atlantic.

The missions he had flown over the preceding days were the culmination of years of training since that first tentative solo flight. Operations against the British Task Force had been taxing, not only because of the extreme low altitude at which they flew but also due to the tenacious response from the British forces. The opening exchanges had been ferocious and already they had lost aircraft and crews to surface-to-air missiles. The analysts in the intelligence cell at Rio Gallegos expected the Task Force to land tonight and it looked like San Carlos Water in Falkland Sound would be the beachhead. If that was the case his targets would already be moving into position and vulnerable to attack. What he could not yet know was that today would not follow the norm even by the crazy standards set since the invasion just a few weeks before.

Today's mission would begin with a rendezvous with one of the precious KC-130 Hercules air-to-air refuelling tankers just off the coast where he would top off his fuel tanks before leaving Argentinean airspace. His targets lay in the heart of The Malvinas and he would need every drop of extra fuel that he could squeeze in.

The tanker join was uneventful and the first four aircraft took their allotted offload. With a ground abort reducing the 6-ship to five, another Skyhawk headed home after a system failure preventing the precious fuel from reaching the tanks. With the Malvinas Islands at the limit of the Skyhawk's range a full load was vital to give them a semblance of a combat reserve. Without it, they had no margin to counter an attack from a Sea Harrier let alone engage in air combat. Even fully fuelled, if they were tied up by the Sea Harriers, they may still have to divert to the airfield at Puerto Argentino just outside the Capital. Carmendez had toyed with the idea of a planned refuelling stop but, even though it was in Argentinean control, the problems of shipping fuel to the airfield meant that it was a precious commodity. The aircraft based at the forward airfield needed every drop of jet fuel that could be shipped in by sea to keep their own operations rolling. Even the transport aircraft which flew in every day to keep the garrison resupplied were dissuaded from refuelling during their short stay. The resupply flights set off from the mainland with full tanks and returned on fumes leaving the deployed aircraft with the benefit of the forward supplies.

The formation rolled off the tanker into the rising sun setting an easterly course for the distant islands. Initially, staying at high level to save precious fuel, they would descend to low level once closer to attempt to approach below the defender's radars. If Carmendez thought his troubles were over, he was to think again many times that day. The coded message from his wingman told him that another of his pilots had a fuel problem. The drop tanks fitted to the Skyhawk were, stubbornly, refusing to transfer the vital cargo. He quickly ran through the options. It was probably another sticky transfer valve, cold-soaked at altitude during the tanking. It might clear as they let down to lower altitude but could he take the risk? He could have the pilot jettison the external tanks and press on but that was risky as part-filled drop tanks could be unpredictable. If one separated cleanly but the other stayed attached to the wing it meant a certain loss of control. Even if both came off, fuel shifting within the tanks might cause a wayward tank to strike the airframe as it tumbled in the airflow and airframe damage was a strong possibility. Much of the soul searching was wasted as, without the external fuel, his wingman would not have enough in reserve to recover to Rio Gallegos. Again he had no choice but to send him back. As the third Skyhawk broke out of formation and reversed its course heading for home, he looked over at the remaining jets. At least he still had a fighting formation and he dropped his two wingmen into a loose defensive "vic."

The range to the enemy coastline wound down steadily. Carmendez expected the tell-tale ping on his radar warning receiver at any moment which would tell him that the long range surveillance radars on the Royal Navy ships had detected him. Intelligence suggested that *HMS Brilliant*, an air defence picket ship, was stationed well to the west of the islands to provide advance early warning of air raids. It would be the first electronic sign that he was entering the combat area. With the long-range Type 996 radar aboard *HMS Brilliant*, he knew that he could press in to about 150 miles from the coast before he risked being detected. Fuel, fuel, fuel; it was the highest priority at this stage and, as he approached the crucial top of descent point, he glanced at the gauge yet again to make sure that his fuel burn was on track. So far it was predictable but with a Sea Harrier on his tail, it would be less so. Once the throttles hit the firewall it would run down at a crazy rate and he would have to separate from the fight quickly or die. There were no diversions on the long sea track between the islands and the mainland and the South Atlantic Ocean was cold and unforgiving in winter. As he looked down at the heavy swell and the angry wind-blown crests of the waves, he had no desire to see whether his single man dinghy snug in its pack in his ejection seat would protect him from the elements and keep him alive.

He snatched the control column hard to the left and right waggling his wings as a signal to his formation that he was beginning the descent. He had deliberately not transmitted the instruction over the radio knowing that sensors on the British ships would detect any transmissions. Why give more warning than was needed? As the jet dropped towards the sea he watched the altimeter as it slowly wound down. By the time the formation passed to the north of Weddell Island off West Falkland, the height was showing well below 250 feet on the radio altimeter and, as the formation finally entered Falkland Sound, he would drop even lower. The harsh forbidding coldness of the South Atlantic gave way to the scrub of West Falkland which flashed past the wingtip as the trailing pair, just a mile behind Carmendez, bracketed the settlement at Fox Bay. He had been briefed that he could expect to find the British landing zones and, most importantly the crucial landing craft, in the lee of the hills surrounding San Carlos Water. He also knew that more warships would be spread out down Falkland Sound and make attractive if rather more hostile targets. The troop ships were the real prize laden with their personnel and stores and, until the landing craft disembarked their precious cargo, they would be vulnerable. As he dropped into the shallow valley, later dubbed "A-4 Alley" by the defenders, the valley sides gave protection against visual detection by the air defence forces and he allowed himself to relax a little. His 3-ship would be in the gulley for only a few scant minutes flying at 100 feet above the ground but during that time would be almost undetectable.

As he neared his expected target area he popped up over the ridgeline into the Sound and, rounding East Head, headed north east into the centre of the combat zone. He eased the jet back down towards the wave tops, the radio altimeter bleeping occasionally as it tickled the bug set just below 100 feet. Almost straight away, Carmendez saw a ship appear in his gunsight and turned hard towards to set up an attack. Closing fast, he saw that it was not a warship but a large white freighter, the *Rio Carcarana*, disabled in an attack by British Harriers some days earlier. The freighter was already listing and would not be sailing again. In the heat of the moment, he failed to warn his wingman and Ensign Carmona, an inexperienced first tourist in the second Skyhawk, released his bombs on the stricken freighter. Frustrated, Carmendez ordered his wingman to return to base with no point in exposing the young pilot to the heavy defences when he had no ordnance to drop. With his bombs gone and only his gun remaining, a strafe pass would be folly against such heavily defended ships.

There was no longer any concern over using the radio now that bombs were falling and, with only two jets remaining in his formation, he called his wingman into tight fighting wing. Easing over to the eastern side of the channel he looked for cover, hoping the terrain would help to shield his jet from the onslaught. He could almost sense the sights of the Rapier surface-to-air missiles coming to bear. As he approached Bahia Ruiz Puenente, almost immediately, he saw a frigate coming directly at him. It was not the ideal attack aspect but at least he would have the length of the ship to aim for. Had it been side-on the bombs might go short or long. With the length of the ship in his sights he had a decent sighting picture down the axis of attack, although with the narrow profile of the ship, it would mean his tracking would need to be very accurate. Left or right and the bombs would drop into the water alongside the warship so there was no margin for error.

He eased his jet even lower to give the British missile operators a harder tracking solution and gently eased the gunsight onto the hull of the ship. Waiting for the crosshairs in the sight to meet over the bow he pickled the weapons and felt the effect on the controls as they were released, immediately making his jet lighter. It was a conscious effort to prevent himself from climbing thereby placing his aircraft at greater risk.

Aboard the Amazon class frigate, the Captain had stood his crew down to a lower state of readiness fooled by a temporary lull and the quiet of Grantham Sound. There had been no advanced warning of the air attack and he was taking the opportunity to feed the crew and redistribute ammunition. The lull was to be short-lived as the lookout spotted the low flying Skyhawks and sounded the warning. Without airborne early warning radars a late contact was inevitable and the Skyhawk was already within 4000 yards and lining up for a bomb run before it was seen. The ship was underway sailing to its nominated station but making slow progress. In poor shape to fight and with few options the Captain called for increased revolutions on the engines and a hard over on the helm opening up to full speed to disrupt the attack profile.

In his cockpit Carmendez could not know that the ship was still reloading her Sea Cat missile system after an earlier engagement and all that the crew had to return fire were two 20mm Oerliken cannons and small arms. His attack should have been unchallenged and, up to that point, his tracking had been good but the unexpected turn by the frigate introduced fatal errors in his sighting calculations. As he pickled his bombs he knew that they would go badly astray. He flicked to guns and let off a short burst of cannon fire as he flashed over the rapidly manoeuvring vessel pulling up to disrupt the tracking solution. Immediately, pulling hard left in a violent wingover, he tried to avoid making himself predictable to the other air defence weapons deployed around the bay. Semi-inverted, he pulled back towards the sea just metres below, returning to the relative safety of ultra low level. As he looked over his left shoulder he saw splashes in the water. The first bomb fell just short and the second passed, harmlessly, over the superstructure and landed in the water beyond. Exasperated, he rolled level and set a course for home looking for his wingman, tense in case the defensive fire found its mark. The Skyhawk had dropped back into loose echelon formation and was closing rapidly as they hugged the terrain. The direct track home would take him north of Swan Island, over Chartres settlement and they would coast out over the Passage Islands.

Overhead, a pair of 800 Naval Air Squadron Sea Harriers had set up a visual combat air patrol over the Sound when they were vectored onto the egressing formation by the fighter controller aboard *HMS Brilliant*. Both pilots pushed the throttles forward picking up speed and descending to 1500 feet to get a better view of the surrounding area. At low altitude the Sea Harriers pulse radar was ineffective and, knowing that any attackers would be well below, they were reliant on the "Mark 1 Eyeball" for a visual pickup. As they passed East of Chartres they spotted the formation of Skyhawks at low level heading for home, tracking rapidly across the nose. The Sea Harriers broke hard towards and engaged.

Carmendez had eased south to avoid a settlement and had been distracted by the challenges of the navigation so he was late to spot the Sea Harriers as they dropped into his 6 o'clock. His wingman should have picked up the attack but was eerily quiet. As Carmendez called the defensive break it was apparent that the wingman had finally spotted the Sea Harrier dropping in rapidly. Carmendez reefed into the turn pulling up to look for safety in the puffy clouds above. The pair split, the pilots conscious that they had virtually no combat fuel to engage in any type of defensive manoeuvring let alone move onto the offensive. They needed every last drop to get back to Rio Gallegos and the cloud might be their only hope.

The wingman in the Sea Harrier formation was first to slot into a firing position on the trailing Skyhawk which was climbing fast. As the pipper came on, the Sidewinder chirp from the newly fitted AIM-9L Sidewinder sounded in his headphones and the pilot instinctively squeezed the trigger. Almost simultaneously, the formation leader acquired his own target and, finding himself perfectly placed, loosed off a Sidewinder at the leading Skyhawk which was looking for sanctuary in the cloud layer. The Sidewinder set off in its relentless pursuit, closing fast as it hit nearly three times the speed of sound in an instant.

The other Skyhawk was less fortunate. The shot had been taken in the heart of the envelope and the Sidewinder guided perfectly striking just aft of the canopy and breaking the fuselage like a match. Released into the airflow and instantly vaporised, the escaping aviation fuel turned into a deadly explosive mixture and ignited in a lethal fireball.

Carmendez cursed not for the first time that day. He should have stayed at low level and run. The Sea Harrier pilots were just as short of fuel as he was with the British aircraft carriers so far to the east. The ships would have to remain there if they were to avoid coming in range of the Excocet missiles fitted to the Super Etendards which meant that the Sea Harrier's combat persistence was also poor. His defensive break, looking for the protection of the thick cloud, was allowing the Sea Harrier pilot to arc his turn and close the range down for a missile shot. He pulled hard and felt the G come on, instantly pressing down on his body, forcing him into the hard canvas covered ejection seat pan. Straining to look over his shoulder, he saw the flash as a missile left the rails of the Sea Harrier in his 6 o'clock. If he could just reach that cloud it might disrupt the infra-red guidance of the Sidewinder that was coming his way but it would be too close for comfort. As he watched, the incoming missile suddenly spiralled out of control and headed towards the ground. He could not believe his luck as the guidance must have failed meaning he had survived the shot but for how long? Now where was that cloud? He could just make out his wingman in his peripheral vision but only long enough to recognise that the aircraft had turned into a flaming fireball and was tumbling uncontrollably. Where was the canopy he thought hopelessly. It should be separating and he should see the tell tale flash of an ejection but there was nothing. At that moment he popped into cloud and the sense of relief was palpable. He jinked a few degrees off heading trying to be unpredictable and to throw the Sea Harrier off his tail knowing that the pilot would be in behind trying to find him on radar. His best chance of escape was to get back down to low level as soon as he could but he knew that timing was critical. As the seconds ticked by his radar warner stayed silent and he began to hope that he had survived the encounter but it was over for his wingman. It seemed that his short life had just ended.

The wingman's name was Ensign Romero.

DAVID GLEDHILL

CHAPTER 1

TWO YEARS LATER IN THE OFFICERS' MESS BAR, RAF BRIZE NORTON

The two RAF officers leaned against the dark oak bar nursing a pint of beer. The room was remarkably quiet and only two others occupied the huge space. In the corner, an attractive woman sipped a glass of wine as she leafed through a magazine taking little interest in the muted conversation. A third man sat alone at the far end of the bar, pointedly, angled away from his drinking companions, clearly not interested in striking up a conversation. His glass of beer was very nearly full and it was some time since he had turned a page of his book. Unusually for the two aircrew, their own beer was going down slowly even though it would be their last pint of real British ale for the next four months.

Normally stationed in West Germany on the Dutch border and close to the town of Mönchen Gladbach, the aircrew were about to embark on a journey that would take them 8000 miles south to begin a detachment with the Phantom squadron at RAF Stanley in the Falkland Islands.

Mark "Razor" Keene, a strikingly handsome fighter pilot, fitted the stereotype. In his mid 20s born and raised in London, he had been flying the Phantom from the fighter base at RAF Wildenrath on the West German border for the last three years. He and his navigator, both bachelors, lived life to the full, their lives shaped by a punishing schedule of training exercises. Once or twice a month the base was locked down and the squadrons fell into a familiar training routine, the spectre of The Third World War, one which everyone hoped would never come, at the forefront of their minds. Carefully scripted scenarios in which the Soviet Union rolled over the Inner German Border and made the armoured push for the Channel ports were run, repeatedly, as Wildenrath and its 24 Phantoms attempted to stem the "Red Tide" flying combat air patrols over the West German countryside. Deterrence was the mantra which said that if the West, in the form of the North Atlantic Treaty Organisation was prepared, the Soviets would never come. Some were more cynical and said it was inevitable. The pace of life on the squadrons was crippling but "Work Hard; Play Hard" summed it up. For the next four months life would change, although from reports which had filtered back from the remote outpost, the work routine and lifestyle "Down South" was even more rigorous.

Jim "Flash" Gordon was the stocky, dark haired navigator his face sporting the classic 1980s Air Force moustache. His relationship with an air traffic control officer at Wildenrath was threatening his bachelorhood and seemed set to turn into something more serious. If things carried on in the same vein, an engagement ring would be on his shopping list in the near future. Hailing from Suffolk, his passion for aeroplanes had steered him towards the inevitable Air Force career. Flying had been his vocation and the prospect of a degree in Biology held few attractions when faced with the choice at high school. More reserved and more experienced than his gregarious pilot, he often found himself forced into the unlikely role of "Duty Adult" acting as the corporate conscience within the crew. What was becoming apparent to their peers was that since being paired up, they had gelled as a team. As their flying skills had developed in tandem they had earned a reputation on the Squadron as the ones to watch.

Razor and Flash lived in each other's pockets but enjoyed the single life. Although austere by modern standards, their rooms in the Officers' Mess on the West German base were merely a stepping-off point for exploring the temptations of Europe. Within the isolated but close-knit British community, displaced from home, a strong camaraderie pervaded. If they chose to stay put, most weekends involved parties and alcohol in equal amounts with a lively social scene being the happy norm. If the party life paled they headed south to the ski slopes and the bierkellers in Southern Germany or the beaches on the Mediterranean only a few hours away.

The weekend was a welcome diversion from the hard flying schedule from Monday to Friday. Working in such close proximity drove their lives. When the 400 knot "office", built by McDonnell Douglas in America and otherwise known as the Phantom, turned upside down it set different rules for both personal and professional relationships. As a pilot, Razor could drive the jet into the ground in seconds and such mistakes were, invariably, fatal as the time taken to recognise the error was often shorter than the time to impact. As a navigator operating the weapon system, Flash's role was to point two aircraft directly at each other, flying at combined closing speeds of 800 knots, and to pass as close as possible yet avoiding a collision. Most times the margin for error was measured in feet and could be particularly dramatic when flying in the appalling visibility typical over the North German Plain in West Germany. Such responsibilities generated either a deep trust or a severe mistrust and there was no middle ground. Fools were not suffered gladly but, once a bond formed, it was hard to break. The pair understood the formula, lived life on the edge and would be friends for life.

Both were coming towards the end of their time at Wildenrath and a posting to another unit back in UK would follow soon. For Razor that would probably be to another squadron. As a "First Tourist" he could expect another operational tour to round out his experience and add to his skills. For Flash, he had already completed a UK tour so he expected to become an instructor. He was hoping that he could persuade his "poster" that he deserved another flying job at RAF Coningsby converting crews to fly the Phantom. If not, his best hope was to go to RAF Finningley to train new navigators before they went off to their conversion units. He should hear his fate at any time and he was desperately hoping to avoid a ground tour. Being a simulator instructor, or even worse a staff officer, was anathema. Flying was his life and the thought of not climbing into the cockpit every day was unimaginable. Making sure his girlfriend followed him or, at least, stationed in the same part of the Country would be the next challenge.

For the next four months they would join 23 (Fighter) Squadron, known as the "Red Eagles", for a tour of duty "Down South" and life would change. Along with his navigator, Razor would trade the flat expanse of Nordrhein Westphalia for the rolling hills of the Falkland Islands.

Inevitably, their discussion focussed on the trauma of the upcoming flight scheduled for the following day. It was a necessary evil to endure and, until the new runway was opened at RAF Mount Pleasant, the C-130 transport aircraft provided the only speedy route onto the islands, the alternative being an even less appealing sea passage. With a cruising speed of just over 200 knots it travelled at half the speed of a commercial jetliner so it would be a long journey. Their early morning call was booked for 3 AM and the flight would take well over 12 hours for each of the two legs; maybe even longer if the winds were unfavourable. The long tracks over the ocean were daunting and, despite the numerous airfields peppering the first leg which could be used as interim stops to break up the 4000 mile journey to the equatorial Ascension Island, the trip was planned as a single hop. These safe havens would only be used in the event of a problem with the trusty C-130 Hercules freighter. Unfortunately, the leg south to the Falkland Islands was a similar distance but without the luxury of a staging base so the transport aircraft would spend most of its time over water many miles from the nearest land. Potential staging airfields were either unfriendly or in countries which were still sensitive about supporting flights into the disputed airspace around the islands. At a pinch they could divert to Brazil or Uruguay but their reception would be less than welcoming. As a consequence, Victor tankers flying from the staging base in Ascension Island, would refill the fuel tanks of the Hercules in mid-air giving it the extra range to reach the remote outpost.

"What have you picked up about Stanley?" probed Razor trying hard to lift the uncharacteristically gloomy atmosphere. "And I know all about the penguins," he said grinning.

"It sounds like quite a challenge according to the mates who did the last detachment," said his navigator. "Operating from 6000 feet of metal will be a bit different to the 8000 feet of concrete that we're used to. How did the check ride go with the squadron QFI?"

"Pretty good. The landing technique is a lot different but at least we're well prepared having operated from Wildenrath. The "rubs" are similar to the HASs in many respects so we're better off than the UK-based crews. At least we've done it before."

"Rubs" were portable aircraft shelters that had been built on the fighter dispersal at RAF Stanley to protect the Phantoms and their crews from the extremes of the South Atlantic weather. Although built from a heavy rubberised material and much less rugged than the concrete hardened aircraft shelters from which the aircrew operated at their home base, they provided a welcome shield from the elements. Despite the protection, the shelters set a number of operating challenges but the Germany-based crew was well used to the procedures and felt comfortable.

"It also helps that we normally fly with the gun in Germany. Apart from the extra weight of lugging a full load of missiles around with us every day, at least the jet will handle about the same."

"So what's the big difference in technique on landing?"

"The approach is at about the same speed but taking the cable every sortie sets its own challenges."

With only 6000 feet of landing distance available, the Phantoms of the fighter squadron made an arrested landing into the cable after every mission as the runway at Port Stanley was too short for normal operations. Nevertheless, as it was designed to operate from an aircraft carrier, the Phantom was ideally suited to the role. In its full operational fit the jet was easily able to get airborne from the short strip needing only about 4000 feet but it was somewhat short for a comfortable recovery, even after the fuel had burned off and despite the help of the brake parachute. No one wanted to park a Phantom in the overshoot at the end of the runway and an arrested landing was the best compromise.

"The technique is to pop the brake chute before landing at about 50 feet on short finals. That kills another 10 knots of speed so the arrival is a bit firm but not much worse than usual. We'll be landing heavy. From what the QFI said the norm is to land on with about 4000 lbs of fuel to give some holding fuel in case a squall blows up. The weather is unpredictable down there. The cable pull out is a lot shorter than we have at base; only 600 feet instead of 1300 so we'll stop a bit sharpish."

"I heard that. I've been warned to keep the straps tight on landing," Flash replied. "One nav was peering over his shoulder on landing and ended up listening to the radar as his head hit the scope with the rapid deceleration. I hear the arrestor crews are pretty good down there. Did you get the brief from the ex Navy carrier guys on how to get out of the wire easily?"

"Yeah, apparently, if you hold position on the power once you're in the cable, raising and lowering the hook a couple of times should disengage the wire and you can taxy clear. It didn't work at Wildenrath but the QFI reckoned that it's easier with the higher cable tension down south. Let's hope it works because, most often, the other Phantom is in the hold waiting for his turn to land on."

"The first familiarisation ride should be fun. We'll have quite a lot to pick up when we arrive and not much time to do it. I hear that the crew we're replacing leaves within a couple of days of us arriving. If we screw up we'll be unpopular. Mind you, the flying sounds good and the airspace is wide open. You can operate from ground level to the stratosphere without anyone complaining. It's a shame the Harriers have gone home to UK. I guess that means it'll be mostly mutual work with our own Phantoms. Has there been any activity from the mainland recently?"

"I heard the Argentinian "snooper" was around last week. QRA intercepted it about 30 miles inside the Protection Zone heading towards the islands. It was probably just a routine monitoring sortie but they prod away all the time trying to see if there are gaps in the radar coverage and listening in to all the radio frequencies. All part of the game I guess. I'm sure we'd do the same if the situation was reversed."

"Are you looking forward to it?"

"You bet I am. A change of scenery is always good and it'll give some challenges of its own. Can't say I'm looking forward to living on a barge for four months but I hear that the Coastel is reasonably comfortable. It's a lot better than the tents or the ship that was being used until recently."

"How has Julie taken it?"

"Oh she's fine I guess. It's the first time either of us have been on detachment for such a long stretch but it's part of the deal I suppose. We'll need to get used to it if she's going to stay in the Service."

"You're right there old mate. No one gets away without detachments nowadays. I had to laugh when the Boss said that the schedule had been cleared in the run up to TACEVAL. What he didn't say was the hooter was going to go off every other week. At least we're out of that for a few months. It's all live flying at Stanley so no Station exercises down there . . . . . yet!"

Their conversation drifted from the immediate to the more dramatic and, inevitably, they began to reminisce. The crew had become minor celebrities in the Phantom force some time earlier when, holding Battle Flight alert, a Soviet Su-27 pilot had defected across the Inner German Border bringing his radical new fighter aircraft with him. Although the "Flanker" had subsequently been rescued by a covert insertion team in a daring attack on the fighter base, much of the advanced high technology equipment had been removed and had been exploited later by western intelligence. At his debrief, the defector had provided a vast amount of information about the new aircraft and its development programme. The episode had been an intelligence coup.

"At least we can be sure that we won't have the same problem during the next four months. There's no chance of an Argentinian pilot wanting to defect to Port Stanley! I hear they didn't think much of it when they were stationed there in 1982. They couldn't wait to leave."

"That's a fact. Shame we didn't get chance to fly against a Skyhawk or a Mirage during our work-up phase. It might have been useful to have some firsthand experience of the opposition. I heard the Boss asked for the French to bring some Mirages up from Dijon to fly against but it didn't happen."

"Mind you, we both got to fly against it in the Combat Simulator. At least we know how the Skyhawk handles. I have to say, I thought it was quite a handy jet. It turns well and even at slow speed you can bring the nose to bear easily. It's a classic delta wing fighter and that engine has quite a bit of poke."

"A mate of mine flew the TA-4 on exchange in Florida. He talked a lot about its handling characteristics. It's a great little jet but we should be able to beat it easily if we fight it properly. It's only armed with rear hemisphere missiles so if we use our long stick and hit it with a Skyflash in the face, we win. No prizes for trying to stay and turn with it."

"Well the chances of us meeting one in the next four months is somewhere between slim and zero so I won't lose any sleep over it. I reckon the hardest target we'll get to fly against is Fat Albert!"

With a lull in the conversation the pilot's eyes scanned the still quiet bar taking in the man and woman who still seemed riveted by their reading material.

"What do you make of these other two," he whispered quietly.

"They have to be heading our way because there are no other flights out of here tomorrow morning. It's the wrong day for the Cyprus or the USA trooper flights so it has to be Stanley. I'm not sure why but neither of them look like military types to me. Have you spoken to them?"

"No, neither seemed to want to chat when I first walked in. Apart from a quick hello they've both been glued to their books. You arrived a few minutes after I did so I left them to themselves."

"Ah well, we'll find out on the Herc tomorrow."

Razor swilled the dregs of his pint around in the bottom of his glass.

"I'm not really looking forward to this flight tomorrow. So . . . . . we've got two choices. We can have another beer and hope that it dulls the pain or we can hit the sack now and guarantee that it will be even more painful."

"Mine's another Tetleys mate!"

CHAPTER 2

VILLA REYNOLDS AIRBASE, ARGENTINA, 1984

Major Pablo Carmendez had been brought up in a poor neighbourhood in Buenos Aires. From a working class family he had been determined at the earliest age to break the cycle and make his parents proud. Like his British counterparts, as a boy he had peered through the fence of the local air base watching the jets takeoff. A camera was out of the question on his meagre budget so his small notebook in which he recorded tail numbers was his only way to pursue his hobby. With growing promise at school the fact that he might actually realise his ambition of stepping into a fast jet cockpit became more of a possibility than a dream. After the award of a bursary from a local college he turned those dreams into reality when the grant funded a private pilot's licence at a local flying club. Once he had the chance to take the controls he showed natural aptitude that meant that his selection interviews to join the Argentinian Air Force were almost a fait accompli. The glowing reports from his flying instructor were enough to get him a place in flying training and, from then on, his abundant skills earned him rapid progress through the ranks.

His defining moment in his career had been the fight for the Malvinas and it had shaped his persona. Up to that time, life on the squadron had seemed almost idyllic. He and his military colleagues had been shielded from everyday pressures and under the military Junta life had been comfortable, insulated from the excesses inflicted on the ordinary people on the streets. In the difficult days following the conflict some of his friends had not fared as well. With the fall from grace of the military leadership their actions fell under closer scrutiny and any suggestion of radicalism attracted immediate attention bringing stresses of a different type. He had been distressed to see some of the once proud pilots on his squadron seeking treatment for mental health disorders and consigned to military hospitals. Post Traumatic Stress Disorder, or PTSD, had proved to be a menace maybe more effective than their opponents. Argentinian losses in the air had been high with over 70 aircraft being destroyed along with many of their crews. In his own fighter-bomber force, the losses to the Sea Harriers had been personal. Short of fuel and at the limits of combat endurance they had been unable to stay and fight over the islands. With more fuel things might have been different and, with better weapons, undoubtedly so. No one doubted the courage and skill of the combat pilots and crews but the outcome had been horribly one sided. He held a grudge and he still felt he had a debt to repay despite the passage of time.

As a line pilot on the squadron during the war he had led formations against the British Task Force and survived. His own Skyhawk had carried pennants recording successes against British warships earning him an enviable reputation amongst his peers. His ability to fly low and fast under fire had earned him decorations to add to his standing. His recent promotion to Major had come with an assignment as the flight commander on the 1st Fighter-Bomber Squadron at Villa Reynolds airbase and he now commanded new pilots coming to the front line, taking them under his wing and guiding them towards operational status. He was hugely respected and still regarded as one of the most capable pilots on the squadron. Operational experience still counted and his job now was to bring on the new generation while trying not to look back. There were plenty of challenges to keep him busy.

Looking out from his office window he could see the line up of Skyhawk fighter-bombers stretching out across the dispersal. It was the usual bustle of a military flight line with utility vehicles pulling trolleys loaded with bombs, gas bottles and spare wheels. His pilots might fly the jets but without the efforts of the technicians these aircraft were little more than expensive toys. A formation taxied out and he watched the canopies closing as they made their way to the runway threshold, the engines whining in the morning air. Flight line mechanics bustled around another jet which had just landed completing the after-flight inspection and preparing it for its next sortie. Another pair of pilots clutching their flying helmets and kneeboards made their way out to the dormant bombers ready to begin another training sortie. Although he couldn't see them, he knew that the weapons carriers under the wings held the practice bombs they would be dropping on the air-to-ground weapons range later that morning.

It was life as usual and he turned back to the file on his desk. As one of the squadron executives his life increasingly revolved around paperwork rather than a map and stopwatch in the cockpit. As he tried to concentrate on the summary in front of him his mind wandered. Tomorrow would be a difficult day as he had promised to meet with the family of a pilot lost during the conflict. It was a duty he should have fulfilled a long time ago but he had always found an excuse to avoid it. Eventually, the formal request from the family to meet with him had brought matters to a head. He had known, deep down, that they deserved answers and he was the only one able to give them. He had been alongside the ill-fated Skyhawk as it smashed into the ground over the bleak terrain of The Malvinas and he was the only one who could recount the story. Too many years had passed and he had finally agreed to fly down to Rio Gallegos to talk to the relatives of the lost pilot. They had questions about how their son had met his demise and, finally, Carmendez would answer them. He had watched as Romero's aircraft had hit the ground. It had been brutal and final and there was absolutely no way the pilot could have survived but the question was how he could tell them gently. The young pilot's death had been swift but gone was gone and, clearly, the family had yet to come to terms with the loss. For Carmendez life went on. For the Romero family something was missing that could never be replaced. With his help could they move on?

DAVID GLEDHILL

CHAPTER 3

ABOARD AN RAF C-130 HERCULES FREIGHTER IN THE SOUTH ATLANTIC

Razor Keene peered through the front window of the C-130 freighter as it plugged into the basket of the Victor tanker. Staring through the functional square cockpit windows the round basket filled the view, the heavy canvas rim vibrating in the airflow outside the cockpit giving the only indication of the immense forces acting on the airframe. The basket shuddered as the hose took up the slack and the pair of aircraft rose and fell in unison. The tip of the C-130's probe was buried in the centre coupling sucking the precious fuel which would allow them to complete their journey. Minor variations in speed were neutralised as the hose ran into and out of the hydraulic drogue unit, or HDU, sheltered within the refuelling pod beneath the wing of the Victor. The slash of the dayglo markings on the pod stood out starkly against the bright metal on the underside of the wing and the blue sky beyond. Green lights in the housing monitored the status of the refuelling operation glowing brightly as the fuel transferred down the rippling pipe.

They were off the Brazilian coast heading south westerly towards the Falkland Islands. It had already been a long trip but there were a good few hours yet before they touched down on the metal runway at RAF Stanley. The air-to-air refuelling probe which protruded ahead of the cockpit and disappeared into the basket was a hastily added modification to give the C-130 the range to reach the distant islands. Ascension Island was a half way stop between the UK and the Falklands but with 4000 miles between the two airfields, without AAR it was impossible to reach them. He watched as the Victor tanker descended slowly to allow the C-130 to stay in contact, the probe shuddering in the refuelling basket as the final drops of the precious fuel transferred from the Victor into the C-130's tanks. Nicknamed "Albert" by the RAF personnel, the venerable transport aircraft was the lifeline to the islands. Not only had it been modified rapidly to act as an air-to-air refueller, it provided the daily "airbridge" bringing personnel and supplies to keep the garrison going. Ships could provide bulk but the C-130 provided responsiveness with the daily flights bringing vital time-critical spares and, most importantly, the mail from home. The new airfield at RAF Mount Pleasant would open soon and allow large passenger aircraft to operate on the route but, until then, the C-130 would remain as the only transport aircraft able to use the short 6000 foot strip at Stanley.

For some time, the C-130 had been in its gentle descent known in the trade as "tobogganing." The Victor normally flew at about 230 to 250 knots which was quite slow for the fighters which were its usual customers. A C-130 could just about make that speed with a fair wind and engines at maximum power but it was uncomfortable and rattled the seams. To bridge the disparity in performance, a procedure had been developed where the Victor tanker made a slow descent ahead of the C-130 allowing the slower aircraft to generate its maximum performance allowing it to make contact. As the C-130 became heavier, yet more height would be traded to maintain contact. These airborne ballets were precarious and formations had descended as low as 5000 feet over the forbidding Atlantic Ocean before the transport crew had received enough fuel to make their destination.

Razor watched the hydraulic drogue unit on the Victor tanker as the green lights on the pod turned to flashing ambers showing that the fuel had transferred and that they had received their allocation. Listening to the chat with the tanker crew on the radio frequency, a note of urgency returned as, topped off, they were ready to disengage. The amber lights flashed rhythmically and Razor watched the Captain as he gently pulled back the throttles slowing the C-130 by just a few knots. The retardation tugged the hose and basket out from the HDU and the C-130 tracked slowly down the line of the hose away from the airborne petrol station. As the pressure built on the coupling that held the probe and basket together, the strain increased visibly and the basket bucked angrily. Eventually, the pull was too great and the mechanical coupling released its grip allowing the probe to pull clear, the basket bobbing violently in the turbulent airflow as it separated. The Captain flew the huge transport aircraft slowly backwards and downwards before moving off to the side of the Victor tanker. As he pulled alongside tentatively he gave a quick gesture of thanks which was acknowledged silently from the adjacent cockpit as the tanker pilot pushed the throttles up beginning the slow climb back up to cruising altitude. Released from its bonds, the Victor tanker climbed rapidly above the C-130, its Rolls Royce Conway engines lifting it effortlessly back to its cruising altitude. It turned away in a climbing arc back towards the sunny climes of its island haven well to the north.

With the excitement over for a while Razor muttered a few words of thanks to the busy crew in the cockpit before handing his headset back to the flight engineer and climbing down the stairs back into the huge cargo area in the rear of the C-130. Without the protection from the headset and away from the cocooned environment of the flight deck the cargo bay was noisy. As he worked his way past the parachute seats fixed along the side of the cabin, he threaded his way through the huge pallets of freight. The stench of the chemical "porta-potty" assailed his nostrils which in the hot and bumpy environment of the cabin had been the final straw for many a less seasoned traveller leading to a few hours of extreme discomfort as airsickness kicked in. His navigator who had strung a portable hammock between shackles on the side of the cabin, seemed immune and had experienced far more tribulations in the hot confines of a Phantom cockpit. At least a C-130 stayed upright. With his bonedome on his head and a light blanket across his torso he was cocooned in the mesh rocking gently with the movement of the huge aircraft. Without deference to diplomacy Razor rapped his knuckles on the hard shell of the green flying helmet causing his navigator to twitch and a flying glove moved upwards to the dark visor pushing it up from the front of the helmet revealing a slightly annoyed pair of eyes. With his rude awakening, Flash wearily disentangled himself from the hammock and his flying boots dropped to the metal floor with a thud. Unhitching the chinstrap he rolled the helmet forward pulling it from his head.

"How far out?" he muttered, the sleep still evident in his voice.

"We just finished the final tanker bracket so we must be just about abeam

Montevideo. It's still a good few hours yet."

"Deep joy! I guess the poke means that it's your turn to use the hammock?"

"How'd you guess," the pilot retorted. "I don't want you to feel guilty that it's actually my hammock!"

"You got the last one in the shop" the navigator replied grudgingly.

"Your lack of planning doesn't constitute a crisis in my book you know."

The seemingly harsh banter was a front. Flash watched as Razor pulled on his flying helmet and placed a foot, tentatively, onto the fabric of the hammock ready for the crazy lurch into the unstable contraption. With a forward lunge he rode the gyrations before settling into a comfortable reclining posture. Flash overcame a childish desire to tip him back onto the cabin floor feeling a little frustrated that he had not been able to acquire a hammock of his own. It made the long ride to Stanley just that little more bearable. Working his way back to his seat he flopped onto the hard webbing of the parachute seat, instantly uncomfortable. Designed to take a fully loaded and well padded paratrooper the metal frame was ill-equipped for journeys longer than an hour. He grabbed his "butty box" which had been handed out by the Air Loadmaster as they had unstrapped at top of climb, from under his seat and began to search through the contents. It was hardly a gourmet feast but the in-flight rations were, undoubtedly, a highlight of the trip. Assembled by Catering Flight at Wideawake airfield on Ascension Island, the white cardboard box held sandwiches, a sausage roll, crisps, drinks and biscuits and would keep him busy for a while. If the food ran out, he was sure the crew would have something extra tucked away somewhere. The navigator was a friend from training days and he was sure he would be well looked after if hunger threatened. Depending on the winds, the long trip south at 210 knots could take up to 13 hours. A rare tailwind would speed things up but knowing his luck they would be charging into 60 knots on the nose.

"Are we there yet?" he muttered, irreverently. Peeling open the cling film that covered the sandwiches he tucked the pliable ear plugs, an essential travel companion, into his ears and began to read his book. With his feet resting up against the pallet in front of him and but for the incessant drone of the Allison turboprops, he could have been in a warehouse anywhere in the world.

Sometime later, the "loadie" tapped Razor on the shoulder and he woke with a start, pulling his bonedome away from his ear so he could decipher the gesticulations. Cupping his hand around his mouth the loadie shouted above the drone of the engines.

"We're about 40 minutes out and we're just about to chop across to "Puffin." One of your Phantom mates is coming up to escort us in to Stanley."

"Outstanding, can we go up to the flight deck for the intercept?"

"All fixed. Go up when you're ready and take your camera!"

"Puffin" was the callsign for the Sector Operations Centre perched at the top of Mount Kent on East Falkland. It housed the hub of the air defence ground environment and was home to the battle managers and fighter controllers for their tour of duty. Most importantly, it and other air defence radars on West Falkland, scanned the skies day and night for any sign of intruders which might constitute a threat to the islands. Although the navigator would have been in frequent contact with the Sector Operations Centre via the high frequency radio as soon as they took off from Ascension, once the C-130 came within range of the islands the crew would speak to them on UHF radio to coordinate their arrival. They were coming within range now and close enough to raise them.

In the cockpit the Captain hit the transmit button.

"Puffin, Ascot 4722."

A pause.

"Ascot 4722, Puffin, go ahead."

The response on the radio frequency was weak and distorted and the Captain clutched his headset to his ear straining to hear the exchange. His message was a routine notification and he continued undeterred.

"Puffin, Ascot 4722, presently 100 miles northeast of the field at Flight

Level 210, requesting initial descent."

"Ascot 4722 descend to Flight Level 100 and call when level."

"Descend Flight Level 100, 4722."

In the rear cabin, the drop in the incessant note as the engines throttled back was received with a great deal of enthusiasm as the weary passengers began to tidy up for the arrival. They had anticipated this moment for quite a while and needed no excuse to get busy. Razor appeared from behind the cargo pallet wrapping the flimsy hammock into a ball and gestured to Flash for him to follow as they threaded their way past their fellow travellers towards the flight deck. Razor smiled at a journalist who had shared the joys of the rear cabin with them realising that it was the woman who had been in the bar last night. She was perched on a parachute seat and looked as uncomfortable as he had been before staking his claim to the hammock. He squeezed past taking a sneaky sideways glance. Apparently, she worked for the Spectator Magazine in London and was quite a looker which made it all the more surprising that she hadn't got the invite to the flight deck.

Karen Pilkington was pretty, articulate and a workaholic and, working for the Magazine, she was accustomed to a male-dominated society such as the one she had been immersed in since arriving at Brize Norton the day before. After the orientation briefings by the staff officer from Strike Command she had been hosted in the Officers' Mess by a team from the RAF Station where the conversation had revolved, almost exclusively, around flying and operations. Since boarding the flight, if she sensed the furtive glances of the other men who shared the noisy cabin of the Hercules, she ignored them. For the first hours she had busied herself making scribbled observations in her notebook, rehearsing her upcoming interviews in her mind and working on the lines of questioning to fit with her concept for the series of articles she would publish on her return. Few journalists had been granted such exclusive access up to now and, with the first visit by Argentinian families of those killed in the Falklands conflict on the itinerary, she had landed a coup. It was an opportunity on which she intended to capitalise. The chance to interview the personnel on the distant islands was granted sparingly and she would be following some heavyweights of the journalistic and literary world who were the only ones who had been given access until now. With the ideas crystallised her attention switched to the stack of pamphlets spread out on the canvas seat next to her. It was research for her next assignment when she returned to London and her work rate never slowed.

With a thumbs-up from the loadie Razor and Flash climbed the short staircase to the cockpit above. As they popped out into the bright sunshine once more, the flight engineer offered them headsets which they donned gratefully remembering to remove the small yellow earplugs first. With a gesture towards the intercom box on the bulkhead, the loadmaster prompted them to plug in the stubby microphone jacks and the headsets burst into life with the in-cockpit chatter. Gesturing to the Captain, Razor settled into the jump seat as Flash grasped the handhold on the seat behind him slotting into the gap between the seats. Unlike the gloom of the aft cabin, sunlight streamed into the cockpit and the visibility forward stretched out for a million miles. Light puffy cumulus cloud dotted the horizon and the dark blue of the Atlantic Ocean unfolded ahead of them. Glancing at the tiny Echo 290 radar display on the navigators station Flash could see the coastline of East Falkland just beginning to paint at the edge of the orange coloured scope. The time base scanned rhythmically left and right arcing across the unfamiliar cheese wedge radar display. He remembered its baby brother from his navigator training but it was a lot different to the scope in the Phantom that he was now used to. At the outer limit of range, the coastline of East Falkland was a reassuring smudge on the radar.

"Cape Pembroke," said the Hercules navigator pointing to the distinctive promontory at the extreme eastern tip of the island. Their professional bonding was interrupted by the radio.

"Eagles check."

"Eagle 2."

"Puffin, Eagles 1 and 2 on frequency."

The Phantoms. It was a tradition on 23 (Fighter) Squadron that, with an airbridge flight inbound, at least one Phantom was vectored onto the incoming flight to say hello to the new arrivals. It was not always possible but became almost a matter of pride, weather permitting.

Eagle 1 and 2, Puffin, loud and clear, how me?"

"Loud and clear also, Charlie 4, 4, plus 8, tiger fast 60," the lead navigator intoned. The code gave the controller vital tactical information and was a ritual on checking in. From this she could tell that the Phantoms had 4 Skyflash, 4 AIM-9L Sidewinders and a fully loaded Suu-23 gun. They had enough fuel to conduct a supersonic intercept and still remain on combat air patrol for an hour. "Albert" was in safe hands.

"Request snap vector for Ascot"

"Vector 040, target bears 040 range 95."

"040 looking" replied the navigator in the lead Phantom already searching the sky for the inbound C-130. Although the AN/AWG12 was a superb albeit unreliable radar even the large transport aircraft was beyond its detection range as yet. On a good day the navigator would pick up "Albert" at about 60 miles. Looking at the C-130's compass, Flash could see that they were on a reciprocal heading; 220 degrees heading for East Falkland. The intercept controller was setting up a "180 intercept" in which the pair of Phantoms and the C-130 would point at each other on opposing headings. With a combined closing speed of nearly 600 knots, the 95 miles would reduce to zero in just over 9 minutes.

"Target range 50."

"Contact 040 range 50," confirmed the Phantom navigator.

"Target," replied the controller.

"Judy."

With just a few brief words the lead navigator had taken control of the intercept and would position the Phantoms alongside the lumbering transport. In the distance, unseen to the C-130 crew, the Phantoms were setting up a carefully choreographed intercept profile. They would descend from their combat air patrol to 2000 feet above the C-130 and turn in at 12 miles. Their final turn would roll them out a few miles behind from where they would pull alongside. In the cockpit of the C-130 eyeballs were now alert, scanning the horizon for the tell-tale smoke trail from the Rolls Royce Spey turbofans powering the fighters. For Razor and Flash it was an undeclared challenge to get the first pick up. With the intercept now in the hands of the fighter crews the radio fell eerily silent, disconcerting knowing that two missile armed fighters were closing inexorably. The horizon remained stubbornly void of smoke.

"Tally Ho 10 o'clock. They went low!" called Flash from his position behind the Captain's seat. With his raised vantage point he could see down through the large side window and the Phantoms had descended below the transport aircraft to maintain tactical surprise. Without a radar warning receiver in the cockpit there had been no clues to the approach direction and Flash's sharp eyes had saved embarrassment. Heads swung around in unison.

There could be no more dramatic sight from the cockpit than being intercepted by an armed fighter jet. The bulk of the Phantoms hove into view with one on each wingtip. The C-130 had slowed in the descent and it was almost impossible to stabilise a Phantom at 210 knots; 250 was a realistic minimum and even then it was uncomfortable but today the fighter crews seemed determined. After the initial manoeuvre, the Phantom pilots wrestled with their jets, uneasy at such slow speed despite having dropped a notch of flap. To stabilise would have meant lowering the undercarriage and what self respecting fighter pilot would do that? To stay in close, they set up a weave alongside, manoeuvring in close proximity showing the functional profile of the F4 Phantom with the occasional flash of the lethal weapon load slung beneath each jet. Down the back of the C-130 cameras clicked away at every window as enthusiastic passengers enjoyed the show. Even Razor and Flash with thousands of hours flying the Phantom between them pulled out cameras and captured the moment. The squadron markings, stylised red eagles emblazoned on the fins and the Falkland Islands crest on the nose, showed their heritage and their loyalties.

As the C-130 let down onto final approach onto the westerly runway at Stanley the disparity between speeds finally became too great and the Phantoms accelerated ahead. The afterburners ignited and the fighters sped off into the distance dropping towards the sea. They were off to pay a visit to the radar site at Mount Kent before dropping into the low flying areas to continue their patrol over the islands. Up ahead, the lighthouse on Cape Pembroke, until recently just a blot on the radar scope, emerged from the haze and the short runway at RAF Stanley popped out of the surrounding landscape, set just a few miles inland on the peninsula.

"OK, only room for one on the jump seat for the landing. Do you want to toss for it?" asked the Captain.

Funnily enough possession proved critical and, as his navigator slid back down the stairs to take his seat for landing, Razor tightened the lap straps on the makeshift seat. Staring ahead at the short strip, he could make out the first detail of his temporary home. Short commands were barked out from the left hand seat as the gear and flaps were configured for the landing, the co pilot making the selections demanded of him. Approaching from the east the stark ocean gave way to the rugged headland as the transport aeroplane began its short descent down the glideslope, the throttles moving a few seconds before the increased note of the engines matched the setting. Through the square windscreen the runway took on its familiar trapezoidal shape tapering to an apex at the far end. The usual stark black of the tarmacadam runway surface was absent replaced by the dull metallic sheen of metal matting visible even from 5 miles away. Small hangars dotted the edges of the runway left and right of the upwind threshold and the terminal building was visible well off to the left towards the end of the strip. Up ahead, the ground rose into the foothills beyond with the peaks of the mountain rising to nearly 1000 feet above the airfield forming a forbidding barrier. The engine note rose again as the huge transport hung on its props dragging its bulk over the threshold onto the landing strip where it thumped down and nodded forward onto its tricycle undercarriage. The note changed as the propellers were pushed into reverse acting against the forward momentum and slowing the transport down to walking speed, the huge wheels under the centre fuselage thumping along the planks causing an uncharacteristic whine. Much lighter after the long flog across the South Atlantic the C-130 turned off at the access taxiway making its short trek across to the parking stand. Ahead, a marshaller waved his illuminated wands receiving a flash of the taxilight in acknowledgement as the freighter made its way towards the terminal building. Within minutes the Allison turboprops were winding down and relative calm returned to the apron. Alongside, another C-130, this one modified as a tanker, was preparing for its mission above the islands and a civilian S61 helicopter started its engine ready to transport its cargo to one of the settlements. There was a functional bustle of activity. Groundcrew positioned support equipment alongside the grey and green fuselage ready to service the transport aircraft.

Clearance given to disembark, Razor stepped out through the forward door from the gloom of the C-130 cabin, the bright light stinging his eyes. He looked ahead at a large blue signboard hastily stuck to the side of the control tower which proudly proclaimed "RAF Stanley." Around him, personnel pulled servicing trolleys into place and unloaded vehicles ready to check the C-130. The crew would fly it out the following day but in the meantime it would be prepared for its long trip home. He aimed for the door marked "Arrivals" with a slight feeling of trepidation. Who knew what the coming months held?

As the aircrew disappeared into the terminal another man climbed down the aircraft stairs. He was glad to be back on terra firma after his long journey that had originated in Whitehall in London. Warren Baird was a "diplomat" attached to the staff at Government House. Ostensibly a First Secretary and responsible for aspects of the secure communications facilities his role was somewhat less straight forward. In reality he worked for MI6 the overseas arm of the Secret Intelligence Services. Although he would normally operate in other areas of the world, his skills made him particularly suited to the problems faced in this small British dependency and he worked closely with his colleagues in MI5. His true role was known only to the Governor and then only in the scantest of detail. Outwardly, his appearance was unremarkable but that was to be expected. Average build, average height, unexceptional features; intelligence operatives blended in with the scenery. The troops around him barely gave him a second glance and he had kept himself very much to himself throughout the flight, avoiding contact with his fellow travellers. They might have shown much more interest if they knew which departments he had visited over the last few days; departments which included the Cabinet Office in Whitehall.

There was an important series of discussions coming up and the Minister responsible for the region was becoming nervous. Warren had been summoned to London to give a personal take on how things were developing and to be briefed on the forthcoming agenda. There could be no mistakes with the stakes so high and keeping track of the Argentinian reactions during these discussions would be the key to success. That was where he came in. He had the means at his disposal, details of which he would not admit to anyone, but they would be brought into play if needed. The technical means by which he kept track of the opposition was for him to know and for others to guess. The intellectual value of his role was his intimate knowledge of the politics of this dependency of the British Isles. He now knew what the Minister and the Governor were being asked to negotiate and, if it came to fruition, it was political dynamite! The local councillors could have no inkling of the initiatives and he could only imagine how disclosure would affect relations with Buenos Aries or Port Stanley for that matter. He had his schedule mapped out and dragging all the way to London had set him back by days. Even so, some things were just too sensitive to discuss over a phone line, however secure.

He followed the line of personnel filing into the Arrivals Hall hoping the queue would be short and that the customs officials had been primed for his arrival. Glancing briefly at the journalist who had accompanied him on the flight he left himself a mental note to check on her itinerary. His interest was not testosterone-driven and, like others around here, he had good reasons to make sure she didn't take too much interest in his activities around Stanley. Some things were best not reported.

Outside the Terminal, a Land Rover from Government House waited, its engine ticking over to keep the cab warm, the driver rubbing his hands vigorously. Unlike his travelling companions Warren would not be taking advantage of the 54-seater Air Force coach that had pulled up alongside the exit ready to make the journey to the accommodation barges and on into Stanley. By the time the coach left he would be well on his way down the rutted track and almost back to the small house he, presently, called home.

CHAPTER 4

RIO GALLEGOS AIRBASE, ARGENTINA

The airbase at Rio Gallegos lies just outside the city boundary to the northwest of the conurbation, its east-west runway bordering on the banks of the river from which it takes its name. Just a short hop away, the mouth of the Bahia Grande feeds out into the South Atlantic Ocean. Head east for 400 miles and the next landfall is on the Falkland Islands where the conflict over sovereignty raged in 1982. The civil air terminal sits to the south of the runway separated from the fighter dispersals on the north side by the runway. At the eastern end, five hardened shelters are grouped around a loop taxiway. At the extreme eastern end of the airfield, the pilot's briefing facility is housed in a separate area linked to an additional hardened aircraft shelter. Towards the centre of the field more shelters cluster around a loop taxiway in groups of four. Extra revetments could house additional aircraft if called upon and were full to capacity in 1982.

Despite the air of menace the lack of funding was beginning to show and the tufts of grass growing through the joints of the concrete taxiways were the least of the problems. The demise of the Junta had caused more than political upheaval. With the A-4B Skyhawk slowing to a walking pace, Carmendez made his radio call as he cleared the active runway, flipped up his visor and pointed his jet along the taxiway leading to the squadron dispersal. He was back on familiar ground as this had been his temporary home for many months during the fight for The Malvinas. His squadron had been deployed here during the war and flew from this very dispersal. At that time they had used the hardened shelters but today he was being directed to the parking ramp which connected the two operational sites. Checks complete and switches safe, he pulled onto the large parking area, kicked the jet around in a 180 degree turn and dabbed the brakes nodding to a halt. The flight line mechanic disappeared under the wing inspecting the undercarriage for hydraulic leaks before reappearing, offering a thumbs-up. He eased the throttle up a notch moving forward just a few inches before applying the brakes for a final time. The chocks thumped into place in front of the wheels before he acknowledged the signal to chop the throttle, quieting the screaming jet engine. As the engine spooled down he opened the canopy and finished off his shut-down checks taking just seconds to replace his ejection seat pins and make the cockpit safe. Pulling off his bonedome and climbing down the ladder he exchanged a few brief words with the mechanic but they were well familiar with the Skyhawk here and he could trust them with the turnround servicing leaving him free to get on with the real reason for his visit.

Later today he was meeting the family of the young ensign, Romero, killed when his Skyhawk crashed over West Falkland on that fateful day in 1982. He had flown down from his new base at Villa Reynolds, where the squadron had returned after the conflict, to make the rendezvous. It would not be a happy event and he wondered how the family would react. His words were carefully rehearsed but he was still not really sure if it hit the right tone. Few parents would understand, or would even want to understand, the patriotic fervour he and his pilots had felt in that fight. Why should they? The loss of a son was a tragic waste and it was doubtful if they would comprehend why they had been asked to make the sacrifice over what they would probably consider to be a remote group of rocks. He would have to play it sensitively. Who knows, it might even be cathartic for him. He was not sure if he had ever sat down by himself and truly mourned his lost comrades. There had been the formal remembrance services of course, and even a few moments of private reflection over a glass of Scotch but was it real grieving? Such thoughts didn't sit well in his technological world. He had often thought about the fight for The Malvinas in the days since the conflict ended. A bleak outcrop distant from the mainland, he wondered about the motivation of the politicians who constantly whipped up the fervour to recover the islands. Sure, many thought that his Country had a legitimate claim over the small dependency but was it truly worth it?

Over 600 of his fellow countrymen, many of them conscripts, had lost their lives in the ill-fated military gamble in 1982. The few Falkland Islanders he had met over the years didn't seem much like Argentinians to him, nor did they seem to want to be part of Argentina. Military adventures in search of territorial acquisitions rarely worked and history was littered with failures. Where the stimulus was financial he had even less patience. Despite that, what rankled was the humiliation he had witnessed when thousands of prisoners of war had been dropped off by British ships at the east coast ports after the war. That, coupled with the scenes in the tabloids of helmets and rifles discarded, carelessly, on the village green at Goose Green on East Falkland after the surrender following the battle left a bitter taste and it was still a source of national humiliation. So far it had gone unchecked. Another military campaign was out of the question and politics would be the new order but he could not throw off the niggling tic.

He tucked his oxygen mask into the helmet and casually lowered it to his side as he made his way across the concrete apron towards the squadron buildings to sign in his jet and make ready for his private ordeal.

DAVID GLEDHILL

CHAPTER 5

RAF STANLEY, THE NEXT DAY

Flash rolled over and, unconsciously, reached out for his girlfriend Julie. Instead of a warm companion, his arm dropped over the side of the narrow cot and he rapped his elbow, painfully, on the metal frame. In the bunk bed opposite the sound of snoring reverberated against the metal walls of the small cabin and, for a brief moment he thought he was back in the Battle Flight shed at Wildenrath. He slowly acclimatised to his surroundings and realised he was nearly 8000 miles away in a small cabin which someone, optimistically, thought could sleep four. Behind him on the small wall between the bunks a dirty, frosted, glass window allowed a small amount of grey light to filter into the tiny cabin. On the floor towards the metal door, two large air force grey holdalls lay abandoned, a few items of clothing strewn across the floor.

The first night had been a blur as Razor and Flash had finally dumped their kit in their new room that would be their home for the coming months. Billeted together they had been allocated a four man room to share and as they would eat, sleep and fly together for the foreseeable future, it would be a relative luxury for only two bodies to occupy the cramped space. The rooms were located on an upper level on the barge and it was a short trek along an outside walkway to the communal area which housed the kitchens, bar, dining rooms and ante rooms. With the Falklands weather raging outside it was a bracing run between the two areas and something of a novelty to wear a coat to go to dinner. "Dressing for dinner" took on a new meaning. The plans to unpack and settle into their cosy hovel had been abandoned in preference to a few pints after dinner but with the lack of space it was a task which could not be put off for long.

As he slowly came around, the noises and smells of his new environment vaguely registered in his subconscious. Somewhere, breakfast was already being prepared and the smell of bacon was filtering through some, as yet unidentified, air vent. The long trip on the C-130 had made food seem unattractive last night but the smell was tweaking his appetite and he suddenly felt hungry. He glanced at the hands of his illuminated watch and groaned. It was an hour before the time at which his alarm clock should have started his day and the "buzz saw" in the opposite bunk seemed insistent that he wasn't going to spend that hour asleep. His only consolation was that some of the sounds that had emerged from his pilot's mouth over the earlier years had been even less eloquent.

He rolled onto his back and pulled the hairy blankets around him. The gesture lasted only briefly as he realised that the temperature in the small space was probably warm enough to boil a kettle. Freezing was not a risk he would face. His mind drifted. On one level he was looking forward to flying in the Falklands and, from the accounts from those who had flown down here, the flying was challenging, fun and varied. Although the Harriers had gone home, the other units were keen to play. Like in Germany he would spend his life at low level operating in the weeds and on the limits. In fact, if the stories were to be believed, the limits were often stretched to beyond breaking point. On a personal level, he was not looking forward to taking four months out of his life. His tour in Germany was already too short and the thought of spending so much of his precious tour in this far off corner of the globe was depressing. Life would be different and, although the social life was supposed to be good, the high life of Stanley town was hardly going to replace the weekend trips to the Swiss Alps where the snow was already deep and the après ski was even better.

He dozed fitfully until the alarm clock rattled its welcome to the day. A thump on the top of the small device silenced the metallic noise and, as he stirred from his pit extracting himself from the tangle of bedding, he realised he had no idea where the shower was located. The day would start, of necessity, with an exploration of his new surroundings.

*

The massive accommodation barge known as the "Coastel" began life housing support workers for the oil industry. After a long journey from the Northern Hemisphere it pulled into the small inlet at the eastern end of Stanley Harbour alongside two other similar vessels providing rooms and living space for the influx of temporary military residents from the UK. Although austere by modern standards, it replaced tents and an aging passenger ferry called the MV Rangatira, dubbed "Old Smelly." In comparison to the ferry the four-berth cabins offered relative luxury and the huge kitchens and living quarters provided a semblance of normal life.

Breakfast over, Razor and Flash walked out into the hastily cleared, rock-strewn car park in front of the three huge barges taking in the morning sea air. Gulls called stridently as they plied the waterfront in a never ending search for scraps of food dropped from a window. Occasionally, the cooks in the kitchens would ditch slops over the side starting a raucous fight for dominance which lasted for many minutes as the gulls wheeled in the air. It was rarely warm in the Falkland Islands even though they shared the same latitude with the English Riviera, albeit at the other side of the globe. Small ports vented steam from the huge accommodation barge into the sharp morning air giving a visual clue to the temperature. In reality, the climate was more akin to that of the Outer Hebrides some 400 miles north of its British cousin. The lack of any shelter between the islands and the South American mainland over 400 miles away, meant that they were always ravaged by strong westerly winds. Even on a bright day such as today, the chill factor cut through like a knife.

Transport was at a premium and only commanders and essential personnel enjoyed individual vehicles. The Boss of the Fighter Squadron was allocated his own Land Rover but even that was shared with the rest of the squadron to top up whatever transport had been requisitioned from a vanquished enemy. For the aircrew, on call 24 hours a day, a regular shuttle of Land Rovers plied back and forth to the Squadron at regular intervals along the rough roads. For the groundcrew, more structured shifts meant a shuttle service plied the technical site at more scheduled times. A few captured Argentinian vehicles supplemented the fleet but with the lack of transport, it was fair game to flag down a passing vehicle for a lift. As they waited along with another crew, the Squadron operations Land Rover pulled into the car park and they hauled themselves over the tailgate into the stark cabin. The thin pad covering the metal seats offered some protection from the pounding which was about to be meted out as the truck moved back out onto the rutted track which led to the airfield. To the left the road made its way towards the island's Capital Port Stanley. Across Boxer Bridge to the right it threaded around past Whalebone Cove and the westerly runway threshold and through the sprawling and rapidly expanding technical site. Looking backwards beyond the flapping canopy as the Land Rover navigated the potholes making its way through the sprawl, they could see "Portakabin City" which had grown up since the airfield had been liberated. It took quite some time before it was safe enough to reopen the airfield after the conflict. The operating surfaces had been littered with unexpended ordnance that had, subsequently, been made safe by bomb disposal experts and armourers. There was still the look of a war zone about the place even years after the conflict and discarded military equipment still lined the road.

Stanley airfield on East Falkland was a collection of rickety huts housing the new military force. Only the Air Traffic control tower had any semblance of permanence and the remaining buildings had been lashed together from building supplies from any source. By far the most popular materials were shipping containers hastily pressed into service as makeshift offices and workshops. RAF Stanley had grown around the main aircraft parking area and the newly extended runway. At 4500 feet, the runway which had survived the war was woefully inadequate for the larger transport aircraft or the high performance Phantoms which now made up most of the movements during the flying day. Only the short takeoff and landing Harriers which performed so well during the conflict had been able to use the original strip until a radical plan had been hatched to extend the operating surface to allow larger aircraft to fly in. A stone quarry to the north western end of the runway had been rapidly expanded and crushed rock by the ton began to emerge on huge trucks, shipped the short distance across the airfield and rammed into place at the western end of the original runway. Once packed down hard, metal planking, known as AM2 matting, had been laid over both the new foundations and the old concrete strip extending the useable landing distance to 6000 feet.

Although a fully armed Phantom could takeoff from the newly extended runway it was still a little short for a routine landing. Rotary Hydraulic Arrestor Gear, or RHAGs, had been installed at each end and at the centre of the strip allowing the Phantoms to land into the cable at the end of every sortie. As a consequence, for the Phantom crews operating from Stanley, it was more like flying from an aircraft carrier than from a normal RAF base and the generous concrete runways they were used to. On the far side of the airfield, temporary hangars, nicknamed "rubs", had sprung up to protect the Phantoms and the support helicopters from the ravages of the South Atlantic climate. The maintenance personnel were particularly grateful as they struggled to keep the temperamental jets serviceable on this remote base. The hangars provided a vital shelter from the wind and rain but for the people as well as the jets. On the southern side, 23 Squadron, nicknamed "The Red Eagles", had taken possession of yet more ramshackle cabins to house the Quick Reaction Alert crews who guarded the airspace.

The new airfield at Mount Pleasant would open soon so not much would be spent on this interim set up at Stanley and in a few short years the temporary structures would be torn down. With the main links to home being via the over-taxed airbridge flights, only operational spares, people and perishable goods arrived by air. Everything else coming to the islands arrived by sea.

All around the airfield, even the smallest unit vied for the most comfortable place to set up its operation. "Plots with a sea view" were at a premium. On the airfield, more of the matting had been laid over the aircraft parking areas and the taxiways giving a firmer surface over which the huge jets could taxy. The air of a war zone was complete as hulks of Argentinean Pucara fighter-bombers still dotted the airfield in varying states of disrepair. Some had been towed into neat rows and were sitting on their tricycle undercarriage even though they showed the ravages of conflict. Barely one had survived without some damage inflicted on the airframe by British troops as they retook the airfield at the end of the conflict. Others tilted forward at impossible angles after soldiers had crippled them in vain retribution following liberation. Other military hardware littering the approach roads ranged from trucks to surface-to-air missile batteries to light guns. Stanley had taken on the look of a huge Meccano set.

Just as he thought he would lose the fillings in his teeth with the incessant battering the suspension was taking from the graded road surface, Razor was distracted by the unmistakeable sound of a Phantom spooling up its engines readying for takeoff. The sound was unique yet familiar as he heard the change in tone as the afterburners lit. He craned his head to catch his first glimpse of his aircraft in its new but unfamiliar environment. The canvas sides of the Land Rover shielded his view across the airfield so he popped his head around the side of the tail flap suddenly hit by the chilling blast of southern air. He tried for a better view staring between the ramshackle buildings, straining to catch sight of the runway as the noise changed from the loud hum to an ear splitting roar. With the afterburners cooking the Phantom sped down the metal strip leaving its wingman in its wake. Razor glimpsed the jet briefly as it passed between two cabins, the twin plumes angled downwards, striking the surface of the runway as the speed increased. Very quickly it was airborne and rose above the buildings popping into clear view, the heat haze shimmering in the cold morning air closely followed by the number 2. With the gear and flaps retracted the aircraft reached tactical flying speed before breaking out into battle formation holding height only feet above the ground. Within moments they were heading off down Stanley Harbour at low level en route to their operational play area. He couldn't suppress a ripple of pride and anticipation as he watched the departure.

The Land Rover pulled up in front of a collection of portakabins and the driver dropped down from the cabin into the inevitable muddy puddle. Although as unlikely an operations complex for a fighter squadron as was possible, the new crew accepted that they had arrived at their destination and followed the driver into the motley collection of shacks. Even the toned-down single storey buildings on the dispersal at Wildenrath looked modern compared to this lash-up. Hopefully, as they reflected over a beer later in the day their surroundings would begin to seem more normal.

Squadron Air Operations consisted of an ISO shipping container accessed via a lean-to entrance of flimsy plywood clad in "wiggly tin". An open doorway led into the main working area giving a semblance of shelter from the prevailing wind which battered the entrance on even the sunniest day. Tall masts sprouting from the roof held aerials providing communications between the duty authoriser who ran the daily programme, to the aircraft via a UHF radio set. Above the austere structure the Squadron Commander's pennant fluttered bravely in the breeze. Sheets of steel planking had been laid down across the approaches to prevent a morass developing but, even so, the surrounding area was littered with rocks and covered in a glutinous mud.

Once inside, although the functions were easily recognisable and similar to those in any other ops room that the pair had inhabited over the years, it had a transient feel. Information boards had been hastily fixed to the wall behind the obligatory ops desk showing the daily flying programme. The Duty Authoriser busied himself trying to piece together the jigsaw of men and machines. The weather states and other operational information such as the serviceability of the base facilities and the vital aviation warnings covered a second wall. In an adjacent ISO container connected to operations by a short corridor, a combined engineering operations and line control team juggled the essential engineering activity, tracking which jets were "up" and giving estimates for when the remainder would be returned to flying status. Unlike, the equivalent back home in the UK, there were no "ops desk lurkers". With space at a premium, anyone who was not directly associated with running the flying programme was noticeably absent and any efforts to poach flying by a hopeful pilot would be swiftly rebuffed. Everything was brutally functional. There was no time for ceremony.

"The Boss wants to see you both," the Duty Authoriser announced, pausing momentarily, secretly enjoying the looks of apprehension on the faces of the newest arrivals.

It's OK you don't need hats," he said, smiling.

The new Boss had a good reputation for being hard but fair, and, although he had served his apprenticeship on Hunters and Lightnings, since converting to Phantoms many years before he had embraced the two seat culture and was popular with the pilots and navigators alike. He had a good pair of hands and was willing to listen in the air. What was more important was that he was a good bloke; something which was vital in the claustrophobic atmosphere on the islands. A minor dictator in this environment had the potential to make many lives a misery.

The new crew were ushered into the stark office, in reality little more than a desk, a table and chairs and a filing cabinet. Luxury had not yet arrived in the latest operational theatre. The Boss gestured for them to take a seat.

"Welcome to Stanley. I know it's a long way from home but how was the trip in the Herc?"

"Pretty long and not that comfortable, Sir, but we're here!"

"I know. The airbridge isn't ideal but some of the troops are still arriving by sea. It's quite a bit longer coming down by boat, although maybe it might be a little more comfortable. It takes some of the guys a week to get here."

He flicked through an open file on his desk.

" We've not served together have we? Tell me something about yourselves; Razor."

"This is my first tour Boss. I've been on 92 Squadron at Wildenrath for nearly a full tour and I'm posted out not long after I get back to Germany. I'm single so I live in the Mess. I can't think of a better way to have learned about the Phantom. You know from your time in RAF Germany that all the flying is at low level. Maybe we don't get the same experience as the UK guys up at medium level but the flying is intense and a hell of a lot of fun. It also helps that we operate from hardened shelters all the time. It'll be quite similar here with the rubs."

"How many hours do you have?"

"I'm not an authoriser yet so I've been filling my boots. I've got 750 hours Phantom already and hope to make that a lot more before the end of my tour."

"Good man, I did the same on my first tour. Flew hard and screwed up regularly but I don't want you following my example! What about you Flash?"

"I'm coming to the end of my tour, Boss, but I've already done a UK tour. I've got nearly 1300 hours on the jet and I hope to get an instructional tour at Coningsby next. I'm also single but starting to think it might be a good time to settle down. Germany can be hard work on the body with all that socialising! Maybe I need a good woman to calm me down?"

"Well I can promise you a quieter social life down here. Apart from the high spots in Port Stanley there's only the bar in the Coastel. Make sure you try the Penguin Ale. It's a taste all of its own. That said, the wildlife is absolutely stunning and there are plenty of ways to get around the islands. Make the most of it. Get out and meet the islanders. They are the friendliest people you will ever meet and will welcome you for an overnight stay without question. You just need to take the time to meet them."

"That's a must Boss, thanks."

"The schedule is hectic and I can guarantee that you'll need a rest when you're done. It's a punishing work cycle during which you'll spend four days on Q and four days flying, on the desk or in the tower with two days off at each end. It's punishing but you should get a decent amount of flying. Even though we're at the end of a very long supply chain, we get quite good priority on spares down here. It's not unusual to have 80% of the jets serviceable for the programme which is way better than back home. The troops are a captive audience. They work hard but play hard too but they do miracles with what we have.

"What's the situation with the Argies Boss?"

"It's been relatively quiet recently. The Electra keeps bouncing off the Protection Zone and, occasionally, it decides to press in a little closer. We picked it up last week when it strayed a little close. It got in to about 150 miles before the Q crews got to it and helped it along its journey. We got some good pictures but it's the old airframe that has been in service for years. There's been some intelligence reports that they have a new version called the "Electrone" kitted out with new electronics by the Israelis. If they do we'll have to be on our toes because everything we say and do and all the electronic burps we transmit will be recorded and analysed back on the mainland. We need to keep them honest and make sure we don't give too much away about our readiness states. Let's keep them guessing shall we?"

"No fast jet incursions though?"

"No, we have good radar coverage out to the west so we can see quite a long way out, right down to low level but we've not seen a hint of any incursions. Mind you, we're worried about the radar head on the south side of West Falkland and we're about to relocate it. There's a new site been identified up on Mount Alice and it should give even better coverage of the approaches. You'll get to see it when you do your familiarisation flights. The Argentinian combat squadrons all moved back to their pre-war bases after the conflict so most of them don't even have the legs to touch us from peacetime locations. If they move back south we'd get some warning and that would probably prompt reinforcement from the UK. Incidentally, we have a rotation planned for next week so it'll get even busier around here when the extra jets and crews arrive. Two jets are going home for servicing and being replaced."

"It's quite a responsibility flying armed every day," said Razor apprehensively.

"You're right. I won't take away the thunder from the weapons briefings but suffice to say that you'll have the rules of engagement to intervene if you meet something that looks like it's anything less than friendly. We practice the procedures regularly so we shouldn't be taken by surprise. Remember, you always have the right of self defence so if anyone shoots at you, you can return fire with equivalent force. Also don't forget that the Rapier crews are live-armed so make sure you follow the correct recovery procedures back to Stanley. I don't want a blue-on-blue engagement because you forgot to wear the correct IFF code, OK? Right, I know there are briefings planned for the rest of the day and I want you flying as soon as possible but not before tomorrow. I want you recovered fully from that trip down here before you climb in a jet. Make the most of the night off and go easy on the Penguin Ale. This will be your last proper free day for a good few months. Any questions for me?"

A slightly nervous crew saluted as they retired from the tiny office.

CHAPTER 6

MOUNT ALICE, WEST FALKLANDS

As if cued by the discussion in the office at RAF Stanley, the clatter of the twin rotors of the Chinook helicopter split the air as it lifted from the helipad at the radar site on Mount Alice on West Falkland bound for Cape Orford. The lift had been delayed for three days waiting for the winds to ease but this morning there was a brief lull and the air was remarkably calm. The remote site on the tip of Mount Alice commanded spectacular views across the surrounding countryside and the crew would take a final opportunity to check the geography for obstructions which might hamper the task as they sped across the bleak landscape.

The AR3D, Type 94 radar built by Plessey in the UK had originally been installed at the site at Cape Orford on West Falkland but the location had proved to be less than ideal. Only accessible by helicopter, from its original location the radar could not see the crucial sea approaches to the island at the critical lower levels. Although it could detect higher flying intruders, anything flying at wave top height was invisible to the radar operator in certain sectors. Hours of testing with Phantoms running in towards the radar head had proved that there were huge gaps in the coverage so the decision was taken to move it up onto the hill at Mount Alice. Despite a narrow road leading up to the new site, it was still very difficult to get to the isolated detachment but from its lofty perch it would guard the approaches much more effectively. The original site had earned the nickname "Cara Cara" after a local seabird and, despite the move to the new location, the name was destined to stick and the signals unit which operated the radars would retain its strange callsign long after the move.

Today, the heart of the system, namely the actual radar head, was going to be transported using a Chinook helicopter. At nearly 12 tons, it was a huge piece of machinery and would tax the Chinook to the limits. To ensure success the helicopter had been stripped of its non-essential equipment and was in "fighting trim" for this challenging move. Just getting the load off the ground would be difficult enough but carrying it slung underneath the massive helicopter over the 15 miles between sites and then climbing the steep escarpment up to its new location would be a true feat of airmanship.

At the old site at Cape Orford, the "hookers", the expert technicians who handled under-slung loads, had carefully secured the strops around the base of the massive radar array. These strops would take the weight during the lift. The radar scanner had been folded down into its transit configuration and protected carefully for its brief journey. Across the site the Chinook, which had set down briefly, spooled up its twin engines and lifted easily into the air slowly edging its way across the dispersal towards its load. The approach was hesitant as the strops were captured as they flailed in the downdraught before being hooked up to the massive helicopter which eased upwards taking the strain. Straps attached to the main structure were pulled tight by the "hookers" who re-checked the load to prevent the radar from spinning around as it lifted. With the slack taken up, the note of the engines changed markedly and the helicopter strained to un-stick the heavy load which slowly stabilised in the turbulent down draft pulling gently against the restraints. With the engines at maximum power it began to rise, imperceptibly at first but soon clearing the masts around its old home. Once safely airborne, the precious cargo began its short hop eastwards to the adjacent mountain.

Over on the hilltop the atmosphere was tense as eyes were peeled, looking for the helicopter on the horizon. A shout went up. Urgent gestures and eyes trained on the camouflaged helicopter as it flew inbound to the north of Knoll Island and made its way along the inlet. As it approached the gully the engines once again spooled up to maximum power and it began its slow climb upwards towards the peak, its cargo revolving slowly on the strop. Any mistakes during the coming manoeuvres would be costly and an emergency jettison might be the only way to save the helicopter and, more importantly, the crew. There was very little ground clearance throughout the climb and, as it crested the boundary fence, the technicians on the ground prepared for the drop.

The trailing lines were snared and the radar stabilised as the helicopter eased slowly over to the final position blowing debris around the site in its wake. Beneath its belly the load swung, precariously, proving to be a handful in the inevitable, unpredictable wind that had picked up and now swirled around the hilltop. The four "hookers" walked the lines slowly towards the drop point and all seemed well until a freak gust channelled between the steel containers caught the slab side of the radar unit. It began to spin dragging the unfortunate "hookers" in its wake as a severe oscillation set in. Technicians around the site sensing impending disaster, rushed over to assist. Three of the four guide lines were quickly weighted down by extra bodies and the swing damped down slightly. The fourth guide line whipped viciously in protest throwing the powerless "hooker" against the side of the adjacent building, forcing the breath from his lungs as he suddenly lost his grip. The unstable load swung dangerously back towards the remaining restraints threatening to crush the unfortunate rescuers with its massive weight.

In the cockpit the pilot felt the effect on the controls just before the loadmaster began to patter over the intercom. The tone in the crewman's voice heightened the urgency and, as the pilot's hand moved momentarily towards the release handle, he contemplated dumping the under-slung load. It was only the risk to the people on the ground which made him hesitate. He could live with the loss of some hardware, however expensive, but he might not cope with the sleepless nights if he crushed the troops below. He pulled up on the collective lever easing on the power lifting the load slightly away from the ground hoping that the manoeuvre would damp the wild swings. Below him, men paid out the lines rapidly trying, desperately, to stabilise the pendulum effect which was building up. With a death defying lunge a camouflaged body captured the errant fourth rope which had been flailing and pulled it tight. As his efforts began to take effect, more bodies joined him dragging the load back under control and the massive swings stabilised. Relieved, the pilot's hands moved back onto the controls steadying the huge Chinook as he eased slowly back down towards the drop zone eager to shed his cargo before the wind caused more havoc.

As the Chinook lowered the radar dish surprisingly gently onto a carriage which had been positioned below, the "hookers" busied themselves unhitching the lifting strops and praying quietly that the load was now stable. As the strops fell clear the Chinook pilot released from his burden eased on a fraction of power. Too much and he might yet blow away the massive radome with his rotor wash. Too little and the rarefied air at the top of the hill may give him cause for a further adrenaline shot through lack of lift. He had enjoyed enough of an adrenaline buzz for one day.

Task complete, the Chinook clattered away towards the landing site down the hill. Safely strapped to the carriage, the radar technicians began to manhandle the massive structure across the site towards the protective radome which had been erected to protect the dish from the elements. The fact the radome was still standing, given the ferocity of the downdraught, was a minor miracle. With the help of a Land Rover which had been hooked up to the carriage it slowly edged towards its new home. Getting it inside and resealing the dome before the incessant wind blew up again was the highest priority. The radar finally edged into its resting position inside the dome and the short outrider legs were dropped to stabilise it in position. Strops were released, the carriage was pulled clear and the structure began to look more like a radar than a collection of components. It certainly looked more serene than it had just scant minutes before as it dangled beneath the Chinook. After a few curt instructions from the NCO who had supervised the arrival, the technicians began to re-secure the panels of the radome protecting the new resident and shielding the radar from prying eyes.

CHAPTER 7

RIO GALLEGOS AIRBASE

Carmendez relaxed in the easy chair in the Squadron Commander's office clutching a mug of coffee, the tranquil atmosphere belying his feelings of apprehension. The Boss was an old friend and they had served together on a previous outfit.

"You can use the crewroom to talk to the family Pablo. It'll be more comfortable in there for you. I don't envy you that one. I never coped well talking to the families after the war. Somehow I never found the right words. Nothing I could say seemed enough to make any difference to their grieving."

He paused sensing Carmendez's tension.

"I'll make sure none of the pilots interrupt. How long do you need?"

"I'd say 30 minutes will do it. To be honest I can't really add much to the official report but I don't know how much of that they've read. I didn't see a lot at the time as Romero was in my seven o'clock as we pulled off target. The first Harrier latched onto him straight away and had a shot in the air before Romero had even seen it. I suspect the first thing he knew was when the jet exploded around him. We were so damned low that it was only seconds before he hit the ground. There was no way he was ever going to get out."

They had both lost friends and words were redundant.

"Take as long as you need."

"Maybe I'll spare them some of the detail."

"Maybe; some things might be better left unsaid."

He made his way along the corridor towards the aircrew crewroom and, as he pushed open the door, Romero's father was being moved into place in his wheelchair. Temporarily taken aback, he remembered that the father had also served in the military but he had no idea that he had lost his legs or of the circumstances surrounding his loss. Recovering quickly, Carmendez walked over and greeted his guests offering them a drink before settling into an easy chair. He hoped that the pleasantries would gauge the mood and lead him into the explanation of the events on that fateful day. He was really hoping that the family would open the discussion and, to his relief, the man spoke up. Had his discomfort been too obvious?

"It's good of you to see us Major and thanks for taking the time to come down to Rio Gallegos. I know you must be busy. Can I introduce my wife and my daughter."

The pause was loaded.

"We all miss him daily."

"Please, it was the least I could do," said Carmendez, quietly.

"You may not know but I served in the Marines for many years and also saw service during the conflict. I was part of the Naval landing party which landed at Grytviken on South Georgia on 3rd April."

"I had no idea," said Carmendez truthfully.

"A group of scrap workers had taken control of the installation at Leith Harbour earlier in March. They'd been dropped ashore from a freighter, the *Bahia Buen Suceso* in the main harbour and raised our Flag. What the Brits didn't know was that the supposed "scientists" in the party were Marines who had been attached to the expedition to check out the defences and to decide whether to take control. Pretty basic the defences proved to be as it turned out. I'm not sure the Brits were serious about protecting things down here before the war."

"They gave some obvious hints that they were pulling back, said Carmendez. "Once they hinted at pulling out the survey ship, *HMS Endurance*, our leadership latched on pretty damned quick. It was a big mistake and sent all the wrong signals."

"Very true. Once we landed at Grytviken there was little resistance and we captured a small group of British Marines who really hadn't expected any trouble from a bunch of scrap metal workers. By the time they realised what was going on it was too late to put up any resistance."

"I'd heard some of those stories from an old friend in the Navy. He said very much the same thing. Do go on," Carmendez prompted.

"There was a lot of posturing during those first few days with messages going back and forth from Buenos Aires to London. Apparently, the Head of the British Antarctic Survey asked us to lower the Argentine flag but it took days to get the message through to us. We did but only after a long delay. I heard afterwards that the Government had told the Brits that we would be leaving and that the mission had no official sanction. Nothing could have been further from the truth. We were there under direct orders so God knows what game they were playing back home. It seemed that we might have been just pawns in a much bigger fight. Our position became difficult and at one point, with the impasse, it looked like they were going to load us onto *HMS Endurance* and ship us out but we knew the Navy had set up a picket line and would have intercepted it well before it reached the mainland. Anyway, by 2nd April things turned hot. A small task force had arrived with a Corvette and another support ship which had more Marines onboard supported by helicopters. The Brit Marines fortified the beaches and the area around the survey site with barbed wire and landmines. As our forces moved in close to shore in the Corvette, the weather turned bad and it wasn't until early the next morning when the leader of the task force demanded that the Brits surrender again. It didn't work a second time and, as our Marines landed in their helicopters, a huge fire fight broke out. The Brits dug in around the inlet and, as the helicopters landed, they opened up with heavy machine gun fire damaging one of the birds. It had dropped its troops but as it tried to return to the ship it crashed on the other shore killing some of the crew. Once the fire fight had started we asked for naval gunfire support from the ship but what a disaster! It had 100mm, 40mm and 20mm guns but they barely fired a shot before the guns jammed. I think we only saw about six shots land before the ship was hit by fire from the shore and had to pull back to sea. In the meantime, our Marines were pushing in towards the settlement but the Brits fought back hard. As we pressed, the ship had fixed its big gun and managed to get a few shells on target. That persuaded the Brits that they would get nowhere and they finally surrendered; or so we thought. As far as we were concerned, we were in control but that message hadn't got out to one of the groups of Brit Marines."

Carmendez listened, fascinated by the tale. He had heard stories of the South Georgia operation before but never first hand. He could only contrast the bloody fighting on the ground with his own more impersonal experiences in the cockpit. The events were no less lethal but there was something about the ruthlessness of hand-to-hand combat. He had also targeted his enemies but he had not looked them in the eye when he pulled the trigger. The man continued.

"I came out of the offices where we'd been sheltering and began to work my way over to where I knew our guys were dug in. As I crawled down the street it had gone quiet and I could see one of the British Land Rovers parked up at the intersection in the road. I was nearly back with the rest of the team and took shelter behind a truck when the RPG hit. I have no idea where it came from but the whole side of the truck disintegrated and I was hit by shrapnel. It shattered the knee on my right leg and took off my left leg just below my hip. I passed out almost straight away. I found out later that it was a Brit fire squad who hadn't heard that their commander had given up the fight."

Carmendez listened to a stream of anti-British rhetoric as the old man branched off at a tangent, reliving his trauma. He shared the horrors of the fight realising that there would be no willingness to forgive and forget. This proud ex soldier was crippled, his life had changed forever and forgiveness would be a long time coming. Despite the torrent of abuse Carmendez sympathised with the sentiments and, wrapped up in the mood, he felt himself drawn in.

"I suppose I should feel lucky to have survived with such injuries and it was only the fact that one of the doctors onboard the Corvette had surgical training that saved me. If he hadn't patched me up and stabilised the blood loss I would have been dead before they had chance to evacuate me. When I got home I looked to the Government for help. There was nothing. I spent months being shuffled between military hospitals and a rehabilitation centre in Buenos Aires. When I was finally discharged and returned home, or what now passed for home, we had lost everything. By then I'd heard my son was dead, my home had been repossessed, my wife was in a shanty and I was penniless. I blame the soldier who pulled that trigger but what can I do? I've listened to the hoop from the Government but talk will never recover The Malvinas. Only action will do that. Unfortunately, my chance to influence the outcome has gone."

"I don't know what to say," said a chastened Carmendez. He had been preparing platitudes to explain the loss of his wingman in combat but he was on a new agenda.

"Forgive me, you didn't come all the way down here to hear the ranting of a bitter old man, you came to tell us how our son died."

Carmendez paused finding it hard to ignore the story he had just heard. He collected his thoughts and tried to shift back to recount the events of that fateful day over San Carlos Water. Somehow his words seemed trite. This was not how he had expected to feel. To his relief, the family listened without interruption.

The mood had been sombre and, he was almost relieved as he watched the airman usher the family from the room. The conversation had, without doubt, taken an unexpected turn. Carmendez had assumed it would be a brief description of how Romero had died and they would move on and seek closure. Instead, he found himself wrapped up in the complexity of a family's tragedy. Alone again, Carmendez mulled over the events on that forgotten, frozen outpost in South Georgia and struggled to understand his conflicting emotions. He went over what he had just heard again with a mixture of curiosity and antipathy. The man was a patriot and to have endured the stresses of the Antarctic conditions on the remote island, suffering potentially fatal wounds, there was no way he could be accused of being a coward. He was bitter and angry with his Country and had every right to be but he was even angrier with the soldiers who had inflicted the terrible wounds. The dilemma Carmendez faced was that this could so easily have been the future for him. Although he now enjoyed the status of combat veteran and was running a fighter squadron, his fortunes could have been so different. Was he himself only a simple misfortune away from the same fate; that of Romero's family? Maybe this had been the wakeup call he had needed and, maybe, he had a decision to make. It was looking as if old man Romero had set him an unavoidable challenge but he was a fighter pilot for God's sake. He was used to logic, planning and precision not ethereal ideas of revenge and intrigue. What was he thinking? In his heart he knew that action was needed and, maybe, if the Government wouldn't do anything about it, perhaps he would. Things had just become very personal. Was it a matter of principle or was there an element of self preservation in there?

A unique chain of events was unfolding and he was beginning to understand just how he could make his mark.

CHAPTER 8

GOVERNMENT HOUSE, PORT STANLEY

Sitting at his desk in Government House on the aptly named Government House Road in Port Stanley, Alexander Sullivan leafed through the official papers on his desk. The green roofed building, distinctive with its large conservatory, nestled alongside Ross Road which skirted the Harbour edge. Overlooking Stanley Harbour, it offered some of the most dramatic views in the Capital.

With his Oxford English accent and countrified dress style anyone could be forgiven for thinking that he was a stalwart of the Diplomatic Service. In fact, he had yet to progress to the senior posts he craved but he believed that one day he would sit in the Ambassador's chair, albeit he had his eyes on sunnier climes. In the meantime, he would bide his time, serve out his penance and make sure that whatever his Governor wanted, he would provide. Well at least that was the image he planned to convey but whether his private actions would support his public facade was debatable.

The Governor was traditional in so many ways but radical in others. The British Government's line for media consumption was unwavering and British sovereignty over the islands would never be compromised. In private, the stance was more pragmatic when discussed in the back offices of Whitehall. The truth was that the British presence in The Falklands was hideously expensive and, in these austere times where every penny spent from Government coffers was scrutinised to the last degree, the constant drive to save money often overrode principles. Every Government spending round was increasingly brutal and the Star Chamber was earning a reputation for making, and breaking, political careers. The hidden agenda, known only to the privileged elite, imposed an unsavoury duty on the Governor which he had been reluctant to accept. He had the doubtful task of initiating covert enquiries to sound out the prospects of power sharing with the Argentinian Government. If even the slightest hint of such discussions surfaced in the press, crisis would ensue. Worse still, if the islanders picked up the merest hint he would be ostracised.

In the process, Sullivan had become a vital conduit for the exchange of views and this had added an importance to his role as an aide which far outweighed his humble role in the daily administration of the Dependency. Significantly, his personal skeleton in the cupboard, namely that his family hailed from Spain, had been overlooked by the security vetting agency when he had been selected for the Falklands position. As the official go-between his activities should have been entirely transparent and above reproach. That his loyalties were less than firmly rooted in London and that his sympathies often lay more with the Hispanic community was a guarded secret which he had no intention of sharing. If Sullivan's surreptitious financial ambitions were added to the mix, a volatile cocktail emerged.

Next door to the Governor's Mansion was the Cable and Wireless Radio Service building that provided the vital links with the United Kingdom. The communications centre, enhanced by complex Government encryption devices since the conflict, transmitted secure messages back and forth to the UK daily. The days of the promised high speed telephone links had not yet arrived and the bulk of the traffic still comprised of signal messages that were entered into the system by operators and sent on their way back to the Foreign Office and the Ministry of Defence in London alongside the more mundane traffic generated on the islands. Highly classified political memos shared the wires with orders for new furniture for the local store. Given the Governor's brief, London was not the only destination and, for the first time in many years, message traffic to Argentina was being authorised.

Over the preceding months Sullivan had cultivated discrete and lucrative links to the mainland. Like any diplomat he had an extensive network of contacts in Embassies around the world. That he still made contact with a personal friend in the Foreign Ministry in Buenos Aries might not be well received in security circles after the seismic diplomatic rift following the

Falklands conflict. For his personal agenda it suited him perfectly. If he was to meet his aspirations he also needed covert communications as open discussion carried risk and was problematic. At present, despite his privileged access, it was impossible to include anything but approved messages in the official communiqués. He could hardly send overt messages to his contact in Buenos Aires and, even apparently sociable dialogue would raise an instant flag with the "listeners", the shady monitoring team at the local air base. Merely adding an address in the Argentinian Capital would raise more than the odd eyebrow. Ostensibly, his formal justification was that he was responsible for facilitating the emerging and highly sensitive dialogue between his diplomatic master and the Argentinian Government. In reality he had an even more clandestine agenda and far more information than the tentative embryonic messages was finding its way to the mainland.

To supplement the official dialogue, a small radio set shared cupboard space with his vinyl record collection in his home on Ross Road and he used it to amplify the discussion. Coded messages were drafted using a single-use message pad and transmitted at pre-arranged times. Although his radio set suffered from limitations of range, he knew that an "Electrone" signals intelligence aircraft regularly probed the Falkland Islands Protection Zone and would always be within range at those critical times. His burst transmission would be received by the analyst down the back end of the converted airliner and recorded for decoding in Trelew. His information would eventually find its way to the desk of the diplomat in Buenos Aires; his key contact in Argentina. It was a tense game because not only the Argentinians monitored the ether but British intelligence staff paid equally close attention to any transmissions from the islands. Unguarded transmissions from British troops at nearby RAF Stanley could provide crucial clues as to how the airbase would operate in war and the British operational security snoopers would capture the evidence and punish the unwary. Some of his traffic could be hidden amongst the daily noise but he had occasionally been forced to leave the Capital and chose a more discreet spot for his transmissions. He was becoming used to the high risk game of tit-for-tat.

The message on his desk today was particularly interesting reading. It was the latest assessment from the Joint Intelligence Committee in Whitehall analysing the likely intent of the Argentinian Government. With the war still fresh in diplomatic minds, this view would form the strategy for the foreseeable future and determine the readiness posture. It was still formative but the assessment hinted at the working of military minds. Suffice to say that if there was any indecision it did not emanate from the Old War Office. Talk of appeasement amongst Foreign Office officials was certainly not endorsed by the military planners.

He flipped down to an annex prepared by the Defence Staff showing planned force levels for the next few years. A full squadron of Phantoms, three C-130 tankers and a squadron of helicopters from the RAF would operate from the newly upgraded airstrip at Port Stanley. The Navy would continue to deploy two capital warships, a fleet replenishment tanker, a fisheries patrol boat and the ever present submarine to patrol the coastal waters off Argentina. The Resident Infantry Company would stay at full strength and the force would relocate to the new airfield at Mount Pleasant as soon as it could be completed. Building was already underway and a small town was emerging from the peat bog just 30 miles to the west of the Capital. Such military strength was at odds with the covert noises emanating from the Cabinet Office which hinted at joint sovereignty but he might turn that division to his advantage. His challenge was how to persuade the decision makers in Buenos Aires that the Foreign Office was serious about change when the military presence was so overt. His ideas, if he could implement them, would be seismic.

CHAPTER 9

THE UPLAND GOOSE HOTEL, PORT STANLEY

Port Stanley was an eclectic collection of brightly coloured houses built within a tightly packed grid of streets stretching away at right angles from the shoreline of Stanley Harbour. The coastal road stretched the whole length of the small Capital and extended beyond the town limits and out towards the Golf Club and Moody Brook to the west. Built from a motley collection of building materials which successive generations had managed to acquire from the occasional ship which pulled into the deep water harbour, the brightly coloured houses with their roofs painted in reds and blues and greens brightened up even a rain-swept day. Shops and the occasional tavern were set amongst the houses whilst, along the waterfront, small jetties extended into the harbour shared by freighters and the fleet of fishing boats. Relatively modern industrial buildings backed onto the port forming the backbone of the local economy. Memorials to key events in the islands' long history dotted the sea shore which was dominated by the hulk of the *Lady Elizabeth* in Whale Bone Cove. After striking Uraine Rock just off Volunteer Point in 1912, the ship suffered a six-foot break in the hull and, after docking for repairs, never left port again. Her presence was now a permanent feature of the local vista.

Bustle was not a description that fitted daily life in Port Stanley and, like the myriad of settlements around the islands, residents went about their business at a measured pace. At night the streets were normally quiet as residents retired to their homes.

The military vehicle pulled up outside the Upland Goose Hotel, one of the few in town and the headlights snapped off. In the ensuing darkness, the distorted conversation from the hand-held radio carried by the driver broke the silence. The red roofed hotel building fronted the harbour alongside the main road through Port Stanley and, although the colour of the bright roof was subdued in the dim light, the long conservatory was brightly lit and welcoming. The lights shone out from the lounge windows and a few locals enjoyed a beer in the warmth of the hotel bar. Considering the islands were flooded with thousands of extra temporary military inhabitants the bar was remarkably quiet.

The aircrew piled out of the canvas covered rear compartment of the Land Rover, the banter flying thick and fast. The squadron duty officer nominated as driver for the evening would forgo a glass of coke with his friends. With transport scarce he would be spending his shift fire fighting problems on the squadron and ferrying aircrew around the airfield. Without the transport he provided it was hard for any of the crews to make the short trip into town as a bus service was an impossible luxury.

Although the Phantoms were tucked away for the night, operational signals were still arriving at the base communication centre, sent out by staff officers in London keen to clear their desks before heading home. As they slept, the duty staff at Stanley would field the questions and fire the answers back to be worked around the corridors of the Ministry of Defence the following day. The "nine-to-five" routine in London was not shared at the southern base and the "can do" attitude of an operational detachment was easily abused.

Razor was first to the bar and ordered pints of beer for his thirsty colleagues. The choice was easy. Only Penguin Ale from the local brewery in Stanley was available on tap. Thousands of miles from home, and with links to the mainland limited, the only alternatives were imported beer in a can or a bottle. Not surprisingly, the cans were easily recognisable and the brands of beer and lager hinted more of Yorkshire and Copenhagen than Buenos Aires. Swift with the order he seemed a little less reluctant to pull out his wallet to pay but his hesitation earned him a barrage of abuse from his vocal colleagues shaming him into buying the first round. As the first beer was downed an attractive woman approached the bar and ordered a glass of wine. Razor immediately recognised Karen Pilkington, the journalist who had shared the long flight down from Ascension Island in the C-130. Her casual attire suggested she was lucky enough to be staying at the hotel rather than aboard the Coastel with the rest of the military residents and she had, obviously, not had to brave the elements outside. Despite the limited number of hotel rooms in town, and even with the conflict still fresh in the minds of the inhabitants, competition for those rooms that were available was not exactly stiff. Visitors from outlying communities were more likely to be invited to stay with friends in town than share the relative anonymity of the hotel and there were as yet few tourists vying for the privilege.

Razor quickly struck up a conversation introducing Karen into the circle. With the addition of the attractive newcomer, the conversation switched briefly from flying and she was quizzed on the reasons for her visit. Like them, her job had drawn her to the remote islands and it emerged that she was producing a piece for the Spectator Magazine looking at daily life post-conflict. For her inquisitors, a major attraction of a night in town was the welcome break from the undiluted diet of military matters and the conversation moved onto trips to meet local families and inevitable stories of encounters with the stunning wildlife at close quarters. What resonated with Karen as she listened to the tales was the fact that the islanders embraced the military personnel as their own. During the brief gaps in the operational programme, everyone had been taken into a home and fed and watered for the night as a thank you for the freedom the islanders enjoyed. It was done without question or compensation. It was a simple token of thanks. The result was that, to a man and woman, military personnel would leave the islands having made friends who would never be forgotten for their generosity and patriotism. The stories flowed freely describing a simple but wholesome lifestyle. Getting around was a little more of a challenge than in rural Suffolk or Nordrhein Westphalia and catching a ride in a helicopter to a social venue was not unknown. In total contrast to a local pub in England the stories of penguins and elephant seals did not seem out of place in this cosy bar in the southern hemisphere. Despite the gentle exchange, as a journalist, Karen was not about to pass up on the opportunity to grill her captive audience in an atmosphere a little less inhibited than the busy base. After all she had a story to write and people were always more interesting than machines and her new acquaintances might be less guarded in the sociable surroundings. She had been frustrated at the close supervision so far and the reticence of the interviewees who had been wheeled out at RAF Stanley, although interesting, had been less than newsworthy. With the beer flowing she found volunteers increasingly willing to regale her with stories. Flying was never far from the minds of the Phantom aircrew and the conversation drifted onto operations at Stanley and of low flying across the barren moors and hillsides around the islands. Keen for more "off the record" snippets Karen didn't dissuade the chitchat. The diet of "war stories" continued unabated proving that life "Down South" could be eventful.

Sitting on alert some days before, the hooter had sounded. After a mad dash to the west they intercepted an "Electrone" electronic reconnaissance aircraft which was probing the Falkland Islands Protection Zone. It was part of the inevitable game of chess which had replaced the shooting of 1982. Each side postured conveying a sense of strength by action to their hostile neighbours while gathering as much vital intelligence about orders of battle and operational deployments as possible. The alert aircraft had been dragged well to the west almost to the Argentinian mainland before making the obligatory identification of the snooper. It was important to know who was probing the zone and why, although the slow speed of the converted airliner was a big clue to its identity. It was unlikely that a wayward Mirage would saunter around the periphery of the zone at such a slow speed. It could be only one culprit; the "Silent Listeners".

Karen eavesdropped intently, wishing she could scribble away on her notepad to capture the rapid fire exchange. Given the chance, she would take the aircrew aside later during her visit to the Squadron and see if she could capture these stories on the record for one of her articles. At this point she bided her time.

So what's the plan for the rest of your stay Karen?" asked Razor jolting her from her thoughts.

"I'm here for another five days," she replied. "The main event is a memorial ceremony that is going to be held at the Argentinian Cemetery at Darwin. It's the first time the Argentinian families have been given clearance to visit the graves."

Razor was momentarily disconcerted by her stunning good looks. She was attractive and not in an "island fever" sort of way. She would have turned heads in any London bar but the effect here was magnified. He switched track to cover his distraction.

"Are you involved in this VIP visit that everyone is talking about?"

"Yes, he's a junior Minister from the Foreign Office and quite influential in the politics of the aftermath. The Editor is quite keen that I ask a few searching questions while he's down here, although I guess he'll be well briefed and rehearsed. I doubt I'll get a straight answer as usual. Rumour is that there are financial pressures in London but any change in the political stance will be resisted quite fiercely down here."

"I stayed with a family out in Pax Port Howard last week, replied one of the group. "I didn't hear any signs of forgiveness or reconciliation. Can't see the locals having any truck with the politicians on that one"

"Without a doubt," said Flash. "I've been down here before and chatted to the islanders. The larger settlements suffered badly during the war and whole communities were locked up during those few weeks. It caused a lot of bad feeling. Why should they talk about their future? They know what they want and they seem to have a firm view on how to get it. I think we're a temporary distraction with so many troops in the area but when Mount Pleasant opens up, things might get back to some semblance of normal life around town."

The conversation dotted around before settling back on safer ground and more beers and wine appeared on the bar. There was little else on which to spend their hard earned cash on the islands. The fluffy seal or Falkland Islands tea mug would be bought much nearer home time. In the meantime, beer was a reasonable compromise. Sometimes it could be a challenge to spend the paltry 50 pence daily detachment allowance they received during their operational deployment.

"Transport's outside," shouted a loud voice from the doorway. "Time to go!"

Time had sped past. Bar stools shuffled back and swift goodbyes were exchanged as the recently arrived Penguin Ale was drained quickly. Karen followed them to the door making her way back to her room but, as he was about to follow his receding mates, Razor sneaked a polite peck on the cheek. With the rest of the group already stumbling out into the darkness and, keen to take advantage of the vital transport, he paused. If the Land Rover left without him, it was a long and cold walk back to the Coastel. He felt a buzz as she paused, the hint of perfume tantalising yet out of place. Her eyes hinted of more but outside, the raucous squawks from the persistent aircrew broke the moment. He smiled again, making polite noises about how much he'd enjoyed the evening. There was a moment of eye contact before he backed away reluctantly breaking the spell.

Rushing towards the Land Rover, its exhaust smoking away in the cold air, the truck began to pull away with hoots of laughter echoing from behind the canvas cover leaving Razor in its wake.

"Very funny," he groaned, attempting to climb aboard the slowly moving vehicle as it moved forward over the slippery road surface. It was a minor miracle he didn't break a leg as he teetered on the towing ball hefting his backside over the high tailgate and flopping into the cabin. Finally installed on the hard plastic padded mat of the makeshift bench seat and gripping the tubular frame to steady himself, he tried to find a comfortable position. It was impossible as the Rover negotiated the rough island roads turning back towards the airbase.

It had been a welcome diversion as he visualised the intriguing face of the journalist. Had she hinted of more to come?

CHAPTER 10

MOUNT ALICE, WEST FALKLANDS

Inside the radome at No. 751 Signals Unit on Mount Alice, the technicians had begun to reassemble the radar. The NCO shouted orders above the noise of the generator unit pushing his men hard. The Boss had made it perfectly clear that he wanted this job finished in quick time and he, in turn, had made his instructions clear to his team. He had friends from his home unit detached to the other remote control post on the northern tip of the island at Byron Heights and he knew that, if there was any delay in getting the radar back online, he'd never hear the end of it. It had become a matter of professional pride.

More important than any personal motives, until the hardware was reinstalled, the temporary gap in the radar cover over the islands would badly affect their ability to detect intruders, particularly at low level. Seeing anything flying in the numerous inlets and valleys that dotted the coastline was impossible and that made them all vulnerable. Byron covered the northern waters but coverage this far to the south and west was patchy with only a single radar operating. HMS Newcastle had been redeployed into the south western approaches as a stop gap but the air defence commander would lose an element of flexibility and the airspace would be just that bit more vulnerable in the meantime. He could imagine just how nervous the Captain would be with his huge vessel tethered within a 20 mile radius, its position broadcast to the monitoring stations to the west. Until the NCO had completed his task and reinstalled the radar, the ship would plug the gap and her radars would feed into the recognised air picture but she was predictable and exposed. The technicians had been left in no doubt as to how quickly they should recommission the radar head.

The hefty stabilising legs had been extended from the sides of the base and had taken up the load. Levelling the platform had been straight forward on its brand new concrete plinth, although shipping the tons of concrete onsite from the temporary cement works had not been a simple task and it was probably the first time the Chinook helicopter had substituted for a cement mixer. The team of technicians were already raising the radar scanner back into its more familiar erect position but a simple failure had threatened to slow the progress. The integral lifting motor had failed prompting endless cursing. A temporary gantry with a block and tackle had been substituted and seemed to be doing the job. As the NCO watched, the scanner reached its apex and huge locking bolts were slotted into place securing the framework. It was nearly ready to resume its relentless rotation.

Thick electric cables were laid out across the floor and disappeared outside through a small gap in the radome snaking away to the control cabin across the desolate, rock-strewn site. Providing both power and control signals to the enormous scanner they were the vital umbilical which, when reconnected, would allow the operators to resume control of the system. Unable to make himself heard over the whine of the generator he made a few unintelligible gestures to his team and opened the small access door, the sudden gap in the protective structure causing the heavy material of the radome to flap violently against its metal frame. He emerged into the brutal wind blast prevalent on the exposed mountain top. They had been fortunate to catch a lull in the weather but the gales had returned with a vengeance and he was glad that they were working inside the dome benefitting from the protection of the bubble. Head down, he struggled against the wind making his way towards the control cabin.

The engineering officer looked up as he slammed the door cutting out the icy blast.

"How's it going Sarge?" he asked still worried about the failure of the lifting motor, contemplating the sombre news that the replacement parts would take a week to arrive from the UK. If the work-around didn't solve the problem he was guaranteed a few sleepless nights.

"It's up Sir," the NCO replied, his face showing his evident relief. "Once we got the gantry in place it was straight forward enough. That lifting arm only just fitted in though. If it had been a few feet longer we'd have been stuffed. It would have been a case of either dismantle the radome or wait for the parts to arrive."

"Bloody well done. The first round's on me when the bar opens tonight. I'll have a chat with them all later but the Boss will be a happy man. What's still to be done?"

"The boys are doing the final calibration checks to make sure it's stable. The electrical work is already complete and the snag on the transmitter is fixed. The routine servicing will take about half an hour and then we'll be ready to fire it up for the test."

"So if I warn the Master Controller at Puffin that we can go live on the hour will that work?"

The NCO glanced at his watch.

"Looks good to me Sir. I'll chase them up and we should be able to meet that."

The officer picked up the handset and hit the direct line to the Sector Operations Centre on East Falkland.

"Sir, it's John Dutton at Alice. We'll be ready for a calibration run at 1300 Zulu."

He listened to the Master Controller watching the NCO struggle with the door against the wind. The howl subsided again.

"Yes, we had a few issues but the team has done a good job. All being well, if nothing was shaken around during the move, we'll be back online as soon as the calibration is complete. The controllers are champing at the bit over here. There's not much to do without a radar and there's only so much housekeeping I can give them. Yes I'll call back in 30 minutes and give you an update"

Back in the radome, as the last adjustments were made, the NCO added the final coordinating signatures to the paperwork and the technicians began to shuffle outside into the fierce westerly winds, their task complete. The NCO would stay inside as the radar was fired up to make sure it was revolving properly on its pedestal. Once the decision was taken to fire up the transmitter he wanted to be just a little farther away. The thought of standing within a few feet of the scanner when it began to pump out megawatts of radar energy seemed just a tad too brave. He wanted a suntan but he would leave that until he could take a spell on a foreign beach once he got home. With a brief signal over the headset the generator outside the radome cranked up a notch, straining to take up the load. The massive motors inside the base began to whirr and the synchronised gears burst into life. Above him the huge scanner began to rotate, slowly at first but gathering speed until it reached its steady state of about six revolutions a minute. It would hold that speed for 24 hours a day for the foreseeable future until it was, once again, taken offline for its next servicing. If all had gone well that would be some considerable time in the future. He cast his eyes over the structure making a final check that the countless components had been reassembled correctly, double checking for friction, pinch points or electrical arcing. All seemed normal as the huge scanner continued its relentless rotation.

With a sigh of relief, he retraced his colleague's footsteps from the radome slamming the door shut and returning to the control cabin ready for the calibration. He would not be the only one who would be nervous for the next hour.

CHAPTER 11

RUNWAY 26, RAF STANLEY

Razor pulled the Phantom alongside his leader, the metal matting of Runway 26 at RAF Stanley stretching out ahead of him through the front windscreen. The coarse surface of the interlocking panels hardly looked fit for use as a runway. The dingy paint that covered the surface in a vain attempt to tone-down the strip to blend in with the surrounding grass seemed futile. The jet nodded forward as he hit the toe brakes on the rudder pedals and came to a stop. In the back Ed Frith the navigator with whom he'd shared a pint in the Upland Goose the night before had already rattled through the final pre-takeoff checks. It was almost a formality as they were so firmly embedded in his mind that Razor had, involuntarily, finished them before they were called. He eased the throttles up looking down at the engine gauges. With the throttles at 80%, the engines stabilised and the RPMs and temperatures holding steady, he flicked off the landing light, his signal to the leader that he was ready. It was strange to see his own navigator in the back of the other jet, staring over at him, checking his jet for any last minute problems or loose panels. For this familiarisation sortie they were flying as a split crew until they had reacquainted themselves with the local landmarks and procedures. Both heads in the other cockpit turned to the front ready for takeoff. The leader tapped his bonedome, the sign that they were about to roll as a pair. At the nod of his leader's head, Razor eased the throttles up to max mil and the two jets began to roll forward, slowly at first. Anticipating the next command he rocked the throttles outboard ready to push forward into reheat. With the jets picking up speed, he slotted tighter into the close formation position, gently guiding the jet with the rudder bars, holding the echelon position, rapidly accelerating. Ready for the second head nod, he was already leading with full afterburner playing the throttles rhythmically to stay in the saddle. He listened to the commentary from the back as the speed built up through 100 knots. The pair seemed tied together with an invisible bond.

"140 Go!" he heard from the back. They were committed to takeoff and any problem now would have to be sorted out in the air. As the weight came off the wheels, the oleos extended to their full travel, the undercarriage suddenly seeming twice its original length as the two lumbering fast jets lifted off, mere feet apart. He held the throttles forward to the firewall the noise of the afterburners from the other aircraft easily audible through the tough perspex of the canopy and his protective bonedome. He could sense rather than see the horizon in his peripheral vision as they flew clear of the ground now well clear of the runway, his whole attention fixed on the jet only feet away. A rotary cycling motion from the leader followed by a further head nod and a pause signalled the undercarriage retraction on his leader's jet. He slammed the red, circular lever on the bulkhead to its up position, the gear on his own jet travelling simultaneously as the undercarriage doors retracted smoothly covering the huge main wheels which had braked to a halt in the wheel wells. The flaps followed and with the massive drag suddenly removed the jets picked up speed rapidly until he sensed a slight closure as his leader pulled slowly out of reheat at 350 knots. His eyes still glued to the other cockpit he was ready for the kiss off that he knew would be imminent. With a wave of the hand he saw the flash of the planform as his leader broke hard away from him prompting a similar reaction. Holding a diverging heading for scant seconds he reversed the turn and they dropped into arrow formation as the leader began the gentle climb around Two Sisters and up the slopes of Mount Kent. Their first event was a tracking exercise for the Blowpipe operators at the radar site on the hill.

Today they were flying their first familiarisation sortie and they were paired with a crew who were coming to the end of their detachment. With an unfamiliar voice from the other cockpit, today's split-crew sortie was a departure from the normal routine. Razor's temporary navigator would offer reminders and advice to familiarise him with the navigation features and airspace procedures which would be a feature of his life for the next four months.

First the Phantoms would attack the radar site on the summit of Mount Kent approaching from random headings to confuse the defenders. Their simulated attack would keep the missile troop sharp. They might decide to return at any time during the sortie so there would be no relaxation on the mountain peak for the next 90 minutes. It was for the surveillance controller in his darkened control room to spot the inbound "raid" and alert the firing team of the approach sector. For this first attack there would be no time to prepare as the Phantoms would hit the site immediately after takeoff hugging the contours of the hill and popping up at the last minute. A late "unmask" would give the operators no time to refine their tracking solution and the fleeting shot as the Phantoms flashed overhead the site would be just as tricky, particularly if they pulled for the safety of low level after the pass. Not only was it exhilarating for the missile teams, with Phantoms flashing scant feet above their heads at high speed, but it offered an adrenaline buzz for the crews operating at extreme low level, manoeuvring hard in the hilly terrain. They had been airborne for less than 5 minutes when the leader flashed over the radome which housed the air defence radar passing just 250 feet above the bubble. Razor in the number 2 had widened the formation and pulled back hard towards his leader, crossing the site on a 60 degree converging heading passing yards behind, only narrowly avoiding the jet wash as they passed through the overhead. For the sake of the personnel on the ground he hoped that if the pass had been for real, the operators had tracked their approach, unlocked the missile heads and would have had a Blowpipe in the air. Privately, he had little confidence in the obsolescent rocket and hoped desperately that the long promised replacement, the Javelin, arrived soon. It would be a quantum improvement and the vital radar units deserved better protection. No sooner had he passed the apex of the hill, the communications masts prominent in his peripheral vision, when the hillside fell away and the terrain opened up on the other side. He rolled hard to the inverted pulling back down for the plain below. A quick spot roll and the world returned to its correct orientation and he pushed up the throttles watching the speed build to 500 knots as they made their escape.

"Stud 9, Stud 9, Go!" he heard as the leader chopped them across to the flight watch frequency.

"Eagle 42."

"Loud and clear, all stations Eagles 41 and 42 on frequency, passing Kent en route Goose Green, low level."

With the simple call other flights in the local area would be aware of their presence and would watch out for them. Some would be keen to avoid their flight path but other marauding Phantoms might use the warning to have a little "nibble" if they happened to be in the same part of the airspace. The game was on!

The navigation exercise planned for the first 30 minutes would acquaint him with the diverse geography. Heading west along the plain south of Pleasant Peak they passed close to the embryonic base at Mount Pleasant which would soon be home to the Phantoms. Razor quickly settled in at low level and took a quick glance at his radar repeater display below his gunsight. It was reassuringly empty as the time base of the radar swept rhythmically left and right, the powerful AN/AWG12 scanning the airspace ahead. A quick check of the instruments and gauges and he transferred his attention to the world outside scanning his visual sector for trouble. A huge bird, probably a goose, flashed down the left hand side causing an immediate comment from the back seat. It had been close and the last thing they needed was one of those down the intake. Birds were a constant hazard at low level and would give the Spey engine severe indigestion if ingested. He unconsciously tugged at his clear visor making sure it was locked down, perhaps the last level of protection if a bird should penetrate the canopy.

Eating up the miles they soon coasted-out over the large expanse of Falkland Sound the water stretching out each side. Hugging the wave tops Razor looked ahead for the small inlet with Mount Moody beyond, the familiar features retrieved from his memory banks. The pair popped up, briefly cresting the ridge before dropping back down to 250 feet once back over dry land. A little jink right and they bore down on the settlement at Chartres the airspeed indicator touching 450 knots. The islanders would be happy to get their daily "fix" as the Phantoms flashed overhead at extreme low level bracketing the houses as they passed. Once they reached the western coastline they would turn north to route offshore along the coast for another tracking exercise at the radar site at Byron Heights.

Unbeknown to them Eagles 31 and 32 had launched just 15 minutes before and were sitting up at 10,000 feet off the western coast looking back towards Falkland Sound. They had already detected their fellow squadron mates on radar and had begun to vector inbound prosecuting an intercept. Staying high out of the visual detection zone they pushed up the speed and began to descend slowly.

"Rackets 11 o'clock" called Flash from the back of Eagle 41. Within the formation, eyes began to swivel looking for the elusive visual sighting. They scanned the horizon assuming the other Phantoms were down at low level with them. Nothing seen!

Up above still holding their height above 5000 feet, the other formation held off from locking their radars to the incoming formation trying but failing to avoid announcing their arrival on their victim's radar warning receivers. On hearing the radio call on the tactical frequency they had lost the advantage but staying up at height made them hard to see. Despite their guile the defenders were alerted. As the range closed down, the urgent commentary in the defending formation was prompting the pilots to gain visual contact but the attackers had the upper hand and could see the outbound pair of Phantoms at low level heading west. From their lofty perch above, the light grey jets, their camouflage optimised for medium level, stood out against the brown scrubland. Just when it seemed they would miss the intercept and fly past, the attacking pair reefed into a tight turn towards each other passing close aboard in a high G manoeuvre pulling down towards the deck rolling in on the pair below.

"Bogeys high 5 o'clock, inwards counter, go!" called Flash from the lead aircraft. Without a thought Razor pulled hard towards his leader who responded as they passed beak-to-beak, preventing the other pair from dropping into missile range.

"Flares, flares, flares" called Ed in Razor's back seat, anticipating the simulated missile firing from the attackers. With each aircraft carrying live weapons, as the call was made, and almost simultaneously, eight aircrew unconsciously made absolutely certain that the weapons switches were set to safe, the firing circuit breakers were pulled and that the risk of stray Sidewinders being launched or involuntary infra-red countermeasures being dispensed was minimal! Mutual self destruction was not on the agenda.

The practice engagement lasted just minutes and after two brief turns the formations separated, one to return for recovery to Stanley and the other to continue with their familiarisation sortie. Adrenaline abated, it was back to the prime mission. The descriptions of the key landmarks which would guide them around the islands would form a matrix that would ensure that they could never become "temporarily unsure of position" – otherwise known as lost – as they navigated their way around the islands in the coming months. As with every familiarisation sortie before them, famous sites such as San Carlos Water, Pebble Island, Fanning Head and Darwin were on the itinerary. These locations had risen to fame during battles in the conflict. Dotted around between those battlefields were sites of crashed aircraft from both sides which the crews would later visit on the ground. There was a final venue to visit before recovering to Stanley. *HMS Newcastle* was operating in the waters off the coast and was singled out for a flypast to keep the Navy team on their toes. It was a well practised routine and broke the monotony at sea.

Flypast complete and with the fuel dropping towards minimums, the call of "Bingo" initiated the recovery and they began the long run back to Stanley airfield. As the range on the needles in the cockpit wound down, Razor felt the tension rising as the time for his first trap into the arrestor cable approached. He had mentally rehearsed the differences between Stanley and his home base eager not to make a mistake on his first day. The airfield should be easy enough to find, sitting prominently on the peninsular at the eastern end of the island but once in the circuit things would become more challenging. He would be popping the brake parachute on short finals whilst still airborne, the short 600 foot pull out of the arrestor cable and the harsh metal runway surface also helping to arrest progress down the strip. Hopefully, the combination of all these factors would bring his jet to a safe stop. Psychologically prepared, he watched Cape Pembroke slip by as they let down.

"Eagles 41 and 42, initials."

The adrenaline kicked in once more as they dropped to 500 feet in tight battle formation for the break into the circuit.

CHAPTER 12

NEAR VILLA REYNOLDS AIRBASE, ARGENTINA

Back in his comfortable home on the outskirts of town close to the airbase at Villa Reynolds, Carmendez closed the book and dropped it onto the growing pile on the coffee table struggling to analyse the jumbled facts. He was in a contemplative mood. His brief research had begun with an account of air operations compiled by two journalists. It mapped out air combat engagements during the Malvinas conflict with stories taken from the firsthand accounts of aircrew recorded during post-conflict interviews in both Argentina and the United Kingdom. He vaguely remembered being taken aside by a researcher in the months following the surrender when he had described the conditions over his own targets. He had come across the description of his sortie, the one during which Romero had been killed, reading with a detached curiosity. The stark description seemed disconnected from the grim and utterly personal reality of the event. Having been compiled from true accounts, many of the stories cut through the Government-issued bluster released on both sides at the time of the conflict mostly making lurid claims of success. The matter-of-fact recollections brought back more sombre memories of his own.

Another book written by a soldier who had served in the British garrison on South Georgia told the story of the recapture in bleak terms and seemed at odds with Romero's recollections. It was telling that many of the accounts of those days only emanated from the British literary press rather than those in Argentina. It was as if his Country had suffered national amnesia at the unexpected outcome. The final piece was from a local Argentinian newspaper in which an investigative journalist had delved into the fate of the veterans after the war. Their plight had, indeed, been a National disgrace and many were left to fend for themselves with little support from an over-stretched healthcare system. The report followed former combatants from all three services, delved into their combat traumas and probed the subsequent nightmares. The story Romero's father had recounted of a family torn apart had resonance and seemed to be reinforced by the journalist's research. Piecing together the disparate facts hardened his view.

His dilemma was how to respond. In the days following the capitulation in Port Stanley retribution had followed and many high profile leaders, particularly military leaders, had felt the consequences. Careers had ended but, for some, high profile trials and, eventually, incarceration had been the outcome. Despite the visible reprisals, too many of his countrymen seemed to live with daily regret of the consequences of the military foray. If he had been able to extend his research to their British counterparts, both leadership and combatants, he doubted he would find parallels. During the days of the military Junta, life on the streets of Argentina had been harsh but it seemed that life for many patriots, even in these enlightened times, was no less harsh. In contrast, scenes of celebration bordering on jingoism had been reported from London.

With frustration growing and his determination fortified, he resolved to act.

CHAPTER 13

OPERATIONS WING, RAF STANLEY

Wing Commander John Fitzpatrick, the Officer Commanding Operations Wing and the Air Defence Commander for the Falkland Islands perched on the edge of his desk in Wing Operations at RAF Stanley. A qualified Phantom pilot, he would have preferred to be flying but the ever growing pile of files and the raft of signals from Group Headquarters in UK was conspiring against him. At least he had a pleasant diversion on today's schedule. He was planned to be interviewed by Karen Pilkington from the Spectator Magazine, this morning and the discussion would be followed by a visit to air traffic control and then on to see the jets holding alert on the squadrons. Like most military personnel, he was slightly nervous about talking to the press. Conversations might drift into areas he would rather not discuss and unauthorised disclosures were guaranteed to cause difficulties back in London. Classified information and freedom of the Press were not comfortable bedfellows and what seemed like an innocent comment in discussion could seem somewhat more contentious as a headline in a newspaper or magazine. If he was honest, he was happier in the cockpit of a Phantom than to be sparking controversy in London with an unguarded remark.

He leafed through the pink covered Secret file on the desk trying to piece together the implications of the intelligence analysis. As Air Defence Commander it was his job to set the alert posture and make sure his forces were able to meet any threat to the islands. The move of the radar to Mount Alice had caused more than a few nervous moments, particularly with the

Ministerial visit taking place this week. Byron was still covering most of the airspace to the northwest and Kent had the approaches to and from Ascension Island covered but he would not relax until the southerly radar was back on line. The extra pair of Phantoms to escort the Minister's C-130 into Stanley had been a prudent contingency but there had been no reaction on the mainland. The air defence frequencies had been quiet and the flying activity routine.

The timing of the visit by the Argentinean families to the war graves was no coincidence and was overtly political. He could see the statements from the Press Office in his mind's eye even now. It would divert some of the media interest away from the real reason for the visit but his biggest worry was the Argentinean firepower demonstration and whether it was significant. The venue at Rio Gallegos was slightly worrying as it pulled aircraft down from the north and within range of the islands. He would need to increase the readiness state during the period. The intelligence seemed plausible and, if it was accurate, having up to a dozen potentially hostile fighter-bombers, fuelled to full and supported by a tanker would be a headache. The intelligence report showed that they would be armed with bombs and missiles and a rogue attack against the new base at Mount Pleasant would make a statement. It was a sizeable force and he would need all his assets in position, both fighters and surface-to-air missiles, should the Argentinean jets head east off the tanker. None of his shore-based radars had the range to paint the assembly area inside Argentinean territorial waters and he cursed the lack of an airborne early warning aircraft. It was impossible to deploy a Shackleton this far south and his request had fallen on deaf ears back at Group Headquarters. The trip would have taken it out of the orbat for weeks with its slow cruising speed and the rejection of his request had been swift. He sometimes wondered where the priorities lay. He would have to push *HMS Newcastle* even further west and hope her Type 965 surveillance radar would give him the coverage he needed.

He dithered briefly considering whether to increase the alert state now and err on the side of caution. He decided to let it ride as his political brief was not to show a military response to the Minister's arrival. The Government Press Officer would lead with the messages in public. No, it seemed that the activity on the mainland was simple sabre rattling and he would not be drawn. Two jets on 10 minutes would be enough for the time being. He'd bring it up to four on the day of the demonstration.

"Miss Pilkington's here to see you Sir, shall I show her in?"

"Yes please Hazel," he replied to his personal assistant, his concentration broken. "Can you bring us coffee?"

The door opened and the journalist was shown into the room, her chic clothes in stark contrast to those of his PA, decked out in her off-the-peg "cabbage kit." He sensed a slight friction between the two women and wondered, briefly, whether he should have insisted on pseudo military garb for the journalist's visit. The largely male-dominated environment was driven by testosterone rather than oestrogen and the balance could be fragile. As he moved around the desk to make his introductions, he was aware that his own flying suit might have benefitted from a trip to the Chinese Laundry. The facilities at Stanley could be rudimentary at times and, with hindsight, a wash and brush up might have been advisable before meeting the press. Unexpectedly, he felt immediately relaxed as he shook her hand and waved her over to the easy chairs in the corner of the office. Her warm smile seemed genuine and he felt instantly comfortable in her company. The deep leather armchairs, at odds with the austerity, were one of the few luxuries he enjoyed and reminded him of the crewroom on his old Squadron in Germany.

"I hope you've recovered from the stress of the trip down," he opened. "I hear you've settled into the Upland Goose. It's a little more comfortable downtown than it would be in the Coastels and it's a massive improvement over the old Rangatira!"

MV Rangatira, fondly nicknamed "Old Smelly" had been moored in Stanley Harbour in the years since the conflict. Home to well over a thousand personnel, it had been a step up from the tent city that had sprung up on the airfield but still left a lot to be desired. Every available space had been converted into accommodation and the rapidly installed helicopter deck and the light anti aircraft guns fitted to the superstructure gave it an air of a warship rather than a coastal ferry which had been its former role in life. The Coastel accommodation barges, in contrast, were another huge improvement bringing some semblance of normal life to the base but the stark bunks were still a long way short of the comforts of the small hotel downtown.

"It's really quite nice," she replied "and it's in a lovely spot just alongside the harbour. The views from the rooms are just incredible. It's hard to think that Port Stanley was a war zone just a few years ago. It seems so peaceful now on a sunny day. I spent some time in the Western Islands of Scotland and I could almost be back there."

"I saw some thought-provoking pictures taken during the occupation showing armoured convoys parked in the road right outside the hotel. They had the town locked down tight in those few weeks just after the invasion."

"I saw that shot in a frame in the lobby of the hotel. It's quite a contrast now with life pretty much back to normality. And yes thanks, it was a long flight down but the aches and bruises are just about gone. I wish I'd known about the hammock trick. Some of your aircrew enjoyed a rather more comfortable ride down than I did with a hammock strung across the cargo bay. I can't say I'm really looking forward to the return leg though. Maybe I'll take a boat home, although I suspect my Editor might balk at the idea of me being gone another week."

"Well I'm all yours for the morning," he replied warming to the upcoming task. Her civilian clothes and the hint of perfume were a welcome break from the drab military camouflage kit that everyone wore around the airbase. No one had told her that perfume and make up were not features of deployed military life. Maybe that was a good thing he reflected before returning to business.

"I've planned a trip around the Station and we can drop in at Air Traffic Control on the way across to the Phantom Squadron if you like. By the way, as we chat, if I drop in too many acronyms and abbreviations I apologise in advance. It goes with the job I'm afraid. Just stop me if I'm talking code and I'll explain. Let me know if there are other sections you'd like to visit because we tend to show visitors the obvious things; the sharp end if you will. I want to make sure we give you a balanced view of what goes on down here. For every Phantom crew there are 20 other people doing the support work in the background and their contributions are no less important, just not quite as glamorous. I'm always keen to show off their good work. The aircraft tend to be the stars but without the support people nothing would move around here. Are there any areas that particularly interest you? Have you decided on the content of your articles yet?"

"Yes and no. The Editor wants some general interest stuff with lots of action pictures and aircraft taking off and landing. The sort of thing that shows why we are still down here; but in my book the best stories are always about people. I'm looking to pick up more on the problems that you face during the daily routine rather than the hardware you have down here," she said. "So many journalists have covered the operations so well before me. I don't want to go over old ground. I'm hoping to get something a bit different."

"I can see that," he replied. "So which particular aspects interest you most?"

"I met some of your Phantom crews last night and they've already told me that I only need to visit the Squadron to get the true picture."

She smiled, letting him off the hook easily.

"Don't worry, I'm only teasing," she quipped, watching him relax visibly. "Can we start with you? The Station Commander gave me a brief introduction when I arrived but said that you'd fill in the blanks. Tell me about your duties. I understand that you're the Air Defence Commander? That must generate a lot of interesting challenges. What if an Argentinian aircraft should intrude? Can you ever envisage having to shoot it down?"

"You'll appreciate that I can't talk about the Rules of Engagement as they are still highly sensitive. Let's say the Argentinians test us all the time," he explained. "The surveillance aircraft are constantly probing the Protection Zone, listening to our comms channels trying to work out what we are doing. They test our reactions almost daily and hope that we drop careless snippets which tell them what we do and how we do it."

"Do you mind if I take notes?"

"Feel free. I should say that some things are still a bit touchy but take notes and pictures as we go. I'd just ask that you check with your contact officer that any pictures you take are cleared before you leave. I can get her to work with you on that. It'll be quicker than waiting for MOD to clear the shots."

Despite his cooperative stance, his military mind urged caution as he envisaged each statement he was about to make regurgitated as gospel in Spectator Magazine. Somehow, jocular comments said more in jest than in truth didn't seem quite so hilarious in print. His scepticism was quickly tested and the journalist was good. Gentle background questions switched in seconds to deep, politically-laced probes about the military posture and intent. Staff officers in MOD were much better placed to answer such aspects and he found himself batting off the subtle hand grenades. He reminded himself to keep his guard up. As the grilling slowed, he made excuses about the time and hastened his guest out of the office, eager for a break from the unexpected pummelling.

Wing Operations was located in the same building as the air traffic control tower and they made the short climb up the stairs to the local control room in the glasshouse on top of the building. As they emerged from the stairwell they were greeted by the local controller clad in tactical green, his headphones draped casually around his neck. After a brief introduction Karen was whisked over to a control console by the controller who began to explain the intricacies of his workplace. The Wing Commander walked over to the Duty Officer Flying, a Phantom navigator from 23 Squadron who was sitting at a small desk at the back of the tower, grateful for a break from his inquisitive visitor. Responsible for setting the flying state and providing advice if a fast jet had a problem, the DOF would assist the controllers with technical advice on the Phantom should a crew have an emergency and things became fraught; a situation all too common. They chatted quietly about various aspects of the days programme as the local controller briefed the journalist, his arms waving as he pointed out the individual flying units from their lofty perch above the aircraft servicing platform. In front of them, a massive C-130 tanker was being prepared for a mission. Closer to them, a second C-130 sat dormant, its doors open apparently ready to accept its crew. It was holding alert ready to be scrambled to support QRA and sat just a few short steps away from the crewroom. In the event of a hooter sounding, the crew would immediately rush to the huge tanker ready to launch in case the Phantoms needed extra fuel for the mission. At any time when the weather turned marginal it would almost certainly launch, particularly if the fighters were airborne.

From her vantage point in the tower Karen could see the rubs across the far side of the airfield which housed the helicopter detachment. Until a few months earlier it had been home to the Harriers which had remained for some time after the war. With the ground attack mission diminished the small jets had provided temporary air defence coverage armed with hastily added Sidewinder missiles. Relieved by the Phantoms they had finally been able to return to the UK for a well earned break from operations. With a custom dispersal freed up, the helicopter detachment has swiftly laid claim to the site and eagerly taken up residence in their new search and rescue base. Freight operations were still centred on the busy parking area in front of the tower but the SAR alert crews could now enjoy a semblance of peace, at least until the hooter sounded. To the east, the sprawling dispersal which spanned the runway housed the Phantoms, most of them also protected from the elements by rubs. Metal covered taxiways linked the operational areas at each side with the runway. In the midst of his spiel, the controller made his excuses as a pair of Phantoms checked in on frequency, calling initials at the visual reporting point just 5 miles to the east. He pulled his headset back over his ears as Karen watched on.

"Eagles, clear to join, surface wind 270 at 10 knots."

He pointed to the smoky trails in the distance just south of Cape Pembroke and heads in the control tower slewed in unison. Binoculars were raised and trained on the approaching formation. The Phantoms dropped lower, the smoke diminishing as the Speys were pushed up to maximum power for a high speed join. The distance between the jets narrowed until they were just a few hundred yards apart, by now only 300 feet above the ground. The DOF looked questioningly at the senior officer alongside him and received a silent nod of assent. The crews in the Phantoms had not been notified that their rejoin was to be under scrutiny and the DOF would have liked to give them a warning that their performance would be "marked". He hoped that 300 feet was the limit of their indiscretion. He could probably sweet-talk OC Ops into the fact that they knew the journalist would want to see a punchy arrival. Beer would change hands if he succeeded.

"Eagles, on the break, Eagle 43 to land into the approach end cable."

"Eagle 44 for overshoot and hold until cleared to arrest."

Both Phantoms racked into a 4G break over the runway and, as each pilot closed the throttles and popped the airbrakes, the speed washed off rapidly. The screaming noise of the Speys died back as the jets turned downwind setting up for the approach. The lead aircraft slowed to 250 knots and as the onlookers watched, the undercarriage emerged into the airflow and locked down. The gear was closely followed by the tail hook on the lead aircraft. Extending slightly the leader began the descending final turn towards the runway threshold as the number 2 ghosted his movements just a short distance behind.

"Eagle 43, finals, gear and hook, to land."

"Eagle 43, clear land, wind 270 10 gusting 15 knots."

"Land, Eagle 43."

"Eagle 44, going round from finals."

As the leader positioned on finals the number 2 pushed open the throttles and stayed at circuit height turning parallel to the runway its landing gear breaking the clean lines beneath the jet. It flew noisily overhead the tower waiting patiently for its turn to land. Gusty crosswinds could cause weathercocking during the approach and more than a few pilots had been given a timely reminder that the Phantom could have some unpleasant vices, operating at the edges of its performance envelope. Anyone in any doubt need only ask the pilots who had flown from the aircraft carriers in the 1970s. Bravado was best avoided and, with the wind nearly down the strip, the leader had no concerns over using his brake parachute to give that extra help with slowing down before entering the cable. As he settled down on final approach, the needles were in the groove and the approach indicators showed that he was spot on the glide path. The radio sounded in the tower.

"Eagle 44, turning downwind."

The number 2 would wait patiently until his leader had been dragged clear of the cable, waiting for the approach end cable to be re-rigged for his own arrested landing.

Karen watched spellbound as the lead Phantom pilot pumped the throttles causing ripples in the smoke trail as it neared the ground. She wondered, idly, whether the crews were the ones she had met last night. The first Phantom was only feet above the ground when something seemed to pop from the back of the jet almost invisible but for the binoculars she had been handed. The brake chute bloomed in the slipstream looking out of place given that the jet was still 50 feet in the air. As it thumped onto the hard metal surface the nosewheel slammed down onto the runway, the tail hook scraping the surface throwing up a shower of sparks. The jet crossed the cable causing a rippling effect as it bounced over the supporting rubber grommets and the hook snatched the metal cable pulling it out from the huge drums at the edge of the runway. The massive hydraulic dampers in the drums reacted to the huge weight of the Phantom damping the reel-out and beginning to retard the forward motion. As the drums took the strain the hurtling mass was swiftly drawn to a halt in just 600 feet. Pulling to a stop the engines spooled up to hold it in place. With a deft flick of the hook the cable dropped away leaving the Phantom clear to taxy down the adjacent access track back to the squadron dispersal leaving a spent cable in its wake.

"And that's how you recover a 56,000 lb Phantom when the runway is too short for a normal landing" explained OC Ops quietly from behind. The journalist had seen many demonstrations but the speed at which the recovery team went about the task of rewinding the cable ready to repeat the process for the wingman was truly impressive. She watched the tiny bodies through the binoculars as they raced about their task resetting the steel wire. In the overhead the other jet droned around eking out the precious fuel, its presence a constant reminder of the urgency. It would take just a few minutes for the cable to be re-rigged and it would repeat the procedure. She jotted a few rapid lines in her notebook as it became apparent that this part of the visit was coming to an end. As she bade farewell to the controller she followed John Fitzpatrick back down the stairs her appetite whetted and eager to see more. After the recent demonstration she wanted a closer look at the Phantoms and was beginning to think that machinery might have more of a presence in her article after all.

The next stop, however, was "Talkdown" where the air traffic controllers would literally talk aircraft onto the ground in marginal weather. As she was ushered into the quiet radar control room her first impression was of total solitude. Dominated by a bank of consoles which displayed the data from the precision approach radar located some distance away on the airfield, the room was eerily quiet with only the vague noise of the other Phantom in the background still awaiting its turn to land. The twin displays on the consoles, one showing azimuth and the other showing elevation gave the precise details of the ideal approach path to the controller. If the talkdown controller could persuade the pilot to follow the ideal glideslope, it would bring the aircraft down onto the piano keys at the end of the runway. The procedure would bring the aircraft down to a decision height as low as 200 feet where the decision would be taken on whether to land or whether to overshoot. It might be very late in the approach when the pilot finally saw the runway but, with help, he would be able to land in the dankest of conditions. With no real diversions on the islands, such weather conditions would cause a good deal of consternation and not only amongst the crew in the aircraft.

As Karen watched, a controller spoke quietly into her microphone in contact with a new arrival. Handed a pair of headphones she slipped them over her head, suddenly party to the exchange between the ground and the new arrival, RAFAIR 5638, today's airbridge flight from Ascension Island.

"Approaching 5 miles, prepare to lose height. Begin your descent now for a three degree glidepath. Left of centreline, approaching nicely. Come left two degrees, heading 258. Above the glideslope, increase your rate of descent."

The sound of the quiet tones of the talkdown controller as she pattered through the sequence persuading the tired Hercules crew back onto the ideal glide path was soporific. Karen felt, unexpectedly, content in the warm darkened room and, as she relaxed in the chair it was all she could do not to allow her eyelids to drop. She felt strangely reassured knowing that she might have been on the receiving end of the same service as she had made the approach to Stanley just a few days before. It had seemed far more dramatic at that moment than it did here in the quiet control room. A tap on the shoulder startled her, breaking the mood, as she was ushered out to her next destination.

John opened the door of the Land Rover and helped Karen back onboard trying hard not to check out her cute rear end as she pulled herself up onto the padded seat. He'd been away too long. Slamming the door shut he walked around to the driver's seat and started the engine. The keys to the vehicle were normally left in the ignition during the working day. Anyone who took an operational vehicle without authority was on a short route to the Guardroom and spell of "jankers" but, despite the warnings, it still happened. He rotated the key and the diesel engine chuntered into life belching fumes from the back end which rapidly blew back through the flapping canvas tail hatch and filled the cabin helped by the strong tailwind. He reversed from the slot outside the tower and set off along the track.

As they worked slowly along the flight line the airbridge flight thumped onto the runway, the turboprops spooling up in reverse pitch ending its long flight from Ascension. When he had described their next stop as Missile City, Karen had formed a picture in her mind's eye. What emerged as they pulled up alongside Missile Servicing Flight was an eclectic group of ISO containers that could not have been further from the image she had formed. The Phantom was a fearsome war machine but without its air-to-air armament it was just a heavy lump of metal not even as agile as the average air show participant. What gave it the edge were its weapons. Outside the strange building sat a number of smart transit containers stacked in piles, their paint schemes obviously fresh from a factory in total contrast to the grubby shipping containers which formed the work complex. This was where the vital weapons were serviced and made ready for use. The austere metal structures housed work benches, test sets and tool racks like any other technical facility the world over. The difference here was that the technicians wore the very same camouflaged battledress as the air traffic controllers rather than the clinical white coats typical of a normal electronics workshop. Unlike the TV repair shop on the High Street, the multi million pound pieces of electronic wizardry lay on servicing trolleys around the bay. Each Skyflash missile had cost the UK taxpayer over a quarter of a million Pounds but a simple slip of a screwdriver in this ramshackle hut could render it useless. More importantly, that might not be obvious until after the trigger had been pulled when a crew's life might depend on its success.

In an adjacent bay a Suu-23 gun pod had been broken down into its constituent parts. Strapped under a Phantom the long pod seemed perfectly proportioned and could wreak havoc with just a short burst of rapid fire, armour piercing cannon shells. With the nose and tail cones removed, it looked much more ungainly. The six long barrels made up the majority of the front half of the pod. Massive loops of ammunition held in mechanical belts wrapped around the breech mechanism and disappeared under the centre frame. The compact electronics pack strapped behind the breech on a metal rack was normally hidden by the squat aft fairing but in the bay was exposed. Another metal canister held the 1200 rounds of high explosive ammunition which comprised the war load on an operational sortie. The rounds had been stripped from the pod and lay in ammunition canisters at the side of the bay the dull metal giving little impression of the lethality of the 20mm rounds. It seemed remarkably like a scene from the local garage and she half expected her car mechanic to emerge from under the trestle. The subject of their attention was far more dangerous than her MG sports car back in London, although questionably less appealing.

Briefings over for the morning, John Fitzpatrick steered Karen towards a remote tent at the edge of the bustling aircraft servicing platform, probably the singular most important building on the airfield. The field kitchen proudly wore the sign "The Packaway Palace" and an amazing aroma tantalised the senses as they pushed the tent flap aside. Once inside they joined the long queue which had formed in front of the serving range jostling with camouflaged bodies that waited expectantly for the highlight of the day. White coated chefs were placing steaming trays of freshly prepared food into the range and eager faces inspected today's offerings. With fresh produce at a premium the chefs cooked up innovative recipes from the ubiquitous tinned "compo" rations. How they produced such incredible meals from such basic ingredients was a constant mystery to the diners.

The next venue for the afternoon would be a visit to 23 Squadron and the QRA crewroom. As she tucked into her food Karen eagerly anticipated the next leg at the Squadron and the chance to dig into some of the stories she had been tempted with last night. As conversation flowed, she could not help but notice the stares from around the dining room. She was, without doubt, the centre of attention and could not fail to miss the glances as she chatted over Lunch. Whatever the reason, she could get used to being a local celebrity. Maybe she'd extend her trip by a few days for some more essential operational research. Outside the flimsy canvas refuge the sound of a C-130 Hercules firing up its Allison turboprops split the air. It rose in crescendo as each additional engine roared into life before reaching a peak as it pulled off the chocks. In the background, the shattering pitch of the reheated Rolls Royce Spey engines of a pair of Phantoms rolling down the airstrip heralded the start of another training mission. It was somewhat different to the normal sound effects in a restaurant in the City. She smiled, distracted, at the Admin officer opposite who had been exchanging pleasantries but realised she could not hear a word he was saying. It was only as the noise subsided that she become conscious that there had been a lull. With the jets gone the conversation around the tent struck up again. This was, obviously, a fact of life for the diners.

Lunch over, they returned to the Land Rover and, once again, joined the road which snaked through the technical site. As the vehicle turned at the road junction the road surface changed from the smooth tarmac of the original road into a rough graded surface of packed rock. This was the new section added after the conflict to give access to the dispersals which had sprung up on the end of the airfield. The ride became noticeably harsher as John eased the Land Rover along the frontage road towards the Phantom squadron dispersal. A grading machine plied the short stretch attempting to reverse the tide and return the rocks to their rightful place on the road. It was a losing battle at times given the relentless volume of traffic that moved between the dispersal and the technical site but she could see the driver whistling in the cab.

From the makeshift car park they made their way towards a squat green building that looked more like a construction site than an operational facility. John pushed open the rickety door to the crewroom and ushered the journalist inside. The odour that assailed them as they entered was somewhat different to the wonderful aroma of the dining tent and rather less appealing. The collective strength of the rubberised immersion suits worn by aircrew who had been enclosed in the impermeable garments for at least six hours, competed with the smell from "Old Smokey", the small furnace which was the only source of heat in the building. He steered Karen over towards a knot of aircrew clustered around the coffee tables in the centre of the room and made the introductions. As she shook hands she unconsciously looked around trying to find the good looking pilot she'd met in the hotel last night but he didn't seem to be around, much to her disappointment. The knot of aircrew huddled around the "uckers" board, a bizarre form of Ludo favoured by aircrew around the squadrons, broke up as the board was hastily abandoned in favour of the attractive newcomer.

"Over to you Karen," he smiled as she was surrounded by green suited bodies jostling for attention. This would be her best chance to collect her quotes to appear in the magazine. He probably should have listened he thought but decided that the best time to exercise the rudimentary censorship would be once the copy was written so he wandered off to chat to the QRA crews lounging around the TV. He didn't get enough chance to drop in to the Squadron other than on his infrequent days when he flew. He resolved to make sure that the never ending pile of paperwork on his desk should not take its toll on his flying hours.

Back around the table, a cup of strong NAAFI coffee in hand, Karen chose her first willing victim. Instantly, she was barraged with facts about the Phantom, its role and life in general. In the background, the video player was blasting out *Monty Python's Life of Brian* for the captive QRA crews and even a visit from a respected journalist would not interrupt that daily ritual.

With a few choice quotes captured in her notebook she pressed for the chance to see the Phantom, that had so recently been the focus of her attention, at close quarters. She was led from the shabby little hut across the metal matting which had been laid over the newly constructed hard standing towards the aircraft. Like most things around the base the operating surfaces were newly constructed yet, despite their ruggedness, had a temporary feel. Just yards away, the brooding QRA aircraft armed with air-to-air missiles and a gun were "cocked" and ready to scramble, their external power sets alongside dormant but ready to fire up at the hint of a hooter. They approached a lone Phantom parked adjacent to the alert aircraft and, even though this one was not on readiness, the missiles slung beneath the fuselage and wings emphasised the reality that every sortie flown from this austere base was live and had a purpose. Any one of the jets ranged around the apron could be called into action at any time and training could turn deadly in an instant.

A flight line mechanic fired up the power set and the huge diesel engine sprung into life belching out fumes, rising in pitch to an uncomfortable whine, temporarily drowning out conversation. The crew hoisted themselves into the cockpits and carried out a few perfunctory checks before returning down the ladder to their guest. The nonchalance as they had flicked a few switches in the cockpit disguised the lethality of the war load beneath the combat jet. A few brief words of warning about what she could but, more importantly, what she could not touch and she was shown up the flimsy steps which protruded from the front fuselage. As she hoisted herself to the upper step and found the toehold in the side of the aircraft skin, shouted instructions from behind, urged her to step over the cockpit wall and onto the ejection seat. Nerves slowed her progress. Settled into the front cockpit, the pilot who had followed her up perched on the canopy rail alongside. He began to talk her around the controls and displays which were the everyday domain for the crews but looked thoroughly alien to the journalist. Despite her years covering stories from around the world she found herself quickly engrossed, fixated by the distorted view of the world through the heavy gunsight just feet in front of her face. It was a unique setting for an orientation briefing as she gazed across the bleak airfield through the perspex canopy. The content of her article was morphing by the minute.

Back down to Earth they slipped beneath the huge jet. its undersides streaked with hydraulic fluid and leaking like a sieve. Her sarcastic comments about the drips seemed to be lost on the aircrew. Maybe this was normal? The Skyflash hung in the semi recessed housings beneath the fuselage and she could not resist a gentle stroke of the sleek white missile body as the pilot talked her through the basics. Glibly throwing in unintelligible terms such as semi active guidance, seeker heads and continuous wave radar, he warmed to his subject. Despite his casual descriptions there could be no mistaking the lethal function of the warhead which he described almost casually. The rest of the technology was merely a means to deliver this section to its target. After a quick detour via the sleek gun pod slung on the centreline they emerged under the dirty back end to view the enormous tail hook and the massive afterburner cans. Soon they were back alongside the Phantom looking at the Sidewinder missiles which she now knew guided on the heat of a target's engines. With the squat forward canards and the large fixed tail fins it was a miracle this thing could fly. On hearing that the small rocket motor powered the missile to three times the speed of sound she suddenly understood how. Although most of this detail would never find its way into her magazine article she found herself intoxicated despite the cutting wind which raced across the dispersal and chilled her through.

She was helped up the rear steps which had been latched across the massive engine intakes stepping into the rear cockpit as the navigator talked her through the engagement sequence in the air, what happened when the motor ignited and the missile sped its way towards its hapless victim. She couldn't fail to spot the boyish enthusiasm as he proudly showed off his cockpit. Unable to ignore her natural pragmatism, the consequences of using this weapon were not lost on her as she listened to the matter of fact descriptions. Surrounded by little more than a high tech delivery vehicle, it was the weapons which commanded attention. It was a deadly game.

As she climbed back into the Land Rover she took one last glance over her shoulder at the ugly but functional warplane. The jet was framed against the setting sun as the light was beginning to fade. In most offices back home things would be winding up for the day and workers would be packing up their desks ready to start the commute home. With a 24 hour operation as the norm, people were gearing up for the next shift. The floodlights above the dispersal snapped on but the technicians were already busy in the rubs preparing the Phantoms for the night flying programme which was about to start. The tempo was relentless.

*

Back at the Squadron Razor and Flash had been selected from a reluctant cast and the lucky ones had, quite sensibly, retired to the pub. For the first time in months the Squadron would be flying from the austere airfield at night. QRA was no respecter of rank and any of the crews from the Squadron Boss to the most junior pilot or navigator had to be able to operate from Stanley at any time of the day or night and in all weathers if they were to be ready to respond. A scramble could just as easily come at midnight as during the day and it often seemed that the Argentinian crews who probed the Protection Zone constantly would feel satisfaction at provoking a launch in the dead of night.

Flash climbed out of the Land Rover as it stuttered to a halt on the northern dispersal, the smell of diesel strong in the air. His attention was already focussed on the jet in front of him, sheltered under the canopy, protected from the persistent drizzle that had blown up from nowhere. The truck pulled away heading back around the perimeter track to the operations complex, its heavy all weather tyres tramping on the metal matting leaving a cloud of spray behind it as it picked up speed. The raucous squawking of the penguins on the nearby Bertha's Beach which he had heard as they set off from operations was unable to compete with the droning power set which was firing up. At any time in the South Atlantic a reversal of seasons was possible and the unpredictability of the weather on the windswept archipelago was a constant concern to the flying supervisors. With the sun already below the horizon, the temperature had dropped and it felt like winter. Flash looked around the rub, the temporary latex hangar which housed the jet, looking for the crew chief who waved in acknowledgement. The external power set hummed alongside drowning all speech as the see-off crew began preparing the aircraft moving around with a purpose. Outside, the sodium lights cast a harsh yellow light across the hard standing giving temporary respite from the darkness around. Stars winked through a break in the clouds in the southern sky suggesting that the shower might be brief, hopefully just passing through. He hoped the weather in the area would be kind. Clutching the chinstrap of his bonedome in one hand and his knee board containing all the sortie details in the other, he walked into the shelter of the hangar enjoying the respite from the wind. To an outsider, the vital scribblings on the kneeboard were hieroglyphics. To him they were the difference between success and failure of the mission. As he moved from dark to light the rub felt welcoming after the bleakness of the airfield and he was struck, as always, by the stark functionality of the Phantom. Most of all, unlike the normal configuration that he was used to in Germany, this jet was armed and dangerous even for a training sortie. The four Skyflash semi-active missiles hung snugly in their semi-recessed housings under the belly of the aircraft. Guided by a radar beam from the air intercept radar, these "semi-active" missiles would do an opponent a great deal of harm. Against a Skyhawk, Argentina's main fighter-bomber aircraft they would be lethal. The four Sidewinder missiles or "9 Limas", hung menacingly on the inboard wing pylons. The heat-seekers could sense the exhaust from the engines of a hostile aircraft and these later versions were sufficiently sensitive to see the tiny amount of heat generated by friction along the leading edges of the wings. They could be used head-on maybe before the enemy pilot could even see his attacker. The most sobering fact was that under the present rules of engagement that had been carefully briefed by the weapons instructor just days before, they were cleared to use them. Any maverick Argentinean pilot who chose to press the claim on this newly liberated British enclave would be at the limit of range in his Mirage or Skyhawk. Flash intended to make sure that, first of all, he would not make it to Stanley with his bomb load and, secondly, that he didn't go home to boast of his exploits.

Razor, had followed just a few steps behind and placing his bonedome gently at the base of the front steps he started his walk round; the first stage of the pre-flight ritual. Stroking the radome which housed the powerful air intercept radar, the AN/AWG12, he began the clockwise circuit around the jet, prodding this and checking the pressure of that. Fuel tanks, skin panels and flying control surfaces received the same meticulous attention confirming a second time that the engineers had prepared the aircraft properly for flight. "Never assume, check" was the old and trusted maxim. With the sounds in the hangar ringing in his ears, Flash climbed up the rear ladder anchored firmly over the massive air intake, and stepped over the cockpit side onto the Martin Baker ejection seat in the back cockpit. After a few deft switch selections he stood up and climbed onto the left canopy rail easing his way gingerly forward into the front cockpit. The bulk of his lifejacket threatened to pitch him off onto the floor twenty feet below but he navigated his way safely past the front canopy and dropped onto the seat in a practised manoeuvre. Speeding through his safety checks which were burned in his memory he was ready to apply power to the jet. Below, as his navigator was checking the cockpits Razor had been checking the status of the air-to-air missiles strapped under the Phantom. All seemed in order and he moved out from the pylon giving a thumbs-up receiving an instant acknowledgement as the power was applied and the aircraft sprang to life. The navigation lights illuminated at the wing tips and the aircraft became a living thing. With an armed aircraft this was a tense stage as it was not unknown for a stray voltage to cause a missile to fire, inadvertently. No one stood in front of the jet during the power-on sequence; just in case! It was a long-standing joke that the reason the navigator applied power was that the pilot would have a ready scapegoat in the event of an inadvertent release. Ironically, it was the one opportunity for a navigator to fire a missile but it was an opportunity that was never taken up. With the cockpit now bathed in a red glow and the gyros winding up, Flash made the perilous return journey to his own cockpit along the canopy rail. The inertial navigation system was soon humming and he began to strap in. It would be a few more minutes before the pre-start checks were complete.

"Eagle 21, 22 taxi."

Eagle 21 and 22 taxi for 26 right, surface wind is 260 at 15 knots."

"Taxy, 21,22."

The noise of the engines rose as the crew chief reappeared from underneath the belly of the jet dragging the heavy chocks behind him. The jet surged forward but, almost instantaneously, the noise dropped off as the inertia was overcome. The throttles closed and, with a nod forward, Razor tapped the brakes before the Phantom popped out into the darkness leaving the welcoming lights of the rub behind. The dispersal was arranged around a central taxiway and as he looked ahead, he could see the nose of the lead aircraft emerging from the rub to the right. The dazzle of the taxi light on the nosewheel door illuminated the bleak dispersal briefly as the jet swung away from them, soon shielded by the bulk of the receding aircraft. The Phantom disappeared into the darkness, its red anti-collision lights blinking away. Again the brakes bit as Razor hit the nosewheel steering button on the stick and pushed on the rudder pedals persuading the big jet to swing right to follow. The greens and blues of the taxiway lights glowed dimly as they began the pre-takeoff checks. It was only a short distance to the holding point and they did not want to be the ones to hold up the departure.

The wind was strong but straight down the runway and the rain still battered the canopy, the drops illuminated by passing sodium lights. As it was already dark, they had planned for a stream takeoff because, although a formation takeoff took the aeroplanes into the air together, at night it could be fraught, particularly on the short Stanley strip. A stream departure was a far more relaxed way to get into the air in the enveloping darkness. Once lined up on the runway as a pair, the leader would roll to be followed 30 seconds later by Razor and Flash in the number 2 shadowing the departure, two miles behind using the radar to stay in contact.

"Eagle 21, 22, clear for takeoff, surface wind 270 at 18 knots." came the distant voice of the Local Controller in the control tower some distance away. The message registered in each cockpit through the headsets. They were clear to go.

The noise of the Rolls Royce Spey engines of the leading Phantom just metres away from them on the runway rose to a crescendo as the lead pilot pushed up the throttles. Flash watched as the reflected glow of their nosewheel light on the runway surface disappeared; Razor's signal to his leader that he was ready to roll. Immediately, the afterburners alongside them split the night sky as thousands of pounds of jet fuel pumped into the jet pipe lighting immediately, persuaded by the igniter rings in the aft of the engines. The jet jumped forward and increased speed, the immense power of the afterburners emphasised by the shimmering shock diamonds in the circular plume. Craning his head to the right around the ironwork which cluttered the back cockpit, Flash watched the jet roll hitting the stopwatch. They would follow soon. The features of the airframe disappeared quickly lost in the darkness replaced by the glow from the reheats. The round glow of the left afterburner was strong but as he peered through the night, he could see that the right afterburner was distressingly dim.

"He's lost a burner," he prompted, stating the obvious, because Razor's left thumb was already hitting the transmit switch on the throttle about to give the vital news to the leader. Razor's call was equally redundant.

"21 aborting," came the urgent tone through the ether as the Phantom, still rocketing down the 6,000 foot strip of metal planking, chopped the throttles and popped its chute. The pilot hit the brakes as the speed slowed but still the aircraft drove relentlessly towards the rocky oblivion in the overrun of Runway 26 at RAF Stanley. After the high speed abort there was no way the jet would slow without the aid of the arrestor gear. The brakes and brake parachute were simply inadequate on such a short runway.

"Tower, confirm hook down," came the worried interrogation from the cockpit.

"Affirmative. Hook down," came the rapid response, the vital information relayed in an instant from the local controller in the tower reassuring the hard-pressed aircrew.

The few moments that passed seemed like an eternity and the bystanders could only wait. Between the crew of Eagle 21 and a certain "Martin Baker Letdown," the colloquial term for an ejection, was the thin strand of steel cable stretched across the runway. The massive hook which the pilot had instinctively deployed was dragging along the metal surface of the runway and should catch the wire and bring the jet to a halt. Unfortunately, the surface of the planking laid over packed hardcore was rough and the hook might yet bounce and miss the wire if the oscillations conspired against them. In the dark night, on the short runway, with a failed afterburner preventing the pilot reaching flying speed, options were rapidly evaporating. A moment's hesitation or a stroke of bad luck might be catastrophic or even fatal.

"21's in the overrun," came the slightly frayed voice from the now stationary jet.

The collective sighs of relief around the airfield were almost palpable. In the cockpit of Eagle 22 still lined up for takeoff, Razor had throttled back and waited for instructions. There was barely a pause before the tower began relaying instructions to the emergency services who would extract the jet from the cable, seemingly unconcerned by the drama. The sick Phantom had missed the centre cable and taken the overrun wire and was sitting mere feet from the end of the strip. The crew felt alone but relieved in the darkness. Blue lights flashing atop the emergency vehicles converged on the airframe and bright spotlights snapped on, illuminating the scene. Emergency crews disgorged onto the metal runway and set about their business. Despite the close call, the incident had moved from an emergency into a routine drill to extract the jet from its predicament. The fire crews were well practised at the art and it would take only minutes to disentangle the Phantom from the cable.

"Eagle 22, Tower, message from your operators. Once Eagle 21 is clear of the cable you are clear to launch to operate with Albert."

The news was less than welcome after the recent drama. This "Albert" was a standard Hercules "trash hauler" which had been modified rapidly to give an air-to-air refuelling capability for operations in the South Atlantic. Although slow and limited in height, it had a useful fuel giveaway and with its electronic surveillance suite it could monitor the local waters. More importantly, it could operate just as easily off the short metal runway as it could from a concrete strip, unlike its larger jet stable mates the VC10, Victor and Vulcan, the latter pressed into service as an impromptu air-to-air refueller to replace tankers deploying south.

They had not expected to intercept the tanker as the mission was to carry out routine intercepts with their "playmate", Eagle 21. No matter, Razor and Flash were in the authorisation sheets for "Ops Normal" which allowed a great deal of latitude meaning they could intercept anything in the airspace. With the missiles strapped under the jet they might just as easily be pulled off to go against a belligerent Argentinean who happened to come their way so a C-130 shouldn't be much of a challenge . . . . . but it was very dark out there.

Safely airborne, the lights of Stanley town slipped past the left wing as Razor held it down along the length of Stanley Harbour, the red anti-collision light winking away on the leading edge of the fin bright in his mirrors.

"Tower, Eagle 22, airborne, switching to tactical"

Flash looked down at the radio box and, unbidden, selected the pre-briefed frequency already programmed into the radio.

"My radio" he muttered to Razor taking over the radio calls.

"Puffin, Eagle 22."

He glanced through the metalwork in front of him which almost obscured the forward view from the rear cockpit of the Phantom. To his left he could see the profile of Mount Tumbledown, vague in the gloom. Almost directly ahead and further east, hidden in the darkness, was Mount Kent, the largest peak of the mountain range which almost shielded Stanley from the westerly winds. Perched at the top was the small, dimpled radome containing the air defence radar that maintained radar surveillance of the airspace around East Falkland. It was just visible silhouetted against the stars in the night sky. The hilltop closed rapidly and, as if reading his thoughts, he felt the pressure through his rear end as the G increased and Razor pulled back on the stick. The jet responded pulling up into a sharp climbing right hand turn taking it safely away from the forbidding terrain. Flash's nerves relaxed.

"Eagle 22, Puffin, you're loud and clear, check state."

He rattled off the coded response giving the GCI controller the status of their weapons and their remaining fuel. The Phantom would recover for a night trap into the cable and would land heavy. With a potential fighter threat from the mainland it was important to keep enough fuel in the tanks to be able to complete a supersonic intercept at any time but between now and then, the remaining contents would be used for training. To the controller tucked away in his small control cabin it was good news. He had a captive audience for at least an hour and something to occupy him for the evening to keep him out of the bar. In the air, the dull red glow of the instrument lights enveloped the crew in the cockpit providing a welcome relief from the dark and forbidding night outside as, well to the west, the flash of a lightning storm broke the gloom but threatened even worse weather conditions to come. Each made a mental note to track the progress of the storm as the sortie progressed. Landing in a thunderstorm back at Stanley was one experience neither of them wished to try. Operating anywhere out to 100 miles away from land, the crew were reassured by the Sea King helicopter sitting on alert back at Stanley. It stood ready to pick up the crew if they hit a problem and had to eject but the wait would be interminable and lonely. During the day the fact barely registered with the aircrew. At night, the South Atlantic waters seemed cold and inhospitable. With a target to intercept the crew snapped into a more comfortable routine.

The controller broke the silence.

"Eagle 22 vector 045 and climb Angels 15. Simulated target bearing 050 range 60. Confirm switches safe."

With "Albert" as the target at the culmination of this intercept, the controller wanted to know that the missiles slung under Eagle 22 would not be causing drama on his shift. As Razor set the heading bug, the Phantom headed even further out into the dark South Atlantic waters to the north of the islands and climbed to its designated level.

"Eagle 22, switches safe," Flash responded as a familiar smudge which he recognised as the radar response from the Hercules appeared on the pulse Doppler radar display in front of him. He refined the contact with the scanner thumb wheel on his hand controller.

"Contact 045 range 45," he replied.

"That's your target."

"Eagle 22 Judy."

The codeword told the controller that Eagle 22 had assumed control of the intercept but there was one more vital snippet of information that the crew needed. It followed immediately.

"Eagle 22, Puffin, identify."

They were to identify the simulated intruder and would roll out behind the target and close to a range where they could establish the aircraft's identity picking out any distinguishing features to help the analysts on the ground. This would be just the type of mission they might expect against an intruding Argentinean intelligence gathering flight.

"Eagle 22, good evening!" came a jovial sounding English voice shattering the myth. The drone of the four Allison turboprops was obvious in the background as the message boomed over the frequency. Flash sensed that the happy response from the C-130 pilot may not be entirely innocent but why did everyone else seem so happy to be flying around in the dark?

Undeterred, he made his mental calculations passing short, sharp commands to Razor to set up the intercept profile. Bringing the radar contact onto the nose, or the "blip" as it was known in the trade, he calculated the target's heading and its displacement away from the Phantom's track and, finally, checked its height. These assessments were carried out in seconds and he rattled off a new heading and altitude to his pilot to establish an intercept course. He would set up a profile which placed the two aircraft on directly opposing headings - "a 180" attack – and, knowing that "Albert" would be slow, he needed plenty of lateral displacement to give the Phantom plenty of turning room. With eight miles separation it would be comfortable and allow him to roll gently round the final turn and carry out a controlled intercept. Any tighter and Razor would be pulling a lot harder and may not be able to hold the height in the heavily laden jet. He would earn his flying pay but why work harder than necessary?

"Take it up to 13,000 feet and set 300 knots" he prompted, refining the parameters, the sums still churning through his brain. As the aircraft climbed, every few seconds he checked and cross-checked the target's heading, height and speed. Even though he knew the blip was in reality a Hercules he resisted the urge to lock up, denying what might be a potentially hostile opponent an indication of the fighter's approach on his radar warning receiver. His caution was to be short lived as, watching the "blip" closely, he picked up the tell tale signs of a rapid change in heading away from their flight path. It was the first sign that this intercept was not going to be routine.

"The target's evading, come right to put it back on the nose."

In the front cockpit, Razor stared at his repeater scope and tweaked the heading to re-centre the target blip. "Albert" was not giving in easily tonight. As the aircraft sped towards each other in the blackness with a closing velocity still over 600 miles per hour, seconds seemed like hours. Flash struggled with the intercept geometry. The profile should have been easy but was being complicated by the evasion. He was suffering in the darkened rear cockpit. After all his efforts, his careful plan was destroyed and he was pointing directly at the rapidly approaching target with only 2,000 feet separating the two aircraft. The radar picture suddenly seemed threatening. As the range reduced inside 10 miles only drastic action would save the profile but he had one important safety call to make.

"Eagle 22, 10 miles, switches safe," he heard as his pilot pre-empted the call.

At least good old "Albert" would not be shot down tonight but if he kept up his belligerent behaviour things might change! Flash stared, disconsolately, at the scope.

"The final turn will be to the left and when I say turn, pull the wings off!"

So much for making life easy he thought to himself. In the front cockpit Razor recognised the predicament. He had been watching the erratic behaviour of the blip on his radar repeater display and Flash's vain attempts to tame it. Even though his navigator had tried valiantly to set up a controlled intercept, his predicament was a gift and the banter would flow thick and fast in the bar later. Razor was already rehearsing the good natured jibes. The tanker pilot had nibbled away at the displacement leaving the Phantom with no turning room and Flash now had a time-critical decision. Turn too soon and the Phantom would roll out in front of the lumbering tanker; too late and they would roll out up to 10 miles behind him. That would give the Hercules crew plenty to crow about in the Pub later. Flash felt isolated in the dark cockpit and only his skill would prevent a verbal pasting.

"Gate," he called prompting Razor to plug in the reheats ready for the high performance turn. The speed built slowly as the sluggish airframe responded but it would soon be checked as the speed was traded for turn performance. Professional pride said he needed a two mile roll out, the standard place to be for any self-respecting fighter crew but the outcome was still far from certain. There were procedures ingrained in his brain for just such an eventuality and he waited for the target to hit the "turn key"; the critical position on the radar scope which would allow him to recover the situation. Once the blip hit 6 miles, a maximum performance turn would do the job. With such a slow-mover maybe he might leave it just a little later to guarantee that he stayed in behind. It hit the magic numbers.

"Come hard left and roll out on …." He snapped out the command, the timing critical. A short hesitation as he checked the compass. "Make it 240 degrees."

"No tally," came the sharp retort from the front cockpit.

His stomach sank. The call meant that Razor could not see the target. With contact the pilot could assist Flash by controlling the turn visually but unsighted, it was all down to the back-seater who would earn his keep by controlling the intercept using his radar. With the G increasing the Phantom began its hard turn, the crew conscious that somewhere just above was hundreds of tons of tanker rapidly closing on the tightly turning Phantom. As he strained against the forces on his body he took a swift glance through the canopy towards the point in space where the tanker should emerge. The tanker's lights should have been visible by now but the night was still enveloping the huge transport. There could be no mistakes and he watched the flight instruments closely as the Phantom whipped around the turn. The height was rock solid never wavering, maintain the precious separation in altitude as the compass rattled around through the cardinal headings. Another sneaky peek through the ironwork but still the visual contact was elusive. In the front, Razor was quiet. Sometimes pilots would hold off from announcing that they had picked up the target to make the navigators work just a little harder; all in the spirit of training of course. On an operational sortie there would be no such tricks. As the blip drifted off the side of the radar scope due to the tight turn, Flash felt the familiar nervousness in his stomach as he stroked the radar hand controller desperately trying to reacquire the target, now hopefully a couple of miles ahead. The small green smudge reappeared, glowing reassuringly on the radar scope as he refined the contact, relief palpable.

Safely in behind they closed in to check the "intruder's" identity, although they both had a good idea what they would find at the end of this intercept. During a QRA mission the goal was to capture the intruder on film but portable night vision cameras had not developed to the point where they could be carried in the limited space on the back cockpit of a Phantom. Night vision goggles were in their infancy and had not yet been issued to the operational crews.

Flash called for the extra speed that would bring them alongside, locking up the radar, prompting the tracking beam to slew onto the nominated bearing, seeking out the target. The steering information popped up onto the pilots radar scope in the darkened cockpit glowing green in the dark. They would follow a choreographed geometric profile which they had practiced hundreds of times before in the months leading up to the deployment. Flash began pattering, tweaking the flight parameters as they closed in.

"Set 280 knots and go up gently. Come right onto 240 degrees, target heading."

"Still no tally," came the slightly nervous reply from the front. "This guy is lights out!"

"Albert" was making them work for a living tonight. If they wanted fuel they were going to have to find him in the gloom. Suddenly, extra fuel seemed unattractive and an arrested landing in the dark seemed somehow appealing. More fine corrections and the target moved slowly down the radar scope, the range reducing steadily. In the front Razor finessed the small changes with stick and throttles.

"Fifteen hundred yards, 8 degrees high, 30 knots overtake."

Finally the target was behaving exactly as it had done so many times before and the profile was in the tramlines. It was easy to think that this was just an up-market computer game but outside the cockpit, tons of steel moved through the turbulent air representing a lethal obstruction. Suddenly, the contact raced wildly across the scope, rapidly moving from left to right. It took seconds for Flash to assimilate the change. Outside in the real world, the aircraft, so close ahead in the gloom, had turned unexpectedly. Flash tensed, subconsciously anticipating a collision that never came. Ahead, the tanker was still well above their flight path. Well, 200 or 300 feet above to be precise. The response was ingrained and automatic.

"Targets turned right, come right gently and I'll roll you out."

This was not supposed to happen but Flash reacted instinctively, the skill honed over many years. Who said operations were easier than training? They inched in towards their quarry.

"Speed back a further 10 knots. Check heading 270 degrees, hold that height. Target is on the nose, 8 degrees high, 300 yards and co speed," he rattled off.

"No tally!"

Impossible. The bright flashing navigation lights of an aircraft could be seen from miles away during a routine intercept and, even during practice "lights out" intercepts over the North Sea, a reflection from an oil rig stack or a reflection from the moon would bounce back from the target's fuselage giving just that sneak peek that reassured a nervous crew. Here in the pitch black of the South Atlantic there was nothing to break the gloom. Tons of metal only yards away, almost in close formation, was totally invisible. This is what crews trained for but why him and why tonight?

"Wait, yes; I've got the beta lights!"

Flash breathed a sigh of relief. His pilot could see the small glimmering lights which ringed the refuelling basket and, although the tanker was 300 yards away, the basket on the end of the 100 yard hose was much closer and trailing well below the belly of the still invisible C-130. With the navigation lights extinguished the small iridescent markers were shining brightly through the darkness. Razor edged in closer when, suddenly, the lights on the hydraulic drogue unit mounted on the ramp of the modified cargo aircraft burst into life above their heads temporarily killing their carefully nurtured night vision. There was a brief flash of reds as the unit charged with fuel before the yellows flashed simultaneously. This apparently erratic behaviour meant that the tanker captain had cleared them for contact using silent procedures the sequence of lights conferring tacit approval to refuel. Razor blinked in an effort to refocus, hoping his night vision would return before the joust with the basket.

"I guess that'll be it then," he muttered. "Gimme the tanking checks. I'm not even sure we need the damned fuel, we could be up here all night."

"The HF is off, radar to standby . . . . . " began the litany from the back seat as they ran through the pre-tanking checks to ready the jet to take on fuel.

Razor hit the refuelling probe switch moving the selector to "REFUEL" prompting the familiar bang as the probe door broke out into the high speed airflow on the right hand side of the Phantom. The massive wind rush was audible prompting the familiar shot of adrenaline which coursed through his veins. The airframe shuddered as the phallic shape of the refuelling probe emerged from the housing suddenly bathed in the red glow of the probe light on the side of the jet. Now the pressure switched and the pilot faced the challenge to jockey his aircraft into position, inserting the refuelling probe into the basket hard enough to lock the mechanical coupling onto the probe whilst driving through the black night in close formation, in turbulent air, at 15,000 feet. Once connected, he had to stay in close formation behind the bucking tanker until the fuel had transferred into the Phantom's tanks and he had to do this without looking at the basket and by listening to commands from the back cockpit. Easy!

In the back Flash prepared for the manoeuvre. He would know if the pilot risked a sneaky peek at the basket as, during the final stages there would be a massive over-correction and a frantic gyration as he tried to compensate. The jet dropped into position astern the basket with slow and deliberate movements as the airflow around the nose trapped the jiggling drogue.

Stabilised six feet behind the basket Flash began to talk him in.

"Right a foot, up a foot, in line, in line . . . . . contact." came the commentary, reminiscent of the old television game show *The Golden Shot*. The basket kicked as the probe rammed home in one final gesture of disobedience before the hose rippled with the momentum passing the oscillations up the line. The whip settled down, the green lights on the HDU illuminated brightly and the fuel began to flow.

Pulse rates slowed, breathing became regular and the minutes passed as the fuel gauge crept slowly upwards. The radio crackled into life.

"Eagle 22, Puffin, stand by for re-tasking."

"Oh great," muttered Flash, "What now?"

"Eagle 22, Puffin, confirm you are still Tiger Fast?"

"Affirmative."

"Roger. Haul off and vector 270 degrees. I have trade to the west range 100 miles. You are to intercept and identify."

"Eagle 22 roger, intercept and identify."

This evening just keeps on giving, though Razor, irreverently, as he retarded the throttles backing away from the basket which shuddered as the probe separated. The Phantom drifted backwards moving away from the darkened shape. He checked the fuel gauge. It was enough.

"Eagle 22, once clear contact Cara Cara on TAD 042."

"To Cara Cara on TAD 042, Eagle 22."

Flash switched frequency and they checked in already on a westerly vector. The controller sounded excited despite the distortion on the radio channel.

"Eagle 22, I have trade bearing 240 range 95 miles, heading 120. Target inside the zone."

"Roger 22, check its height?"

"Showing Angels 25."

"Eagle 22, looking," called Flash knowing that there was no chance of a contact at such long range. He stroked the thumbwheel more in hope than expectation as the jet began to climb to 23,000 feet.

The target's behaviour could mean only one thing. The Argentinian Electrone was up tonight and had come to listen in. Within seconds a contact appeared on the radar scope and Flash took a closing heading to intercept. Maybe tonight would prove more productive than they had anticipated. The range closed relentlessly but at 40 miles the closing velocity rolled off rapidly signalling that it had turned away.

"Eagle 22, I show the target turning."

"Confirmed. Target is now heading 270 and leaving the zone. Eagle 22, haul off."

The frustration and disappointment was tangible and they both felt an unexpected urge to press on despite instructions. With sanity re-established, Razor pulled the Phantom around heading back towards Stanley. There would be no airborne rendezvous tonight. The Electrone had called the shots and was not staying around to play.

"Cara Cara, Eagle 22 is complete and returning to base."

That was enough fun for the night and it was time to get back on the ground.

"Eagle 22, is on recovery. We'd like a hand-off to Base for radar vectors for an instrument approach."

"Roger 22, make your heading 150 and descend to 3000 feet on the QNH, 997 millibars."

Razor read back the instructions from the controller and began his recovery checks in preparation for the approach. It was still pitch black as they descended towards the ground but they could just see the lights of Stanley appearing in the distance. Back to civilisation he thought distractedly, although on second thoughts, civilisation and the Falklands could be a contradiction of terms in comparison to his home town, London. Loaded with the extra fuel which they had been unable to burn intercepting the Argentinian snooper he pushed the speed up, the needles flirting with Mach One but remaining just below the magic figure, careful not to drop a sonic boom on the unsuspecting population. They ate the miles passing overhead the airfield at 5000 feet before inverting and dropping, rapidly, to 1500 feet a few miles east of the airfield.

"Eagle 22, ten miles finals, contact Talkdown now on Stud 5 for ILS monitor."

"Stud 5, roger, goodnight."

As they chopped across to the Stanley frequency the lights of the Capital stood out and, by working back eastwards, the slightly dimmer outline of the base emerged from the black hole. After the drama of the evening it took little discussion before opting for an approach without the help of the fancy onboard electronic aids.

"Tower, Eagle 22 is converting to a visual approach I'll call you initials."

"Eagle 22, Stanley Tower roger."

"Tower, 22 initials."

"Clear to join, Runway 26 right hand, surface wind 270 at 20 knots."

Running in from initials and descending ever lower, Razor peered down at the short Stanley runway. The runway lighting consisted of omni-directional lights spaced 1000 feet apart down the length of the strip, interspersed with uni-directional lights which could only be seen from the approach direction. As they broke into the circuit, the runway was etched bright on the ground and from the break height of 500 feet it suddenly seemed very short, emphasised by the surrounding darkness. The G came on as the Phantom pitched into the circuit and Razor grunted as it took effect, pressing him down into the unyielding ejection seat. Extending the speed brakes into the airflow, he pulled harder, manoeuvring the aircraft into the downwind position washing off the speed and slowing for the final approach. As the airspeed indicator hit 200 knots, he ran through the downwind checks.

"Speed brakes in, Landing gear down . . . . . "

The rumble of the undercarriage could be heard even above the jet noise in the cockpit as it extended into the airflow giving a reassuring clunk, locking into position.

"Fuel is 4000 lbs, makes the on speed 148 knots." He was about to earn his flying pay yet again as he manoeuvred for his first night trap into the cable at Stanley. Looking ahead, he picked out his landing point feeling the familiar adrenaline buzz.

"OK where's the runway?" he muttered.

Where it had glowed just moments before, it had been replaced by a pitiful series of barely glimmering white omni-directional lights and Stanley had descended into virtual blackness.

"Oh well, here goes," muttered the resigned pilot pointing his jet at the black hole, the tiny runway now barely visible, suddenly seeming woefully inadequate. Used to operating in Europe with 8000 feet of concrete, placing ten tons of screaming Phantom onto the concrete runway would hold his attention. With only 6,000 feet of metal matting, relying on the approach end cable and the arrestor hook to bring the massive fighter to a stop was a whole different game. Tonight, on this darkest of nights, it seemed to be taking on crisis proportions.

It became quiet in the front cockpit and Flash could sense the tension as they began the final turn. Still only the meagre omni-directional lights glowed back as the nose lowered, passing 500 feet in the descent. Suddenly as they lined up on final approach, the full majesty of the approach lighting blinked on as if the controller had hit a switch. The relief from the front cockpit was almost audible. The engines hunted as Razor adjusted the power to cushion the landing, pumping the throttles to adjust the descent. Scant feet above the ground he dropped his hand to the chute handle popping the drag shoot into the airflow before the jet had even touched down. This would give the maximum retardation before the jet hit the ground and might even make it possible to stay down if the hook jumped the cable. The jet thumped onto the metal matting in true carrier style instantly losing speed. In the back, Flash braced his body and turned to watch over his shoulder anticipating a successful trap. If he wasn't careful he'd be listening to the radar as his head was whipped forward by the retardation. If they missed the cable they would need an instant response from the engines to allow them to go around for a further approach, the manoeuvre known as a "bolter" from the days when British Phantoms operated from aircraft carriers. The sodium lights which marked the position of the cable only 1,300 feet into the runway flashed through his peripheral vision as he looked for the tell tale ripple of the tapes which would show that the hook had snared the wire.

Had they? Hadn't they?

In the dark it was hard to tell and there was a short uncomfortable moment in limbo as they both tensed trying to decide whether to push the throttles through the gate into afterburner and go around again. There was a momentary rise in power as he hesitated followed, immediately, by the vicious retardation as the hydraulic arrestor gear dragged the aircraft to a shuddering halt in just 600 feet of runway.

200 miles to the west the Electrone turned northwards towards Trelew air base, its electronic recorders filled with new data for the spooks to analyse.

*

Karen relaxed in the comfortable easy chair and reflected on all she'd seen today. The makeshift ante room in the Coastel was still quiet, the first diners only just emerging from the dining room. The Station Commander had promised to join her so work was not quite done for the day. Her minder had disappeared temporarily and she was glad to have a few minutes alone for the first time today. The small notebook packed with her tight cryptic script was beginning to fill up and she was pleased with progress so far but she added a few extra notes as she reviewed the interviews.

Never far from her thoughts were her Editor's words before she had set off on the long voyage. The broad areas he had asked her to cover were fairly clear and she planned to capture life at RAF Stanley and aboard the Navy ship if she could blag a ride out there on a helicopter. Both topics were "feel good" stories and the Services were still riding high in the public approvals ratings so they would need to be positive portrayals. Come to think of it, every single person she had met so far had been positive, motivated and kind and she had little appetite to portray them in a bad light despite her journalistic intuition. The memorial service would almost cover itself and she suspected she could almost sit down and write the piece in advance. She sensed that nationalism and politics would be stripped bare at the cemetery and it was certainly no time for sensationalism. That left the visit by the junior Defence Minister and its impact on local politics as her major piece. There was undoubtedly scope for a revelation or why would he have travelled so far but whether he would let his guard drop was the key. Her only time to pin him down would be in Heritage Hall after the meeting but she had only been scheduled for a short 10 minute interview. At least any decisions would have been taken by then and he may even have a breaking news story for her. Now that would be a telephone call she'd be happy to make. More likely, if the script followed the norm, he would have to return to Whitehall and clear the line with the Minister and the Cabinet before it was released. By then the rest of Fleet Street would be scrambling for a headline and would hear the news at the same time. Her problem was still that she needed the killer story; the incisive piece of journalism; the potential Pulitzer Prize winner but so far, she didn't have it. It would have to be a political angle that provided the solution but, as yet, she couldn't see where it would come from.

Her minder had pointed out the small booths along the corridor, the telephones providing the only link back to normality. As she waited, she would call the editor and see if anything had emerged from the daily briefings about the Ministerial visit.

*

In the bar, pints of Penguin Ale were slipping down and tribal groups from each unit had formed. Razor watched as the attractive journalist was ushered in by the Station Commander and the small group of Station executives congregated at the end of the bar. He switched his attention, reluctantly, back to his navigator.

"Well I guess that gets us night current in theatre, night tanking qualified, QRA qualified and night VID qualified all in one go," Flash said as he leaned against the bar. Razor smiled.

"OK share it with me" he replied

"It's a hell of a way to get qualified on the C-130 tanker. I've never tanked from one of those at night before."

Flash stared back. He was the sortie authoriser and "adult" member of the crew. He was the one supposed to exercise supervision and make sure they complied with all the rules. He was the conscience and the decision maker and they had just broken just about every unwritten rule as well as a few of the more significant written ones. With the Hercules tankers only operating on the islands it had been impossible to schedule a training sortie back home. He had missed the chance to add a tanking serial to the familiarisation sortie when at least they could have run the event in daylight. He blanched.

"Just don't tell the Boss!"

Razor watched as the Station Commander made his excuses and the small group began to break up deciding whether this might be his only opportunity of the evening. He left Flash nursing his pint and his conscience and walked over to Karen Pilkington. The project officer was fawning over the Station Commander and seemed temporarily distracted as he pushed up to the bar.

"I was hoping to catch you before I left," she smiled. "How was your flight?"

"Thank goodness for stars is all I can say. It was darker than a pitch-black panther, covered in tar, eating liquorice at the bottom of the Black Sea. Now where did that come from?"

She laughed, sympathetically, at the bizarre joke.

"Seriously", he continued. "Once you head north of the islands there are no lights between here and Brazil. It was a good job I had Flash along or I'd have been lonely."

They chatted easily for some time but Razor was conscious of the minder who was once again hovering in the background. His reservations about journalists were rapidly evaporating and if he could keep the conversation on safe topics he might survive the encounter unscathed. The meeting at The Upland Goose had broken the ice and, despite his reservations, the conversation was enjoyable moving on from local issues and military life to stories of shared haunts in London. It seemed that despite the geographical gulf between here and home - they were, after all, moored in the harbour in Port Stanley - they had quite a lot in common.

"How's your room down at the Upland Goose?"

The hint was strong.

"Good, why?"

"Ahh, just wondered. We're crammed in two to a "cell" here and it gets a bit claustrophobic at times. It must be nice to have a bit of privacy. Do you feel like showing some sympathy and sharing it for a few hours?"

"I got a lift up here with a couple of the C-130 guys and I think I have transport arranged for later but . . . . . If you can get hold of a Land Rover for the night, the hotel bar might still be open."

Razor looked around the bar.

"Just a minute," he said as he spotted the duty officer and walked over. A few brief words later he wandered back clutching a precious set of keys in his hand.

"I'm not flying until later tomorrow but I'll have to get these wheels back by breakfast. Will that work or am I . . . . . ?"

"Looks like you just fixed it," she said quietly, careful to make sure the conversation wasn't heard by any of the others nearby. She smiled, picked up her bag from the floor and whispered in his ear.

They made for the door.

DAVID GLEDHILL

CHAPTER 14

VILLA REYNOLDS AIRBASE, ARGENTINA

Carmendez pulled out the file from the cabinet and laid it on the desk. Where were the details of that weapons demonstration? It was due to be flown in just a few days time and he had seen the Operation Order recently. If he remembered correctly, air-to-ground targets would be set up on a weapons range and formations of fast jets would push through the airspace for the benefit of the VIP guests. Lots of noise, plenty of action and loud bangs for the punters. Tankers had been allocated in support and would refuel the participants before they ran past the targets. Yes; here it was.

He opened the document and scanned the details. Excellent; right there in the annex he could see which squadrons were taking part and his own squadron number was right there. They were providing a 4-ship and would be loaded out with 500 lb Mk82 bombs and each Skyhawk would have a full load of high explosive incendiary rounds in the guns. The 6th Air Brigade from Tandil airbase in Buenos Aires province were tasked to provide another 4-ship of Mirage 5s from the 1st Fighter-bomber Squadron with another 4-ship of Mirage IIIs from the 3rd Interceptor Squadron for the air defence serial. Both the 1st and 2nd Fighter-bomber Squadrons from his own base at Villa Reynolds were also tasked.

As the Flight Commander, he would push to lead the formation and he felt confident the Boss would not object as he was spending more time than ever down in Buenos Aires fighting off the budget cuts. He would have a chat with the squadron programmer straight away and fix the details. Digging deeper he saw that a temporary weapons range would be set up in the Bahia Grande off the coast of Rio Gallegos with the tanker towline offshore to the east. The run-in lines were parallel to the coast passing just a few yards to the seaward side of a visitor viewing area positioned on the shoreline. Splash targets set on huge pontoons would provide targets for bombs, their large floating panels easily visible to the pilots in the air but also to the spectators on the bleachers. They would also be used as strafe targets for the air-to-ground gunnery. He leafed through trying to locate the execution paragraph. The squadrons from the northern bases would deploy southwards to mount the sorties from a forward operating base close to the exercise area. The Brits would love that. After takeoff each formation would route first to the tanker which would be flying on the tactical towline and, after topping off to full, they would hit the targets dropping live weapons at three minute intervals. The whole event would finish with a simulated combat demonstration with the Mirages engaging the Skyhawks in mock air combat for the crowd. Hopefully all the live ordnance would be expended in the mock attacks if his embryonic plan was to work.

Flipping over the page he scanned the section covering the details of the air-to-air demonstration. The Mirage IIIs flying from Comodoro Rivadavia would be loaded with AIM-9B Sidewinders and a further pair of Mirages would provide novel air-to-air targets. Running ahead of the shooters the flare droppers would deploy a sequence of long-duration flares which would descend slowly under parachutes providing a "hot spot" against which the heat-seeking Sidewinders could be fired. To the missile, the bright chemical concoction would mimic the heat from a target's engines looking more attractive than the real thing. A carefully choreographed flight profile would ensure that, as the lead aircraft finished the flare drop, it would pull up and out of the line of fire to make sure it did not become an unintended target. Hopefully, the missile would see the flares as an attractive alternative to the Mirage's jet engine and home on the flares. It was always a spectacular demonstration in front of a crowd even if it did give the weapons staff a headache trying to work out the safety trace. Fired over the sea, a Sidewinder could travel up to 5 miles boosted by the onboard rocket motor. A wayward missile which failed to acquire the flare could easily fall to ground amongst the watching crowd. Now, that would cheer up the Generals and make the headlines.

The rest of the document was typically turgid and went on at great length detailing logistics, communications, command and control and on, and on, and on . . . . . There were no surprises.

This could give him an ideal opportunity for what he had in mind. If his plan was to work he needed at least two or three of the 500 lb weapons and the gun was a bonus. He would have preferred the missile demonstration to have been much later in the schedule as the thought of a pair of armed Mirages airborne at the same time and in the same airspace was a worry but he would have to work around it. He needed much more information if he was to have a chance of making the rest of the plan work and, more importantly, if he was to survive the sortie. There were some big "ifs".

Picking up the phone he dialled the number for the intelligence cell.

DAVID GLEDHILL

CHAPTER 15

THE UPLAND GOOSE HOTEL, PORT STANLEY

Karen nestled into the crook of his shoulder enjoying the warm glow after their gentle lovemaking. The rays from the rising sun were just breaking through a crack in the curtains throwing a dim light over the bed. She knew time was short and Razor would have to leave soon.

"So why do you do it?" she asked.

"Lots of reasons" Razor replied "but will this go in the article?"

"I could put it down to an unnamed source. After all, I'm hardly in a position to expose you am I?"

They shared a smile at the double entendre.

"I started like any other plane-crazy youngster. Watching the jets at air shows, hanging around the fence at RAF stations with a camera. It only really sucks you in once you join the Service."

"Why only then?"

"It's not a job, it's a way of life, maybe even a calling. You could never really retire from it, not like civilian flying. Some people think it's just a few years training and then it's all fun and frolics on the squadron. It's not at all. Officer training, elementary then basic, then advanced flying training. Follow that with one of the most intensive courses you could imagine at the

Tactical Weapons Unit learning to drop bombs and fight in air combat. They don't take prisoners during that phase. Only then do you get to fly your operational jet. Once at the conversion unit it's another four months hard slog to get to grips with the operational stuff. Even when you hit the squadron it takes up to a year to get operational. It was five years of my life before I was declared "Op."

"It must be hard; but fun and challenging."

"True but the worst thing is you're only as good as your last trip throughout the whole process. Get it wrong and you can be suspended and out on your ear in days. Most of the guys I started out with at elementary flying training fell by the wayside. I think only two of us made it onto a fast-jet squadron."

"So why not do something easier?"

"Have you seen the Phantom?"

"My first sight was through a grimy cabin window in the Hercules but I got to have a good look round yesterday up at the Squadron."

"Once you've seen and smelled "The Rhino" there's no going back. It's like the best aphrodisiac ever imagined. Not that I'd know about that," he bantered.

"So what next?"

"You mean after I look you up in London when I get back?" he asked.

"I'd like that Razor, I really would."

"Really?" It was quiet for a moment. "Well I guess another squadron tour but it'll be Leuchars in Scotland probably. Almost a prison sentence for a Londoner! Maybe I should push for Wattisham. It's a bit closer to home."

"That would suit me."

"What about you? Do you enjoy being a journalist? Must admit, I've spent my service career avoiding you types. I don't know what went wrong tonight."

He laughed as he felt a hand tighten on a sensitive part of his anatomy. He squirmed to avoid the, potentially, painful experience.

"I enjoy it for the most part. Many of the people I interview can give as good as they get. For the politicians it's mostly a game. They thrive on the exposure and it's a challenge to break through the usual drivel of the Party Line. This assignment is actually a welcome change for me. Most people down here seem intent on getting the job done and keeping a smile going. I imagine a few bombs going off around the place might change things though."

"Yes, we're a bit of a priority target at Stanley if they decide to have another go at us. Have you interviewed any of the locals yet?"

"Just one or two residents who I met in the hotel. I'm interviewing the Governor later and he seems to be quite an impressive character. Everyone who has met him says he's full of presence which is a surprise in such an out of the way place."

"They hold the occasional cocktail party at Government House and a few of the guys from the Squadron were invited. They say he's quite a charmer. So have you had to play the hard bitten hack yet?"

"What *are* you suggesting Flight Lieutenant?" she said as she propped herself up on one elbow distracting him instantly as the sheet fell away. "I'm always the ultimate professional."

"I'd guess just walking around in those tight jeans would get most people around here singing like canaries."

She hit him playfully and he feigned pain at the unprovoked attack.

"Seriously though, are there any down sides?"

"Oh yes."

"I don't believe you."

She flopped back down onto the pillow.

"When it gets into silly season, particularly as TACEVAL approaches, the

Station goes into lock-down about twice a month. The hooter goes at "Oh Dark Early" and we're expected to be at work within a few minutes without even taking a shower. That's despite the fact that you then sit around waiting for hours until the jets are loaded and ready to check in. As for breakfast . . . . . "

"Surely it's a bit more normal on a routine flying day?"

"It should be if we got to fly all the time. I fly maybe twice or three times a week and the rest of the time I get to do my secondary duties. For the new boy that means keeping the tea bags stocked up in the coffee bar and the biscuits resupplied. You should hear the moans when that goes wrong."

"Just think, you could get a job stacking shelves at the supermarket when you retire. You've had the ideal apprenticeship. It can't be all bad though?"

"No it's not. When I strap that jet to my arse and hit those burners on the runway I get the biggest rush of adrenaline in the world. You can't beat turning upside down at 500 knots overland."

"So what's the biggest negative?"

"Without a doubt, losing mates. I've been lucky so far. We lost a jet last year and the crew were killed. It was flying at low level chasing a Harrier in the low flying area up near Osnabruck. The pilot got tied up in a rolling scissors at low level. As he pulled back down he got the nose buried. Even though he pulled the wings off – almost literally – he didn't have enough Gs available to recover. The jet hit the ground still doing 400 knots. Neither of them tried to eject. It was a hell of a wake in the bar that evening but I cried my eyes out later that night."

She pushed herself back up on her elbows and looked closely. The tears were still not far away as he retold the story. She kissed him lightly. What the hell was this feeling? He turned away looking, distractedly, through the slit in the curtains.

"The real issue is that every single person from the youngest airman to the senior leadership is driven. Oh there's frustration but everyone really wants to get the job done. The trouble is some people are happy to step on others on their way upwards but I guess that's no different to any job in any company in the world."

"So how driven are you?"

She watched closely for his response but he had drifted off, lost in thoughts that he was not yet ready to share.

"So did I pass the interview?"

"Oh there's plenty there to fill a whole article, " she said playfully. "Maybe I'll get my psychiatrist friend to analyse the transcript."

She lifted her face towards him and kissed him gently. Little prompting was needed as things stirred again, the clock, temporarily, forgotten; the flying programme a distant distraction.

DAVID GLEDHILL

CHAPTER 16

THE INTELLIGENCE SECTION, VILLA REYNOLDS AIRBASE

Carmendez caught the eye of the airman behind the desk in the outer office.

"Is he in?"

"He is Sir; he's in the vault. Go through, he's expecting you."

Carmendez walked through the cluttered office and pushed open the heavy security door peering into the windowless intelligence cell where he could see maps and charts arranged around the wall. Unsurprisingly, two maps dominated. The borders of Chile were clearly marked on one with the tactical airbases highlighted and tagged. Notes attached on stickers denoted obscure facts about military dispositions that were unreadable from this distance but were obviously significant to the staff. The map which interested him most was immediately alongside showing the Islas Malvinas. The geography was hauntingly familiar and it brought back stark memories of the days operating over the rugged terrain during the conflict. The two new British air defence sites at Mount Alice and Byron Heights dominated the approaches to the western island and bright red circles marked the extent of the low level radar coverage over the sea. It made the risk seem more personal. Coloured push pins marked out the military bases at Stanley, Mount Pleasant and Mare Harbour. The main HQ, Headquarters British Forces Falkland Islands, was still located at the airfield at Stanley. A new facility which would house the headquarters lay just south of the new airbase but according to a handwritten note was not yet operational. The final link in the chain, the radar station at Mount Kent, lay northwest of the Capital on one of the highest peaks. Its dominant position gave it an uninterrupted view of the surrounding countryside and Carmendez took a close interest in the photographs attached to the map which showed the installations in close up. He speculated on their origins. The radome on top of the peak gave the radar an unobstructed view for many miles to the north and west so it was not only the fighters that would give him a challenge as his plan unfolded.

The intelligence officer beckoned him over and they exchanged a quick greeting before hunkering down over a bulky file laid out on the desk.

"Sir, good of you to come over. We don't see too many pilots in here, especially not ones with your reputation."

Carmendez shrugged off the compliment.

"No, it was good of you to see me at short notice. We're involved in this live-fire weapons exercise and I thought I'd get an update on any local issues. Have you been briefed on the details?"

"We have, Sir. It's the hot topic at the minute. The Base Commander is all over it and he's asked for daily updates at his morning briefings. The Russians are showing an interest and we've had an AGI parked just off Rio Gallegos for a week now. Make sure you watch what you say on UHF because it's all going down on tape and it will be back in Moscow by the end of the day. The Brits are also listening. We had a Nimrod electronic intelligence aircraft operating from the Malvinas flying up and down the coast outside territorial waters just yesterday."

"I will, thanks for the tip."

He stored the vital piece of information away thinking that radio silence might be a prudent tactic once his mission was underway.

"Speaking of the Brits, I hear they have a big event coming up."

He hoped his not too subtle question would not attract interest but the switch of topic had been a welcome lead-in to his main area of interest.

"They do. There's a VIP visit planned for the same day as the weapons demonstration which might be significant. I doubt our exercise pushed their agenda but it's unusual that it's all coming together at the same time. We've caused them a few sleepless nights and they've brought forward a "Fiery Focus" air defence exercise to next week. They deploy extra Phantoms down to the islands from UK for that exercise and normally operate at Stanley for about a week. After it's over the aircraft recover to UK but they normally take the opportunity to rotate the jets that are based on the islands. Our guess is that they have to go back for major servicing. With the heavy flying task down here and the fact they fly with weapons all the time probably puts quite a stress on the airframes."

"We'd probably do the same. I remember during the conflict that we had to send some of ours back here to Villa Reynolds. At least the maintenance facility turned out the replacements on time for a change. Sorry, go on."

He was keen not to lose momentum whilst the intelligence officer was happy to talk.

"We think this VIP visit is quite significant. One of their senior Government ministers is due to visit Stanley at the same time and it doesn't seem to be connected to the exercise. Traffic suggests he may already have arrived. We know there's been a lot of discussion about a new Constitution for the islanders so it might be connected with that but I can't say too much at this stage. we have some channels open to see if we can take advantage and we're trying to influence the direction with some diplomatic efforts underway. Even I'm not cleared for most of what's going on in the Defence Ministry but let me tell you what I can."

Carmendez settled back in his chair listening keenly.

"We know that, although the Minister has a global brief, since the conflict he's been a major player in regional matters around here. He's in the Foreign Office and works directly to the British Foreign Secretary. He's very influential both in Washington and on the South American continent and he's been lobbying the US State Department hard for their support. He's also been involved in discussions with Brazil and Chile and we think that has to do with operating rights. The flights in and out of the islands are seriously affected by weather and their refuelling plans have virtually no flexibility so if anything goes wrong and they can't take fuel, they often have to fly all the way back to Ascension Island. They desperately need diversions so, realistically, that means Brazil or Uruguay. Montevideo has been quite supportive and Brazil has been given quite a few sweeteners to play along. Rio ruffled a few British feathers during the war when they impounded the weapons on a Vulcan that diverted in with a broken refuelling probe. The buzz is that relations have thawed and they are back on an even keel. Chile is different. It's about the only bolthole on the mainland for fighters based on the islands. The weather in the Malvinas is unpredictable and if it clamps-in they rely on the air-to-air refuellers to extend their sortie duration. Once the tanker gets down to minimums they have no choice but to divert. Funnily enough we haven't been approached to allow them into Rio Gallegos! That means the airbase at Punta Arenas in Chile is their only viable option. To get into Punta Arenas they have to route across the Magellan Straits and come very close to our airspace on the way."

"That might look quite provocative to an air defence commander. Do we have any procedures in place?"

"Supposedly so but I suspect it would still cause a flutter at the Air Defence Ops. Centre if it happened."

"Sorry, I distracted you; you were talking about the Brit Minister."

"He's visiting the new base at Mount Pleasant quite soon. Normally we wouldn't know about a VIP movement but there was a careless comment in one of the routine logistics signals which gave it away. We intercepted it and, piecing other bits of information together we know he'll visit Government House to meet with the Governor and they'll both attend a meeting of the Islands Legislature at Heritage Hall in Stanley the next morning. That's the morning when our weapons demonstration is planned. We don't think that's significant and the timing seems to be coincidental. There are also a few journalists in tow. They're running a lot of pieces about the islands in the British Press at the minute. They've picked up on our event and are calling it "sabre rattling". It's a big thing for them and they're still worried about our intentions. One hack has even decided that this is a mission rehearsal for another air attack on the islands. His piece is quite provocative and it crossed my mind that he might have been speaking to some of our air planners. They could do worse than copy it and stamp Secret on the top and bottom. It would work quite well in my opinion."

Carmendez nodded thankful for the diversion.

"Any increase in the readiness posture? Are the Phantoms still on 10 minutes alert?"

"They are. Still just two jets on state. They'll be moving up to Mount Pleasant in the not too distant future. The dispersals up there are coming along well and the imagery shows that they are being fitted out with comms and power as we speak."

"That's good. Well, I mean it's good that they haven't increased their numbers on readiness."

"What you might not know is that the VIP party plans to drive up from Stanley on a military coach and do a bit of media stuff at the new airbase. The timing coincides with our live drops and it seems to be well choreographed. They plan to transmit some material live to UK and I suspect they may accuse us of being provocative. The best of luck to them I say. If they're using the usual green RAF coaches it'll be a bumpy ride. That's a rough ride on that new road from Stanley."

Carmendez thanked the intelligence officer and made to leave.

"Mind if I take a look at the maps? Anything sensitive on there?"

"No Sir, help yourself" said the intelligence officer as he turned and returned the file to the secure cabinet.

Carmendez took one last surreptitious glance at the map of the islands taking in every detail of the order of battle and the key locations of the defences. He didn't want to draw too much attention or to make his interest too obvious. The young analyst had no need to be drawn into his plans. The VIP visit was a real stroke of luck and perfect timing.

His mind was racing as the plan slowly crystallised.

*

Back in his office, Carmendez digested the information he had been offered. An attack against the British Headquarters had a certain synergy and would make his point well, particularly given that the Minister would be in town and its destruction would reinforce the vulnerability of the military installations. He had to be certain that the target suited his goals and weighed up his options analysing the strengths and weaknesses of each possibility before making his choice. Coming to the decision was a defining moment

He pulled out a low flying chart which he had already cut down to size focussing on his area of interest. The rectangle filled with mostly sea contained Rio Gallegos airfield to the western end and the Capital of the Malvinas, Port Stanley, to the east. Placing a strike ruler on the chart he circled a spot on the western coastline of the distant islands; his designated coast-in point. With his protractor positioned over the TACAN beacon located on the base at Rio Gallegos, he measured the range and bearing of the rendezvous point for the tanker and ringed the point over the South Atlantic Ocean. It was very close to this point where he would complete his air-to-air refuelling before he was expected to make the attack run to release the weapons for the assembled crowds. Connecting the TACAN beacon to his coast-in point with a long line on the map, he measured the bearing along which he would fly to make landfall on the coastline of the Malvinas. At some stage as he headed east towards the islands he would lose the radio signal from the TACAN beacon. At that point he would be on his own until he could work out his position once he coasted-in. Marking the line with timing marks he worked out how long it would take from leaving the tanker to arriving over the islands. Once off the tanker if he headed in a south easterly direction from the rendezvous he would intersect the radial from the radio beacon and could head off towards the distant islands. He had little need to calculate fuel figures. Those were indelibly etched in his mind from his sorties in 1982 and his Skyhawk would be, if anything, more lightly loaded this time. With resurgent memories, the vast expanse of ocean between the mainland and the islands emphasised the loneliness of the flight. As soon as he committed, he would be alone and unaided in his task. Even if he succeeded and survived the attack his reception on his return would be uncertain. He risked being branded as a pariah but he would worry about that later. Choosing a number of interim navigation points over the islands which would help him to navigate across the barren terrain he finalised his route. Joining up the navigation points he measured the tracks and added more timing marks. His final goal was marked with a target symbol and he spent some time checking the surrounding geography and choosing lead-in features for the attack run.

With his planning finished and conscious of the noises in the corridor outside the office, he stuck the map back into his drawer and locked it away. The last thing he needed now was questions over why he was showing an interest in this particular route.

From here to there seemed to be an insurmountable goal but his mind was made up.

DAVID GLEDHILL

CHAPTER 17

NO. 751 SIGNALS UNIT, MOUNT ALICE, WEST FALKLAND

Fingers tapped on consoles as technicians and controllers ran through their final checklists making sure that the radar was operational. The reinstallation seemed to have gone without a hitch but the massive transmitter, which would eventually send the radar pulses out into the ether, had been firing into a dummy load protecting itself from a potentially fatal short circuit. The test mode protected the delicate electronics until the technician was happy that all was well and he was ready to hit the transmit switch. Sitting at his engineering console, he refined the display controls setting the picture to his liking, cycling through the modes, checking every aspect. The Phantoms would be on frequency soon and he needed to return the system to the intercept controllers as soon as he could. It had to be ready. They had money resting on it after a bold bet between mates.

"Radar coming up in two minutes," he heard in the background from the engineering officer at the rear of the cabin putting adding pressure to his task. He ran through the final checks before holding his thumb in the air and, as the scope burst into life and the heavy ground returns began to paint behind the sweeping time base, he breathed a sigh of relief. The first transmissions were the most dangerous and the orange glow of the cathode ray tube seemed strangely comforting as its dull blaze returned, casting dim shadows around the room.

Alongside, the mini communications panel lit up and the intercept controller hit the button to take the call.

"Intercept Console."

"Master Controller, here. Eagles are airborne and en route just passing Fox Bay. They'll be pulling up in a couple of minutes. Ready to take them?"

"Affirmative. The radar's just come up and looking good. Chop them across to TAD 024, standing by."

He turned back to the scope and waited for the fighters to check in. Seconds before he had been staring at a blank scope and, worryingly, he was now about to take control of a pair of Phantoms using a totally untested radar system. His wait was brief.

"Eagles check."

"32."

"Loud and Clear."

"Cara Cara, Eagle 31 and 32 on frequency."

"Eagles, loud and clear, how me and check your weapons state?"

"31, loud and clear also. Eagle 31, Charlie Four, Four, Plus, Eight, Tiger Fast 60."

"Cara Cara, Eagle 32, you're loud and clear, same."

"Roger Eagles, vector 270 for the play area."

"270, roger."

The pair of Phantoms were ready for the calibration runs. Very soon he would know whether the new site on the summit of Mount Alice had solved the detection problems that had plagued the radar in its original location on the coast. With any luck, from its new perch on top of the mountain it would be able to detect low flying targets in the western approaches before they coasted-in over West Falkland.

There was plenty of fuel onboard the Phantoms and the gentle manoeuvring expected during the calibration runs would use little of the precious Avtur. For the crews it would add plenty of hours to their log books today but they would be on task for a considerable time, boring holes in the sky before the fighter controllers were happy that the radar was recalibrated. For the fighter controller this was his utopia. On a routine sortie, the moment a navigator in the fighter picked up the target on his radar he would take control of the intercept leaving little for the controller to do but monitor the airspace. Today, the controller would exercise close control throughout the sortie giving some much needed training. He would control the set ups and choreograph the fighters' moves all the way in to the intercept position. Happy days.

"Eagle 31, as fighter, vector 320 degrees and climb flight level 150. Eagle 32 as target vector 180 degrees. Climb flight level 170."

The controller was in his element. In the cockpits, boredom set in as the Phantoms manoeuvred languidly in the upper air. In the control cabin the tapes were running, capturing each frame of the radar display. The data was recorded and would be analysed in minute detail at a later stage by the scientist from the Radar Signals and Research Establishment from Malvern who had been sent to the remote hilltop for the very purpose. The analyst made copious notes as the fighters separated on yet another serial, the radar tracks burning bright on the cathode ray tube. The controller vectored each to a point in space where the nominated target would start its run back towards the islands, varying the altitude to gauge potential holes in the radar coverage. He was particularly interested in the picture below 5000 feet in the western approaches. If another attack ever materialised, it was from that area where it would most likely originate. Argentina lay a mere 400 miles to the west and just a short flight would threaten the vital installations on the islands, his own location high on the priority list. Alongside him the scientist clutched his clipboard taking copious notes as the sortie progressed. Once he sat down to analyse the data he would know just how effective the relocation had been.

"Eagle 32, say your height."

"500 feet, Eagle 32."

"Roger, as target come left heading 090. Maintain height."

The Phantom still painted brightly on the radar despite having dropped down to low level and it was a promising trend. With the Phantom pilot complying meekly starting yet another low level run towards the radar head, the "blip" remained reassuringly solid on the scope. If this had been a real target flying inbound the controller would already have been vectoring fighters to intercept. Today the fighter would arrive at the merge but it would find only its compliant playmate. There would be no mistakes in the air today.

"Eagle 31, as fighter, vector 240 for cut off."

He watched as the tracks on the scope followed his instructions, the fighter converging on its simulated prey. His gizmo flashed across the scope as he made the calculations for the intercept geometry crunching the numbers in his head. This would go on for at least the next hour but he, for one, was having fun.

*

"Eagle 31 is joker. Cara Cara, Eagles are complete and inbound for Measles and then RTB. Thanks for the service. Eagles, stud 10, stud 10, go!"

"Eagles, clear to tactical and thanks for your help. Good day."

As he pulled off his headset glad for the break, the controller pushed back his chair and made for the door. A "Measles" was the clue that they were about to witness a tracking exercise for the MANPADs operators. That meant a rare flypast over the site and he didn't want to miss it.

The bright sun made him squint as he pushed open the door to the control cabin and emerged into the daylight. Not even time for a coffee as he heard jet noise in the valley to the west.

CHAPTER 18

QUICK REACTION ALERT, RAF STANLEY

In the crewroom on the Squadron the video player was pushing out the obligatory movie. This morning, Monty Python had been given a well earned break and a new title which had just arrived on the overnight airbridge flight was breaking the monotony. The alert crews spread out on easy chairs around the TV, their places sacrosanct. Woe betide anyone, including the Boss, who tried to grab the Q seats. Retribution would be swift. Home based QRA crews were spared the hum drum of normal squadron life, closeted away in the "Q Shed" for their stint of duty. With little external pressure they could concentrate exclusively on the heightened boredom of a 24 hour QRA session. In the hastily cobbled-together crewroom at RAF Stanley, space was at a premium and they shared the limited room with other squadron crews who were preparing to fly on training sorties. Those not involved were dissuaded from adding to the clutter.

Life in the crewroom was tranquil given that they were transplanted from normal life. For the flying crews, a flying suit was the order of the day until just before they walked for their jets but for the alert crews there could be no such luxury. The thick "bunny suit", worn under the heavy immersion suit was designed to protect them from the ravages of the cold South Atlantic waters if they were unlucky enough to eject. As a sop to comfort during the long tedious periods of alert, the upper half of the heavy rubber suit was undone and tied loosely around the waist using the arms to hold it in place. If the suit was zipped up inside the building they would quickly be overcome by heat exhaustion. Even in a cold cockpit the thick rubber neck seals and heavy impregnated rubberised fabric was hot and cumbersome. For these crews the suit was their insurance policy against coming down in the icy local waters, surely not suited to the comfort of crewroom temperatures. Sometimes back home they would be allowed to dispense with the bulky internal G suits as missions were unlikely to involve any hard manoeuvring. The target at the end of a QRA intercept was more likely to be a Tupolev Bear on the "Milk Run" to Cuba than a fighter. With the potential to meet an Argentinian Mirage which was far more agile, flying without a G suit was not an option at RAF Stanley.

In synch with its rudimentary external appearance, the inside of the crewroom was equally austere and functional. A telebrief set, giving a constant and direct link to the Sector Operations Centre at Mount Kent, emitted a regular bleep from the corner of the crewroom. The sound, which became embedded in the psyche after 24 hours on Q gave the crews the confidence that the link was live, albeit at the risk of driving them crazy. Alongside, the high frequency radio set offered a chat frequency used by the islanders in the remote settlements who would pop up for a regular chat and discuss their diaries and routines with their fellow inhabitants. For the crews it was a welcome diversion and the means to plead with a host for the offer of bed and breakfast away from the military routine of RAF Stanley. The hospitality of the locals was legendary and welcome and the simple acts of hospitality formed bonds of friendship which would never be forgotten. It was almost unheard of for a crew to be unable to secure a visit to a settlement for the night. Next to the radio, the field intercom linked the crewroom, via a hastily installed wire, to the Ops Room. An occasional metallic rattle would be the summons for a formation to make its way for the out-briefing prior to escaping the cosy confines of RAF Stanley for a few hours.

Alongside the communications equipment sat the legendary heater which had probably seen service in the trenches of Flanders. Temperamental in the extreme, a ritual lighting ceremony each morning would take the chill off the crewroom and make the temperature bearable even in the cold winter conditions. Many an unwary Phantom pilot or navigator had nearly lost fingers when trying to coax it into life. Its eccentricities were forgiven when it finally, often reluctantly, burst into action throwing a pleasant warmth around the room.

This particular afternoon the atmosphere was relaxed. A few bodies lounged around catching up with exploits from the "fleshpots" of Port Stanley the previous evening, or at least those who had been lucky enough to have purloined the squadron transport and to have enjoyed a brief respite from the constant readiness. Although it failed to make the list of the top 100 venues for night clubs on the South American archipelago, a night in the Globe Tavern drinking Penguin Ale was a welcome diversion from military life. The Upland Goose Hotel was a positive luxury. Only the crews on R and R were lucky enough to escape the claustrophobic confines of the local area for a luxurious 24 hours.

What no one could know was that today was the calm before the storm.

CHAPTER 19

GOVERNMENT HOUSE, PORT STANLEY

"That's me finished for today Mr Sullivan. I'm away home now."

"Goodnight Susan and thank you," replied the aide barely glancing up from the files arranged on his sumptuous antique desk. With furniture sparse on the islands, particularly antique furniture, the deep mahogany veneers and the dark green leather inlay on the desk top formed an immediate impression on visitors who entered the Governor's outer office, in stark contrast to the norm. It was one of the more pleasant trappings of power in an austere community.

He waited for some time, listening for other noises around the now quiet building, reasonably confident that he was alone. Burning the midnight oil was not unusual for Sullivan as there was little to occupy his time at home and tonight was no different. Entertainment, such as it was in Port Stanley, revolved around family life, the radio and the few pubs. Despite his passion for reading, his bookcase could only hold so many books and his appetite was limited by the cost and delay in acquiring new volumes from home. He longed to be able to browse his favourite bookshop off Leicester Square in London once again. The Governor was long gone. He had left Government House some time earlier and caught the afternoon flight in the FIGAS Islander to Pax Port Howard in West Falkland where he was meeting the local islanders to discuss some development plans. He would not return until the morning, reinvigorated for the keynote meeting to come.

Satisfied that he really was alone he pulled a file from the base of the pile and opened it at a recent enclosure. Releasing the loose-leaf entries he selected a few significant candidates from the carefully numbered and registered documents and laid them out carefully. The minutes of the Governor's meeting with the representatives of the Island's Legislative Council had been quite illuminating as were the latest policy edicts from the Foreign Office.

He had sent his regular radio transmission to the mainland earlier in the week but a message he had received by return had come as a surprise. It was the first time his short transmissions had elicited a direct response and, nervous that the burst transmission might have been intercepted, he promised himself that he would make the point clear in his next transmission. He had no desire to turn this into a dialogue and even less desire to compromise his position. One-way traffic was the only safe option in this highly monitored environment and the risk of discovery was high. His compensatory pay check, deposited regularly in an overseas account, was a motivation but liberty was even more important if he was to enjoy the windfall and fulfil his political ambitions.

His contact on the mainland was pressing for sight of original documents and he had anticipated this probability for some time. How else would he prove the veracity of the information? Encoding the mass of data was out of the question and it would take hours to transcribe the documents even if he had the means to send a copy unnoticed. There was only one viable alternative and he would have to resort to old school methods. He pulled out a single lens reflex camera from his briefcase, screwed the wide angle macro lens into the camera body and set it on the desk. He had discounted the idea of finding fast ISO 400 film in Port Stanley which might make photography in the darkened office a little easier. The flash gun which he snapped into place on the hot shoe of the camera would have to do. He hoped that the quality would be sufficient but there would be no way to check because developing the film was out of the question. Holiday snaps of official documents were hardly the norm in the quiet Capital. With the curtains tightly closed, hoping that the flash would not attract attention shielded by the heavy lining, he went back to the desk. Propping a document on a typing stand, the header and footer luridly stamped with the word "SECRET", he began to capture the images. He winced as the flashgun popped and whirred with each exposure, the noise of the tiny capacitor sounding like a siren in the quiet office as it recharged.

The last document returned to its place in the files, he packaged the small film cartridge in a box with the address of his Argentinian contact clearly marked on the front. The box was placed in a second envelope carrying the address of a London-based forwarding service. On arrival the box would be forwarded to the recipient and a significant charge debited to the sender's account, expressly for the discrete service. He would drop in to the British Forces Post Office at Stanley tomorrow. That way the package would be anonymous amongst the mass of mail which originated on the base every day. He returned the files to the security container in the corner of the outer office and spun the combination lock. With the camera and envelope safely returned to the briefcase and, after one final check around his office, he clicked off the desk lamp and made his way out of the door.

DAVID GLEDHILL

CHAPTER 20

RIO GALLEGOS AIRBASE, ARGENTINA

Carmendez walked across the familiar dispersal taking in the atmosphere. It was a hive of activity. He had led his formation down from Villa Reynolds the previous day and his Skyhawks were once again parked alongside the squadron. Armourers scurried around the jets preparing them to accept the live weapons. Before any live ordnance came anywhere near any of the aircraft there were safety checks to complete to make sure they would operate correctly and, most importantly, safely. It was ironic for a piece of equipment designed to destroy. Only very late in the process as pilots taxied towards the runway were the safety pins finally pulled and the bombs made live. Up to that moment discretion was the watch word. Test sets would be plugged into umbilicals and checks made on weapons systems to monitor for stray voltages or for anomalies on the circuits. Only then when the armourers were happy were the bomb trolleys pushed alongside.

Carmendez exchanged a greeting with the crew chief who was supervising the loading. They talked briefly as Carmendez quizzed him to make sure the correct weapons were being loaded onto the correct jets. The Operation Order called for a mixture of stores mainly 1000 lb bombs and 500 lb bombs. Although he had a little latitude, he wanted to make just a small change to his own load. He had been allocated four 500 lb Mk 82 bombs with contact fuses. Given the fuel restrictions he would face as he made his way east, he had asked for only three to be loaded. To keep the symmetry he wanted one on the centreline and one on each of the wing pylons. The crew chief didn't need to know why. He also made sure that there would be no changes to the loads without his say so and the chief was under no illusions about the consequences if there was a screw up. A quick check on the markings on the cases of the squat, ugly weapons confirmed that they really were live weapons; just an arming key away from their mission.

Satisfied with progress, he looked across the dispersal towards a formation of Pucara light attack aircraft which were being armed. Unlike the Skyhawks they were being loaded with rocket pods which carried the 2.75" unguided rockets. Not quite as lethal as his own load they were, nevertheless, effective and perfectly suited against convoys or dug-in troops. He had fired the rocket cans in the past and had even used them on the Skyhawk but, for his purposes, he wanted the more predictable ballistics of the iron bombs. Unguided rockets could have a mind of their own at times and the target he had in mind was tucked in amongst other buildings. He could not guarantee that there would be no collateral damage but that was a risk he would have to take. He had a precise effect in mind and intended to deliver a clear message.

The targets for the firepower demonstration would be ranged off the coast but within easy sight of the viewing area. In addition to the panel target, a small rocky island had been designated for the live drops of the thousand pounders to give a visible detonation. The pilots would use a variety of attack profiles depending on the type of bomb they had been tasked to drop. For the first run attacks, or FRAs, the formation would approach at low level and drop retarded 500 lb dumb bombs. The drag fins at the back of the weapon would snap open in the airflow slowing the bomb which would fall behind the flight path of the fighter-bomber and impact well after the attacking aircraft had cleared the target. Other Skyhawks armed with free fall 500 lb bombs would employ a loft attack profile. At a suitable range from the target the attacker would pull up into a steep climb and release the weapon at the apex of the pull. The inertia would literally lob the bomb ahead of the aircraft striking the target from a distance. An escape manoeuvre would ensure that the attacker was nowhere near the explosion and debris hemisphere once the bomb exploded. The fuses would be set with both contact and airburst settings to ensure that the spectacle from the ground was at its best. During live weapon drops, these settings were critical. For a heavily armoured or protected target a contact fuse attached to a rapidly moving bomb ensured maximum destruction. A bomb which exploded just before it reached its target would break up into thousands of pieces and spread lethal shrapnel around the vicinity. For lightly armoured targets this was enough to cause lethal damage. Warheads were specifically designed and optimised against different types of target to elicit maximum damage. For each drop the effect of the high explosive charge in each bomb would provide a show for the guests and it would all look particularly spectacular but he didn't intend to be around to witness the event.

Glancing back at his jet the arming sequence had begun. A bomb loader had pulled alongside and the long forks were already positioned under the bomb casing as the armourers strapped it tight to the cradle. It wouldn't do if it parted company from the loader during its short journey across the tarmac. The operator eased it upwards, manoeuvring cautiously underneath the delta-wing fighter-bomber. Once in place, a deft flick of the control lever raised the lethal cargo up towards the weapon pylon. More frantic action as an armourer aligned and mated the two components before locking lugs snapped in position holding the bomb in place on the pylon. With the straps released and a thumbs-up from the armourer, the driver moved back to collect his next weapon.

Carmendez worked his way along the line checking and rechecking the rest of the aircraft in his formation. Significantly, he looked for any air-to-air missiles. They were not planned to be fitted but he wanted to make absolutely sure. There was nothing he could do about the full load of HEI ammunition in the guns as that would be expended as part of the spectacle but he didn't want any surprises with random Sidewinders. Finally content he stepped back, the sight of the "aircraft armed" warning boards placed alongside the jet ominous, causing just a ripple of anticipation. Only he knew what the next 24 hours would hold.

As he walked away, and despite his dire warnings, a fourth bomb was loaded onto the centreline station on his jet. It was a mistake which would later come to be his undoing.

CHAPTER 21

GOVERNMENT HOUSE, PORT STANLEY

"Alexander, come in would you?"

Replacing the phone in its cradle, Sir Ronald Chilton, the Governor of The Falkland Islands eased back in his chair and watched the large door from the outer office as it swung open. Alexander Sullivan had been in Port Stanley for some time and had acted as aide to his predecessor for a short time. His calm, efficient demeanour was popular with his masters and he seemed unflappable. Why the young diplomat had been sidelined in such a remote outpost was a mystery but the Governor was grateful for the anomaly and trusted him implicitly. There was no preamble as the aide took his seat.

"I've just been on the phone to Sir Michael Crowe in the Foreign Office and he updated me on the Minister's brief. We've had a long discussion on how to play this forthcoming meeting and I think we are agreed. We can't be seen to be giving any latitude to Buenos Aires at this stage. The wounds are still a little raw in London and even more so locally. Despite that, Sir Michael has serious reservations over how long the Treasury will carry on funding the military build up. The money for operational tasks comes from Treasury contingency funds rather than the MOD's central budget. Those funds have already provided the wherewithal for the new base facilities at Mount Pleasant but, even so, there are already mutterings in the corridors of MOD Main Building. They've been asked to take up the strain starting next year from within their core funding. The Junior Defence Minister is not happy and he's threatening to take his protest to the Star Committee. As always, money seems to override morals and principles."

"I can see that it wouldn't be popular in the MOD, Governor," said Sullivan. "They are already suffering from cutbacks after "Options For Change" and they are only just getting to grips with the new figures. I have contacts in the MOD and they tell me that they are under pressure to make ends meet. Adding the annual running costs for Mount Pleasant will not be insignificant."

The two men were quiet for a few seconds and Sullivan, deliberately, waited for his mentor to respond. His goal was to report the agenda not to drive it so for now he would hold his counsel. His plan was best served by subservience.

"Diplomatic channels are still open since the repatriation of the prisoners of war. With the imminent visit by the families to attend the memorial ceremony they will not be too keen to sever the links any time soon. Sir Michael has asked me to sound out my old contacts in BA to see if we have any wiggle room over a shared arrangement on Sovereignty. I'll have to play this very carefully. It has to be seen to be a strong and principled negotiation. Any hint of compromise and the islanders will feel that we've sold them out."

Chilton had been a junior diplomat in the British Embassy in Buenos Aires for some years in the 1970s and had developed the usual diplomatic network of contacts during his service in the South American Capital. Despite his ingrained affinity with his South American neighbours he was cautious over the developing initiative to "repatriate" the "Islas Malvinas". His sympathy could only extend so far and the rights to Sovereignty were extremely tenuous even by Latin American standards. His brief when he was posted to Port Stanley had been to assess the mood post-conflict and to decide whether the islanders aspirations were met better by linking with their neighbours. Although the public principles were clear - and the Prime Minister had been unerring in the desire to retain British control - Government finance would become, as always, the driving factor. Principles were negotiable once the Treasury became involved. His tentative suggestions for renewed tolerance after his arrival in Stanley had been predictably and firmly rebuffed by the Head of the Falkland Islands

Council. No one in this community had any desire to see an Argentine Administration reinstated and memories of the heavy-handed treatment by the Argentine Military Governor when he imposed martial law after the occupation were still strong, particularly amongst the older residents. The occupation had been swift, unexpected and brutal. During those brief months before Liberation, islanders had been displaced from their homes and vain attempts to introduce Spanish as the daily language and to drive on the right hand side of the road had been hugely unpopular. It would be a long struggle if the Governor was to persuade the Kelpers that their future lay with the mainland and not the British Isles.

"My view is that, as much as they hate the idea, reality will dictate that by 1990 these islands will be forced to consider life as part of Argentina. We can't keep up the airbridge for ever and life will continue to be austere if everything continues to be imported from the Northern Hemisphere. Local links are vital and Chile can only offer so much. I can't see how spirit can override the practicalities of geography."

"I see that," said Sullivan, "but they already stand a good chance of improving living standards. The new deep water port of Mare Harbour will allow all manner of goods to be imported. Building materials will become more plenty and consumer goods will begin to appear."

He hesitated having pressed harder than he had intended.

"All true but if the air links to the mainland are improved people could get back and forth with ease. Think of cruise ships docking more regularly and the East Coast ports on the mainland becoming easily accessible. Life could be so much better."

Sullivan bided his time knowing that decisions had already been taken. It was a skilful battle of wits.

"Well I'm going to have to keep up my best poker face with my old contacts in Buenos Aires. It wouldn't do to show weakness so soon would it? Heavens knows, I have a strong hand but if they even had an inkling of London's real intent we would never make progress. Why would they concede anything? They could play the waiting game with a guaranteed outcome."

"Very true Governor that wouldn't do at all."

The stony face implied acquiescence but Alexander Sullivan had his own agenda. Little did Chilton know at this stage that it was somewhat at odds with his own party line and driven by motives other than politics and diplomacy.

The coming days would determine the islands' future, one way or another.

CHAPTER 22

THE ARGENTINIAN NAVAL BASE, TRELEW

The four turboprops hummed steadily as the "Electrone" electronic surveillance plane accelerated down the runway at Trelew. Modified for the signals intelligence mission, the extensive array of electronic equipment in the aft cabin was in stark contrast to the innocent looking exterior. To the casual observer it was an airliner, although this guise did not stand close scrutiny. With the lack of windows and the clusters of aerials adorning the fuselage, its task was far removed from its former role. Rather than moving people between airfields, it had become a highly complex and capable electronic snooper and today's mission was to test out the British defences.

Safely airborne, gear and flaps retracted, the Captain released the crew to move around the rear compartment. Operators began to fire up the receivers and run through their post takeoff checks. The galley was active and the coffee was brewing. The flight engineer cleared technicians to apply power to the systems and lights winked on as radio receivers sprang into life. Soon they would be listening to each and every radio or radar signal which was transmitted in the vast area of ocean off the coast of Argentina. Some would be fascinating, some would convey crucial intelligence but most would be simply boring. All would be captured by the state of the art data recorders. The crew set a south easterly course away from Trelew, gaining height as the Electra turned towards the disputed waters off the Falkland Islands.

*

Back at Rio Gallegos, Carmendez carried out his walkround but cursed once he looked at the weapons loaded under the jet. Despite his orders, the idiots had loaded four Mk82 "retards". It was too late to fix it and he, certainly, had neither the time nor the inclination to attract additional scrutiny. He would just have to live with the drag penalty, although given the chance, he could jettison the extra weapon into the ocean if it proved to be too much of a "dragmaster". The mistake was a hindrance and set his mind racing as he recalculated the penalty of the extra weight, re-computing the vital fuel figures in his head.

A relieved Carmendez dropped onto his ejection seat pleased to be finally in the cockpit, cinching tight his lap straps, pulling his butt into the hard canvas seat covering. The flight line mechanic handed him the top strap and he twisted the seat harness buckle as he slotted the strap into place. The other strap followed and he snugged them down tight, gripping him firmly to the seat. A flick of the "go forward" lever and, once again, he could move freely, unconsciously checking the lanyard which connected him to his rubber dinghy in the seat pack. It was a habit developed over the years of training, and was one last check that his means of survival in a cold South Atlantic would not drift away on the tide. Today, if he needed the survival dinghy, he wondered whether he might be better accepting his fate rather than an unpredictable reception when he returned. He pulled on his bonedome shutting out the noise of the outside world temporarily.

As he fired up the systems he checked the indications for the weapons. All looked good as each bomb registered on the status panel. With his checks complete and tuned into the Tower frequency, he waited patiently for the rest of his formation to finish their own checks. Looking down the line he could see groundcrew darting under the jets as they cross-checked systems and buttoned up panels readying the jets for departure. Deft hand signals communicated wordlessly between the pilots in the cockpit and their see-off crews as the nominated taxy time approached. He could not fail to notice the dark green bombs hanging menacingly on the weapons pylons under each jet. Whether they would actually be dropped today depended on how the next 30 minutes played out.

"Viper 2's ready."

"Viper 2, roger."

The remainder of the formation gradually checked in and he received a final thumbs-up from the pilot alongside.

"Gallegos Tower, Viper taxy."

"Viper taxy, Runway 25, QNH 1013 millibars."

"Taxy for 25, Viper."

"Viper, message from your operators, your serial is on time and Esso is on station."

"Viper Lead, roger."

The tanker was on the towline. Perfect. He flicked his thumbs sideways which elicited an immediate response from below as the chocks were pulled away. A touch of throttle and the jet moved forward; a dab of the brakes to confirm that they were working and a tweak on the rudder pedals to confirm his nosewheel steering was active and he pulled off the slot. Round the corner and he moved briskly towards the armament safety slot where an armourer would carry out last-chance checks on the weapons before clearing him to take the active runway. In his mirror the remainder of the formation followed his lead and he experienced that familiar shot of adrenaline as the well practised routine unfolded. The pre-takeoff checks rattled by and soon he was stationary again allowing the safety pins to be pulled from the bomb carriers, the runway just metres away. The armourer presented the metal pins with their bright red tell-tale, one for each bomb, with a flourish. He was ready. The technician worked his way gradually down the line of jets in turn, each tucked in echelon ranged along the small armament dispersal, engines whining. A thumbs-up from the number 4 passed back along the line eventually repeated by his wingman who raised the final thumb. They were good to go.

"Tower, Viper takeoff."

"Viper, clear takeoff, wind 270 at 12 knots. After departure call Gallegos Zone on 345.7."

"Takeoff, Viper."

He pushed up the throttles moved to the near side of the runway and watched his wingman cross over and line up alongside. He had briefed two pairs in 20 seconds stream and once the second element had lined up he pushed the throttle to the firewall checking the response of his engine before takeoff. With a final nod from his wingman he hit the transmit switch.

"Viper, rolling, rolling, go."

As the Skyhawk accelerated, the wingman in tight formation, they took off down the centreline. They had a rendezvous with Esso.

CHAPTER 23

GOVERNMENT HOUSE, PORT STANLEY

"Minister, it's very good of you to speak to me."

On the other end of the phone the cultured tones of the senior politician in Buenos Aires was slightly muffled as they exchanged pleasantries in the time honoured fashion. The fact that the two countries had so recently been at war might have been inconsequential as the ethics of the cocktail party circuit dominated. Such tradition would survive future skirmishes, no matter how serious the stakes yet, despite the verbal ballet, topics eventually turned more serious.

"The Foreign Secretary has asked me to open discussions concerning how we move forward. I should say at the outset that Sovereignty is not open for discussion and I have been asked to stress that fact. I can, however, explore other avenues that might lead to a diplomatically and mutually acceptable solution."

"That is most disappointing Governor. You will know that my own Prime Minister could never be seen to accept anything other than the return of Argentinian control over the islands."

"Perhaps Minister, " he replied, ignoring the indelicate use of the word "return", but after the recent unfortunate events he is hardly in a position to make demands over what was taken by force and merely returned to its rightful inhabitants in the same way."

"Indeed, and we now see that those events were most unfortunate, Governor. Please be assured that we would never resort to force again and a political solution is the way ahead. He seeks a diplomatic compromise."

"I do believe I can go some way to producing such a solution Minister; with your help of course."

"I'm intrigued."

"Clearly, I must embrace the wishes of the people and the representatives of the Island Legislative Council should be included but at this early stage we could lay some groundwork before we bring them into the discussions."

"You must know that we regard the dispute over the Islas Malvinas as a bilateral issue between London and Buenos Aires."

"Of course but you must also respect that we place the islander's wishes at the top of our list of priorities. Nothing must affect their right to self-determination."

"It is so difficult to talk over the phone so maybe I can have our aides draw up an agenda for exploratory talks. Neutral ground would probably suit both of us at this stage would you not think?"

"Indeed; I hear Zurich is pleasant at this time of the year."

If only his counterpart knew how much leeway he had been offered. The facts that the Sovereignty issue was by no means a closed book and that at the heart of the question was a desire in Whitehall to save money were bargaining chips he would play carefully. If either fact came out at this stage he would have little left with which to negotiate. Although apparently robust, having recaptured the islands, if London was seen to play loose with the islander's futures and, heaven forbid, it came out in the Press, the Prime Minister would appear weak and that could never be countenanced! These would be critical negotiations if he was to sell the plan locally and he was, undoubtedly, treading a dangerous path.

On his desk the portable recording device whirred away capturing the conversation so that every nuance could be analysed later. Unbeknown to him, his would not be the only copy of the conversation. Next door, in

Sullivan's desk drawer, another recorder was capturing every word and this copy would attract the same scrutiny but from a different analyst. The person to whom it would eventually find its way might not be quite so objective in how it would be interpreted.

DAVID GLEDHILL

CHAPTER 24

THE GLOBE HOTEL, PORT STANLEY

In the bar of the Globe Hotel set back from the Stanley waterfront, the two men had already finished their first lunchtime beer and the second pint was following. The Penguin Ale was going down well and, as inhibition faded, confidence rose and the scuttlebutt flowed.

"I was talking to Jennie this morning. She's the book keeper in the Governor's office and she was telling me a few things. That aide, the one who keeps himself to himself, Sullivan I think his name is. She reckons he's a bit dodgy."

"He comes over alright I'd say. I met him at one of those evening events a few months ago and he seemed like a decent sort. He was quite the hero during the war. He stood up to a couple of soldiers when they occupied Government House and stuck up for some of the women. I heard he only just escaped a beating. One of the soldiers was about to rearrange his head with a rifle when an officer intervened and stopped him. It was a close thing though"

"Maybe so but she told me he's been making a bit of a nuisance of himself and that's being kind. He made some pretty lewd suggestions to one of the young clerks at a cocktail party the other week. It frightened the life out of the young lass."

"What sort of suggestion?"

"Let's put it this way, if you were her father you'd be taking Sullivan aside and explaining a few facts of life to him. Let's just say I don't think marriage was on his mind, more like some practice for the wedding night if you get my drift."

"So he's on the prowl then?"

"Without a doubt."

"He wants to go careful around here. He should know by now that nothing goes on in Stanley that doesn't get out. He's been here long enough to understand that, if he so much as burps, it'll be common knowledge on the radio network the minute he's shut his mouth."

"So what was the full story?"

"Just a bit of boasting to try and turn a young lass's head. Offers of Champagne in the Governor's conservatory for a start but that wasn't all he suggested before she excused herself. We all know where that would have led don't we?"

"Well maybe we just need to have a few of the lads have a quiet word in his ear sometime? It can't harm can it?"

"Maybe I'll have a chat with Jeff and Steve. They might like a change from wrestling with sheep. It'll be a treat for them."

"Maybe a quiet word will remind him how we behave around here."

They drained their glasses and headed out the door.

CHAPTER 25

OVER THE BAHIA GRANDE OFF THE ARGENTINIAN COASTLINE

Carmendez could see the coastline in the distance off the right wing as he led his formation over the Bahia Grande towards the refuelling rendezvous. They had broken through the scattered overcast into clear blue skies and, as they coasted out, the cloud had broken up completely and the Atlantic Ocean stretched away to the limit of visibility. He was grateful that he would not have to fight through the murk once he made his move.

Pulling alongside the C-130 tanker, already refuelling a Mirage, he dragged down his visor to kill the glare. In the first Mirage, resplendent in its green and brown splinter camouflage, the pilot's head was motionless, fixed on his references on the underside of the lumbering tanker. The second Mirage moved relentlessly towards its in-flight coupling with just a slight oscillation as the pilot played the basket in the final stages of the approach. The probe sank home and the jet settled in the slipstream alongside the first.

Carmendez knew the pilot well; a fellow combat veteran of the Malvinas campaign whom he had met on a number of occasions after the conflict. Captain Raul Hernandez was an experienced Mirage pilot with well over 1000 hours on type. They had dissected the reasons for the defeat in minute detail and the analysis had been helped by copious amounts of malt whiskey. His campaign had been frustrating. The Mirages had pushed forward aggressively in the early stages of the conflict, employed as a fighter sweep to persuade the Sea Harriers to engage in air combat to the west of the islands. Canny British commanders with only limited numbers of Sea

Harriers had recognised the ploy and refused to be drawn. Frustrated by the reticence, the logical move to embed the fighters within the attacking formations of Skyhawks and Daggers had not been pursued leaving the Mirage pilots frustrated and under employed. They had been relegated to making limited feints against the task force facing the operational reality that, once over the islands, the Mirage pilots were on the limits of their fuel reserves and had only enough combat fuel for 30 seconds manoeuvring in the area and could not even consider using afterburner. Had they been able to do so they would have fared better but, without the vital extra thrust they gave a huge advantage to the Sea Harrier pilots. Tactically, the Argentinian fighter-bomber pilots were committed to avoiding detection rather than confronting the combat air patrols aggressively. As a consequence, Hernandez' squadron had failed to claim a single air-to-air kill throughout the campaign despite losses to the Sea Harriers. Like Carmendez he held a grudge.

Carmendez couldn't fail to be impressed. With only two C-130 tankers in the inventory, opportunities to practise air-to-air refuelling were few and far between. Nevertheless, the Mirage had plugged effortlessly into the basket and made contact first time. As he watched, the second Mirage hit turbulence and the hose whipped alarmingly in the airflow before the oscillations damped down. He could see a pair of air-to-air missiles hanging menacingly below the pylons under the wings, the slim white missile bodies fixed to the launchers. From the Operation Order he knew that they were the older AIM-9Bs which were the original versions supplied by the Americans many years before. When the Mirages had been delivered, the French had provided first generation Matra Magic missiles but even they were too valuable to waste on a demonstration event. With the rudimentary uncooled seeker heads of the bravos, the pilots would be forced to manoeuvre into the target's "6 o'clock" before the missile would acquire the heat of the engines and be able to track. Later versions were much more capable but for the purposes of the firing demonstration these would be just fine. It was also fine by Carmendez who saw the Mirage as a threat to the successful outcome of his plan. The second Mirage on the far wing hose was, to Carmendez's relief, not armed. The planners had allocated two missiles to the primary firing aircraft rather than one missile on each jet as he would have done. Instead, slung beneath the centreline of the second Mirage was a large "Lepus" flare pod normally used for illuminating a target during a night reconnaissance mission. Massive flares dispensed by the pod, much larger than the small self defence flares carried by tactical aircraft, burned for up to 20 seconds providing a visible target for both the heat seeking missiles and the cameras. For the firing exercise they would provide a huge infra-red source which would confuse the obsolescent technology in the aging AIM-9B persuading the seeker that it should follow the flare rather than the heat of the engines of the Mirage dropping the flare. More importantly for Carmendez, the second unarmed Mirage could not influence his mission in any way leaving only Hernandez as a cause for concern.

Once the Mirages were topped off they were marshalled off to the far side of the formation by the tanker captain and his own pair was called in astern the hose. With a reassuring "thunk" the probe slotted into the basket first time and fuel flowed. He was quietly smug as he registered that the Mirage pilots had watched his efforts before they peeled off to make their way to the start point. With the tank contents increasing he relaxed. He wanted his fuel tanks full as every last drop of Avtur would be vital to his goals.

The refuelling was quick and efficient and soon the lights on the hydraulic drogue unit above his head were flashing away signifying that he was full. Time was now of the essence. He would make his move once the remaining members of his formation slotted into position behind the wing hoses. Once astern they would be infinitely less flexible and unable to influence events leaving only his wingman to worry about. Before they caught on he would open up the range to the point where they could not overhaul him even with full fuel tanks, particularly carrying a heavy bomb load.

The impending mission needed no more mental rehearsal. He had gone over the opening moves in his mind a hundred times and it should be the least risky part of the scenario. There would be people in the corridors of power in Buenos Aires who would be less impressed with his actions but he secretly hoped that there would be others who would applaud him. He was, after all, a patriot. Nothing he would do today was for himself even if he risked being branded as a maverick.

With the second element still refuelling he cleared his formation's departure from the tanker and eased away on a diverging flight path, his wingman in tow. He turned southerly before hitting the transmit switch. He had made the first move and from now on he was diverging from the carefully briefed plan for the firepower demonstration. It would not be long before alarm bells began to ring on the ground but he suspected the first to realise would be his own wingman. He would force the issue.

"Viper 2, RTB."

"Say again Lead."

"I say again, RTB, I have other business."

He hauled the stick left and began to descend to low level to drop out of radar coverage but in his mirrors he saw the other Skyhawk follow him down.

"Viper 2, tactical, tactical, go!"

"Viper 2."

"You're loud and clear."

He paused phrasing his words carefully. How could he get the wingman to go home without drama? Bluster would be pointless and his intentions, although maybe not yet obvious, were clearly not in line with the briefing. Rather than heading at medium level towards the start point he had turned south easterly and was descending. Hopefully, the youngster would realise that compliance would be the least line of resistance.

"Luis, my business is in the Malvinas. These weapons will make my statement but you don't want to be a part of this. RTB now."

"I can't let you do that Lead. This conversation is between us. Let's take it home before it's too late."

"Negative, don't screw this up. RTB. Now!"

"Let's go home Lead or I'll be forced to engage."

Just what I need thought Carmendez. A wingman with a conscience. The kid's gutsy though. He only has a load of cannon shells onboard. Whether Carmendez had any intention to comply was already moot. He had no idea if the exchange had been monitored and, already, news of his plans could be whipping up the chain of command and the events it would unleash would form unexpected alliances against him.

The radio altimeter bleeped its warning as he dropped through 1500 feet, the dark blue of the South Atlantic Ocean stretching out to every horizon. Fortuitously, his wingman's Skyhawk was not carrying a Sidewinder because without a flare dispenser on his own aircraft Carmendez might already be dead. Like his wingman, he had a full load of high explosive cannon shells in the DEFA cannon but he hoped desperately that they would not be needed.

"Viper 2, I say again, RTB."

*

Back on the mainland, a signals intelligence operative listened intently. He scribbled notes on a shorthand pad, ripped it off and signalled to the other airman in the room

"Get that up to Buenos Aires Central quickly!"

DAVID GLEDHILL

CHAPTER 26

THE AIR DEFENCE OPERATIONS CENTRE, BUENOS ARIES

Colonel Hector Baldini in the Air Defence Operations Centre scanned the huge back-lit perspex situation display. Behind the transparent screen, a clerk perched at the top of a large ladder, tagging symbols on the board using a grease pencil, marking the positions of the force elements assembling for the firepower demonstration. The map of the coastline etched in green was dominated by a strangely luminescent grid that delineated the lines of latitude and longitude superimposed over the coastline. He glanced down at the small computer screen that had recently arrived on his desktop. A few blue tadpoles swam across the display representing some of the aircraft in his area of responsibility. If the computer technicians were to be believed in a few years time these screens would replace all the manual totes and he would be doing business on a TV screen. As yet unconvinced, he switched his attention back to the massive screen at the front of the operations room.

A temporary weapons range had been established by NOTAM on the coastline just south of Rio Gallegos. From the tanker towline about 80 miles northeast the participants would let down from medium level to a holding point 14 miles away. From that initial point they would run in for the drops at low level at 420 knots. It was just two short minutes from the initial point, after final arming, in which to set up their bombing pass. The formations had been scheduled to run through at three minute intervals during the 15 minute demonstration culminating in, hopefully, a spectacular finale. After the pairs had gone through a 6-ship of Skyhawks would fly a coordinated first run attack on crossing headings, dropping their weapons within 15 seconds of each other, in pairs. A Mirage would follow a minute later and fire Sidewinders against a parachute flare dropped by a second aircraft. If all went well it would be a crescendo of noise and smoke but, to make it work, the timing had to be perfect to the second. The Air Force needed this to reassert its credibility. There had been way too much negativity recently and the re-equipment programme depended on making a good show.

A red track was making its way slowly northwards at the edge of the display. The morning airbridge flight from the Malvinas was heading towards Ascension Island already well north of his area. The 200 mile circle around the islands marked with a dotted "advisory" ring rankled. Imposed after the conflict, ostensibly it had been established to protect shipping operating in the waters around the islands. It was nothing more than an engagement zone and with his fighter background he knew exactly how the rules of engagement would be couched. Weapons free out to the limit of the "Falkland Islands Protection Zone" would be the order of the day. More tracks plied their way down the airway just off the coast heading towards Buenos Aires almost reaching the end of their long international flights. Some had originated as far away as Europe and he could visualise the travellers enjoying one final stretch before strapping in for landing.

So far things were progressing to plan. The Mirages had departed from the tanker on time and the two jets were established in the hold at their assigned heights. The first formation of Skyhawks had just arrived at the datum and would be stacked in height for deconfliction. The remaining Skyhawks were on the tanker and should be leaving shortly, setting off towards the datum at medium level ready to descend into the stack when cleared. He had been listening to the radio calls as they had refuelled and all had gone perfectly. No last minute glitches, no spokes contacts, no fuel transfer failures, no nervous radio calls. So far so good.

The plan for the weapons demonstration was clearly laid out in the Operation Order and, as the Air Defence Director for the mission, he was responsible for its execution. From the moment the "Flash" signal landed on his desk, Colonel Baldini's poise was shaken. With the arrival of the unexpected message he now had a far more pressing matter. The exchange between the pilots could not be misinterpreted and something odd was in train. A symbol on the tote showed a formation detached from the main force as a pair of Skyhawks headed south easterly. That there was an unanticipated diversion from plan was now clear but why had he been slow picking up the significance? How had he missed it? Re reading the text of the disconcerting exchange between the pilots there could be only one reason. There was only one destination to the south and east and it lay 400 miles east of the start point. The Islas Malvinas. It was unambiguous. The fact that a Government Minister and the Chief of both the General Staff and the Air Staff were probably already arranged on the temporary bleachers on the windy shoreline awaiting the arrival of the aircraft for the demonstration did little to ease the pressure on his ulcer which gnawed away in his gut.

He stepped down from the dais and moved over to the radar display assimilating the information rapidly. The tanker towline was marked on the scope as was the position of the initial point for the bombing range. He could see the radar contact of the C-130 tanker making its way slowly around the towline but a second blip had, undoubtedly, broken out and its IFF response had not reappeared. As he watched the primary radar contact faded. A glance at the situation tote and he could see that there were two Skyhawks astern the tanker still refuelling. For whatever reason Viper formation had split up and one element was heading away from the initial point rapidly.

"Why have we lost primary contact on the formation that just left the tanker" he barked, knowing the answer before he posed the question. The radar contact which until minutes ago had glowed brightly had disappeared meaning that the huge radar dish just outside his control room had lost contact. In turn that could only mean that the aircraft had descended. The IFF response from the black box onboard the fighter-bomber which should have confirmed its path towards the holding area was absent. All that showed now was the electronic slash of the secondary radar return from the air-to-air refueller.

Out on the ops room floor a controller was moving between consoles plugging in his headset and making rapid calls to try to establish the reason for the change of plan. His furrowed brow suggested he was not hearing the replies he hoped.

With his conflict of priorities, Baldini began to craft a reversionary plan to resurrect the demonstration running order. He hoped vainly that this was the only contingency plan he would need. Without more information he could only guess at the pilot's intent but another glance at the signal left little to the imagination:

" . . . . . my business is in the Malvinas. These weapons will make my statement . . . . ."

"We'll need to go with the fallback plan if the second wave of Skyhawks doesn't make the time at the gate. Get onto Striker formation leader and warn him to hold at the exit datum after his live drop. I'll run him back up to the start line if Viper formation is late. We can't have gaps in the running order or there'll be hell to pay. He'll need to do a dry pass if necessary. The Chief of The Air Staff is sitting in those bleachers for God's sake. I need to know why Viper is heading south east and I need to know now. Who's in Viper Lead?"

"I'm on it now Boss" said the Mission Director still making frantic requests over his headset.

"I say again, who's the formation leader in that pair?"

"Carmendez from Gruppo 5 at Villa Reynolds, Boss."

"What the hell is he playing at? I don't know what's going on but that Skyhawk is way off track. There's no way he's making for the entry gate on that heading. Get me the Assistant Chief of Staff at the Defence Ministry on the phone and quickly!"

The phone buzzed back immediately.

"Sir, it's Baldini at BA Central. We have a problem here."

CHAPTER 27

OVER THE BAHIA GRANDE OFF THE ARGENTINIAN COASTLINE

Carmendez's heart sank as the wingman dropped into guns tracking range behind him but, fortunately, an instinctive reaction buried deep in his psyche saved his skin. As he racked on 90 degrees angle of bank, a stream of cannon shells passed harmlessly past the wingtip, noticeable by the tracer rounds within the lethal trail. A second later and it would have been game over. His wingman was determined and would not be that naive again. He had enough rounds for maybe three bursts before the magazine was empty so there might be two more bursts if Carmendez was to survive. The hasty guns pass spat the wingman out to the side and Carmendez watched as the youngster flew a text book lag pursuit roll around the slowly descending Skyhawk slotting back into his 7 o'clock. The irony was that Carmendez had coached him through that very manoeuvre so many times during air combat training sorties and now it was being used against him in a deadly encounter. It would have been easy to negate the basic fighter manoeuvre as he had done so many times before but Carmendez didn't have the fuel to spare. For once he needed avoidance rather than engagement and had to outrun the Skyhawk without throwing too much of his precious jet fuel out of the jetpipe. This was a perilous defensive game and he hoped he hadn't taught his former student too well.

Carmendez's best defence was to seek out the safety of ultra low level as he had done so many times during the conflict and he eased it down further concentrating on holding it rock steady at 50 feet above the waves. A straight and level target flying at extreme low level was the hardest air-to-air guns target imaginable. Normally in air combat if the target turned it offered a simpler tracking solution with the arc of turn presenting a planform. In a straight and level pass the fighter hovered behind and above until the point of commit, at which stage, a very uncomfortable bunt-over induced a rapid descent towards the sea. If the line was good the target would pass briefly through the gunsight, hopefully with the aiming pipper passing through the target's fuselage. If the line was out, the bullets would fall harmlessly into the sea. If the ensuing recovery was not performed at maximum G, the fighter would strike the water behind the target. He watched as the wingman set up on a perch above and slightly offset. He had learned well and was hoping to drag the sight through as he manoeuvred using lateral displacement to avoid the potentially deadly push towards the sea. Although it gave a lower probability of kill, it offered a higher chance of a lucky strike and a much safer recovery manoeuvre. Anticipation was the key and he waited for the exact moment as the wingman committed nose down pulling the sight on, the nose of the other aircraft coming to bear. The small profile became almost invisible even at such close range, the Skyhawk angling down crazily, tracking relentlessly, closing the range down. Carmendez tensed predicting the moment and, when he judged that the other pilot would pull the trigger, he pulled the stick hard back into his gut and began a steep climb, disrupting the line in a crazy defensive manoeuvre that he hoped would destroy the accuracy of the tracking solution. The move was timed to perfection and, as his head cranked over his shoulder to stay sighted on the attacker, he could see the slash in the waves where the rounds fell harmlessly into the water. Maintaining the pull, he eased into a wingover watching the wingman's tentative recovery from the firing pass before rolling inverted and pulling hard back towards the waves passing behind the wingman hoping to make him lose sight. As he checked his heading he could see he had drifted off. The engagement was dragging him south of his planned track. He set the wings level returning to 50 feet above the sea hoping that his wingman would be disorientated and lose him as he ran. It was easy to lose a low flying target but his brown and green camouflage, optimised for hiding over barren South American fields, was not ideal over the blue ocean. Illogically, he hunched down in his ejection seat willing himself to appear smaller. Surely, after two healthy bursts the wingman must be nearly out of rounds but the engagement was not yet finished. Carmendez watched with growing trepidation as the Skyhawk pulled alongside just yards away, the bonedome in the cockpit facing in his direction, the dark visor lowered and menacing. The ploy had failed and his wingman had more situation awareness than he had given him credit for. He had taught him too well and could only cling to the hope that it would not now be his downfall. It must have been near impossible to see the fleeing Skyhawk at ultra low level and yet here was his prospective nemesis back on his wing like a limpet.

Carmendez eased up, his efforts futile at present. He would save the edge-of-the-envelope flying for when it was needed. Maybe the second burst had emptied the gun after all? In the other cockpit his former friend who had just made every effort to kill him was gesturing, furiously, pointing back towards the mainland. Carmendez gave him a kiss off, still hoping to avoid the final confrontation. Without warning, the jet lurched manically towards him, the top side flash dramatic before it closed rapidly. With an empty gun and out of ideas, they were entering the last ditch response. The wingman had opted to ram him and it seemed that was prepared to take them both out in a final effort to stop him. Carmendez pulled up to counter the lunge in a classic high yo-yo-manoeuvre rolling over the top of the rapidly closing fighter-bomber and passing feet above his rival's canopy. As he flashed clear he reversed the turn pulling hard back towards the aggressor, scant feet above the sea. The other jet matched his counter the pair lifting clear of the waves, the crazy gyrations continuing. As they entered the next rolling pull the young pilot made a fatal error and allowed the nose to drop. Eyes locked to his former leader, he failed to respect the sea just 200 feet below and the over aggressive reversal towards the other Skyhawk buried the nose as he slashed downwards. Realising his error he rolled upright and reefed the stick hard back but it was too late. Despite the legendary nose authority of the delta wing jet, the Skyhawk wallowed, the speed washing off alarmingly as the nose came up, the trajectory still inexorably downwards. With insufficient power to halt the rate of descent, the fighter-bomber smashed into the sea. The plucky but ill-fated pilot was too low to eject as the airframe disintegrated around him before tumbling over and over in a plume of spray and disappearing beneath the surface.

Carmendez was stunned. This had not been in the script and he had suckered his young wingman into an early grave. The feeling of remorse was almost unbearable. As he resumed heading still stunned by events, the radio which was tuned the air defence common frequency, burst into life.

"Vixen Leader check your weapons state?"

The call was from the Sector Operations Centre.

"I have 2 Sidewinders and a full gun."

"And your Number 2?"

"Negative, he has only a flare pod."

"Stand by for instructions."

With only two elderly AIM-9Bs, the Mirage pilot was about to be diverted in pursuit.

Carmendez's escape was by no means guaranteed and this further if not totally unexpected complication was unwelcome. How had they reacted so quickly to his plan? He had expected that his rapid descent below radar cover would have gone unnoticed but apparently not. After the unplanned tussle, it was vital that he now saved fuel and he began a gentle climb back to medium altitude for the first leg of the transit to the distant islands. It would probably bring him back into the coverage of the coastal radars but he had little choice and, with his move detected, of little consequence. His route was predictable within a few miles and he had nothing to lose. He would descend back to low level once he was closer to his quarry.

He bugged the heading on his compass and pointed towards the Falkland Islands.

CHAPTER 28

ON THE HIGH SEAS, WEST OF THE FALKLAND ISLANDS

HMS Newcastle had been underway for some days since pulling out from the mooring at Mare Harbour. The heavy seas overnight had abated and she was ploughing through a gentle chop about 100 miles west of Weddell Island mounting the air defence barrier. On the bridge the Captain scanned the horizon for a visual sighting on a fishing vessel which the lookout had reported when the comms box buzzed. He picked up the handset.

"Captain."

"Sir, we've just picked up a hit from some Argentine Air Force communications we've been monitoring. I think you might want to hear some of it. It's quite sensitive stuff Skipper. Can you come below?"

"I'll be right down. Officer of the Watch, you have the ship. Course 290."

"Aye Aye, Sir."

He moved to the rear of the Bridge and made his way quickly down the stairs, the rungs rattling as he made his descent. The intelligence cell was a dismal space buried in the bowels of the vessel and the notices on the door made it clear that the regular ship's company was not welcome in this secretive empire. As he pulled the watertight door closed behind him a rating pointed to an operative hunched over a radio receiver, playing with a manual tuning dial refining the frequency. The electronic display danced in tune to an unseen discussion.

The man flicked the earpiece back and passed him a scribbled transcript.

"Skipper, we just picked this up on UHF. I'm tuned into one of the air defence HF chat frequencies at the minute and it just lit up."

The Captain pulled on a headset and listened to the garbled discussion on the HF radio, the background noisy and distorted. He wished his Spanish was better. Although English was the international language of the air it was not uncommon for the Argentinians to chatter away in their native tongue to frustrate the listeners. He read the short extract again assimilating the implications.

"What do you make of it?"

"I thought with your background as an intercept controller it might make more sense to you Sir. From what I can make out one of the Skyhawks just broke formation after taking on fuel from a C-130 tanker. He was about to take part in a live weapons demonstration in the coastal area. It was NOTAM'd as active a few weeks ago and we've been hearing quite a lot of chatter as they've been setting up. If our intelligence is correct we're expecting some live weapon drops quite soon. The pilots are on a tactical UHF frequency and this one is the ground controllers chatting to the Sector Operations Centre. His unexpected departure has thrown the whole show into confusion."

"What happened with this guy?"

"I was listening on the tanking frequency and everything seemed normal. The calls were routine and it sounded like he filled to full but just as he was about to head inbound to the initial point there was a rapid exchange within the formation which I couldn't make out. My Spanish is good but we're at the limit of range for this frequency and there was a lot of break up. I know this sounds crazy Sir but if I didn't know better I'd say he just lost his wingman. It's very weak but we've had intermittent detection on a personal locator beacon. How likely is that? What could he be doing?"

"Funnier things have happened in these waters" he said quietly. "Thanks. You were right to let me know. Keep me in the picture if you get anything else. I'm going up to the Ops Room, let them know I'm on the way"

*

The Principal Warfare Officer was staring at the radar display from the main air surveillance radar. The Type 42 air defence ship was well equipped with both surveillance and tracking radars and its Type 1022 and Type 965 long range air surveillance radars gave the crew an extended air picture almost to the Argentinian mainland from their present position. The shorter range Type 996 three dimensional target indication radar and Type 909 fire control radars controlled the weapons. From their western picket station he could see virtually all the airspace along the Argentinian coast at medium level, although targets at low level would be much closer to the ship before they could be detected. The surveillance operator had been monitoring the Argentinian exercise with interest as a regular stream of aircraft had made their way from Rio Gallegos and Rio Grande in the south. They had converged on the Hercules tanker towline in preparation for the anticipated live serials before heading south into a holding pattern. Before starting his shift he had dropped into the intelligence section and had seen a print out of the Operation Order for the exercise, intercepted some days before during routine monitoring. A careless radio operator had transmitted the classified document in the clear and it had been transcribed appreciatively by the intelligence staff down below. Sometimes routine monitoring of the signals traffic hit pay dirt and this was one such occasion. Armed with the details from the op. order he knew exactly what he should be watching for on the radar display. Up to now all had gone to plan but he had a feeling that the tracks that had faded from the display were not following the script.

*

Carmendez dropped the Skyhawk to within feet of the waves. It was way too early to need to fly at this height but it was quite a while since he had operated below 100 feet. It was a skill hard won and easily lost and took constant practice to maintain the edge. The encounter with his wingman had rattled him and, if he was to survive today, he might well need these skills again later. As the slight chop on the wave tops registered in his peripheral vision he began to feel comfortable, once more back in his element. He reefed the stick left and pulled the nimble fighter into a hard turn trying to hold a constant height and speed. Ballooning away from the ground was a mistake which cost many pilots their lives during the conflict and it might be an error he could ill afford to make today. It was important to hold a rock steady height during a bombing run because the weapons trajectory and ballistics relied on precision. Consistency guaranteed a weapon on target. The most dangerous phase was post-target when the adrenaline shot hit. Allowing to jet to climb, framed the airframe against the sky creating an easy target for missiles or guns tracking radars. His radio altimeter showed a steady 100 feet although, as the aircraft turned hard at low level, the warning flag occasionally flickered on as the radio signal skated across the surface of the waves reflected away from the jet rather than back to the sensor. Back on heading and once more straight and level, the needle settled again at 100 feet. He hadn't lost it yet.

*

"Unidentified contact, 275 range 100," came a disembodied voice on the combat net, the owner hidden from view somewhere across the darkened ops. room. "Looking for a height."

"Designated Track 007," came a different voice over the net. The PWO stared intently at the new contact well to the west.

"The contact shows low level."

*

Back on track, Carmendez relaxed. He'd save the hard stuff for later when it was really needed. He would stay low to avoid detection but there was little difference between flying at 100 feet and 500 feet in terms of when he would be detected. The really low altitudes made it harder for a hostile weapons systems to lock on and, more importantly, for the missile to track and fuse. If his dead reckoning was correct he would make landfall at Beaver Island which was just west of Weddell. It would take a few minutes after landfall to precisely locate his position but that first check would be vital to success.

Had he been fitted with a radar warning receiver he might already have registered the first bleeps from the long range surveillance radars which were recording his presence but, as it was, he pressed on in blissful ignorance. As yet, he had no idea that he had company in the form of the

British warship to the east.

*

Onboard *HMS Newcastle* controlled panic ensued and the tension in the ops. room rose a notch.

"Track 007 reclassified Zombie 007, high speed, low level, heading east."

"Bridge, PWO, high speed track inbound, suspected hostile, no squawk, request clearance to engage."

"PWO, Officer of the Watch, Captain's off the Bridge, I'm trying to get him back now."

On the Bridge the harassed watch officer, loathe to make such a vital call, almost pleaded over the tannoy urging the Captain back into the hot seat. His job was to navigate the ship not start a new Falklands conflict. Below decks, the PWO recognised the urgency as the potential hostile, now 80 miles away and closing fast made a turn towards the ship. Recurrent nightmares of Exocet missile launches against sister ships during the conflict plagued him and, if this was for real, he needed to get a Sea Dart shot away without hesitation. His first priority was to protect the ship and her Company. If this was an Etendard, the missiles would be in the air well before they could see the attacker, the first sign probably a paint from the Agave radar signifying that they had been singled out. It would be too late if he allowed the approaching jet to overfly the ship. He must pre-empt with an opening shot from the Sea Dart system. Delay could risk a reduction in the probability of kill and they might miss the chance. He searched vainly for alternatives to lethal force coming up short. What other options did he have? He picked up the radio mike.

"Puffin, 3 Lima 4 Tango on TAD 043, I show high speed contacts, bullseye 286 range 47. Suspected hostile, request instructions."

In the absence of direction from the Captain, someone else could worry about this one too, although putting the onus back on the command chain at the Sector Operations Centre would take time. It was probably time he didn't have. Ultimately it should be the Air Defence Commander's call but self defence overrode the rules of engagement. He might not be contactable in the remaining minutes if the PWO was to save the ship and launch a valid shot. Things were spiralling out of control.

"3 Lima 4 Tango, Puffin, on TAD 437 my scope is clear."

Why? His own radar picture should be feeding into the recognised air picture. They should be seeing the same information. That decided it. There would be no help there.

"Magazine, PWO elevate 2 Sea Darts, NOW!"

A startled armourer in the magazine just forward of the Bridge hit the switch which began the loading sequence for the massive surface-to-air missiles. Mechanical arms raised the missile bodily onto the track and pushed it forward with surprising speed. With a massive clang and the associated noise of precision mechanical gears, the missile moved to the front of the bay and rotated vertical. Huge doors in the deck above slammed open and the missile was thrust skywards by the launcher mechanism. As it popped into the open air, another massive clang registered the limit of its travel as it hit the end stops. Within seconds the launcher rotated downwards to a 45 degree angle and slewed around onto a westerly direction. Within seconds, priming commands were relayed from the radar and the Sea Dart was armed and ready to fire on the PWO's call. Alongside, the second Sea Dart mimicked the first both now primed for a shot.

"Puffin, my contact bears 286 range 43, high speed, low level, closing on my position. I say again, request clearance to engage."

On Mount Kent a bewildered fighter controller stared at his blank scope and wondered how he could approve a request to engage without any tangible evidence of a raid. This type of screw up was all too familiar as they had begun to mix live operations and simulations on exercises. He checked his consoles for signs of a training scenario in play. Nothing! Without any other ideas he took the safe option.

"3 Lima 4 Tango my scope is clear, weapons tight, repeat weapons tight."

In the adjacent Operations Room, the harassed Master Controller who had watched events unfold was desperately trying to contact the Air Defence

Commander on the phone. He needed top-cover and he needed it fast. The phone rang in the office of Wing Commander Ops at Stanley.

"Sir, the Master Controller at Kent here. Newcastle is reporting a high speed contact at low level, west of Weddell. My scope shows nothing and I have no idea why his feed is not showing on the recognised air picture. I'm worried he's in training mode and they haven't warned us but what if it's a real contact? If it is, we haven't much time. All our Phantoms are on the ground with only a training pair taxying for takeoff so I can discount an exercise by the Phantom Squadron."

"Scramble Q and get them on CAP over East Falkland," the Air Defence Commander replied. "If this is for real I want a back stop up there between that inbound track and Stanley airfield."

The Master Controller pointed at the QRA tote board, simultaneously making a wind up signal with his right hand. His intent was translated instantly by an alert intercept controller. who hit the scramble claxon, immediately triggering a response in Wing Operations at RAF Stanley. The telebrief repeater in the QRA crewroom on 23 Squadron stuttered its warning.

"Eagle Ops alert 2 Phantoms . . . . . "

DAVID GLEDHILL

CHAPTER 29

OVER EAST FALKLAND

At the radar unit atop Mount Alice, the surveillance controller's eyes followed track 007. He had been monitoring the contact for a short time but he, involuntarily, began to take more interest as the ship ran through its engagement sequence. This was happening too often and it frustrated the hell out of him. A high sped low level track was everyone's nightmare scenario so the PWO on the ship should warn them when they ran these simulations. The sequence had run to its conclusion but, for once, the track had not been deleted and it sill glowed brightly on the display heading east.

He was about to hit the transmit switch to raise the PWO on the ship when he paused. Was this a real track? If it was, it wasn't a Phantom because the first wave had yet to launch. He rolled his track ball onto the contact and allocated the height finder. It showed 300 feet.

His reverie was broken as the QRA control frequency chattered into life.

"Eagle Ops alert 2 Phantoms . . . . . "

The track headed relentlessly east and his blood pressure rose a notch.

*

As the features on the coast began to break out of the haze Carmendez readied himself. He needed a good fix as he coasted in and strained to pick out the feature he had chosen as an entry point. Beaver Island should be to the north and the smaller Staats Island on his nose. If he rounded Staats

Bluff he could route through the gap south of Hotham Heights and on into Chatham Harbour. From there a run easterly over Queen Charlotte Bay, tracking across the flatlands of West Falkland would lead him to A-4 Alley at Carcass Bay Hill. He'd be exposed over the low terrain but, by then, he'd be following a familiar route, the one he remembered from so many years before. The one that had led to the fateful events of that infamous day in 1982.

He could see an island ahead but the ground to the north was too far away and seemed to be higher than expected. As the coastline flashed under the wingtip he had no choice but to ease the track southerly to see if he could identify a feature. He banked hard right and, as he straightened up on his new heading, he scanned the features over his left shoulder and edged closer to the rugged coastline. He had no spare fuel to waste and the familiar nerves heightened his predicament. He needed to be heading east not south. This wasn't Weddell and if he'd been further north he would have seen New Island. That had to be Settlement Hill he could see which put him some miles south of where he wanted to be. A promontory was barring his way and, if he found a small airstrip beyond, he must have coasted-in at Port Stevens. The wingtip dipped as he slipped through the tight gap in the coastal ridge. Sure enough the tiny airstrip appeared on his left and he recognised Port Stevens Bay. Quickly recalculating, he moved his thumb down the map clutched in his hand and highlighted his new position, mentally recalculating the heading to the next turning point. He hit the stopwatch and the second hand began to track around the dial. There was an easy route through and, although he was a little closer to the radar site on Mount Alice than he would have liked, at least, being this close they would have lost contact with him by now. He had flown into their "dark area, the gap in coverage immediately around the radar dish.

*

In the control cabin on the hill, the surveillance controller played with the gain controls trying to regain contact on the target which had disappeared. Had the PWO finally deleted it? Was it really a training target? Attempts to raise the ship had failed but comms were notoriously unreliable with it positioned so far west. The track was very close to the point where it would enter his dark area and he wondered whether QRA had been launched in vain. At that very moment a second track popped up on the screen about 20 miles behind the first contact and he rolled his marker over the new contact and hit the button to enter it into the system. Track 008. A further check with the height finder registered a slightly higher level but, as the contact updated with each successive sweep of the radar, the height reading was already winding down showing the contact descending fast towards the deck. Its heading was almost identical to the first and aiming directly at the radar site. Without hesitation, he hit the air raid alert and the claxons rang out across the site. If he was wrong the embarrassment did not bear thinking about but survival outweighed sensibilities. There were now two high speed low level contacts coming right at him and it seemed that *HMS Newcastle* had already had a stab at destroying the first hostile. Now where the hell had it gone?

*

In the Mirage, Captain Hernandez had no way of knowing which route the Skyhawk pilot would take but he knew that his options were limited so he would have to make a guess. Would he take the harder but safer option of a northerly track through the hillier terrain to the north of East Falkland or the more open but simpler southerly route over the flat ground of Lafonia, risking detection? He plumped for the easier challenge and set a course for the southern tip of the islands. He had no maps to help him navigate and he was relying on memory from those fateful days during the war. His instructions were vividly clear but a lot different to the last time he had entered these waters.

"Engage."

This time his target was not a Sea Harrier. This time his target was Carmendez's Skyhawk. With his obsolescent Cyrano pulse radar scanning the airspace he knew there was no way to break out a low flying fast jet over 20 miles in front. He would need some luck if he was to succeed. He began to let down painting the coastline on his radar recognising the inlets around Weddell Island. He had used this fix point before. If he was going to bet money, he reckoned that the Skyhawk pilot might use A-4 Alley as a screen for his run across to East Falkland Island and it might provide an obvious choke point. During the war it had been a sanctuary from the intrusive air defence radars onboard the ships in San Carlos Bay but, today, it could provide similar cover for Carmendez's Skyhawk. If he took some cut off and ran directly over Fish Creek Hill and the plain north of Fox Bay, he might intercept him west of Swan Island. He relished the challenge knowing who was in the jet just ahead of him and hoped that he could get to him before the defenders intervened. Otherwise it might get messy. Whichever way the next 30 minutes panned out it would be far from easy. At least his opponent was not armed with Sidewinders he thought gratefully but it was more than he could say for the resident Phantoms if they entered the fight. The thought prompted his own weapons checks and he flicked the master arm switch to "*Arm*".

*

With the hooter blaring, there was frantic activity on the peak at Mount Alice and bodies tumbled from doorways rushing around the rock-strewn site making for their duty stations. With the realisation that the high speed target was going to pass almost overhead the controller's decision to hit the panic button had transmitted the bleak message emphasising their impending fate.

"Air raid warning red. Air raid warning red. Air raid warning red. Take cover."

The air defence platoon struggled with the protective cases snapping open the reluctant clasps and hauling out the Blowpipe missile readying for firing. The Platoon Commander listened intently to his earpiece still digesting the severity of the situation willing the controller to add the word "exercise". No such caveat came. The bullseye calls from the fighter controller in the adjacent control cabin registered dimly and the significance was still slow to develop. The situation seemed surreal coming without warning. Transferring the meagre information onto his plotting reticule he glanced at the map. Somehow "Measles" exercises were so much more relaxed he thought to himself. Training took over.

"That puts the hostile over Port Stevens. Look down the bay."

He raised his pointing stick on the approximate bearing to the target and the operator swung the heavy launch tube around bringing the Blowpipe to bear.

*

Carmendez was now hugging the surface only feet above the surface. His radalt buzzed occasionally as he flirted with his minimum height keeping him sharp. As he ran down the bay and across Knob Island he felt the familiar buzz of adrenaline. Up Hoste Inlet, and he could see the pimple on the hill to his right which was the air defence radar at Alice. Hugging the contours of Mount Moore he had no choice but to pass close to the air defence site as the gorge climbed and narrowed ahead of him.

*

The operator clipped the aiming unit onto the firing tube and hefted it onto his shoulder. The Blowpipe was a strange contraption with the huge bulge at the front of the firing cylinder which held the fins of the missile. After launch the missile literally flew through the ring of the fins dragging them out of the tube, by then attached to the missile body. An antenna on the front of the tube transmitted guidance signals to the missile in flight and, if the operator could track the target and keep the crosshairs aligned, the missile would strike its victim. It was a big if!

Listening to the commentary from the platoon commander he peered through the sight and registered a flash of movement against the background. He was dropping into the familiar routine that he had practised so many times against the Phantoms. Apparently, this time it was for real and he was struggling to track the camouflaged airframe which was breaking out from its surroundings. It was not the familiar air defence grey of the Phantoms with its brown and green splinter camouflage, frighteningly familiar from the aircraft recognition training sessions. A Skyhawk! As he pulled the trigger, he tensed, anticipating the pause before the first boost motor fired, popping the missile out of the tube into free space. As the missile emerged it seemed to hang in the air only a short distance in front of the firing crew. The sustainer motor fired up and it accelerated away in a plume of smoke towards the Skyhawk which had reached the apex of its climb and was already rolling inverted pulling hard back downwards towards the inlet beyond. As it reached its terminal velocity the missile would fly into a "basket" centred on the crosshairs of the aiming sight where it would be captured by the operator who tried his best to track the elusive aircraft. Once captured, he would steer it to its target using the tiny thumb wheel on the trigger grip. Electronic commands transmitted to the missile would refine its flight path by moving the control fins in unison. If he was close enough to the target after the short duration of its flight, a proximity fuse would detonate the warhead and send out a deadly shaped charge towards its victim. If it struck the airframe it would prove lethal as the charge ripped through the tightly packed flight systems.

*

Carmendez could see the crest of the rising gulley and anticipated the manoeuvre. As he popped out of the narrow valley he rolled inverted watching the ground rotate into the top of his canopy and pulled hard back into a seemingly terminal dive. This was the scariest manoeuvre any pilot ever performed. With the ground a scant few feet above the canopy, continuing the pull guaranteed oblivion. The rapid roll back upright meant survival but timing was critical. Too late in rolling to the inverted position and every weapon in the local area would track easily as the aircraft became an undemanding target framed against the sky. Too gentle on the pull and the result would be the same as the aircraft ballooned. Too late on the return to upright flight and the hard ground would be an unforgiving neighbour. The roll when it came was perfectly timed and, as he sensed the mountainside falling away in front of him, he heard the reassuring ping of the radalt in his headset as he skirted the falling ground descending towards the shimmering bay below.

He was oblivious to the smoke plume behind him which followed his path unerringly.

*

The operator had trapped the fast jet in his crosshairs and was silently impressed at the skills the pilot was demonstrating. After cresting the ridge he had returned to low level almost instantly once more benefitting from the camouflage which threatened to make the airframe invisible again. He was certain it was not the Phantom against which he trained regularly, the delta wing planform distinct and different. A quick flash of the blue and white roundel through his magnified sight confirmed his thoughts. It was a bloody Argie! He had a flashback to 1982, sitting in a dugout on Fanning Head, a Skyhawk tracking up Falkland Sound and he tensed involuntarily disrupting the tracking. There was only a few seconds flight time remaining and it needed maximum concentration for those last moments.

As he had fired, his target had been an easy shot standing out in stark contrast against the bright blue sky, its dark camouflage highlighting the airframe but, as it had descended moving back into the obscurity of the surrounding terrain, it became much more demanding. Barely visible now, he followed the gyrations as it twisted and turned descending towards the bay. His mental clock ticked down and he warmed, anticipating the impact. Suddenly, the target blended back into the background and the crosshairs drifted off at the vital moment. He tweaked the sight hoping for peripheral movement against the background terrain but it had vanished. The target was gone.

"You bastard!"

The operator watched as a fireball detonated in his field of view. He was not to know but the missile had impacted off the left wingtip of the fleeing Skyhawk, the charge driving harmlessly into a giant boulder. It had been close but not close enough.

*

Oblivious to the tension in the British Headquarters to the east but aware he was now the subject of unwelcome attention, Carmendez popped up over the ridgeline at the entrance to A-4 Alley. He had not even been aware that the missile had been fired so there had been no stress. It was only when he saw the flash of the detonation off the left wing that he realised that he had had a close shave. At least if it had hit him he would not have died tense. A quick look to the northeast set him his next challenge as he dropped into the obscurity of the gulley cocooned by the ridgeline on each side. The cloud had formed over Mount Usborne and was sitting firmly on the hilltops. Short of routing well to the north there was no gap through and he would have to route to the south over the open plain and past the new airbase at Mount Pleasant. It wasn't his preferred choice but he didn't have the fuel to take the northerly detour. He would be on the limits as it was.

The sensation of speed was magnified as the Skyhawk flashed along the infamous valley towards the old killing ground in San Carlos Bay. Beyond lay his target and his destiny.

CHAPTER 30

OPERATIONS WING, RAF STANLEY

John Fitzpatrick, watched a Hercules pull onto the slot outside his office in Operations Wing at RAF Stanley, the Allison turboprops rattling the metal window frames. The ring of the phone was barely audible over the din and he strained to hear his PA in the outer office. He was still rattled by the turn of events and the direct line from Mount Kent had been hot.

"Sir, you're not going to believe this but you've got the Air Defence Commander from Buenos Aires Centre on the line!"

He could not suppress the feeling of astonishment. Surreal. They had faced each other anonymously across the 400 mile stretch of ocean since he had arrived but this was the first contact with his counterpart on the mainland. It was undoubtedly unexpected and set a startling precedent.

"Wing Commander, good morning and please forgive the unusual intrusion. This is Colonel Hector Baldini. I'm the Sector Controller at Buenos Aires Centre. Thank you for taking my call. We have a situation developing and I think you need to be aware of some facts."

Fitzpatrick adopted his best poker face, wasted over the anonymous phone line, his reply tentative and non committal.

"My pleasure and quite a surprise to speak to you. Go ahead Sir."

His tone was tense and formal.

"As I'm sure you know, we are conducting a live weapons demonstration in the Bahia Grande. It's been planned for many months and we issued a NOTAM well ahead of time. It was to have been a routine event for the benefit of some military officials and local dignitaries but we seem to have experienced an unplanned turn of events. It seems from the radar plot that a Skyhawk is missing and believed to have crashed in the coastal waters close to Rio Gallegos. We have SAROPS underway but no sign yet of the pilot."

"I'm sorry, I hope you find him."

Despite their differences, the loss of an aircraft formed a common bond amongst aviators.

"Thank you Sir, I appreciate the sentiment. I hope so too. A young pilot and he has a promising career."

"I'm not sure how I can help you unless you need C-130 support. I can launch the alert Hercules which is fitted with Lindholme gear if it helps."

"That will not be necessary but thank you. The crash site is within range of the coastal-based helicopters and they are searching the area as we speak. No, I'm afraid it's the other Skyhawk which is the problem."

"Another Skyhawk? Go on," he replied, immediately attentive. He was about to understand the context of recent events.

"One of our aircraft was refuelling from a C-130 tanker. It is being flown by a Malvinas veteran, Major Carmendez."

"Yes I'd heard," he said, immediately realising his mistake. He could only have known the name from one source and that was signals intelligence and his information should have been protected a little more carefully. The transcript of the brief radio exchange had landed on his desk shortly before the call. His poker stance had been weak and he had been too casual in his reply. The short pause reinforced the error.

"Yes, indeed. Anyway, just after he left the towline he disappeared from radar cover. It was completely unexpected. His track should have taken him at medium level down the coastline towards targets near Rio Gallegos but his track diverged. You'll understand my reticence so please don't press but we picked up an exchange between the pilots on a tactical frequency shortly afterwards. Within minutes we picked up a personal locator beacon on "Guard" frequency."

Fitzpatrick scribbled a note. Why hadn't he known about the beacon? It should have been picked up by his outlying units and reported back. What if it had been one of his own aircraft? That debrief was for later.

"My concern is that the other Skyhawk hasn't yet reappeared on our radar screens and we have excellent coverage down to very low level in that area. We can only assume he headed east."

The revelations were not unexpected.

"We think he's heading towards The Malvinas and he's loaded with Mark 82 bombs. We have no idea of his intentions or his target!"

"Is he carrying Sidewinders?"

"No, he's not but he does have a gun loaded with high explosive incendiary rounds."

More notes scribbled on the pad.

"There is one more complication."

A pregnant pause.

"We instructed a Mirage III to follow with instructions to engage. The pilot has a full missile load but he is some miles behind. I had hoped he would catch the Skyhawk before he left our airspace but I realise now it was a vain hope. I have now lost radar and radio contact with the Mirage so I'll be unable to haul him off. I'm afraid I shall have to trust his common sense and discretion but both aircraft have enough fuel to make landfall over the Malvinas. I will make transmissions on the distress frequencies now we have spoken but I doubt it will be of use."

"Thank you, Sir, for your candid admission. It might make my task a little easier."

"Please let me reassure you that the Government here has nothing to do with this initiative. I must leave the response to you if he penetrates your airspace. You will understand that I cannot officially recognise the status of that airspace but I understand that you will need to react appropriately."

"Likewise, Sir, I'm sure you know that I cannot discuss rules of engagement but I'm afraid a high speed low level penetration would be seen as a hostile act. He would run the risk of engagement by any of our weapons systems deployed on the islands. I'm afraid I cannot guarantee his safety."

"Sir you must do as you see fit, as I would do in your situation."

The implied threat was hollow given that a Skyhawk fighter-bomber was at this minute heading east at high speed towards an, as yet, unknown target followed by an armed fighter.

Fitzpatrick thanked his counterpart terminating the call and immediately dialled the Sector Controller at Mount Kent. The aircraft bearing down on the islands was an intractable problem and he was not sure that, in the heat of the moment, his Phantom and Rapier crews would appreciate the difference between a bomb-armed Skyhawk and a missile-armed Mirage. They both carried blue and white roundels and that in itself was sufficient grounds to respond.

Carmendez's fate was not yet sealed but he faced a hostile reception as well as a Mirage pilot in hot pursuit.

CHAPTER 31

NO. 23 SQUADRON CREWROOM, RAF STANLEY

Razor and Flash had been relaxing in the slightly battered easy chairs, the incessant drone of the television in the background repeating the cult movie. The scramble message, when it had come was concise but slightly chilling, heralding the unknown.

"Eagle Ops, alert 2 Phantoms. Vector 280, climb Angels 25, contact Puffin on prebrief, scramble, scramble, scramble, acknowledge."

Mayhem!

The action from the QRA crews was immediate and urgent. Immersion suits were hastily pulled over startled faces as the Q2 navigator rushed over to the telebrief box in the corner to acknowledge the message before following through the door to the flight line behind his rapidly disappearing pilot. The groundcrew were sprinting ahead and the flight line mechanics were already pulling the huge protective weather cover off the nose of the nearest alert fighter. Razor and Flash sprinted to their own jet closest to the crewroom occupying the favoured spot as the primary jet. The rear steps were fixed in place over the engine intake and, as they rounded the front of the jet, they sprinted up the steps towards the cockpit. Below them the see-off crew fired up the external power set and moved into position to assist with the strap-in.

As Razor dropped onto his Martin Baker ejection seat he was already hitting the start button for the right hand engine. The battery powered gas turbine starter was a boon for QRA and the Spey engine spooled into life breaking the calm across the dispersal. In the back Flash pulled on his bonedome, clipped the microphone lead into his personal equipment connector and began to align the inertial navigation system. As the tell tale caption began to flash away on the delicate instrument he hit the transmit button on the floor of his cockpit.

"Wing Ops, Eagle 1, on frequency, scrambling!"

"Eagle 2's on, scrambling!"

The sound of the Speys in the number 2 jet could be heard over the noise of his own and he pulled at his lap straps plugging them into the harness box. Safely strapped to the bang seat he gave a thumbs-up and the flight line mechanic placed the top seat pin into the stowage in front of him and disappeared down the steps which were pulled clear. His seat pan firing pin followed, his ejection seat live. Less than two minutes later, with a few rapid checks completed, both QRA jets taxied off the slot to cover the short distance across the metal matting to the in-use runway completing the pre takeoff checks on the roll. As they approached, the local controller was clearing the takeoff but it was a formality. A short backtrack to the end of the runway with Q2 in close trail and the Phantoms swung back around to line up. Nothing stopped a Q launch short of a major systems failure and the only way to prevent these jets from rolling was an authenticated cancellation message which would never come. The reluctant, still cold Rolls Royce Spey engines were persuaded into burner and, after a quick nod and thumbs-up from the Q2 pilot, the lumbering aircraft rolled reaching takeoff velocity and lurching into the air with gear and flaps travelling.

*

The Sector Controller had ended the call to his Commander and turned back to the master tote board to monitor the progress of the scramble. The scripted sequence of events at the Phantom squadron was underway and he could imagine the noise on the airfield as the fighters rolled down the runway. He stabbed the direct line to the master controllers at Mount Alice and Byron Heights and set up a conference call. With both of them waiting in anticipation he began to recount the facts he had just learned from his Boss.

The Electrone snooper droned along still flying over international waters but slowly approaching the boundary of the exclusion zone to the south.

"Captain, Comms, I just detected something weird. I've been monitoring a couple of Phantom radars but I just got two hits from the area of Falkland Sound. I know this sounds crazy but it looks just like a Cyrano air intercept radar from one of our own Mirage IIIs. There's no doubt about the location. It's overland in the Malvinas. I've checked the bearing about three times now."

The Captain in the left hand seat in the cockpit gazed through the window at the endless expanse of water, considering the information carefully. He knew of the firepower demonstration but how that connected with a hit from a Mirage over the Malvinas was impossible to understand. How could the two events possibly be related?

"Keep watching it and get that message back to Buenos Aires on the flight watch frequency. They need that information right now!"

*

In the surveillance room at Byron Heights closest to the Electrone's position, the surveillance operator heard the radio transmission and the vector from the automatic direction finder on his console pointed directly at the Electrone's track. There could be no doubt about the origin. The message to the mainland was encrypted so there was no way that he could decipher the content but, even so, whatever was going on would be of interest to the Master Controller. He hit the direct line to Puffin. As he waited for the connection the radio chattered.

"Eagles airborne, Stud 11, stud 11, go!"

QRA was airborne and vectoring outbound.

DAVID GLEDHILL

CHAPTER 32

GOVERNMENT HOUSE, PORT STANLEY

The corridor was eerily quiet as Karen Pilkington walked out of the Ladies Room in Government House. With some minutes to kill before her interview with the Governor it felt odd without her ever present "minder" in tow and strangely intrusive wandering along the corridor alone. She could hear the low tones of a man's voice on the telephone in an office and, her journalistic interest piqued, she held back from the open door just out of sight and listened. It was probably not the way to endear herself to her escort if she was discovered eavesdropping but from the few snippets she had picked up she was intrigued. The conversation was becoming more anxious.

"I can't speak now. This is not a secure line."

Unseen by Karen, Sullivan glanced nervously at the open door.

"I'll make sure you receive the transcript but I'll have to use our normal line of communications. Can you confirm that the "favour" has been deposited as agreed?"

Stopping short of implicating the speaker, the cryptic comment left little to the imagination. The tone became businesslike once more.

"I have some very interesting angles which might affect the forthcoming negotiations but now is not the time."

If the journalist had been able to see the speaker she would have noticed that he was sweating profusely. She could, however, sense a hesitance as, occasionally, he shut off the conversation if it strayed too close to the mark. The exchange was riveting and might have been a routine discussion between staffers but for the reference to a "favour". Why would a "favour" be deposited if the discussion was over transcripts of routine discussions? This might make an interesting story she thought. Indiscrete leaking of information from the Governor's inner circle but to whom, she wondered? Who was the mystery recipient of the call? Maybe some minion in Whitehall trying to keep his political master one step ahead of the game? Scandal in the Foreign Office; subterfuge on the islands, she mused as she unconsciously drafted a dramatic headline for the magazine.

A glance at the nameplate identified the Governor's aide, Alexander Sullivan. Withdrawing back along the corridor discretely she returned to the reception area scribbling a hurried reminder in her notebook, promising herself that she would follow up when she got back to London. Hopefully this man's background would offer up a lead as to why he might be negotiating using other peoples information. Suddenly, a faceless bureaucrat was the potential star of the show from her brief trip.

Glancing at her watch she realised that she should be with the Governor. Where was her minder when she needed her? The transport was due to leave for the ceremony in less than an hour and she couldn't afford to miss it. The wheels would leave on time and there would be hell to pay back in the editorial office if she missed the key event.

With the corridor once again quiet, a door opened and Warren Baird, the First Secretary watched her retreating along the corridor. He had struggled to hear the conversation but what he had overheard troubled him even more than her presence and demanded action. First Secretary was not his only role in life and, as the resident representative of the security services, his role in the Falkland Islands might just have become immeasurably more complex. He suspected he knew the likely response from his colleagues at "The Firm" in London and was certain that his friends in Gower Street would show more than a passing interest. If Sullivan really was taking money for information he would have to be stopped, and quickly. The big question was where was the information being directed? If it was to the mainland there was a serious leak which would need prompt resolution. Sullivan was playing a dangerous game if he was making direct contact with an Argentinian whether with the Governor's blessing or not. If money was involved he doubted that his masters would countenance such a blatant act of treachery so soon after the conflict. His only reassurance was that powers far higher up the food chain than he would take that decision. His dilemma was what to do about the journalist who had unwittingly stumbled into this mess. Her journalistic activities might become rather more complicated if she was targeted for surveillance. Her destiny had unexpectedly become his responsibility.

DAVID GLEDHILL

CHAPTER 33

HEADQUARTERS BRITISH FORCES FALKLAND ISLANDS, EAST FALKLAND

As he entered the Combined Operations Control room in the Headquarters of the British Forces Falkland Islands he knew that momentous decisions were imminent and Wing Commander Operations positioned himself on the dais taking in the detail of the tactical picture. With the huge displays fed from the Sector Operations Centre at Mount Kent he could now see as much as the Master Controller up the hill. There could be no hiding from the responsibilities of command and equally, there must be no confusion over his orders. There was simply not enough time to consult with the leadership in London. The call would be his and his alone.

The communications circuits had been hectic as people within the decision chain sought to understand what was going on but, more telling, sought to cover themselves. He had been given all the pieces of this jigsaw, he just needed to think it through logically. He knew that he had a rogue pilot out there. The Argentinian commander had made that perfectly clear. What other factors would shape his decision? The high speed track had penetrated from low level from the west. He knew it couldn't be a Phantom because he knew exactly where each jet was located and they were all accounted for. The intruder's behaviour since popping up on radar was consistent with harbouring hostile intent and there could be no doubt that it was the Argentinian jet. The rules of engagement were clear and unambiguous and it met every parameter. The Argentinian Air Defence

Commander had been explicit and it was down to him to neutralise the rogue jet. The other contact in hot pursuit had to be the Mirage and if he could avoid a confrontation, all the better. If not, so be it. His options were limited; he really had little choice. The voice in his ear broke his chain of thought.

"What are your instructions Sir?"

"Wait one. I'll get back to you."

He wasn't going to be rushed. This decision had to be right and he gave himself the vital extra moments before coming to his decision; for better or for worse. He hit the mini comms.

"Master Controller this is the Air Defence Commander, you have clearance to engage, acknowledge."

They were simple words with enormous significance. He was on a secure line so there was no need to authenticate his directive. He had just made the biggest decision of his life and because of it, someone would die. As yet he didn't know who that would be or how soon it would occur. What he could be sure of was that there could be no other outcome.

As he watched the huge tactical tote he spotted a further complication. The Electrone surveillance aircraft which had been skirting the airspace was about to penetrate the Falkland Islands Protection Zone. On a normal day it would be intercepted and photographed before being escorted safely away from the islands.

Today was not a normal day.

CHAPTER 34

OVERHEAD MOUNT PLEASANT AIRFIELD

The pair of Phantoms headed outbound climbing into the bright blue Falklands sky. The crews ran through the weapons checks settling into a familiar routine but for once the ordered calm was soon to be shattered.

"Eagle check"

"Eagle 2."

"Loud and clear. Puffin, Eagle 1 and 2 on frequency, Eagle 1 is Charlie 4, 4, Plus, Eight, Tiger Fast 60, switches safe."

"Eagle 2, same, switches safe."

"Eagle 1 and 2, Puffin loud and clear, anchor left in your present position, look 090."

In the rear cockpits, the navigators punched buttons on the inertial navigation systems entering the combat air patrol position into the kit. The needles on the instruments slewed around registering the range and bearing to the designated position just overhead Mount Pleasant airfield over East Falkland. If the jets became separated this would be the rendezvous point.

There was an evident question. Look for what?

In the back of the lead Phantom, Flash glanced at his map absorbing the detail of the surrounding terrain. They were just south of Pleasant Peak and beneath the Phantom he could see the new base at Mount Pleasant emerging from the peat, the new concrete structures stark in the sunlight. The fresh concrete of the runway thresholds stood out bright against the green background of the surrounding peat bog and the new operational complexes which had recently sprung up, dotted the perimeter. Most obvious was the huge hangar built to house the enormous transport aircraft which were about to begin operating the airbridge flights making the interminable trek south so much more tolerable. It would become a familiar navigation feature for the aircrew that would follow in the future.

For the time being the Phantoms would hold in the overhead scanning the airspace for the elusive contact that was worrying the air defence controller. Whatever was out there it had been significant enough to generate a scramble.

"If something's inbound from the west, the ridgeline to the north will shield it. We need to push the height up so the radar can see over the ridge."

"Yep, that makes sense." He hit the transmit switch.

"Eagle taking it up. Make the CAP height 5000 feet."

"Eagle 2."

The Phantoms pulled up from low level holding tight battle formation just one mile apart. As the lead jet levelled at 5000 feet, the wingman climbed even further, building in a tactical height separation above his leader. It would make it just that bit harder for an aggressor pilot to get a visual pick up on both aircraft simultaneously. They had no idea at this stage whether they would meet an "Ace" or a dullard but they would leave nothing to chance. They would get one opportunity to decide. Flash glanced over at his wingman taking in the smoke plume from the Spey engines trailing out behind the formation. At this height they stood out clearly but he had little choice. Much higher and they wouldn't get the height off in time if they vectored against a potential target and any lower and the target would be hidden behind the hills. This would have to do. In the nose of each fighter the AWG12 radars scanned the airspace ahead, the pulse Doppler mode primed to pick out targets from amongst the ground clutter. If there was an intruder to be seen they would see it.

"Eagles, sitrep," he prompted, the radio frequency frustratingly quiet since they had checked in. What was going on?

"Eagles this is Puffin, Cara Cara reports bogeys inbound. The targets faded around Fox Bay. Targets are high speed, low level, heading east, strength two."

"Roger, Eagles on CAP and ready for trade. Request instructions."

In their minds the scenario was shaping up along familiar lines and, so far this exercise was becoming predictable. They had followed this script many times but that illusion was quickly shattered.

"Eagles you are clear to engage, I repeat, clear to engage, Puffin authenticates Zulu Delta."

In the cockpits, the implications sank home and the adrenaline buzz was instant. Flash immediately cross-checked the authentication code from his decode on his kneepad and realised that it was genuine. They had just received an authenticated clearance to engage. It was unprecedented.

"The code's good," snapped Flash. "Puffin, say the position of Eagle 4 and 5."

"Roger, they've been vectored north against a further track. Presently 340 range 32, heading away, climbing to medium level."

A stray formation of Phantoms was the last thing they needed stumbling unintentionally through the fight.

"Confirm they are talking to you?"

"Affirmative, they're with me on TAD 042."

"Eagles copied."

"Your targets last seen 270 range 38 and 42, high speed, low level."

"Looking."

Whatever was inbound was fast and in a four mile trail formation. With the other pair well to the north, and instructions which left little to interpret, anything which came up on the scope was hostile. Flash stared hard willing the radar to show a contact. Finally the years of practice were at an end. This one was live and the coded authentication left nothing to decipher. It gave authority to use the weapons strapped underneath the Phantoms without further recourse to the controller. They had been cut loose.

"Shit!" he muttered.

"Want to make me feel any more nervous?"

The intercom went quiet. For now nothing needed to be said.

CHAPTER 35

THE ARGENTINIAN MILITARY CEMETERY, EAST FALKLAND

The Argentine Military Cemetery holds the remains of 237 Argentinian soldiers killed during the conflict. Located west of the Darwin Settlement it lies close to the site of the former battlefield outside Goose Green. Surrounded by a simple picket fence, each grave was marked with a simple white cross. After the war, as each soldier was identified from dog tags or personal items, they were interred in the hallowed ground with a Christian ceremony and military honours. Those who had fought them acknowledged their sacrifice at the hands of their political masters.

Sentiment ran deep for many reasons and on both sides of the divide. At first, the islanders had been reluctant to allow the cemetery to be established at all preferring to repatriate the fallen to Argentina. For its part, the Argentinian Government had seen the cemetery as a political statement leaving a tangible, albeit grizzly Argentinian presence on the islands. Compromise had prevailed and the simple memorial had been established which had slowly become more structured and permanent. It had taken much discussion before the planned visit had been approved. The Governor had championed the cause as the first tangible gesture of reconciliation but the islanders maintained a dignified resistance to the concept until compassion won them over. Politics aside, the cemetery was a simple memorial to the lives lost. In death there were no enemies.

The group of mourners clustered around the large white cross which dominated the skyline. It had been a simple service administered by a military padre from the base at Stanley. The thin sounds of the hymn sung by the knot of mourners had followed the prayers heightening the solemn atmosphere amidst the stark beauty of the local scenery. As the Army bugler sounded the Last Post a lone Chinook flew past in tribute. The noise of its engines briefly drowned out the sound of the haunting refrain but as it cleared through, the final notes prompted tears from the families still clustered in small groups and holding each other for support.

Karen Pilkington made a few hasty notes in the ever present notebook before snapping a few discrete photographs of the small assembly. Despite the ferocity of the battle in the local settlement of Darwin and, despite the fact that this had been one of the greatest victories of the campaign, she felt only sadness. The rows of regimented white crosses stark against the dark peat of the surrounding countryside were a tangible sign of the human cost of war. It mattered not that they had been the enemy. She focussed the camera on one old man who, hunched immobile in a wheelchair wept quietly. The woman next to him draped her arm around his shoulders in support. He looked from this distance like a defeated man, his head drooped in grief. To Karen, not used to the role of photographer, the clicking of the shutter seemed somehow intrusive.

With the simple ceremony of dedication over the mourners were escorted back to the helicopter site, their short trek completed in silence. They were to be transferred to Mount Pleasant where they would be put on the bus for the short journey to Stanley stopping off at the site of the heaviest fighting on Mount Tumbledown on the way. Afterwards they would visit the Capital before being returned to Mount Pleasant for the flight home.

Karen watched quietly, snapping a few more photographs. To the south the clatter of the returning Chinook helicopter shattering the solemnity of the occasion breaking the mood and bringing her back to the present. As it set down adjacent to the cemetery, the rotors slowing as the engines shut down, the mourners began to file towards the camouflaged machine ushered along by their military mentors.

Karen sat down on a small section of wall that seemed strangely remote from the crisp white fences which had been erected around the cemetery. She had little time to spare as she too had to be aboard the helicopter but her mind flicked back to the urgent words spoken into the phone in the office in Government House. The name on the door had been nagging at her since she'd read it but the reason why had been elusive. Alexander Sullivan she mused for the hundredth time when suddenly it clicked. There had been an incident some years ago and one of her fellow journalists at the magazine had picked up a nice little assignment in Gibraltar for a few weeks. It stuck because she had felt slightly guilty at her feelings of envy as she had been assigned to cover a boring conference in Lancaster House. The facts of the case had been inconclusive at the time but her colleague had returned fired up with the idea that there was more being concealed than was being admitted. Conveniently, the subject of the investigation, a British diplomat, had disappeared and there was rumour that his rapid departure had been orchestrated to defuse the situation. What emerged was a tawdry case implicating him in the disappearance of a girl in the tiny dependency. She was convinced the diplomat's name was Sullivan. If she could connect the dots between the incident in the Mediterranean and an apparently devious conversation in the South Atlantic she might have the bones of a story that would make the rest of her assignment here into mere padding. Her notebook re-emerged and after a few brief notes she made a promise that she would do a lot more research on Mr Sullivan when she got back to the office in London.

She watched the first of the families filing into the cavernous cabin of the helicopter which had settled onto the makeshift helipad. It was a relatively short trip across to Mount Pleasant where they would transfer to their coach. She pulled the camera bag onto her shoulder and began the short walk to the helicopter, her thoughts still on events in Gibraltar.

DAVID GLEDHILL

CHAPTER 36

GOVERNMENT HOUSE, PORT STANLEY

Located in a large building next to Government House, the Cable and Wireless office in Port Stanley was, literally, the hub for communications traffic into and out of the islands. Before the war it had been the only way to make a telephone call. In the months after Liberation the single secure line which had allowed the Governor to talk to Whitehall without fear of hostile monitoring had been slowly supplemented. The level of effort had increased exponentially and, recently, more lines had been added at Stanley airfield utilising the military satellite communications networks. The RAF Tactical Communications Wing had embarked on a massive upgrade with mobile communications terminals now able to send messages via satellites in space. Hundreds of phone calls were being made daily and a constant stream of signal messages flashed back and forth to UK every hour. Despite the increase in military traffic, the Cable and Wireless office remained as the hub for the locals.

Also a constant was that each and every line was monitored and "loose lips" would be punished for indiscretions. Communications security was taken very seriously indeed and the "listeners" took great delight in punishing the unwary. At times Warren Baird wished it was not quite so rigidly enforced. As the resident "spy", indiscretion provided him with much of his daily fodder. Once the new Headquarters on the edge of the airbase at Mount Pleasant was set up, a large part of the routine signals traffic would transfer to the new facility. It would benefit from more of the very latest in communications technology but, in the meantime, having to route traffic through this small organisation suited his purposes perfectly.

Warren punched a numbered code into a keypad on the door and let himself into one of the most secure offices on the island. He waved at the operator hunched over a small box in the far corner of the room as he made his way to a control desk. The operator was playing with his new toy. Called a personal computer, if the experts were to be believed, the thing would revolutionise the way this business operated. Based on a small electronic chip called a 286 processor it had the potential to allow signals traffic to be recorded. You could even write letters using a thing called a word processor. Rumour had it that it might even replace the typewriter and Roneo machine.

Every single radio message or telephone call which came through the communications hub was recorded. It was impossible to say anything on the island networks without it being captured on one of the massive reel-to-reel magnetic data storage tapes which revolved constantly on the huge machine in front of him. Every day the operator changed the reels and the master tape was sent back to the UK to be analysed by shadowy figures at the Government Communications Headquarters in Cheltenham.

He sat down and played with the controls of a tape recorder. Running the tape back he hit play and listened intently. The measured tones of Alexander Sullivan filled the headphones. Stopping the recorder he paused, distractedly rubbing his chin. The indecision lasted only briefly as he picked up the telephone dialling a familiar number which set a handset ringing 8000 miles away. The phone was answered instantly.

"Baird in Port Stanley here. We seem to have a problem which requires quite urgent attention." He began to recount the recent conversations. . . . .

"No that's perfectly clear, if not a little unexpected. I'll get onto it immediately."

CHAPTER 37

MI6 HEADQUARTERS, CENTURY HOUSE, LONDON

The modern tower block in Westminster Bridge Road, Lambeth was the least likely setting for one of the most secretive organisations in the Country. This had been the home of Military Intelligence Division 6, better known as MI6 since 1964, throughout the depths of the Cold War. Behind the drab facade, successive generations of agents had masterminded the most sinister plots from anonymous offices, unacknowledged by Government.

In a third floor office, its elegant surrounds at odds with the bland exterior, the two men relaxed in red-buttoned Chesterfield sofas. There was none of the austerity of the other Government departments in neighbouring Westminster. Covert budgets had a number of advantages, not least of which the ability to make office life slightly more tolerable.

"I understand you've been in touch with Baird in Port Stanley. I have to say his revelations came as a bit of a surprise. Who is this chap Sullivan?"

"He's a minor aide on the Governor's staff. He was a bit of a rising star in a former life but caused a few problems during his last overseas posting in Gibraltar. I'll fill you in on the details in a moment but, unfortunately, there's more to it than that."

"Why did I suspect there would be?"

The conversation faded at the discrete knock on the door as an assistant carried a mahogany tea tray, laden with china cups and saucers, into the room. She placed it on the regency coffee table and withdrew quickly. It was quiet until they were certain that they were, once again, alone.

"It seems there are a few facts hidden in his service record that he wasn't quite open about during his security vetting. I'm not sure if it was deliberate subterfuge but he was a tad sparing with the facts. He admitted to his background but I'm afraid the vetting agency failed to dig deep enough to uncover the truth."

"And might these be things we need to do something about?"

"They most certainly could be."

The visitor began to expand on a rather murky past.

"It seems our friend Alexander Sullivan, or should I say Alexandro Solvedo as he was known to his dear Mother, was born in the Basque region of Spain. The parents were radical in their views and he had quite a grounding in the politics of separatism. That much came out during his original vetting but didn't seem relevant to the jobs he was applying for at that time and, crucially, a job he was subsequently given. Regrettably, it became more relevant at that stage. It seems he has a penchant for the small former colonial enclaves because he had applied, successfully, for a tour of duty in Gibraltar."

"Why am I not getting a warm feeling about his character. Go on."

"It seems his loyalty to the Crown was less important than his apparent desire to see these principalities secede. In the case of the Gibraltarians, unlike the Basques, he had no issue with their views on self-governance. It was all to do with idealism but influenced by "filthy lucre." He was later found to have earned rather more during his tour of duty than his Government salary would suggest. And that was only the funds that we tracked down. We think there was more hidden away than we uncovered."

"So why wasn't he brought to book for espionage if he was taking cash for information? That seems straight forward to me."

"As always it was the burden of proof. He's a slippery character and he managed to come up with a plausible reason for the extra funds. We couldn't produce anything that we could have used in court. We can't even admit that GCHQ exists for goodness sake never mind that they produced evidence of shady deals. I should warn you that we may face a similar problem this time. Much of the evidence in the latest incident is circumstantial."

"So our man is not the upstanding country gent that his public persona suggests?"

"It gets worse."

"I find that hard to believe."

"There were some strange goings-on. It seems he had rather too much contact with the Spanish mission in Algeciras just across the border in Spain. It would appear that the Spanish delegation at the annual talks was particularly well briefed on the British position during the annual "Bilateral" that year. Those are the talks which discuss the status of Gibraltar, by the way. No one could work out why the Spanish Mission Leader always seemed to be a step ahead of us, unless, of course, our delegation was "leaky" which would have explained it all. It would also explain the source of the suspect cash."

"Maybe our man is developing a theme here."

"But there's yet more."

"More?"

The older man grimaced.

"The most serious accusation was over a girl in the Gibraltar Embassy who went missing. Nothing was pinned on Sullivan but there were strong suspicions that he was involved and he was interviewed by the local Police. Naturally with his diplomatic status they were unable to get beyond the initial questions other than to determine his status. They were less than thorough and the investigation drifted off at a tangent. The local Spanish newspapers picked up on the story and reported that a British diplomat was "helping with enquiries" and, as you can imagine, it provoked the usual anti-British rhetoric. The Spectator magazine reported it too. The girl was never found and there were never any satisfactory explanations for her disappearance. There were reports that he had been seen with her that night in quite a few of the bars. The local yobs who the Police latched onto were clearly innocent and were released without charge. At that stage, the Governor decided that Sullivan's actions were somewhat suspicious and, with local tensions rising his hand was forced."

"But Sullivan wasn't charged?"

"No, and to be frank, the interviews in the Embassy gave him so much leeway that his alibi was barely tested. Even so, there was enough doubt to ease him quietly into a posting where it was felt that he would have less diplomatic influence, hence his posting to Stanley."

"But Port Stanley hardly qualifies as a diplomatic wasteland at the minute. The politics are torrid!"

"He moved down there in late 1980 and he's been down there for well over three years. It must have been the perfect political backwater at the time. The conflict was barely a spark in Galtieri's devious mind at that time. Sullivan actually came out of that little fracas smelling of roses and achieved some notable successes before he was deported with the Governor after the occupation. He became quite the local hero at one point. Up to now his recent record in the Falklands had seemed solid."

"I think I've heard enough and thank you for bringing it to my attention. What with the stuff going on in Port Stanley at present I think we have enough circumstantial evidence to act, don't you? We can't have sentiment clouding the picture. I for one don't believe in allowing renegades to operate freely."

"He does seem to be a constant irritation, does he not but I'm afraid there's another complication."

"More? How could it be worse?"

"I'm afraid the journalist who is on the islands to cover the memorial ceremony seems to have been dragged in unintentionally."

"What has she uncovered? Can't we just slap a D Notice on her to keep her off the trail?"

"We could but it seems she may have overheard rather too much than is healthy. Baird is not sure that she's rumbled Sullivan yet in terms of his past or his motivations. That said, once she returns to London and starts digging who knows how much she'll uncover. No, it seems she caught part of a conversation between Sullivan and a third party. We suspect he may be talking to the Argentinians and she now has a lead to chase."

"That seems to be an impossible dilemma doesn't it? We can't go interfering with the workings of the free press now can we, particularly when the Whitehall Press Office issued the invitation to her Magazine Editor to attend the memorial ceremony. You'd best leave that one with me and we'll decide how to play it. What's her name; Pilkington isn't it?"

"It is. She's a bit of a rising star and quite unpredictable. Let's just say she's not averse to holding politicians to book if the need arises. The Foreign Office is quite sensitive about negotiations over Sovereignty. I doubt they'd want her digging into one of the diplomats affairs, particularly as the memorial service was supposed to generate a "feel good" piece."

"OK, leave that with me. I think I have a good feel for the issue. Let's keep this internal for now shall we? I need to discuss options with the Director. We'll need his guidance on how this develops."

As the visitor left the room, the ominous tone would have been evident even to a casual observer.

DAVID GLEDHILL

CHAPTER 38

GOVERNMENT HOUSE, PORT STANLEY

Back in Port Stanley, the phone on the Governor's desk rang at the most inopportune moment. He was due at Heritage Hall for a pre-meeting with his aides within minutes and his car had already pulled up at the main entrance. His PA was scrupulously efficient and would not have forwarded a call if it was not important. He could not afford to ignore a call from the Argentinian Foreign Office at this delicate stage of negotiations and it might be crucial to the discussions he was about to have. His proposal would be clear and should be attractive but he was still not certain that Buenos Aires would see it the same way. Surely he was offering a lifeline to them after the shambles of the invasion and the subsequent surrender but the unpredictability of the Latin mind never failed to surprise him.

He picked up the phone but rather than his diplomatic contact in Buenos Aires, the voice of the Air Defence Commander at the military headquarters greeted him. The news was simply unbelievable. An Argentinian Skyhawk bomber flying over the islands? Impossible! Where on earth was it headed? His thoughts tumbled out, random and uncoordinated. Please don't let it attack the airport at Stanley. The people on the ground up there were packed in like sardines and, with just one bomb in the technical area, there would be carnage. His schedule interrupted his train of thought and, with his meeting looming he cut the discussion short and headed out.

As he left the building walking quickly towards the waiting car, his mind raced. He began to think over the implications and none of the solutions he reached were particularly sound. He would return the call to the Air

Defence Commander as soon as he got to Heritage Hall and find out more about what they were doing about it. This was their business after all and this was why such an array of military hardware had been assembled in these few acres. The military firepower was deployed for this very contingency so that they could respond precisely to this type of aggression. He had rehearsed similar scenarios endlessly during quieter moments but he now realised that they had all reached predictable endings. In his mind's eye, an attacking force of hostile Argentinian jets had always been dispatched neatly by the friendly forces. Faced with reality, the variables were huge and the outcome was less predictable.

The car moved off for the short drive to the conference hall. He hoped the situation was under control and the fact that he was woefully ill-equipped for such life and death decision making was becoming increasingly clear to him.

CHAPTER 39

OVER EAST FALKLAND

The radar scopes in the Phantom cockpits were empty but the stakes were raised. Only recently, a training exercise staged to keep the defenders honed had very nearly gone wrong when a formation simulating an Argentinian fighter-bomber attack had almost been engaged. To the best of their knowledge the only other airborne Phantom formation was heading north away from land. There was, certainly, no one operating to the west. Whatever the controllers had detected on their early warning radars was not friendly and a track approaching at high speed and low level from the west demanded a closer look.

"Eagles," called Razor over the radio, "Switches live!"

He flicked the toggle switch on the weapons panel from "*Safe*" to "*Arm*". The "*Selected*" light glowed steady designating the front left Skyflash missile and the "*Ready*" light illuminated as the missiles responded to the electronic command. Under his feet in the semi-conformal missile launcher, the Skyflash missile tuned in to the frequency of the continuous wave radar and began accepting priming commands. Once the radar was locked-on and, with a touch of the trigger, the missile would be on its way towards its designated target. He flicked briefly to Sidewinder and cycled through the missiles making sure that each was ready. Reselecting Skyflash he returned his attention to the radar repeater watching the display for signs of activity.

In the back, Flash stroked the thumbwheel setting the scanner a few degrees down, the radar beam striking the ground at a point over Falkland Sound scanning a narrow swathe of airspace where he expected the target to appear. Anything which flew across the flat expanse of water and onto the low lying plain would be detected. Over the flat topography, if a hostile fighter chose the southerly route over Lafonia it would easily be visible. To the right and below, the massive ridgeline, the backbone of East Falkland, rose to nearly 1000 feet. From their elevated position the radar might even see targets on the flatter plains to the north. Closer in, there were some deep gulleys that might shield a cunning intruder but even if the target dropped into one of those valleys they should see it.

The scope remained frustratingly blank.

*

To the southeast, the Falkland Islands Government Air Service Islander headed west towards Falkland Sound only 1000 feet above the ground. The short hop from Stanley had taken only 20 minutes and the pilot had already let down for his approach into Goose Green airfield. At slow speed and heading away from the Phantoms on their combat air patrol it was invisible to the radars. With the Phantoms changing directly to the tactical frequency the flight watch frequency was quiet and the pilot was unaware of their presence.

The four passengers in the small cabin tightened their straps for the landing gazing from the large windows at the surrounding scenery and the crystal clear waters of Darwin Harbour. The grass airfield was easily visible on the rising ground above the settlement, hemmed in by low boundary walls, a 20mm anti-aircraft gun still guarding the entrance to the airstrip adjacent to the Darwin road. Spent cartridge cases and ammunition boxes littered the surrounding hedgerow, the detritus of war blighting the landscape, a reminder of the fierce battle that had raged in 1982. At one time this gun had defended the Argentinian garrison and the squadron of Pucara fighter-bombers that had flown from the airfield, against air attack from the Harriers and Sea Harriers of the task force. Now, merely a hunk of scrap metal, in the course of time it would be removed as the islands slowly returned to normal. On the airfield, the hulk of one of the Pucara fighter-bombers still obstructed the landing strip, the charred wreckage lying where it had come to rest, its take off run halted by a BL755 cluster bomb from a

British Harrier. Although an inconvenience, the Islander needed only a short landing and takeoff roll and the pilot was used to working around this obstruction. He landed on far shorter strips at other settlements and it was this feature of the Islander's performance that made it ideal for operations in this remote landscape. He banked gently over the water and made his final approach over the small settlement with its brightly coloured roofs, landing just abeam the shattered hulk before backtracking along the grass runway towards a waiting Land Rover.

Normally, he would drop his passenger and the mailbag and be off on his way without delay. Today, however, the pilot closed down the left engine and waited. Warren Baird climbed from the cabin and made his way over to the waiting Land Rover where the driver stood patiently. In the cabin, the passengers had already returned their attention to their books and the pilot played around with cockpit switches readying the aircraft for departure. The two men engaged in brief conversation before shaking hands, the short meeting over. The parka clad figure returned to the Islander, opened the small door and climbed aboard strapping into the empty seat prompting an increase in noise as the left engine wound up immediately. The Islander slewed around and began its takeoff roll towards the west.

The man alongside the Land Rover watched the small aircraft lift off and bank sharply towards the settlement. After a sporty flypast for the benefit of the residents it pulled up and wheeled northwards towards its next destination rapidly disappearing into the distance. The noise of the engines faded being replaced by the noisy calls of the gulls in the harbour below. Warren Baird climbed into the warm cab of the Government Land Rover and started the engine. Putting the vehicle into four wheel drive he bumped across the rough ground back to the road, churning up the damp ground. He set off northwards away from the settlement towards Darwin whistling happily. The villagers would have to wait for the later flight for the mail delivery. He would make one final phone call from the public call box in the Post Office in Darwin just to make sure the plan was still on track. He would make sure that his words were cryptic but hoped that the listeners would be busy today and that his call might be lost in the midst of the routine traffic. He did not want to advertise his activities to any more people than was absolutely necessary and what he had planned for later in the day was not something he would care to share.

DAVID GLEDHILL

CHAPTER 40

APPROACHING FALKLAND SOUND

In his cockpit, Carmendez hugged the contours of the small valley as he headed northeast following A-4 Alley. He passed a small gap in the ridgeline and caught a brief sight of Swan Island in the channel before the valley closed around him again. Glancing at the map on his knee he could see another gap coming up and, as it neared, he cranked on the bank and pulled hard towards the small rift. Wings level again he popped out into the clear airspace of Falkland Sound quickly taking his bearings. He was about to make a crucial decision and with a look towards San Carlos Bay his options narrowed. The clouds had formed on the hilltops as the cold Atlantic air was forced up over the peaks to the north condensing over the warmer landmass and masking the high ground. There was no way through. He turned hard onto east holding the Skyhawk at low level, scanning the area for fighters. It was an illogical reaction but the last time he had crossed this stretch of water he had been about to brave the hail of defensive fire from the British ships in the Sound. Hopefully, today's passage would be easier but having passed so close to the radar site at Mount Alice he felt sure he must have tweaked the tiger's tail.

As a precaution, he had dialled up the flightwatch frequency on his VHF radio and was monitoring the local traffic. Listening for the routine position reports on this frequency he hoped to check for any other traffic in the area, particularly fighters. The last thing he needed at this critical stage was a close aboard pass with an Islander commuter plane or even worse a chance encounter with a fully armed Phantom which might possibly be his last given the parlous state of his combat fuel reserve. So far the frequency was quiet but that meant nothing. It could be many minutes between position checks. From the intelligence reports he had devoured back at Villa Reynolds he knew that the fighters switched to a tactical frequency once they entered a training engagement so they might be airborne after all. He had no time to scan the range of frequencies so he might have no advanced warning other than his eyes. It did little to calm his nerves.

The short distance across the Sound was covered in minutes and the low-lying coastline of Lafonia appeared in the windscreen to either side of the heavy gunsight glass. To the right lay Goose Green which had been the scene of fierce fighting during the war. Back then it had been heavily defended with 20mm and 35mm radar-laid anti aircraft artillery. Those systems were long gone, removed to UK as spoils of war, so the airspace should be quiet now. He cursed the lack of a radar warning receiver which would have alerted him to any radar threats. He knew that the Rapier missiles were dug in much further to the east but a forward deployment was not unknown but, hopefully, he would have an easy passage for a few miles yet. In its absence he was relying on his eyes. The risk of encountering fighters grew greater the farther east he flew and he began to search the skies ahead methodically for the tell tale smoke trails. If they followed their normal tactics the Phantoms would be down with him on the deck and hard to see. He scanned the horizon moving his head left and right to see around the ironwork of the windscreen suddenly catching a movement in his peripheral vision to the right and above. The bright red Islander was climbing gently and already above him as he hugged the wave tops. The small passenger plane held a steady azimuth in the canopy and, as he watched its passage, it dipped a wing turning onto a new heading. Already well above him, he doubted the pilot could see him as he jinked slightly passing directly underneath and coasting in over the flat plain. The frequency remained quiet and he felt confident he had not been seen.

*

Four miles behind in the cockpit of the Mirage III, Captain Raul Hernandez was working hard. He knew he had closed down the range and was only a few miles behind the Skyhawk but the rate at which his fuel gauge was dropping was making him nervous. He reckoned he had 10 minutes combat fuel at most and as he coasted-out at Fox Bay and entered Falkland Sound he could not believe his luck. He had fired up his radar and there on his scope at 30 miles was a pair of contacts. They were well above him which was a huge surprise as the Phantoms rarely flew high. Had they been down at low level they would have been lost amongst the ground clutter but by easing up to a higher level they had solved his detection problem. He refined the contact, tweaking the scanner control on his throttle, staying in search mode to avoid alerting the crews of his presence. Hopefully, they would not detect him on radar. They were flying in line abreast just a mile apart and, although they were not his target, if they found the Skyhawk first maybe they would do his job for him? If nothing else they should tie up the rogue Argentinian pilot and maybe prevent him from penetrating any further east. It might give him the opportunity for a snapshot with one of his missiles. He cursed his luck. The squadron had recently received the Matra Magic infra-red missiles which were much more capable. Unfortunately, because the AIM-9Bs he was carrying had been planned to be fired against a flare for the benefit of the VIP visitors, he had been allocated the older weapons for the live demonstration. Unlike the AIM-9Gs on the Phantoms, his own early generation missiles were much simpler, had to be fired closer to the targets 6 o'clock and were completely vulnerable to infra-red flares which the Phantoms carried. He had no quarrel with the Phantom crews but if he had been sitting in their cockpits he might be less than thrilled to see an Argentinian fighter over the islands, be that a Mirage or a Skyhawk, and would respond aggressively. He would have to take care. The cloud on the hills to the north was making the scenario more predictable and he guessed that the Phantoms must have opted for the clearer air to the south of the ridgeline. If he got too close to the hills and became trapped above a solid cloud layer he would never get back down to low level. With his limited fuel that would be the end of his mission. He edged closer to the heavy clouds and eased up to the base of the solid overcast to check its height. It looked clearer out to the east where he predicted he would overhaul the Skyhawk. That was the killing ground where the merge would occur.

*

"Eagle 1, contact bearing 100 range 25 miles," called Flash from the lead

Phantom.

"Contact."

His wingman could also see the bogey but as Flash had called it first he assumed the tactical lead for the intercept.

"Taking it down."

The Phantoms began a rapid descent to lower level. They had no interest in staying unseen and wanted to advertise their presence to the intruder. If this was a Skyhawk it could not carry head on weapons so they had the advantage. If it was a Mirage III it might be carrying the R530 semi active missile which was inferior to the Skyflash they carried but still able to threaten them, particularly if they gave the opponent an easy look-up shot. If it was a Mirage they would have plenty of warning as their radar warning receivers picked up the engagement sequence, alerting the crews of a firing. They were confident that the missile could easily be defeated by tactics.

The navigators in both Phantoms were now glued to the small radar displays buried in the cockpits.

"Single bogey heading east, low level," called Flash receiving a quick blip on the radio from his wingman in acknowledgement. He barked a few quick commands to Razor to set up a closing heading for a front quarter attack. He planned to lock up at 10 miles launching a Skyflash missile as soon as the target came within range. On his wing, the other navigator would stay in search mode looking for other targets and guarding against a surprise attack. Unbidden, his pilot had pushed the speed up and the airspeed indicator edged towards 500 knots. A little fast at this stage he thought but better fast than slow. It would also cut down the smoke trail behind them. The cut off was good and he was rapidly closing towards the target's extended centreline. Not knowing if his opponent was fitted with a radar warning receiver he held off with the lock until he was ready to commit the first Skyflash missile. He did not want to give advance warning of his intentions but with clearance to engage he had the advantage. Even so, he was edgy and needed reassurance.

" Confirm I've got this right Razor, we're clear to engage, right?"

"Affirmative, clear to engage and authenticated."

The acquisition markers closed around the blip on the scope and he squeezed the small trigger on the back of the hand controller, the penultimate act in the sequence. The radar faltered in its scan, pointed at a position in space some eight miles ahead of the Phantom and entered its acquisition phase. After some brief electronic wizardry it centred on its target and began to track. The indications on the display switched to full lock mode and Flash made his final assessments.

"Heading 090, range 6 miles on the deck, in range, clear to fire."

Razor pulled the trigger committing the missile to its deadly mission. After a brief pause the express train left the station in a cloud of smoke. It corkscrewed downwards towards its target, apparently tracking accurately. In the cockpit all looked well on the display and Flash mentally counted down the seconds to the kill. For a five mile shot he anticipated the time of flight should be about 15 seconds. In the front cockpit Razor watched the smoke trail as it marked a path towards its intended prey. Suddenly it nosedived into the peat bog and the smoke trail extinguished.

"Missile trashed, continue," he transmitted, the frustration clear.

The unseen intruder had survived . . . . . for now.

"No kill." A pause. "Tally Ho, it's an A-4," he transmitted the excitement instant. His wingman to his right was not yet close enough to identify the opponent but the call left no doubt.

To his navigator, "Coming down the left hand side, I'll commit left." To his wingman, "Bogeys now!"

*

As Hernandez skirted the base of the overcast he suddenly spotted the fur ball below. The Skyhawk was turning hard and both Phantoms had hauled around and were beginning to gain ground. If this went to its natural conclusion he could make his escape without needing to intervene and leave the Phantoms to do his job. Despite its turning performance there was no way an unarmed Skyhawk loaded with bombs and short of fuel could hold off a pair of Phantoms for long. He pointed his nose at the trailing Phantom to keep it in sight but in doing so he had made a fatal mistake. In the nose of his fighter the Cyrano radar was transmitting its deadly siren call.

*

"Rackets, 6 o'clock," barked the navigator in the back cockpit of Eagle 2, his radar warning receiver alight with the radar emissions that had struck the antennas mounted in the fin cap of the Phantom. On the display a solid vector pulsed its warning, the I Band signal from the Cyrano air intercept radar generating a squealing audio tone. A pulse light on the small display verified the threat generating an instant reaction in the cockpit. He craned his neck to search the area behind his aircraft.

"Tally, 6 o'clock high, nose on tracking. Keep it coming hard left. PULL!"

In the front the pilot transferred his attention from the Skyhawk and looked over his left shoulder towards the unexpected threat. His navigator was calling the shots as he strained to pick up the visual contact.

"Seven o'clock high, two miles closing, keep it coming hard left."

"Tally Ho. Shit it's a Mirage!"

The arrival of the second threat came out of the blue; literally. Whilst it might look clear cut on a huge tactical display in the Sector Operations Centre, up here in the spinning cockpits it was far from clear who was friend and who was foe. As they faced-off across the circle the blue and white roundels on the Argentinian jets was enough evidence for the Phantom crews. They were over the Falkland Islands and that was enough to declare the unexpected arrival as hostile.

Razor increased the pull, the needle on the G meter touching 7G, and pushed the throttles forward to the firewall engaging full reheat. He strained his stomach muscles as the G came on, warding off the onset of dimmed vision. Around his lower legs the G suit inflated and, in the back, his navigator grunted under the strain. The speed stabilised and only when he relaxed slightly did it begin to creep up slowly, eventually reaching 420 knots, his best cornering velocity. He rolled the wings to match the Mirage's flight path and watched for a reaction in the other cockpit. He had fought the Mirage before and knew that, with its instant turn capability, speed was life. If he allowed this to degenerate into a slow speed flat turning fight he would lose. Simple as that.

*

The Mirage pilot cursed his luck. The Phantom crew had seen him and were already reacting. The decision came in a split second which was fortuitous as he might not have had another chance. If this Phantom tied him up and the Skyhawk could avoid the wingman it would make its escape from the "circle of joy". He pulled the sight onto the massive airframe listening for the tone from the 'Winder". The growl, when it came, was strident but the aspect worried him. The Phantom was centred in his sight but the turn had increased the angles off and he could see mostly top surfaces. The engines were slowly being shielded by the airframe. So what was his missile seeing? He knew the limitations of the old AIM-9B and the shot would be fleeting. With only two missiles onboard he needed to save one for the Skyhawk but this Phantom was persistent. He pulled the trigger committing one of his precious rounds. Under the wing the missile's electronic brain received the signal pulse which fired up the thermal batteries and brought the electronics into life. A few brief commands to the seeker head and the autopilot and the motor fired up producing instant thrust from the rocket. The frangible links on the launcher rail were overpowered instantly and the missile shot forward from the rails accelerating quickly to nearly three times the speed of sound in a cloud of efflux. It sped away from the jet and corkscrewed towards its target.

*

"Missile defence! Flares, flares, flares," called the navigator as he registered the significance of the smoke trail. Hitting the dispense button on the ALE40 control panel he watched the counters click down. In the front cockpit, the pilot yanked back the throttles in a classic chill defence, reducing the huge infra-red signature from the afterburners and allowing the jetpipes to cool even if only for a few seconds. Anything he could do to make the jet less significant to the infra-red seeker or to confuse the inbound missile would help. On the Phantom's missile pylon the countermeasures dispenser began to eject a sequence of pyrotechnic flares which, milliseconds after leaving the squat container, ignited in the airflow and separated from the turning jet. The chemical cocktail in the flares rose in intensity, each tiny payload in the sequence burning spontaneously and generating a hotspot, replicating a mini jet engine.

The Sidewinder missile streaked towards its target, the small reticule in the dome of the missile registering the heat from the target's engines. It tracked the pinpoint sensing the movement away from the central null. Occasionally, the electronics sensed a drift and sent small corrections to the autopilot kicking the guidance fins on the forebody of the missile into action. Following a spiralling flight path it closed unerringly on its target when, suddenly, the inanimate electronics sensed a change in the signature. An attractive alternative had appeared and another, and another. The missile switched its attention and tracked towards the new quarry, its radio fuse searching for an airframe on which to trigger.

In the Phantom, the crew could do little more than wait as the smoke plume snaked towards them, the rippling white plume marking the flight path of the missile. With the Phantom's speed beginning to wash off, the effect of the defensive reaction now obvious, the pilot could do no more. He re-engaged the reheats and hoped for the best. Just when their fate seemed inevitable, the missile passed underneath the right wing and corkscrewed harmlessly towards the ground. Seconds before it struck, the timer for the self destruct fuse operated and it blew apart spreading shrapnel into the peat bog. The flares had done their job.

*

With only one missile remaining and still engaged, the Mirage pilot was running out of options. The Skyhawk could be anywhere and his rash decision to shoot at the Phantom had probably secured its escape. He was faced with a life or death match with a hugely superior weapons system. The Phantom might be heavier and might not turn as well as his own Mirage but, flown well, its Skyflash missiles and AIM-9G Sidewinders were a fearsome challenge and he had a significant disadvantage. He glanced at the fuel gauge. He had just 500 kilograms of combat fuel in the tanks which would be gone in an instant if he used the reheat. Down in the weeds at low level was not where he wanted to be. In the upper air, the Phantom would be less manoeuvrable, lack the nose authority of his own fighter and it would be a more uneven fight. He did what was, probably his only choice. He did not have the fuel to spare so he pointed his nose at his opponent in the hope that he would feel intimidated and wash off even more of his precious speed. Down here he was in the Phantom pilot's domain. It might still be a fight for his life.

*

As he passed the Skyhawk, Razor pulled hard towards the fighter-bomber and made angles before the pass, already part way into his turn before the merge. Initially, the Skyhawk pilot jinked towards but then extended keeping his wing down in a classic feint, showing no interest in entering a turning fight. It was obvious that he was trying to find an easy exit and disengage. It was a crucial piece of intelligence for the Phantom pilot. An aggressive opponent would not have allowed him to take such an advantage so quickly and would have threatened him at the merge. That the Skyhawk pilot chose an extension manoeuvre suggested he would prefer to escape. It was a defensive rather than an offensive reaction. Whatever the Argentinian's thoughts, he was outnumbered, had narrowly avoided an engagement by a "smoking telegraph pole" and he must be rattled. Razor maintained the hard level turn with his wingtip only hundreds of feet above the ground, his nose tracking around the horizon. As he stared over his shoulder at the receding fighter-bomber his wingman passed through his 6 o'clock close aboard, the two aircraft momentarily coupled. He pulled the stick even harder, watching his G meter which hovered close to the maximum limit. If the Skyhawk was not to escape he must try to bring his gunsight to bear on the fleeing target.

*

In the number 2 Phantom the crew were fixated on the Mirage on their tail and everything else in their confined world had become irrelevant. The more he pulled, the more the pilot washed-off speed allowing the Mirage pilot to arc inside the turn, ever closer. He would, eventually close in to set up for a guns kill. This was exactly the situation he had trained for throughout all those simulated air combat splits back home on the squadron and he would not allow that. Think F-5 he told himself. How many times had the American aggressor pilots flying their Northrop F-5s talked about this situation? He had to use the strengths of his own jet and exploit the weaknesses of his opponent and, at this point, had one crucial factor on his side; fuel which bought him time. His opponent was on the limit of endurance and could not stay and fight for long. If he could hold him off for a short time his opponent would need to disengage and run for home at which time he would be vulnerable. Another huge advantage was that there was a bolthole on the doorstep and it was only available to one of the duelling opponents. Mount Pleasant was a mere five miles away and with its 8000 foot runway he could burn his own fuel down to absolute minimums. Even if he stayed in full afterburner for the next 15 minutes he could still drop his jet onto the long concrete runway leaving only fumes in the tanks. It was more than his opponent could do and, if he did consider the same option, he could guarantee an unfriendly reception on the ground at MPA.

OK concentrate, he urged himself, listening to the commentary from his navigator in the back as he unloaded the controls, picking up an extra few knots as he watched his opponent's reaction. Nothing; the Mirage continued its predictable turn; pointing, pointing. By easing off on the G the speed increased by a few precious knots and he began to increase the radius of the circle, imperceptibly at first. As soon as he had some turning room he would take this fight into the vertical. To follow, the Mirage pilot would need to use reheat. Still watching over his shoulder and still defensive, he could see that the Mirage pilot was matching his moves although, with the planform of the upper surfaces of the delta wing jet now visible, he must have backed off a little. It may be that he was unable to use the full turning capability of the jet and he, undoubtedly could not engage reheat. it told him that his opponent was not yet ready to try for a missile shot. If intelligence was correct and he was only carrying AIM-9Bs, there should be no risk of another shot until the nose came to bear. To release another missile, the pilot would have to put his gunsight onto the Phantom to lock the Sidewinder seeker head to the heat of his engines. While he could see the top surfaces of the Mirage the Phantom pilot knew he was safe. He continued to nibble away, biding his time, slowly widening the circle keeping his jet close to the ground making the other pilot work hard. At this height, so close to the ground, the Mirage pilot would have one eye on his opponent and another on the rocky terrain. One slip and it was over. The ground was an unforgiving opponent and the probability of kill was 100%.

*

As Carmendez watched one Phantom he caught a movement in his peripheral vision and, involuntarily, winced as the wingman flashed close aboard within feet of his cockpit. There was a dull thud as he hit slipstream and the Skyhawk bucked against the forces exerted by the disturbed air. He tightened his grip on the controls resisting the rapid roll but, as quickly as it occurred, it was over. Switching back to the leader he could see the other jet pulling high into the vertical, no longer a threat. It was the break that Carmendez needed and he pushed for the deck taking a small turn-away trying to separate from the "circle of joy". If he could hold the diverging heading for a few moments and find the anonymity of low level his pursuers might stay wrapped up with the Mirage and he could yet make his escape.

*

Razor had been making angles on the Skyhawk slowly and was employing every basic fighter manoeuvre in the book to sweeten the shot. The goal was tantalisingly close just off the edge of his gunsight but he did not quite have that extra G to bring Skyhawk under the pipper. The nose stubbornly refused to shift that final few mils to bring the target into the Sidewinder seeker head's field of view. With the needle on the G meter registering the limit and the angle of attack already well above 21 units he could not risk that extra pull that would give him a growl from the Sidewinder. He was close to the ground and loss of control was possible at this height. If he could stabilise his position he might be able to talk Flash on to a lock and get a Skyflash missile away.

"PULL!" he heard from the back cockpit.

With caution forgotten and, without question he responded instantly as his wingman whipped past the cockpit in an opposing turn just yards away, filling his vision. There had been no time to ponder his mortality and hesitation would have been fatal. As the nose gyrated upwards, the altimeter increasing rapidly, he lost sight of the Skyhawk beneath him. With the horizon once more at a sensible angle and, by now, well clear of the ground, he risked a glance at the G meter. The needle was firmly lodged beyond the tell-tale red bug and It had registered 8.5G. With external full tanks hanging beneath the wings, hopefully still here, he had overstressed the airframe. Gingerly testing the controls to make sure the jet was intact, he breathed a sigh of relief as it responded normally. He was not yet safe. Where was the Skyhawk and, more importantly, where was the Mirage.

"Shit, that was tense" said Flash from the back cockpit. "That was a close-aboard pass if I ever saw one. I've lost the bogey do you still have him?"

At this moment, and without a G meter in the back he was still blissfully unaware of the consequences. Razor dropped the wing and stared down at the rolling landscape beneath but his concentration was broken. There was no sign of the Skyhawk. He pulled up to 5000 feet and tentatively checked the feel of the controls despite the protestations from the back cockpit. Everything seemed to be working but he could easily have damaged the airframe. He cursed inwardly as he admitted his error to his navigator. Until he got this jet checked over he was out of the fight.

"Puffin, Eagle 1, heads up. One bogey heading east, high speed, low level."

They now faced the classic dilemma. Unless he could get his eyes back on the elusive Skyhawk, it would be down to the base defences to engage the hostile fighter-bomber. If he pressed eastwards he would penetrate the base defence zone and may himself come under attack. The Rapier crews would be monitoring the engagement on the air-to-air frequency clutching hairline triggers.

"Eagle 1, this is Puffin, climb to 15000 feet and stay with me on this frequency. Head 090 degrees and stand by."

"Eagle 1 climbing."

Where the hell was Eagle 2?

*

After the close pass, the pilot of Eagle 2 had paused to collect his thoughts, not easy at 500 knots. He, momentarily, held the wings level and extended away from the fight listening to his navigator who's head was screwed backwards over his shoulder at an impossible angle watching the bogey. A steady patter flowed from the back, the commentary describing the air picture perfectly.

"He's eased the turn. At your 8 o'clock in a gentle turn, top up, nose off." The unsighted pilot tried to visualise the tactical situation from the words before recommitting into the fight. If the Mirage began to threaten, the commentary would revert to commands to make sure the Phantom did not become a victim. In his mind's eye the pilot timed his pitch back. Far enough away and he would give his navigator time to turn his attention back to the radar and try to lock up and release a Skyflash missile. It was a huge challenge under threat, although this was what they had practised for every day of the week for the last 10 years. If he timed it right, the navigator would lock and he would squeeze the trigger before they reached the minimum firing range of the Skyflash. Too close and there would simply not be enough time for the missile to go through its arming process. The Mirage would regain the advantage with its superior turning performance.

"Range now?" he asked.

"Three miles," came back the response, instantly. Four miles would have been better and it was still close but time was pressing. The decision was marginal. He yanked the stick hard back into his gut and, as the huge aircraft came around in a flat turn just above the ground, he called his navigator bringing his back-seater's head into the cockpit.

"Tally Ho," he called as the Mirage appeared exactly in the front canopy exactly where the commentary predicted. He glanced at the radar repeater scope in front of him watching the elevation markers on the radar moving methodically, searching for the elusive blip.

"Contact," he heard from the back seat "Trying for a lock!"

He looked down at the indications on his missile control panel. The *"selected"* and *"ready"* lights were glowing for the rear-left Skyflash missile.

"Good lock," he heard as the indications on his radar display flashed fleetingly before settling down in a full track display. He looked for the steering dot on his radar display, moving the control column urgently, pulling the dot towards the centre of the circle giving the missile its best chance of success.

"Hold Fire," the navigator screamed from the back. "Min range!"

He had hesitated too long and they were too close! If it was fired, the missile would have insufficient time to separate from the Phantom, go through its arming sequence and fuse on the target. Even if it did, they stood every chance of flying through the debris zone and writing themselves off in the process. His finger twitched on the trigger but he resisted the urge to pull. Seeing the Mirage closing at a crazy pace he adjusted his flight path looking for yet another minimum separation pass. If he gave this guy turning room at the pass he would arc the turn and be in a firing position before you could say Fox 2! The pilot knew exactly what he would do. He rocked the throttles outboard and smashed them to the firewall engaging full reheat on both Speys. The engines spooled up and both crew felt the kick as the burners lit.

"Left to left pass" he called to orientate his back seater. The navigator screwed his head to the left peering through the ironwork between the two cockpits. A speck appeared in the canopy rapidly growing in size taking on the familiar profile of the Mirage. After the merge, the pilot would probably lose sight again so it would be up to him to keep the air picture. In this situation against an agile "low wing loader" he knew that the pilot would probably repeat the last manoeuvre and he anticipated the G forces. They had few options but to repeat the separation manoeuvre to gain the elusive range to pitch back for another Skyflash shot. This time he suspected the fight would go vertical.

The Mirage flashed past with only yards between the jets at a combined closing speed of 1000 miles an hour. The confrontation was over in seconds and once again his head was on gimbals looking at the planform of a Mirage as they arced upwards in an oblique loop.

"He's got to be out of gas soon. He's in a gentle left hand turn at about two miles, staying on the deck. Make your pitch back to the right and I'll try for another lock Take it back down onto the deck."

"Roger that."

"He's got to be short of gas!"

The assessment seemed to be more of a plea than a fact.

"Makes sense this far from home. Let's finish this!"

They extended, the pilot dropping the wing to keep the Mirage in sight, desperately waiting for the elusive range. The manoeuvre had dragged them around onto an easterly heading towards Stanley and they knew that the Mirage pilot had to be nervous about his fuel state. With the range from his home base increasing and the fuel gauge needles decreasing he could only hold the poker move for so long. With the separation increasing he might elect to turn and run for home at any moment. It would be the smart thing to do. However this panned out, once they pitched back they would get only one chance for the shot. The Phantom pilot's nerves gave first and he pulled the stick hard over, engaging the burners to maintain his speed as he turned. He wanted the airspeed indicator at 420 knots when he came out of the turn.

*

In the Mirage, Hernandez looked down at his fuel gauge yet again. He was bingo fuel and had to go home. The Skyhawk had made its escape and he had no quarrel with the Phantom crew. After the next pass he would separate and climb to high level to make his escape. It was tight but he could do it.

*

The Phantom steadied up on west with the back-seater buried in the scope. A blip appeared slightly right of the nose and he moved the acquisition markers around it squeezing the trigger on his hand controller. The radar scan stopped, entering a conical scan centred on the target's position, searching for the contact which should be in the radar beam. Its electronic brain registered the response and switched to full track mode bringing up the firing symbology in both cockpits.

"Three miles, in range, clear to fire," called the navigator urgently. The window was tight.

The pilot pulled the trigger and there was a pregnant pause as a new command was sent via the electric string to the missile. He resisted the urge to pull the trigger again knowing there would be a lag before the missile left the launcher. The noise of the hydraulic rams, suddenly loud in the cockpit, announced the departure as the huge semi-active missile was forced away from the underbelly into the airflow beneath the Phantom. Once in free airspace the rocket motor ignited and the missile sped away trailing a massive smoke plume, tracking unerringly towards the closing Mirage.

"Fox 1," he called over the radio.

*

In the Mirage cockpit, Hernandez suddenly heard the screech of an RWR warning announcing an unwelcome event. The small display burst into life showing an I Band radar signal which could only be a Phantom radar. It was in his 12 o'clock exactly where he expected the attack to come from. His tactical options flashed through his brain, demanding decisions in a split second. If he broke to the beam to defeat the missile he was dead meat offering his tail to the Phantom. If he pressed on and the missile worked he was also dead. The break was the lesser of two evils so he pulled hard to the left watching the strobe on his RWR track around to his 2 o'clock then 3 o'clock. The strident tone was unrelenting and he finessed his heading to keep the threat on the beam. Surely the pulse Doppler could not track through that, he thought. The piercing tone continued to ring out its warning and, as he levelled the wings, he stared at the smoking trail coming ever closer. Suddenly the cockpit was quiet and, simultaneously, the Skyflash entered a violent corkscrew upwards as it lost the tracking information before spiralling downwards and disappearing under the wing of the Mirage. With his heart pumping and the adrenaline flowing he dropped towards the deck and accelerated back across the islands towards the mainland. The descent would cost him more of his precious fuel. Behind him the Phantom brought its nose on.

*

"Shot trashed," called the navigator as the radar broke lock and returned into search mode, well before the missile had timed out.

"Confirmed," he heard from the front as the pilot watched the gyrations from the Skyflash as it dived into the peat bog. Ahead he saw the familiar planform of the Mirage as it turned belly up to him and dived for the safety of low level.

"He's running on west," he called.

With little to do now that his target was in front of him, the navigator switched his full attention to the radar scope. Pulse Doppler was useless in a tailchase so he flicked across into pulse mode. Although the screen suddenly flooded with noisy ground returns from the reflections from the terrain, if carefully handled it should be possible to break out a target from the clutter. Even if he was unable to intimidate the fleeing Mirage pilot by trying to lock on, if his pilot could close the range down to a mile and keep the escaping Mirage in sight, they could fire a visually-aimed Sidewinder.

"Eagle 2 is engaged, running west at high speed," he called to the other Phantom still unaware of Razor's predicament. "Bogey, two miles on the nose."

"Can you see him?"

"No, I just lost him against the background. He's at low level. He must be about two miles ahead but I lost him as he descended. He's right on the deck. Can't be much above a hundred feet."

"Still looking on radar but I'll be lucky breaking him out at two miles."

"Hold it, I think I just got a flash, just left of the nose Bringing it left 10 degrees."

The navigator adjusted the ground returns hoping to see the tell-tale blip separate from the band of noise on the radar. The lower the target, the closer it would be to the noise and harder to break out. This Mirage pilot was flying so low it would be a miracle if he found him on radar. He took a glance out of the canopy and could see Choiseul Sound to the south. That put them just short of Goose Green. All around them the flat landscape was a dull beige. The Mirage camouflage blended in perfectly with its surroundings.

*

Hernandez looked again at his fuel gauges. At 500 knots he was eating the gas and would never make it back to base holding this speed. He eased the throttle back to 80% and watched the fuel flow drop back to a more sustainable level. The move would cost him a few knots and he watched as the airspeed indicator settled back slowly to 400. He could see the tell-tale smoke plume from the Phantom in his 7 o'clock in the mirrors. So far it had not closed down the range but it was only a question of time now. He gingerly eased the heading left trying to avoid a wing flash which the Phantom pilot might pick up. He concentrated on keeping his height down below 100 feet. Up ahead Falkland Sound stretched from left to right. If he could diverge from heading, the Phantom crew might lose him.

*

As they screamed past Goose Green the navigator had a brief flash on the radar just left of the nose. He called a correcting heading just as the contact faded again, playing with the radar controls, refining the display trying to break out the elusive target. This guy must be really low. In the front the pilot's eyes darted left and right peering through the armoured glass of the windscreen, looking for that tell tale flash. There it was just left of the nose and hugging the scrubland. He called it to his back-seater who, instantly, refined his search. Up ahead the glassy water caught the sun and he knew in an instant that he had won. As soon as the Mirage coasted-out he would have him. Blending perfectly with the scrubland, over the water the low flying jet would stand out like a dog's balls and more importantly would be much easier to detect on the radar. He bided his time.

*

The Mirage crossed the coastline at Kelp Harbour and the pilot suddenly felt vulnerable. The Phantom was doggedly sticking to his tail and he had nowhere to hide for the next 15 miles. He gritted his teeth and concentrated on flying as low as he could. In his peripheral vision the waves whipped past as he concentrated on the radio altimeter. He held the stick rock steady.

*

There it was, as clear as day. As soon as the Mirage crossed the coastline and emerged over the water it stood out plainly. The Phantom pilot eased up and nudged the throttles forward to increase the speed and close the range down. There was no problem keeping sight now. He had to take the missile shot before the Mirage reached the sanctuary of West Falkland and he edged closer and closer until, eventually, he reached firing range. With his increased height, the Mirage had disappeared below the massive radome of the Phantom and he faced a precarious manoeuvre to take the shot. Tensing, he bunted over, pushing the nose towards the ground, waiting for the target to appear in the gunsight. There it was; smack under the pipper and the line was perfect. He made one final check of the weapon switches. Sidewinder was selected and he waited for the growl. The height began to wash off rapidly as the Phantom descended towards the ground but his wait was brief. The strident tone of the missile seeker head sounded in his helmet as it acquired the jet pipe of the Mirage. The warbling metallic tone steadied and he squeezed the trigger. With a loud whoosh, the Sidewinder left the rails and accelerated towards its quarry as the pilot pulled hard into the recovery manoeuvre taking his jet away from the rapidly approaching water. He pulled up and dropped the wing watching the smoke trail guiding downwards towards its prey.

*

Hernandez saw the flash in his mirrors and the chilling signature of the smoke trail as the missile was fired. With no chaff and flares he could only break towards the incoming missile in the vain hope that the turn would shield his jetpipe. He cranked on the bank and the Mirage veered left in a defensive manoeuvre. It proved to be a vain hope. Looking over his shoulder watching the missile guide straight towards him he increased the pull on the stick but, flying at such a low altitude, he made his final fatal error. With his jet turning hard he let the nose drop and the jet flew lower still. The wingtip grazed the water causing a rapid slew and the retardation drove the nose hard down and it struck the water. The Mirage cartwheeled in a plume of spray before striking the sea and disappearing instantly. Hernandez made no attempt to eject.

*

"Fox 2. Splash one bogey, heading west."

A simple statement.

The Phantom reversed its course back towards Stanley pulling up as it turned.

CHAPTER 41

BLACK EAGLE CAMP OUTSIDE RAF STANLEY

The Rapier surface-to-air missile was ready on its launcher, today no different to any other day. A product of the Cold War designed to shoot down Soviet bombers attacking bases in West Germany or the UK, it was equally capable in the similar climate and rugged conditions of the South Atlantic. It, and its crews, had gained vital combat experience during the conflict and the operators were confident. RAF Stanley was protected by Regiment units deployed from the UK and Germany on rotation. From their deployed "hides" around the airfield they scanned the skies for intruders which they hoped would never come. If they did, however, they were ready.

A Rapier fire unit was made up of eight gunners from the Royal Air Force Regiment and was the basic fighting element to defend the RAFs airbases from air and ground attack. The gunners operated the wheeled launcher, the tracking radar and the missile support and supply vehicles. Designed to be mobile, the system could be repositioned by the ubiquitous Land Rovers. Compact and easy to hide, the surveillance radar mounted in a small radome, could detect targets flying at all levels out to about 10 miles and up to 20,000 feet. The radar would see an incoming raid and, because the launcher could rotate through 360 degrees, it could cover all aspects around its dug-in position. Fitted with four ready-to-use missiles, with more available that could be reloaded rapidly from the resupply vehicle, it would be ready to respond within minutes. Once launched, the missile tracked to its target following commands fed in by the tracking operator using an optical sight and a small joystick. A transmitter and aerial provided a command link between the operator and the missile in flight. The tiny warhead, unlike the Sidewinder on the Phantom, was designed to strike the target so technically, it was a "hittile." In combination with small arms, the system was lethal against low flying aircraft and helicopters.

Black Eagle Camp, just outside the perimeter of RAF Stanley, was home to the air defence detachment. From this headquarters the Rapier fire units were deployed around the airfield in a defensive ring protecting every possible avenue of approach. Each of the pre-surveyed sites gave a modicum of comfort for the gunners in their peacetime posture. Access tracks allowed them to get into, and out of, the remote sites easily. This was not, however, a "nine-to-five" operation. Gunners spent 24 hours a day at the sites and lived and breathed air defence during their stint on duty. Small cabins constructed from purloined shipping containers had sprung up at the established sites and they enjoyed a modicum of home comforts in the makeshift camp.

Further out from the Capital the real pre-surveyed sites, which they would use if the hooter sounded, were less obvious. Access routes were carefully camouflaged and, although the firing plinths had been surveyed, home would be a tent if the balloon went up. There were no obvious clues that this was where the missiles would be located, protected from all but the keenest eye or a roving satellite. Even when occupied they would, suddenly, be far harder to spot from the air.

At the Rapier hide closest to Black Eagle Camp it was a day like any other day. The oncoming shift had run the daily maintenance schedule and made sure the fire unit was in a fully operational state. The radio checks and static line checks had proved the communications links and the oncoming battery commander was happy that his unit was ready. The portable generator which provided the power for the system electronics hummed rhythmically in the background and the missile launcher was gyrating gently as it ran through a built-in test routine. The Commander walked across the scrub to the crewroom, as the tin box in which they lived was grandly named, and pulled open the huge door. Things had settled back down after the Phantom QRA aircraft had launched. Inside, chairs and tables offered a little comfort during the times when they were not conducting training runs with the Phantoms or the Hercules. One of the gunners handed him a "brew" and he sat down with the precious newspaper which had arrived on yesterday's airbridge flight. News from home was still sparse and they relied on the British Forces Broadcasting Service radio station to keep up with World affairs. The tinny sound of the radio hummed to the beat of the latest offering from a 70s band. The life saving "blueys", the forces aerogrammes which arrived daily from loved ones back home were the essential lifeline. Yesterday's mail run had contained not only his "bluey" but a rolled-up copy of The Sun newspaper and his first task was to check out Page Three. He listened idly as the team outside shouted commands to align the fire unit and to bring it back up to readiness. The routine was well practised and needed no input from him. His job was to catch up with events from "Blighty." The small arms training wasn't planned until 10.30 and in the meantime he could put his feet up and admire the model who smiled out at him from the newspaper.

The volume of the radio box which connected them to the Sector Operations Centre was turned down and the steady chat which was increasing in tempo was drowned out by the radio station. He was oblivious to the drama unfolding just to the east.

That was before the claxon sounded.

CHAPTER 42

APPROACHING THE FALKLAND ISLAND PROTECTION ZONE

In the cockpit of the Electrone the Captain stared from the front window listening to the soporific drone of the turboprops. All he could see was open ocean but the northern coast of the Islas Malvinas lay somewhere out there.

"Captain to Navigator, range to the coastline now?" he queried.

"Just over 200 miles Captain. Zone penetration in three minutes."

This was all part of the plan that they had briefed carefully a few hours ago. Today's mission profile, planned weeks ago, had them penetrate the FIPZ by 40 miles before turning west in a feint. They would then tickle the edge of the zone hoping to provoke a reaction from the QRA Phantoms at Stanley. With their sensitive radio receivers and their hours of endurance they should easily be able to keep the fighters at arm's length. Providing they didn't press their luck they should be able to remain well outside the zone until the fighters ran out of fuel. It was a game of chicken with their opponent's supersonic capability but one thing they had in their favour was a generous fuel load. If the QRA C-130 tanker was launched that would be a different ball game. That would mean the fighters could operate to the edge of the FIPZ and beyond bringing them within easy range and vulnerable to interception.

Down the back end, sensitive receivers were tuned to the air defence frequencies and any response on the unencrypted channel would be instantly intercepted. Exactly what response their flight path would provoke was yet to be seen. If it followed the usual pattern the air defence controller would launch the alert birds but with Q already airborne it would be interesting to see whether they diverted a training sortie. He was pretty certain there were only two alert aircraft but all the Phantoms flew armed as they knew well from past interceptions.

"Keep an eye out for the Hercules Ecko 290 surveillance radar. Let me know if you get even a sniff of the refueller. Comms; listen to the air defence common and let me know if there are any more QRA scrambles or if any other flights are diverted in our direction. If they are, we carry on running west."

"Will do, Captain."

He gestured to the co-pilot who took control of the lumbering aircraft, stood up from his seat and eased over to the navigator's plotting table, glancing over his shoulder at the track drawn on the map. It ran on a south-easterly heading to a point north of the Capital Port Stanley known to those who had occupied it during the war as Puerto Argentino. A large 200 mile radius circle had been superimposed over the islands showing the extent of the air defence control zone. Although his Government rejected the arbitrary limit he knew that the Phantom crews would be less dismissive. For him it was important tactical data and once they penetrated that ring he knew he would provoke a reaction. Even if they subsequently withdrew, staying in the general area around the islands would warrant an interception. After the next turn the track headed west to a further navigation point to the northwest before running directly at one of the radar sites on East Falkland. This was their most vulnerable point and they would withdraw at the earliest sign of a reaction. He was keen to avoid being photographed as the new antennas which had sprouted from the upper surfaces during a recent refit would give away the role and capability of the new equipment which had been installed. The overseas vendor had been keen to avoid too much publicity but business was business, as he had made clear. Who the Argentinians listened to was none of his affair. He gestured again to the co-pilot and eased his way down the back of the aircraft. His first port of call was the comms console where the operator was listening to the air defence communications channels.

"What have we got?"

"Hey Captain, we've got the usual callsigns on frequency. I recognise a lot of the voices from our last trip. All the "Eagles" are using the same callsigns so the new arrivals must have been absorbed by the resident squadron for their stay. The reinforcements came in on Ascot callsigns a few days ago. I'm hearing a few new voices but most seem to be the ones who have been here for a few weeks. The guys on Q are new. Not sure if they are the detachment guys or new on the squadron. QRA launched about 15 minutes ago and headed west. It's been quiet since apart from the occasional tactical call."

The Captain moved over towards the intercept operator who was monitoring the air intercept radar frequencies. He plugged into the console next to the technician who was hunched over the desk with his hand clutched to his headset, frowning. They switched to a quiet intercom channel to chat.

"So why the frown?"

"I'm struggling with this one. I can see the Phantoms clearly. I've watched them too many times to be confused. Trouble is I'm getting other hits in there too. They're not the usual run-of-the-mill stuff either."

"How so?"

"I've had some hits from comms but that's not uncommon. We often get random UHF contacts from ground sets. It's the higher power stuff that's confusing. I even thought I got a hit from a radio altimeter just now. If I didn't know better I'd say we had some of our own aircraft flying over the western island!"

"Impossible!"

"I know but tell me that's not a Cyrano air intercept radar," he said pointing to a string of electronic scribble on the display in front of him. "I can't explain it but I know what I'm seeing!"

At that minute the comms operator banged the table to attract his attention, his headset pushed back from his ear, beckoning.

"You're not going to believe this but all hell just broke loose on frequency. There's an engagement going on down there and it doesn't sound like the usual training stuff."

"Missile guidance signals detected" called the intercept controller. "Bearing 170."

"World War 3" had broken out and, suddenly, the ether was full of unusual electronic emissions. The mission was proving far from routine.

CHAPTER 43

MOUNT TUMBLEDOWN, EAST FALKLAND

Alexander Sullivan pulled his Land Rover off the road. There were few places along here where he could hide its presence but from the vantage point at the top of the ridge alongside Mount Tumbledown he could see for a good way in both directions. The road was clear and his task wouldn't take long. He began the short climb up the escarpment and the effect of the exertion came as a surprise. By the time he reached the peak he was breathing heavily and he promised himself that he would improve his exercise regime or at least make a start. From the overlook he could see the road to Mount Pleasant snaking away into the distance disappearing from view as it rounded the hillside. He had chosen the spot for its uninterrupted view to the east and the view back towards the Capital was breathtaking. Seeking out the rocky outcrop that he had found a few weeks before he began to pull away the stones that covered the small cave where he had hidden the radio transmitter. He must choose a new spot. Leaving it in one place for too long risked it being discovered and he suspected the listening post at Port Stanley must already have some suspicions. He placed the last rock carefully aside and reached into the gaping hole feeling for the transmitter. His fingers fell around the strap and it made a noisy scrape as he dragged it from its temporary resting place covering any sound made by the shadowy figure that approached silently. He didn't see or hear anything so the blow from behind came as a total surprise. He slumped forward knocked instantly unconscious.

The assailant moved the limp body roughly over to the neck of the tiny cave and kicked aside a few of the carelessly discarded stones. Picking up the, apparently, lifeless body he manhandled it towards the dark hole and pushed it head first into the opening. There was no way that the victim would be able to turn around once inside the small space. A few hefty shoves and Sullivan's body disappeared head first into the orifice.

Warren Baird looked down at the bleak hole in the ground. He hoped his subterfuge had worked and that he had covered his tracks. The drive from Goose Green had been arduous and it had been a long, cold wait before Sullivan's vehicle had appeared, although he had known that it would. The aide may have thought he had covered his trail but the clues had been there if one had known where to look. Baird had been alerted by the listeners that there had been transmissions from this general area and it had not taken long to find the cryptic notes which Sullivan had concealed in his office giving away the location of the transmitter. The idiot could at least have committed the hiding place to memory rather than write it down. That error had sealed his fate. He began to stack the heavy stones back in place sealing the makeshift tomb. Escape from the narrow confines was impossible.

Sullivan had made his final transmission. It was a fitting end for a traitor who would never have the chance to make use of the funds lodged in the numbered account in the Cayman Islands. No one could ever find this tomb and any evidence of its whereabouts had been destroyed.

He could not drive both vehicles back to Stanley and the disappearance of Sullivan's Land Rover might generate questions. A quick search was inevitable once it and the aide were found to be missing so he would have to move it at least a short distance away from here. He certainly didn't want to attract attention to this lonely outcrop or even worse, have anyone visit in the near future. The makeshift vault was sealed well enough and the cave entrance had returned to its natural state, invisible and natural against the surroundings. Even the wildlife would struggle to gain access but he would not leave it to chance. He stacked a few more heavy stones against the opening making sure to keep the weathered side in view. Stepping back he inspected his work and, satisfied turned to leave making his way back down the short incline towards the waiting Land Rover.

He would move the vehicle back along the Stanley road a short distance.

There was a pull off not too far away and, providing he wasn't seen dropping it off, it should be discovered soon. Maybe a tug on a plug lead or two would be enough to make it seem like it had broken down. It would have been just like Sullivan to have tried to walk back rather than wait for a lift from a passing vehicle. Some poor sap might even hijack it and then they could answer the questions. The walk back to his own Land Rover would take time but it was well concealed from the road and he just could not take the risk.

The last thing he needed now was a Phantom, or even worse a helicopter to fly past before he could sort things out. He trudged towards the waiting truck hoping that the keys were still in the ignition. Please God he hadn't buried them with the corpse.

DAVID GLEDHILL

CHAPTER 44

OVER EAST FALKLAND

Back at Mount Pleasant the search and rescue Sea King had just lifted from the apron outside the new Air Terminal. The crew had been inspecting the modern alert facilities at their new squadron home next to the massive Tristar hangar from where future SAR crews would hold their vigil. They had watched the families of the Argentinian war dead file from the Chinook helicopter, which had touched down moments before, and climb onto the waiting bus. The female RAF escorting officer had waited patiently as the journalist captured a few brief images of the scene and they had both climbed aboard before the engine revved and the white bus pulled away. It was a short 30 minute ride to the Capital Port Stanley. As the Sea King cleared the airfield perimeter the Captain gestured upwards, attracted by the presence of two Phantoms that flew high over the airfield heading west.

*

Scribbling her final note on the ceremony in her ever present notebook, Karen Pilkington pulled open the camera bag and lifted out the precious camera. She had already removed one roll of film at the ceremony and it was stowed safely in the pouch. She wound on the second roll, opened the back of the camera and popped the film safely into the protective plastic canister. She had used a number of exposure settings so, hopefully at least a few photographs should be usable. It was not the first time she had wished a cameraman had accompanied her for the visit and just hoped her skills had been up to the task. Capturing a unique event was a heavy burden and it had taken all she could muster to calm her nerves. With the camera reloaded and her interviews completed she sat back for the short ride back to the Capital.

*

As the helicopter made its way eastwards the Skyhawk was already closing down the range to its target. Carmendez had followed the track of Darwin Road towards Stanley hugging the foothills, the stick flicking left and right in unison with the contours. With the pressure off, his mind drifted back to that day in the crewroom which had started this whole roller coaster. It seemed like years ago. He had shaken off the Phantom for now and, as he approached the lower slopes of Mount Tumbledown, the presence of a vehicle off to the side of the road vaguely registered. Ahead, the road disappeared around the hillside but another vehicle making its way along the road appeared just in the edge of the windscreen and quite hard to see behind the ironwork. His next action would be an act of pure, irrational folly. Nothing in his plan had suggested a target of opportunity and all he registered in that split second was the chance for a snap shot. Illogically, he drew the pipper on to the vehicle and squeezed the trigger, sensing the vibration through the airframe, letting go with a long burst of HEI allowing the rounds to track through the military vehicle. Something felt wrong as the dust was thrown up from the fall of shot yet he held the trigger longer than he should, walking the line through the vehicle. Transfixed by the scene he kept firing, the bullets ripping into what he now recognised as a white civilian bus moving slowly along the rough road.

*

Karen stretched out her legs across the space in front of her making the most of the empty seat alongside. The British contingent had taken seats at the front of the coach; the Argentinians choosing to maintain a detached separation had congregated towards the rear. She was grateful for the extra leg room and flicked open the seat belt that chafed her hip. Suddenly released she felt much more comfortable and relaxed despite the pounding of the bus tyres over the pockmarked road surface. She was barely aware of the subdued thumps from the rear of the coach before mayhem erupted around her.

The high explosive incendiary bullets thumped into the unprotected bus and it shuddered under the onslaught. With its tyres shredded it slewed towards the edge of the road with the driver struggling to maintain control and, as the wheels drifted over the banked shoulder, it rolled over and began to slip down the long incline towards the rock strewn bundu. With nothing to arrest its progress it continued to roll, uncontrollably, as the windows shattered and the lightweight framework buckled, folding inwards destroying the integrity of the cabin. Inside the bus the passengers screamed as they were thrown around, struck by flying debris and seats which had been torn from their mountings. Peppered by shards of flying glass horrific injuries were inflicted on the hapless passengers in seconds.

Karen was unable to take in the juxtaposition of the horizon as the green peat appeared through the shattered windscreen but above her head. She was lifted bodily from the seat and thrown across the wildly rotating cabin, bodies flying through the air around her. She felt the sting of hundreds of tiny sharp projectiles tearing at her body and was only vaguely aware of the seat frame, torn from its mountings which flew towards her at high speed. She tensed.

As the bus rolled to a standstill once again upright, there was an eerie calm. The door had burst open and a whole section of the front of the cabin had been ripped away leaving vast gaps in the structure. There were groans. The escorting officer eased herself to her feet, gingerly, feeling her damaged arm to see if it was broken. It seemed in one piece although she was covered in blood; who had shed the blood, she had no idea. Disorientated, she staggered away from the wreckage stunned at the carnage around her. The aircraft, and it seemed as if they had just been attacked by a jet, had flashed past and disappeared bringing back harrowing memories from the conflict. Although it had been too fast to see the markings on the fuselage she had come to recognise the Phantoms which operated from Stanley and that was not a Phantom. She recognised the Skyhawk and had seen them at air shows back home in the UK. Only one country operated those aircraft in this region but why was it over the islands? It was unfathomable as it had attacked the bus which was full of Argentinian mourners going back to the Capital after the dedication ceremony. How could they possibly be a target? Madness.

Looking back at the bus she listened for signs of life trying to decide her next action. She was an officer and supposed to act calmly in this type of situation but she felt only fear. The smell of spilt fuel was overpowering and she resisted the urge to retch. Struggling with her dilemma and wanting to run, she heard the sound of an approaching helicopter, its clattering noise splitting the air. Her overpowering sense of relief was tinged with a feeling of guilt.

*

Already some miles distant, Carmendez snatched back on the stick pulling out of the unplanned strafing pass, stunned. What had he been thinking? He pulled hard around the escarpment hugging the foothills and pressing towards his target. He had come this far, evaded his attackers and still had bombs onboard. Port Stanley lay ahead but there was a nagging doubt. As he had flashed past the bus at 400 knots he was sure it was white. The intelligence report had said that the bus carrying the Minister should have been wearing green military camouflage and it should have been heading west towards the new airfield. The bus had been heading east towards Stanley. He twitched as he drifted below the 100 foot minimum height he had bugged on the radalt prompting a piercing warning tone from the instrument. It was too late to go back on his actions now and he put the scenes he had just witnessed behind him. His concentration switched back to the target analysis he had run at the Squadron and an image of his target on Stanley Harbour, formed in his mind. He had work to do.

*

In the cockpit of the SAR helicopter which was paralleling the rough road the crew were beginning to prepare for landing-on at Stanley. For them the sortie was nearly over when the Captain spoke on the intercom.

"Ah sweet Jesus, I can see a smoke plume off the side of the road. It doesn't look good. We need to check this out. It could be a traffic accident. Graham, stand by to winch down. I'll try to find a place to put down but I'll set you down first if I can't."

Up ahead, the source of the smoke was still unclear but an ominous pall rose into the air. Wresting the cabin door of the Sea King back on its tracks, the winchman pulled the metal hook which dangled from the winching mount towards him and clipped it onto the shackles on this lifejacket ready for the short drop to earth. If the Captain found a landing spot it would take seconds to unclip, meanwhile he was ready for a winch down. Behind him the navigator positioned himself at the winch controls, ready. The noise level in the cabin had risen and the intercom was now the only way to communicate as the helicopter approached the scene. He looked over at the navigator who gave him a thumbs-up and he dropped his feet over the edge of the cabin preparing to launch into thin air. The pilot was back on the intercom.

"I can't risk setting down. That peat looks unstable and it's covered in rocks. I'll go into the hover alongside and we'll put you down and then try to land nearby. If I can't find anywhere better I'll land on the road. Come up on "scene of search" frequency once you're on the ground."

"Will do. Ready to winch down."

The navigator moved alongside the door and clipped his own strop to the cabin wall. The winchman was already in the open door his bright dayglo immersion suit standing out against the scenery beyond. With a quick gesture he pushed away from the lip and was instantly suspended below the winch spinning crazily in the turbulent air below the rotor blades. The navigator steadied him in space and after another thumbs-up hit the down button on the winch panel and the winchman started his descent. The helicopter was now rock solid alongside the scene of the accident and the navigator could see the shattered wreckage of the white bus below which had only minutes ago set off from MPA. He had watched it drive away from the Terminal. How could things go so bad, so quickly?

"He's down. Clear to depart," he said as the Captain twisted the collective lever initiating a gentle ascent. As the helicopter moved upwards and clear, the downdraft from the rotors subsided and the grey helicopter backed off slowly.

On the ground the winchman pulled off his bulky bonedome and stared, incredulously, at the shattered wreckage. As it had tumbled down the slope, the sides of the bus had folded in on themselves deforming the once symmetrical shape almost beyond recognition. Virtually every window along one side of the bus had shattered. The thing that caught his attention was the line of holes through one of the panels that had been torn from the bus and now littered the peat. Although he was no weaponeer, he recognised the signature of incendiary rounds. This was no simple road traffic accident. Something bad had happened here. His first irrelevant thought was that the Phantom crews at Stanley would have a lot of explaining to do after this shambles. His next thought was for the survivors. He just hoped there were some. He ran towards the wreckage as the first dazed survivor began to stagger out of the shattered door. Steam was rising from the rear of the vehicle and there was an overpowering smell of fuel. He would have to be quick as one spark threatened to turn the scene into an inferno.

The young officer was first to emerge and appeared stunned but otherwise seemed to have survived remarkably unhurt. She was not his major concern. Others, also apparently uninjured emerged, flopping onto the grass nearby way too close to the smoking wreckage. He shouted, urging them to seek refuge further away from the bus. Approaching closer he could see the mangled remains of a wheelchair whose occupant was still trapped in the tangled mess. The old man was clearly dead, crushed by the metalwork of the windscreen as the bus had tumbled. There was nothing to be done. Likewise, the driver had taken the full force of the huge metal upright and was disfigured beyond recognition. The hardened veteran of many a road traffic accident, the winchman had seen all this before. His priority was not those who had perished but to try to save anyone alive and, particularly the injured. Others would cope with the aftermath. Working his way inside the shattered doorway, he began to work his way along the line of seats stopping at each row and checking for signs of life. The front of the bus had taken the full impact and most of those in the first rows had succumbed to their injuries. As he reached row four, a groan alerted him. One young lady was moaning softly but, clearly, still alive. Her body lay at an impossible angle and had suffered impact injuries in the crash. He pushed the seatbelt aside which had been unclipped thinking that, if it had been fastened, it might have saved her life. He lifted her gently from the seat. With the overpowering smell of fuel still hanging in the air, normal medical protocol would have to be ignored. He pulled her back down the aisle as gently as he could, off the vehicle and away from the bloodbath. Laying her out amongst the other dazed survivors he urged a man to tend to her as he sprinted back to the bus, his heavy immersion suit slowing his progress. He prayed that the inevitable fire held off for a while longer and that the spark, when it came as it would, occurred when he was outside the bus. With his heavy survival gear he ran the risk of being trapped inside and it played on one of his worst fears, the nightmare of being trapped in a burning tomb. It kept him awake at night. Miraculously, the inevitable held off and he slowly pulled more people off the bus, each trip back tiring him a little more. Knowing there were still more survivors, he turned to make another run when there was an ominous silence followed by a whoosh as the spilled fuel ignited. The fabric of the vehicle acted like tinder and the flames increased in intensity within seconds. There was nothing more he could do and he collapsed on the ground exhausted. The Sea King had set down some distance away and, as he turned his head, he could see his crew running towards him. He realised that in his haste to pull out the survivors, he had forgotten to give any updates on the radio. He had saved many lives but the reality was that in the burning hulk, many more would perish. Shaken by the unexpected turn of events, he lay back and breathed heavily. His body ached. Slowly he was aware of a shadow and the young RAF officer stood over him.

"I can't find Karen Pilkington who was with me. Did you find her?"

He had met the journalist just last night in the bar. Stunned at the thought, he pulled himself upright and looked back towards the bus which was burning fiercely. He ran back to the shattered door without a thought for his own safety. The tangled mass of seating barred his way and he frantically pulled at a loose section uncovering the mess below. The floor of the bus had buckled as it had tumbled down the slope distort the structure. As he peered into the muddle he could see the shape of a body, badly injured. Despite the flames he tore away at the loose shards of metal trying to get closer. The camera lying next to the body confirmed his fears. It was Karen. Adrenaline helped in this situation and he found reserves he didn't know he had despite years as a winchman. He felt the rubber of his neck seal on his immersion suit melting and it burned his skin. The heavy material of his immersion suit gave him some protection but the heat on his face was intense and he could feel his skin begin to blister. The smell of singed human hair was strong and he realised it was his own. He ripped the final distorted seat mounting away and pulled himself as close as he could. It didn't look hopeful. Karen's legs were trapped by a twisted seat frame and she looked to have suffered heavy trauma from flying debris. Her pretty face would not be quite so pretty in future. Despite the injuries she stirred so she was still alive. Any time there was a breath there was a chance. The flames were raging at the back of the bus and moving ever closer. He struggled to remember where the fuel tank was located on this vehicle and hoped that it was at the front because when the flames reached the tank there would be a massive explosion. He manoeuvred himself alongside and pushed his arms in behind her distorted torso. He gave a slight pull to see if he would be able to free her but there was no give. It was all or nothing and the smell of fuel grew ever stronger. With the flames coming ever nearer he doubled his efforts finding untapped reserves. Tugging hard against the obstruction, her trapped body still refused to move. Frustrated, he twisted against the wall of the bus trying desperately to get a better purchase. Her legs were still trapped and her sudden groans made him back off. As he struggled for what he could not know was the final time there was a huge flash as more of the spilled petrol ignited and tracked quickly towards him. The exposed padding from the seats acted like a huge wick and it quickly spread. He had little choice but to think of his own survival. After one last futile pull he was forced to withdraw down the aisle and jump clear leaving the body of the young woman inside. The flames quickly engulfed the hulk. As he resigned himself to her fate he was consumed by an immense feeling of guilt that he had been unable to save her. As he walked away from the burning wreck, the looks on the face of the young officer somehow made him feel responsible. The navigator spotted the symptoms and quickly pulled him aside away from the survivors and began to talk quietly but urgently. The rest of the crew dragged the injured back from the scene urging the walking wounded to move away from the growing inferno.

*

Despite the potential damage to the airframe, Razor and Flash were reluctant to haul off with the job unfinished. The geography had to make the Argentinian predictable. If he ran north he would be forced up by the foothills of the mountain range and become easily visible as he crested the ridge, skylined above them. To the south the flat plains and coastal strip would give no place to hide and, again, he'd be easily visible. The curve of the lower foothills meant that he had to be following a track around the lower slopes which made it even more likely that Stanley was his target.

Razor strained his eyes looking for the tell tale flash of movement against the terrain. In there somewhere was a Skyhawk with a full bomb load and hostile intent. In the back Flash played with the controls of the radar but overland and with the target already well ahead he would be lucky to get a chance detection. In this environment the "Mark 1 Eyeball" was still the best sensor. The RWR had fallen silent.

"MEZ in five miles," Razor heard from the back cockpit knowing it would be suicide to enter the base defence zone at high speed in hot pursuit. There it was! A tell tale glint and the Skyhawk appeared briefly as it flashed over the peat bog, its camouflage blending in well with the surrounding countryside. It was tantalisingly close and he just needed to get the range down a little more to close inside parameters and get a Sidewinder away. It would be a worrying bunt manoeuvre as he pushed the nose of the Phantom down to get that elusive growl from the seeker head.

"MEZ boundary, pull up Razor. He's still out of range," said Flash, resignedly. Seconds later the radio burst into life.

"Eagle 1, haul off, haul off," they heard from the controller emphasising their predicament. Rapidly entering the Rapier's lethal zone and with no options left he complied, pulling hard on the stick and starting a zoom climb to height, the speed rapidly dropping off. He had no desire to make his Phantom appear any more threatening than it already looked. It was down to the Rapier crews now.

*

The intercept controller watched his fighters head north from their previous play area. His request to the Master Controller to be allocated a pair of Phantoms to monitor the intrusion by the Electrone had been readily granted. The Phantoms had just completed a mutual intercept over East Falkland but they still had plenty of reserve fuel so there was no need to divert them via the QRA tanker. The IFF response on his radar display had changed and they now wore his squawk signalling the change of controller, their height showing clearly on his radar tube. They had pulled up from low level and were approaching 15000 feet rapidly so, very soon they would check in on frequency and he would vector them towards the intruder.

"Master Controller, Intercept Console, what's our status?"

"Weapons free!"

They both knew the implications. They had watched, fascinated, as events had unfolded in the south, first with *HMS Newcastle* and then Mount Alice. The raid had been declared hostile and the QRA Phantoms had been vectored onto the low level targets. This track to the north was undoubtedly the Electrone. Its speed, height and flight pattern all fitted the normal profile but today, however, its role was more sinister. It had obviously been assisting the bogeys with electronic intelligence during their penetration and that made it an accessory to the events unfolding over the southern part of the islands.

"Master Controller, this is Byron, I hold track number 009, from me, 360 range 170, heading west, request instructions."

On the hill at Mount Kent the Master Controller switched his attention. He had been riveted by the events over East Falkland and had taken his eye off the ball. So used to watching the surveillance aircraft ply the waters he had not thought this through. He had vectored fighters to intercept the track and he knew it had left Trelew and popped up in the usual area but was it the Electrone? He needed confirmation.

"Byron, Puffin, identify."

He would cover his arse and check with the Air Defence Commander. Hitting the direct line to the Wing Commander's office at Stanley, he paused. No reply. Damn! The response from the controller at Byron was instant.

"Roger, identify, request further instructions."

"Checking, I'll call you back."

There was no reply from his Boss. This one would be down to him and it was time to earn his keep. He had rehearsed a similar scenario in his mind's eye so many times but this was different. He had a hostile Argentinian, presumably a Skyhawk from the radio calls, being chased by a Mirage which had been declared friendly. Despite that fact the Mirage had been splashed by the Phantom crew. They must have been attacked to have responded with deadly force. That made all the Argentinians in his airspace hostile in his mind. This surveillance plane had helped the raid. Its presence was no coincidence and it must have given information to the attacking pilot. Signals from the Electrone had been intercepted by the surveillance team. It was participating in a hostile act against the islands. It was fair game and his mind was made up. If the visual identification was positive the intruder was looking at a missile. He tried the direct line to the AD Commander one last time . . . . . still nothing.

"Puffin, this is Byron, sitrep?"

What a time for an update he fumed but despite his frustration he began a brief summary.

*

After picking up the blip on his radar, the lead navigator in Eagle 4, now well north of the melee had chosen to approach his target from the stern sector. Like the controller on the ground he had recognised the profile, slow and predictable, typical of the tracks normally flown by the Electrone. The pair had chopped across to a discrete control frequency and were no longer hearing the frantic, clipped radio calls from the other Eagle formation. Trust his luck he thought. World War 3 breaking out over Lafonia and they were being pulled off for the milk run against the snooper. Approaching from the south he had been pulled into a beam intercept coming up from the Electrone's flank. The converted airliner was already running for the mainland and, although not a tailchase, the intercept seemed to be taking an age. The closing velocities were much lower than a head-on attack and it tracked down his scope at a pedestrian pace. In reality the aircraft were still closing at combined speeds of over 500 miles an hour but time seemed almost to stand still. The radar contact drifted away from the ideal approach and he made a few heading adjustments to keep the intercept on the rails. With the banks of electronic gear aboard the converted airliner he had thrown the usual caution to the wind and locked his radar to the blip on the screen. The full track display gave him all the information he needed to prosecute the identification profile even if it meant advertising his presence to the target. Another barked command and his pilot brought the Phantom to within a thousand feet of the intruder's height. He had no need to camouflage his approach. He wanted these guys to know they were coming. There was no way an Electrone could outrun a Phantom with full fuel tanks. On the wing, his number 2 was looking at the same information and guarding against other potentially hostile bogeys which might be in the airspace and out to set a trap. There had been Mirages down in the south and there was just the possibility that this could be a decoy set to lure them into an engagement. The target was showing inside 10 miles still crossing his nose and he increased his rate of commentary to the pilot to try to talk his eyes on. No academic two mile roll out today. They wanted an identification and they wanted it quick. If it came when they were still five miles down the road, all well and good. As it was, he did not wait for long.

"Tally Ho, 1 o'clock 4 miles," he heard his pilot transmit over the radio, alerting both the controller and his wingman.

Glancing from the right hand side of the canopy the navigator stared hard. Now that the pilot was visual he didn't need instructions from the back and four eyes were better than two. He fixed the point in space where the radar pointed and there it was.

"It's the Electrone!" he called to his front seater picking out the distinctive over-wing engine configuration.

"Eagle 4 identifies one Electrone, Hostile, Hostile, Hostile, acknowledge!"

In the darkened ops room at Kent the Master Controller hesitated for just a moment. His decision had been made and the hostile call merely reinforced it.

"Clear to engage, I authenticate Foxtrot, Mike."

"Check that mate," called the pilot prompting his navigator to quickly check his authentication codes on his kneepad.

"Bloody hell, it's for real. That code checks out. We're clear to engage."

Without further thought the pilot reached down and flicked the master arm to "*Arm*", selected the Sidewinder missile and checked the coolant was on. He was rewarded with a solid growl in the headset, the seeker head instantly picking out the strong infra-red response from one of the Electrone's engines. The nav looked down again at his radar display for one last time. The target was firmly inside Sidewinder range at this height. A slow speed straight and level target with look up. It was a sucker shot.

"In range, clear to fire!"

The pilot pulled the trigger.

*

In the Electrone, the crew had watched the tell tale indications on their warning equipment as the Phantoms had conducted the intercept. There was no change in the tone as the Phantoms began to turn in behind. As the crew had not selected the Skyflash semi active missile, the continuous wave radar had not fired up so there was no warning to the operators of the recent escalation. The monotone of the locked-up air intercept radar from the AN/AWG 12 continued and the strobe began to drift around into the stern hemisphere as the Phantoms closed. They had watched this scenario unfold many times over the last couple of years. In the cockpit, the pilots stared ahead unable to see into their own 6 o'clock but waiting for the Phantoms to pull alongside. In the darkened rear cabin the electronics operators stared at their electronic displays as they had done so often before. No one aboard the Electrone was aware that the stakes had changed until the Sidewinder missile ripped into the port outboard engine exhaust. The warhead detonated sending a shower of lethal shrapnel radiating outwards from the missile body. The small supersonic shards ripped into the structure splitting open pipes and spilling combustible liquids onto hot metal.

*

The Phantom pilot watched as the smoke trail from the Sidewinder extinguished as it struck its target. It had boosted all the way to its target driven by the rocket motor in the tail of the missile. A shower of debris erupted from an area between the twin engines on the port wing. More debris tumbled as the missile warhead exploded sending more shards of shrapnel into the fuselage of the large aircraft. He watched in morbid fascination as the propeller on the inboard engine, damaged by the warhead of the Sidewinder, shattered into pieces sending a disintegrating blade through the fuselage. The Electrone began to lose height streaming smoke.

"Mayday, Mayday, Mayday, Snitch 27 on Guard. Major structural failure, lost power on two engines, attempting to ditch. Our present position is 40 miles north of Pebble Island."

There was silence on Guard frequency as the UHF transmission would only be audible out to about 100 miles from the stricken aircraft. The only potential benefactors who might hear the distress call were those responsible for the Electrone's demise. Even so, the controllers acted from instinct and calls were already being made to scramble the SAR Sea King helicopter. The QRA C-130 tanker would follow shortly equipped with multi seat life rafts and, if they were needed, would drop them into the water. Little did anyone know that one Sea King was already engaged on more macabre duties. In the Phantoms, the crews watched, fascinated, as the smoking surveillance plane lost height rapidly. It was the ultimate irony but having prompted the "emergency" their role under international conventions was now to act as scene of search coordinators until help arrived at the crash scene. And a crash was inevitable. Sitting well back, one on each wing, they followed the stricken aircraft in loose trail as it descended towards the sea.

*

Back over East Falkland, Carmendez jinked back onto track easing ever lower. Having thrown off the Phantom he had hugged the lower slopes of Mount Challenger skirting south of Two Sisters before cranking hard left through the gap to the west of Sapper Hill. His target lay at the extreme end of the town and he wanted a straight run in down Moody Brook and along the line of the road into the Capital. His initial point was very close to his target where the road crossed the neck of the valley. Short of attacking from the east which would put him very close to the defences around the RAF base, he had no choice. Timing was not critical and he would adapt. As he pulled hard around the small hill he looked ahead for his lead-in feature. There it was. He straighten up checked the heading – 092 degrees – and made his switches live. The bombs were armed and he was committed. He clenched his teeth and looked ahead through the sight glass.

CHAPTER 45

HERITAGE HALL, PORT STANLEY

The Community Centre and Conference facility was built towards the edge of town on the road to Moody Barracks to celebrate the Liberation of the Islands. Its location was not a coincidence as it was the same road that saw Argentinian troops march into the Capital on that dark day in 1982. Since it rose from the peat it provided a focus for the emerging importance of the Falkland Islands Legislative Council. The conflict brought an added emphasis and urgency to the daily workings of the institution and with a constant stream of visitors from the UK, remarkably lacking in the years before, the Council needed somewhere slightly more modern than the Town Hall in which to host meetings. Constructed of pristine new brick which had been imported through the new deep water facility at Mare Harbour the materials had been trucked down the new road to Stanley. The smart modern image was a source of pride to the residents. The frontal road snaked along Ross Road alongside Stanley Harbour leading to the impressive portico in front of the building. With its smoked glass entrance hall and imposing flagpoles it was a stunning example of the new vibrancy and optimism and a stark contrast in style to the old buildings which flanked the road. Some more traditional residents called it "The Carbuncle" but, secretly, held a strong sense of pride in the new identity.

Inside the conference room in Heritage Hall, officials sat around the long mahogany table, the meeting well underway. The positions of the attendees said much. On one side, the British Minister was flanked by the

Commander of British Forces, Falkland Islands. Seated opposite, the Governor was alongside the Leader of the Legislative Council on his right. The atmosphere was cordial but the fact that the Governor had chosen to join the islanders was not lost on the visitors. It sent a powerful message about loyalties despite his sinister yet unspoken brief.

"It's not for us to take decisions today", explained the Governor, "rather to lay out a series of potential options. Let's be clear, Sovereignty is not up for negotiation and the Prime Minister has been forthright about the Government's views. The wishes of the people are paramount. That may, or may not, dictate how Buenos Aires views the negotiations."

"I'm pleased to hear that" replied the Head of the Council. "You know our position here. I can, categorically, state that the residents would not countenance any actions which show weakness in our resolve. We are British and wish to remain so."

"You can rest assured on that issue", said the Minister. "It is not London's intent to impose any policy which would transfer rights away from the Council nor is it to follow any path which does not reflect your vision for the future. The Prime Minister asked me to make that crystal clear. Our concern is to place the future financial strategy on an affordable path and ensure that you remain protected and able to exercise your democratic rights."

"I'm grateful for the Prime Minister's reassurance, Minister. I understand the need for financial constraint but none of us would wish to see the economic trauma inflicted on us by the Argentinians repeated, would we?"

Heads nodded along the length of the table and the Minister felt slightly anxious at the sudden, collective scrutiny.

"Assuredly so. Our thrust should be to see where we can build bridges and to establish links again with the mainland where possible and prudent. Although Brazil has to be seen to favour their South American neighbour in public, we are hearing reassuring noises that they will show rather more tolerance in private. We all know that Chile will be positively enthusiastic and will set up air links at the earliest opportunity once Mount Pleasant is commissioned. With scheduled flights to UK beginning as we speak it won't be long before LAN Chile is operating a scheduled link to the mainland. The new harbour is already allowing much better capacity via the sea lanes. It is more than able to take a container vessel which will revolutionise the economics. Once MPA is complete we can reallocate capacity to facilitate imports for the islanders."

The posturing continued at a tedious pace as minor officials were invited to outline potential strategies. Despite the importance of the discussion, in the warm and comfortable venue, heads began to nod.

*

Carmendez made a final check. Master arm switch to *"Live"*, bombs selected and ready, fuel checked. The pipper in the gunsight jumped as he uncaged the sight and it began to gyrate gently in concert with his pressure on the control column. If he had been about to attack the military headquarters he would have been well short of his goal. The fact was he had decided against the military option, choosing instead a softer target. He could see the houses of the Capital in the distance which he reckoned were just beyond his target but he would pull off before then. The road ran along the shoreline and somewhere to the right of it would be Heritage House. There it was. His real goal was the Conference Centre packed with Government officials and, more importantly, a British Minister.

The brand new building stood out against the older houses with their colourful tin roofs and he caught a glint of reflected sunlight from a window which picked it out. He eased the stick gently right lining up the predicted impact line with his target. He sensed the tiny building beginning to grow in the gunsight. Moving the pipper onto the impact point he refined his aim waiting for the precise moment to release the weapons. At the point when he could no longer resist the desire to bunt forward, the release cue flashed briefly and he pickled the bombs. A glance down; two bombs away and the lights extinguished. Damn; he'd had a hang-up. He squeezed the trigger again prompting the third weapon to leave the jet milliseconds after the first two. With the ground growing too large for comfort he pulled back sharply on the stick pulling out from the steepening dive. The Skyhawk grazed the rooftops its jet efflux throwing up debris and began to climb away. He admonished himself. It was a rookie mistake. He had nearly left it too late to recover.

*

As the meeting broke for coffee officials left the room to make hurried phone calls before the summit resumed. The Governor and the Minister poured drinks before moving off into the corner for a brief but private huddle. Quiet conversations resumed around the table as private agendas were pursued. Dialogue was suddenly disrupted by the sound of a low flying jet which passed at high speed and, obviously, very low level overhead the Hall. The military commander winced visibly and rose from his seat, apparently seeking out a telephone. He would be asking questions very soon. Officials were used to the sound of jet noise and Phantoms tracking noisily down Stanley Harbour were a daily occurrence. The piercing squeal which split the quiet of the room was much different and the looks on the faces around the table registered surprise. No one predicted what was to follow.

The two 500 lb bombs found their mark. As they struck the western wall of the hall the contact fuses triggered blowing the structure apart. The wall collapsed removing the support for the roof which followed immediately. Minor officials who had moved into the offices at that end of the building to make their calls were killed instantly. Some died as a result of the blast from the huge explosions but others were crushed by the massive weight of the roof beams which collapsed into the void. The domino effect as the internal walls collapsed like a pack of cards destroyed the integrity of the structure and it was reduced to rubble. The conference room at the eastern end of the building escaped the worst of the damage but was still devastated. The thin internal wall succumbed to the blast which ripped through the remaining structure, shattering instantly and turning into hundreds of small wooden spears which radiated outwards from the core. The main wall of the conference room was more substantial and built with breeze blocks but it was still not strong enough to withstand the force of the blast. As the shock wave drove, inexorably, along the building internal walls were flattened causing yet more destruction. The blast upended the heavy mahogany table which only moments before had been the centrepiece of the room. It probably saved the lives of the Governor and the Minister as it skewed across the floor setting up a temporary barrier shielding them from the blast. Anyone standing upright managed to do so for just a few brief seconds before being thrown around like rag dolls. In the corner, the VIPs had dropped to the floor as the shrapnel flew over their heads peppering the wall behind.

Although the blast lasted mere seconds, to those caught up in the ferocity it seemed like hours. As the dust and debris subsided there was an eerie calm split only by the hiss of escaping water. What had been a bustling conference venue minutes before had been transformed into a massacre. An internal alarm sounded feebly but its warning was wasted on the stunned survivors. Within minutes the sound of the siren of the local fire engine could be heard rushing down Ross Road towards the shattered building. Telephones around town were already ringing and the local telephone exchange was saturated.

Governor Chilton had taken the full force of a flying breeze block square in the chest before being bowled over. The impact had crushed a number of ribs one of which had penetrated his lung. His laboured breathing was evidence of the severity of his injuries and, although he was alive, the trauma might yet prove fatal unless he received rapid treatment.

Peering through the dust and mayhem the Minister could see nothing at first. He pulled himself to his feet, remarkably uninjured, and looked at the chaos around him, unconsciously brushing his sleeve trying to remove the brick dust which had covered him. It was a futile attempt and his action had been habit rather than a rational attempt to improve his appearance. In a quiet moment later, he would feel a little embarrassment at his vanity. Moving over to one of the delegates who lay sobbing on the floor he could see that she had been badly cut by the flying glass and he blanched at the sight of her shattered limbs that would be, forever, disfigured. Snatching up a bottle of water which had been thrown from the table he offered her a drink as he cradled her head. It was a feeble response and for the first time in many years he felt utterly powerless. Despite her wounds she would heal and would survive. She was one of the lucky ones. Looking across the room his eyes fell on a decapitated corpse and he, involuntarily, shuddered at the swift and unexpected fate of the victim. That corpse had only minutes before been thinking about what to serve for dinner or putting together a shopping list. He had been more fortunate.

*

Carmendez pulled off target climbing to 500 feet above the harbour and made his second mistake. The third bomb which had left the Skyhawk moments after the first, had dropped long, falling into the midst of the houses next to Heritage Hall. With its fuse set to airburst, the case of the bomb had shattered before it struck the ground spreading tiny shards of deadly shrapnel across the residential buildings. The small but lethal projectiles ripped through the thin walls of the houses acting like mini bullets. Designed to destroy armoured military targets the thin walls and tin roofs were no barrier and the destruction was instant.

Stephen Lucking was sitting at the kitchen table, drinking his tea as he had done every day for the last 20 years. He died without fanfare, never knowing why he had become a pawn in the intrigue of international politics. His immediate neighbours, fortunately visiting friends at the other end of town, would return to find their home destroyed. Further along the street another shard passed through the cabin of a parked Land Rover lodging in the engine block and ensuring that the truck would never drive into Stanley again. The quiet suburb of Port Stanley had become a war zone once more.

Smoke rose from the bomb site marking a second funeral pall in just a few minutes.

CHAPTER 46

BLACK EAGLE CAMP, OUTSIDE RAF STANLEY

At the deployed site close to the airfield, the fire unit commander had been listening on the air defence control frequency, riveted by the radio calls from the Phantom crews as they engaged. Astonishment followed the controller's call on frequency when the intruder had been declared hostile and he could see from their reactions that the other gunners were equally amazed and tense. Professionalism had quickly reasserted itself. Looking west towards the Capital from the elevated hide, he caught site of a fast jet hugging the coastline along Stanley Harbour. With a glance at the Rapier control unit he looked for a tell-tale friendly identification from the IFF interrogator, immediately switching back to the target not wanting to lose sight. Nothing! Barking a quick command he prompted his team back to their positions raising the pointing stick allocating the target to the gunner now hunched over the tracker. The controller up the hill at Mount Kent rattled instructions in his ear and he struggled to assimilate both sources of information. As he stared at the jet it straightened up and seemed to hold a steady course for a short moment. He could have sworn he saw something drop from underneath but the pressure of the engagement took priority. This was no time for diversions. The weaving fighter pulled up coming clear of the urban sprawl and standing out against the background. Suddenly, framed against the hills behind, the jinking Skyhawk made an easy target sweetening the shot for the gunner at the pedestal. He momentarily reflected on the magnitude of his instructions before training kicked back in and he dropped into the familiar pattern of actions which had been instilled in his brain through the years of training.

"Target hostile, we are clear to engage, fire at will." His voice sounded alien. "Single target, follow my cue."

The gunner stared through the optical tracking unit. The pointing stick had given him a coarse search bearing and he began a methodical search in elevation to acquire the Skyhawk which had steadied up on its egress heading. He quickly located it and switched to track mode refining the picture tweaking the joystick on his control station to bring the fleeing jet into his crosshairs. The fire unit slewed around on its pedestal and the four Rapier missiles, strapped onto the launchers, two per side, elevated, pointing at the distant quarry. One final check of the IFF warning light which remained out. The gunner hit the firing button. It had been less than 10 seconds since he had been given the crazy command to fire but it seemed like an age as he refined the solution. The missiles, still on the launcher, tracked the outbound Skyhawk inexorably. There was a brief pause before a loud crack split the air and the firing sequence initiated. A gout of flame erupted from the rear of the lower missile turning into a plume of smoke as the missile sped away from the launcher gaining height in seconds. It followed a snaking corkscrew path as it sped towards its target, tiny flares at the rear just visible to the trained eye. A TV tracker on the fire unit followed those tiny flares which had fired up on the base of the missile as it followed its course. Computers in the fire unit calculated the difference between the line of sight to the receding target and the position of the missile in space. Electronic commands sent via the data link refined its trajectory causing the corkscrew to intensify. As the operator refined his tracking solution using the stubby joystick, the missile flew into the tracking beam still closing rapidly on its target. The time of flight was short given that the missile was, by now, travelling at twice the speed of sound and the target was only three miles away. With a virtually straight and level flight path the operator kept the crosshairs embedded on his prey easily. As the missile entered the end game, the contact fuse in the nose of the projectile, already armed, would detonate the small two kilogramme blast warhead once it struck the thin airframe.

*

There was a massive crash at the rear of the fuselage and Carmendez felt an immense and immediate shudder through the controls which suddenly stiffened. The master caution warning rang out through his headphones causing him to glance down at the central warning panel. It flashed, urgently, littered with red and amber captions and his heart sank. Such a collection of failures could only be bad news. His first thought was to push out a "MAYDAY" call so ingrained was the reaction, but having just dropped a weapon on the town below, he felt sure that he would not receive much support from the garrison that he had just attacked. His head swivelled around and could see damage to the wing where shrapnel from the missile's warhead had torn through the skin and ripped away the structure. Torn sections of metal were shaking manically in the airflow. Amazingly the warhead had failed to detonate fully or he would be history but he was worried about another noise he had detected. It emanated from the jet pipe area and, looking behind, he could see he was trailing smoke from below the wing. If fuel was escaping he had a potentially catastrophic combination. A quick check of the throttle and he could feel that he still had control over the engine so his thoughts turned to tackling the problems. The fuel gauge seemed steady so the pressing urgency was the amber "*HYD*" caption warning of major degradation to the hydraulic supplies for his control surfaces. Sensing the scale of the damage the trembling through the controls made more sense. At least he was still flying and, thankful for small mercies, he assessed the remaining captions, analysing the problems methodically. A red "*HYD*" would have been easy and he would already have been pulling the ejection seat handle as the controls froze, starved of the vital hydraulic fluid. Even so, the precious fluid might still be venting overboard. Another flash of the master caution light caught his eye as the generator caption flashed intermittently before coming on permanently. A further complication. What little spare capacity he had was now slowly ebbing away as the electrical services placed an impossible load on the tiny battery deep in the guts of the jet. He began to load-shed getting rid of all but the essential electric-powered services. He was not quite ready to turn off the radio yet as that was his final link with the unfriendly world outside but he was reaching the point where, even if he could diagnose the problems, there would be a limit to what he could do to recover the situation. Unless he got on the ground quickly the decisions would be taken for him and one thing was certain; this jet would not be making the trip back west towards the mainland.

He would need the hook as, with the jet in this parlous state, he would be taking the approach end cable. While he still had utility pressure he would get that action out of the way, even though it should release and lower under the effect of gravity. He slapped the lever hard downwards and saw a reassuring glow from the illuminated handle. What other choices might he have? He could eject leaving his fate to the manufacturer of the "bang seat" or he could try to put this thing on the ground. Hobson's choice and, either way, his reception committee would be hostile. Glancing out of the cockpit he could see the metal runway at Stanley up ahead inviting him to drop in and it crystallised his thoughts. With the wind behind him, the controls were becoming more sluggish by the minute and, as the speed dropped off and handling became ever more difficult, he would not have the luxury of flying a circuit to bring his crippled jet back into wind for the approach. He would commit to a downwind landing. Turning towards the closest threshold of the airstrip he eased into a slow descent struggling with the reluctant jet, coaxing it towards the ground and safety. The cable stretching across the runway looked inviting and would be his salvation.

*

Razor dropped the right wing and looked down at the Skyhawk trailing a thin plume of smoke in its wake. The Rapier crew had called the engagement on the air defence frequency and the flash as the missile had found its mark had been visible even from his lofty perch, high above the MEZ.

"Puffin, Eagle 1 going to Stanley Tower."

"Give me Stud 1, Flash."

Not waiting for the acknowledgement from the controller, the back seater switched to the air traffic control frequency.

"Stud 1's up!"

"Tower, Eagle 1 on frequency. Holding in the overhead and Tally with the bogey."

"Eagle 1, loud and clear."

The controller's response sounded slightly frenetic.

"He's long finals and he's taken a hit and smoking. Looks like he'll be taking the downwind cable. Are you speaking to him?" said Razor.

"Negative Eagle 1. I see him and I confirm his hook is down."

"Roger, I have 15 minutes to chicken fuel. I'll land back into the approach end cable once you've pulled him clear."

"Eagle 1, roger. I'll get onto arrestor and chase them up. Call you back."

The intensity of the smoke trail increased as the pilot struggled with the crippled aircraft, the power increasing to hold the approach angle. Even though he had just tried to destroy the Skyhawk he empathised with the struggle. If he was to survive, the Argentinian needed to get the jet down on the ground; and quickly. The urge to stay with the jet would be strong but, sometimes, a "Martin Baker Letdown" might be the smarter option. There were still four Phantoms airborne and Razor's fuel gauge was dropping visibly. His own wingman had been heavily engaged with the Mirage and couldn't be far behind, probably also on fumes. He was damned if he'd divert to the mainland if the Argentinian pilot blocked the runway. They could bulldoze the Skyhawk off the strip if needed. Trimming the throttles back to save fuel he watched with a morbid fascination as the jet approached the threshold.

The local controller trained his binoculars on the crippled jet. At this stage of an approach, he would normally be giving clearance to land but, without contact with the Skyhawk pilot, he was reduced to the role of casual observer. He swung the binoculars towards the fire section seeing blue lights already flashing on the tenders, the fire crews fanning out from the doorway climbing aboard the emergency vehicles. He held off for a few final moments knowing that a cable engagement was inevitable before hitting the crash alarm prompting an instantaneous wailing over the public address system.

"Put out a crash warning," he barked at the air traffic assistant.

Across the airfield, the unexpected visitor lurched, drunkenly, over the threshold before crashing onto the metal planking of the runway. The hook scraped the metallic surface generating a shower of sparks behind the jet pipe before catching the wire and pulling it from the massive rotary hydraulic drums at the edge of the runway. As it paid out, the coarse fabric tape attached to the arrestor cable shimmied as it bounced on the runway surface, a visible sign that the hook had made contact. The Skyhawk dipped forward on its nose oleo as the retardation took effect, slewing off line towards the side of the runway, drawing rapidly to a halt. Fire engines careered down the runway, bearing down on the smoking airframe. As they pulled to a stop, clustering around the jet, hoses reeled out and a plume of water and foam issued from the nozzles covering the shattered airframe, dousing the flames.

"Tower, he's in the cable but this could take some time," called the fire chief over the radio.

Razor took another look at his slowly reducing fuel contents and winced.

"Roger Tower, can you scramble "Albert" to top me off? And a message to my operators; we're Zulu 20 and we'll need overstress checks on the ground. Best they get a new jet on Q!"

"Roger, I'll pass that to Eagle Ops," replied the harried local controller.

There was a scene of utter confusion around the Argentinian combat jet. The water which was spreading in a huge arc around the airframe made the metal surface of the runway slippery. Technicians held back waiting for clearance from the fire chief to approach the hulk. Firemen struggling with high pressure hoses trained a stream of foam onto the airframe masking the shattered wingtip where the missile had impacted. An RAF Police Land Rover had pulled alongside, its blue flashing beacon adding to the air of chaos, its occupants waiting for the moment. The massive fire tenders, toned-down with green paint rather than the vivid reds or yellows of their civilian counterparts, masked the view from the control tower prompting a constant stream of questions from a nervous local controller. As the foam was washed off by the constant jet of water, the gashes from the missile warhead re-emerged, clearly visible along the fuselage and wing sections, pock-marking the surface. The jet would never fly again. Underneath the wings the bomb racks were eerily empty with one exception. A single Mk82 bomb still hung from a pylon. Whether it was a misfire or had been saved for another more sinister purpose was a question for later. At least it would not wreak further havoc.

In the cockpit Carmendez allowed the stress to dissipate and closed down. His fleeting thought after all the concerns over fuel was that he had engaged the cable with enough in the tanks to return to Argentina. It was a bitter irony. That he had just ended many lives was not on his mind at that moment. He stood up and pulled off his flying helmet, glancing nervously around, devoid of the usual swagger. There were no steps to assist his exit and he made his way tentatively over the fuselage behind the cockpit dropping down onto the upper surface of the wing, ungainly as he lowered his feet onto the external fuel tank. Turning, he grabbed the leading edge easing himself carefully to the ground where he was grabbed, unceremoniously, by the waiting military policemen. His flying days were over. Handcuffed and bundled roughly into the rear compartment of the waiting land Rover he was joined by two armed guards ensuring any vain thoughts of escape were quickly dispelled. The Police vehicle took off at speed picking up an escort as it cleared the active runway its blue light flashing away, marking its progress.

There was a frantic urgency as the recovery crew eased the tension on the arrestor cable and it fell clear of the hook. The cable began to retract back into the massive hydraulic drums alongside the runway, a technician at the control box alongside the runway monitoring its progress. A towing arm was connected to the nosewheel of the Skyhawk but the bulldozer which waited on the access track, its engine idling noisily, left no doubts that this jet would be moved clear by force if necessary. Overhead the jet noise emphasised the pressure on the team. Unnoticed, an armourer plugged a safety pin into the bomb rack making sure that the live weapon, which still hung menacingly on the pylon would remain fast. It might still be armed and it was certainly still lethal but he would make it safe once the jet was clear of the runway. More importantly, a Provost Marshall officer had already spoken quietly in the armourer's ear giving firm direction and was now directing a photographer who snapped shots of the ominous load. The pictures would find their way into evidence in a forthcoming trial. The presence of the weapon on the jet graphic proof of the facts that would probably consign the pilot to prison.

In a touch of irony, a captured Argentinian Unimog utility vehicle revved its engine taking the strain on the tow bar and began to pull the Skyhawk along the metal matting. The short run to the access taxiway was rapid and the still smoking jet turned off on its final journey to an isolated dispersal where the weapon would be made safe. Its future was as evidence in a court case rather than the operational mission intended by its designer. At best it might find its way to a museum as a grizzly exhibit.

In the overhead, a second Phantom joined the first and they droned around the pattern waiting for their own chance to use the arrestor system. The pilots were eking out the precious fuel and the moment the runway was clear they would land. The option of diverting to the mainland was one to be avoided given, undoubtedly, heightened tensions which the events of the last hour would have caused. There had been enough missiles expended today and they had no wish to test their procedures for diverting to the bolthole in Chile. As the recovery crew worked frantically a second pair of Phantoms broke into the circuit before climbing up to join their playmates in the holding pattern adding to the stress on the ground. The recovery team would be hard pressed to land four on in quick succession with the clock ticking. If they could not clear the runway soon the C-130 which was holding at the far threshold would be launched to top-off some thirsty Phantoms.

*

The Land Rover pulled up at the RAF Police Headquarters and a bedraggled figure, still wearing flying gear, was manhandled from the vehicle and ushered inside.

CHAPTER 47

THE HOSPITAL, PORT STANLEY

The toned down military ambulance with its gaudy red crosses on white circles emblazoned along the side idled outside the hospital in Port Stanley the rear doors wide open waiting for its passenger. In a cruel twist of fate, the King Edward Memorial Hospital had been destroyed by fire just months before and the makeshift facility left much to be desired. As the doors of the hospital pushed open, a trolley emerged flanked by a fraught military medical team, out of place in their camouflaged uniforms. Other hospital staff clustered around the entrance, watching silently as the trolley was pushed towards the waiting vehicle. The Governor looked pale and, clearly sedated, was unable to acknowledge the well wishers. The decisions had been taken rapidly with the temporary facilities hopelessly inadequate for such casualties and a transfer to the military hospital offered little better prospects. With the extent of his injuries, it was touch-and-go whether he would survive the trip back to the UK.

Hurried phone calls to the military headquarters had put on hold the departing airbridge flight and the waiting jet was being reconfigured for its priority passenger. Protesting travellers had been warned of a 24 hour delay to their repatriation as space was made for the emergency traveller. Back at the hospital door, the Governor's wife spoke quietly to a doctor as she too watched the trolley being lifted aboard. She would ride in the military staff car which would accompany the ambulance for its short trip to Mount Pleasant.

As it pulled away along St Mary's Road a small knot of well wishers doffed their hats watching silently as the ambulance begin its journey. As it turned left along Reservoir Road the street was lined with islanders who burst into a spontaneous but muted ripple of applause waving Union flags. The ambulance picked up speed joining Darwin Road, making its way towards the Ring Road.

In the staff car, the Governor's wife dabbed at her eye as she waved goodbye to people she had come to see as friends, her life inexplicably transformed in just hours. She could not rid herself of the disturbing air of a funeral cortege rather than a flight home to England. The familiar landmarks passed the window and, feeling an overwhelming regret that she was leaving after such a relatively short time, she gazed sadly at the ambulance ahead. Despite the austerity, Port Stanley had been kind to them and she was leaving behind genuine friends. It would be hard to stay in touch given the gulf in geography between the two countries but she would try.

The small convoy accelerated as it headed westwards along the main road to the airfield. Normally a 30 minute journey, the delicate condition of its passenger would mean this run would take a little longer than normal. The driver winced as he hit the inevitable pothole. It would not be the last he would hit along the short stretch of road.

*

Officials in Whitehall and Port Stanley had already reacted to events and communications circuits chattered as highly classified signals began to be exchanged. With media reports making headlines in London, diplomats in Buenos Aires had not been spared and harassed staff were preparing defensive briefings to explain the presence of a combat aircraft on the airfield at RAF Stanley.

It would be a long day and an even longer night.

CHAPTER 48

MOUNT PLEASANT AIRFIELD, EAST FALKLAND

The convoy turned off the main road and entered the military complex at Mount Pleasant. Word of events had travelled fast and groups of servicemen snapped to attention saluting the vehicle as it passed, registering their solidarity. The Governor had been popular with the troops and they were determined to acknowledge his sacrifice. The ambulance moved across the large dispersal towards the waiting Tristar, spared the usual trauma of a military check in procedure. Its passenger would receive special treatment and be sensitively handled throughout the forthcoming journey. The stretcher, festooned with drip bags and other medical apparatus, would ease the stress of the flight somewhat but, at best, Sir Ronald Chilton would be a long time in rehabilitation and would, certainly, never return to the islands. At worst, he might not survive the long voyage across the world. His vision, or rather his masters' vision, for a future linked to Argentina had evaporated at the precise moment that fateful bomb had been dropped from the Skyhawk. Unbeknown to the staff who fussed around the gurney, a replacement Governor had already been nominated and he was known to be much more traditional and conservative in his views.

The forward passenger door of the Tristar freighter, specially fitted out for the medevac. duties, was open allowing the stretcher to be eased gently aboard taking its place in the gap created by the swift removal of rows of seats. As the passengers filed back onboard led by the Defence Minister, homeward bound at last, few could avoid a surreptitious sideways glance at the patient on the stretcher. They had heard the local news reports broadcast on the British Forces network but here was the graphic illustration of the horrors of the unprovoked attack on the Capital.

With the remaining passengers loaded and its engines whining, the Tristar eased away from the Air Terminal and began the long taxy to the easterly holding point of the main runway. It would take off to the west but, far from heading towards the mainland, it would turn north easterly for the long leg towards its interim stop at Ascension Island. A short turnaround to refuel would see it carry on to the UK with minimal delay. With a casualty onboard normal procedures were expedited without question. Within 24 hours it would span the globe and deliver its cargo to the waiting medical teams at RAF Brize Norton where the Governor would be handed off to a specialist trauma team.

Established in the climb, the crew in the cockpit of the airliner settled down for the long flight. The pilots released the cabin crew to begin serving coffee, although, unlike a normal airline service, pre dinner drinks were less alcoholic than the norm. As the altimeter spun upwards through 5000 feet, four Phantoms pulled up from below the wing line and slotted into close formation, two on each wingtip. In a gesture of defiance they held station for a short time, their weapons easily visible from the cabin windows. With the runway now clear but events in flux, there would be no further risks taken. The fighters would not leave their charge until it was safely out of range of the islands and well on its way to Ascension Island. On the ground, radar controllers scanned the airspace for pop-up contacts. This was one flight which would not be caught unawares.

As the navigation system registered the airliner's departure from the Falkland Islands Protection Zone, the outer pair eased out before pulling up and rolling away from the Tristar in a dramatic flourish, leaving a single Phantom on each wingtip. The departing pair set up a combat air patrol searching to the west scanning the empty skies, guarding the departure route. They would stay there for as long as the fuel permitted.

In the cabin, the manoeuvres prompted an enthusiastic dialogue amongst the passengers but were lost on the Governor, his breathing laboured and his cheeks pallid. His wife whispered quietly in his ear giving him a running commentary of events outside, even if it would only ever register in his subconscious.

*

The convoy conveying the Governor to the airport had not been the only one to drive along the rough Stanley highway that day. Earlier, two military utility vehicles had rattled along its graded surface led by a military police Land Rover. In the back of the leading vehicles the coffins were laid out in stark rows, the simple gold plaques identifying the innocent victims. A single coffin lay alone in the rear of the last vehicle carrying the body of Karen Pilkington the only British casualty of the attack on the bus. Her trip home would be a poignant contrast to her arrival. The Union Flag covering the casket seemed incongruous in the makeshift hearse.

A LAN Chile Boeing 737 charter flight had shared the ramp with the Tristar airbridge aircraft for most of the day and was being prepared for its flight. The passengers on the return trip would be somewhat more subdued than the eager tourists who had disembarked some hours before. Their itinerary visiting nature reserves and wildlife colonies offered fun and escape but within minutes, the survivors of the attack on the coach would be emplaned for their short but sombre flight back to Rio Gallegos. The blinds in the departures terminal had been drawn closed as a mark of respect as the solemn procession had passed. As the convoy entered the apron it had separated, the majority of the vehicles moving slowly towards the Boeing, only a single vehicle breaking out and heading towards the Tristar before pulling up alongside the open doors of the baggage holds. Without ceremony but with dignity, the coffins were loaded aboard the respective aircraft for their journeys home. The sole escorts snapped to attention and saluted as each coffin disappeared into the hold. From the windows of the Tristar a few passengers watched the sad cargo being loaded, silently offering their own contemplative eulogies.

CHAPTER 49

PORT STANLEY JAIL

As Carmendez was led in handcuffs from Port Stanley Jail towards the car which was waiting to take him to the Courtroom, he glanced at the sandwich board outside the store opposite. The headline in the Penguin News was stark:

"Rogue Attack by Argentinian Aircraft. Twenty tourists killed. Heritage Hall destroyed."

This was his first inkling of the consequences of his actions and it was not the way he had intended it to be. How had he managed to get it so wrong? The headline should have said Government Minister killed in daring attack instead of the bleak suggestion of cold-blooded murder. There could be no leniency and a charge of murder seemed inevitable, even to him. His accusers would struggle to interpret the facts unless the military authorities released the information about his mission but he suspected that justice would be transparent here. With the facts from the radar units and the fighter jets on record his actions would be glaringly obvious and his fate assured.

He was roughly bundled into the van, his treatment becoming less civil as the details of his alleged crime had filtered out to the security forces. Although he was facing a civilian trial his escorts were military policemen and were somewhat less accommodating than their civilian counterparts. The handcuffs were backed up by 9mm Browning pistols. His treatment might be fair but it would not be polite.

As the van moved off he could sense the accusatory looks from people ranged along the road. No smoked windows in a Black Mariah for him. The small cluster of reporters had easy access as the vehicle pulled away and the cameras snapped incessantly through the windows adding to his feeling of vulnerability. It was a short journey from the Police Station to the Town Hall which housed the courtroom and the locals had turned out in force. For the first time he began to appreciate the protective custody and he suspected his reception on the streets might be somewhat more hostile if left to his own devices. Within the hour he would know his fate and it did not seem attractive.

The Land Rover pulled up at the courtroom where more armed guards waited, this time porting Sterling sub-machine guns. The vehicle door banged open noisily as he was bundled out and ushered in through the rear doors.

CHAPTER 50

MI6 HEADQUARTERS, CENTURY HOUSE, LONDON

The patrician figure adjusted the knot in his tie and smoothed down the tails of his impeccably tailored Savile Row suit, easing himself gently into the captain's chair behind the imposing mahogany desk. He had considered his words carefully and there must be no ambiguity. Nuance across an open phone line was impossible and his agent in Port Stanley would need to understand his instructions implicitly. The discussions with the Prime Minister had been tense and, as always, the politician had been worse than useless in offering guidance. At the first hint of a scandal, they took the line of least resistance and it would be left to him to resolve the mess, as he had expected. Cradling the phone he fussed with a paperweight listening to the clicks on the line as the call was routed via a maze of exchanges between London and Port Stanley. A familiar voice answered but the exchange of words, if it could be described as such, was brief.

"Warren? Good to speak to you. I've been keeping up with events at your end. Things have moved rapidly, have they not? Can I assume you took care of our minor irritation?

He listened, his response rather more edgy than he intended. He had a rehearsed line and would not be diverted by excuses. Maybe that was one skill he had learned from his political masters.

"Unfortunately, it would seem we have rather too many loose ends. I think we need to consider a more permanent solution."

He frowned at the negative response from his operative on the distant islands. His carefully crafted direction was being misconstrued and he felt uncomfortable. Whatever the events in Stanley, he could find out later and, in any event, this was far too frank a discussion for an open line. It just was not like Baird to be quite so unreceptive.

"I'm well aware of that but if it's found that there is a case to answer, and let's face it, it's rather obvious given the press headlines, then the judge will have no option but to send the hearing to a higher court. They're not equipped to hear cases of such gravity in Stanley. After all, we're talking about a murder and we all know what that would mean if it comes to the High Court in London. Imagine the feeding frenzy it would generate amongst the media. I know our relations with Buenos Aries are less than stellar but imagine the impact of sentencing one of their military and not even following military protocol. No, the position would be intolerable and the Press would have a field day, Old Chap. Not something I could countenance."

It was drifting into discussion rather than the sharp directive he had intended to issue. His man in Stanley seemed to think that this might be a conversation. The look on his face betrayed his increasing disquiet and his response was, undeniably, curt.

"The loose ends; do tidy them up!"

The message seemed to be sinking home, finally, and there was a distinct lull in the exchange. Anxious to end the call, he framed his reply extremely carefully but precisely.

"I think you follow my meaning. I don't want that pilot appearing in the High Court in London *under any circumstances*. I'll leave it with you. I'm sure you understand."

He pressed the button on the cradle disconnecting the call.

"Marjorie, could you come in please. I'd like to sent a note to Number 10."

CHAPTER 51

THE MAGISTRATE'S COURT, PORT STANLEY

The Town Hall served as the Post Office, the Falkland Islands Court of Law and even as a dance hall and was home to the only resident Magistrate. His normal legal fare was to adjudicate on whether an errant islander was guilty of the occasional traffic offence or, maybe, to provide arbitration in a neighbourhood dispute. His diet was uncontroversial with a charge of murder almost unique in the islands' history and the complexity was taxing his legal abilities. He had already spent some time on the phone to an old colleague from student days in London, tapping his expertise on recent precedents. With the clock showing he was already five minutes late for the allotted hearing he donned his robes and made his way to the courtroom.

The lawyers, or what passed for lawyers in this tiny law abiding community, had set the scene succinctly. From his bench at the head of the Court he listened to the last of the witnesses, hastily assembled to appear before the opening hearing. His first task had been to establish identity and there could be no doubt that the pilot sitting before him was the culprit. He had, after all, been taken into custody as he climbed down the steps of the Argentinian jet which had landed, badly damaged, at Stanley airfield. He had quite arrogantly confirmed his identity in the chaotic aftermath and made no attempt at subterfuge now. Logically, there could be no confusion over who, or rather what, had been responsible for the carnage at Heritage Hall. The initial investigation by the Police had identified three impact craters; two in the Hall and a third in the street beyond. The weapon found hanging on the aircraft was compelling evidence. Not that it would influence his decision, but he was appalled at the apparent and total lack of remorse from the pilot. His demeanour seemed supercilious, almost egotistical. The video footage from the Rapier surface-to-air missile system had been presented on a hastily rigged video recorder and the grainy evidence with images of the offending jet being engaged over the Capital were reminiscent of the television footage from the conflict. Numerous eye witnesses had linked the jet to the attack on the Hall describing the camouflage scheme precisely. There could be no confusion between the Skyhawk and the resident Phantoms and a few had even seen the weapons leave the aircraft, although most had missed the precise moment of impact. Those that might have borne witness had perished. It took very little imagination to link events with the attack on the bus despite that fact that there were even fewer witnesses. A Phantom pilot had testified that he had seen the Argentinian Skyhawk in the vicinity and, given that the Phantoms did not carry bombs, that their cannons had not been fired and that the Harriers had long since returned to the UK, the list of potential aggressors was small. In his mind the two incidents were inextricably linked.

The Magistrate struggled to remain neutral given the appalling loss of life and the death of the local resident trapped in his house as fire raged around him was difficult to ignore or to forgive. He had known the man and he had not deserved to die in this way, an innocent party to what seemed to be a blatant act of revenge. The overriding principle must be that justice must be seen to be done, albeit, he might already be guilty of a degree of pre-judgement. The Press would latch onto any suggestion of prejudice and that would be his poison chalice. So far, the accused had been silent other than to confirm his identity. Whether he would be more forthcoming would be apparent very soon and an unfamiliar wave of trepidation washed over him as he offered the pilot the opportunity to speak.

The words of the Spanish interpreter chattered in unison and he listened carefully to the apparent tirade. The motivation for the attack was becoming clearer and it would complicate matters further. What unfolded was a tale of injustice and nationalism which would undoubtedly fall on biased ears in the Island's Court. At times he wondered why this small outcrop of rocks in the South Atlantic raised such jingoistic passions. Inevitably, the rhetoric made his course of action easier to determine and he took little time to reach his decision. His gavel sounded harsh and disturbed the Clerk of the Court from his apparent reverie.

"The accused will rise."

The words seemed detached.

"Having heard the facts before me I am convinced there is a case to answer. I am firmly of the opinion that the severity of these matters is well beyond my jurisdiction nor do I feel you would receive an unbiased hearing on these islands."

At least it was out and in the public domain.

"The allegations are too controversial and will provoke emotions that would be hard to control in this small and law-abiding community. I rule, therefore, that the case be transferred to the High Court in London for trial before a jury. I will seek a date for the hearing. You will be flown to the United Kingdom at the earliest opportunity; Court is adjourned."

"All rise," said the Clerk of the Court and chairs scraped back in unison.

With the Magistrate framed by the Royal Coat of Arms on the wall of the courtroom, Carmendez, who felt slightly purged after his oratory, finally appreciated the severity of his plight. With the Magistrate making his way back to his chambers and the Court officials beginning to disperse, the few reporters scuttled away to file their copy, eager to make the headlines with an exclusive. He was led out between the two heavy-set military policemen down the long flight of steps. The darkness of the stairwell was ominous.

Once alone, the Magistrate, divested of his official robes, pulled out a weighty legal volume flicking swiftly to a passage which he had barely consulted since his days at law school. He had more distant colleagues to consult and the process was unfamiliar. Hopefully, the phone lines from the island would not delay the vital negotiations. Such a case was unique in his jurisdiction but he was confident that the decision to refer the case to a higher court was the right one. It was a contingency he had contemplated many times over the years but little had he expected that it would occur with such controversy.

He picked up the phone waited patiently for the Cable and Wireless operator.

"A London number please."

CHAPTER 52

PORT STANLEY JAIL

Back in his cell in the small jail attached to the Police Station in Port Stanley, Carmendez lay on his bunk as he contemplated the events of the last few days. The unexpected decision by the judge to send him to London had unsettled him. Was it really only a few days since he had sat in his office and gone through the Operation Order? Events had moved rapidly once he had made up his mind and the irony of his plight was not lost on him. He had survived over 20 combat missions over the islands in 1982 and yet, here he was, incarcerated having been shot down by the very weapons he had successfully avoided in actual combat.

The impact of his actions on South Atlantic politics was undeniable. The attack had been dramatic and had made the headlines on the islands. He could have no doubt that he would have been headline news in Buenos Aires because even the smallest scuttlebutt concerning the islands was worth a few lines inside the tabloids. Something like this should have made the front pages. To make the front cover of the Penguin News had not exactly been the limit of his ambitions. He wondered whether those same headlines would be plastered over the broadsheets in London and the around the rest of the world.

Having flown combat for so many years and, honed by his time in the cockpit, he should have been able to penetrate the defences unscathed. He had no difficulty even now rationalising his motives and was convinced that had he made it back to Gallegos he would have found ample support for his actions. He struggled to work out where he had gone wrong executing his final mission. His recall of events as the sortie had unfolded was perfect and he was pleased by his performance but the attack on the bus had been hasty and ill considered. Those Argentinian families had not deserved to die and he would live with that rash decision for the rest of his life. He regretted the loss of life deeply. When he had made the fleeting contact as he had come around the valley he had assumed that the bus was the military transport carrying Government officials to the meeting. It would have been logical that they were on their way to the new airbase at Mount Pleasant where security was tighter and the facilities better suited. There were a few details that didn't yet add up and, since his arrest his captors were being tight lipped. How could he have possibly known about the memorial ceremony unless the intelligence officer back at Rio Gallegos had shared it with him? He could have expected that the analysts would read the newspapers from the islands. That would be reality versus speculation and it must have been reported at some stage, surely? On the other hand, if he was brutally clinical, the attack on Heritage Hall had been spectacular and totally effective as a statement of intent. His only regret was that he had hoped that only those involved in the political process would die. Many of the victims were islanders and some of the casualties had little time for politics. Their mistake had been to be in the wrong place at the wrong time. As the arguments went around in his head he realised that he had become immune to the consequences of hostilities and that the acceptance of casualties had become routine. Was he really that blasé about killing?

Broken from his deliberations he glanced over his shoulder, sensing a movement in the corridor. In the shadows he could just make out a figure visible in the dim light. He had been warned that he was locked in for the night and he was the only prisoner in the cells, so there should be no reason for anyone else to be in the building other than his jailer who had been silent for some time now. The movement was unexpected.

"Turn around and keep your eyes on the window," said the mystery visitor in muted Spanish. "If you don't do exactly as I say you'll regret a missed opportunity."

"Who are you?" he asked, feeling faintly embarrassed to be conversing with a stranger whilst locked away in a cell.

"You don't need to know that Carmendez, just listen. Outside the back door is a Land Rover. The keys are in the ignition. You know the way to Stanley Airfield I presume?"

"No. I wasn't exactly given a guided tour on my way here but I'm sure I could work it out easily enough I guess."

His inquisitor knew his name. Should that be a surprise or not? After all, he had become infamous rather quickly. The man, and it was clearly a male voice, continued unabated.

"There's a security checkpoint between Boxer Bridge and the technical site. You have no ID so I wouldn't recommend you try to get through it in the vehicle. Even though it's a military truck they carry out 100% checks and they're thorough, so don't think you might get lucky. Ditch the truck before you get to the checkpoint. It's only a short walk beyond that to the Air Terminal and there are always aircraft parked there overnight. There are mobile security patrols throughout the quiet hours so keep your wits about you. If you're to make an escape you'll need to have your story straight and work on your accent but I recommend you try to avoid being stopped. There aren't too many Spanish speakers around here anymore. If you're challenged, how about some tale of an emergency call-out to help an islander? FIGAS, the air service, uses Britten Norman Islanders for the local trips but it would be unusual to fly this late at night. There are sometimes medical emergencies which need an evacuation flight from a settlement in the small hours so it's not impossible. I'm sure you'll come up with something to seem convincing. Don't forget, with Phantoms on quick reaction alert there'll be someone in the control tower at all times so be discrete. With luck, they'll be downstairs and you'll have the engines started before they realise what's going on. You're a pilot I'll leave it up to you to decide how to get back to the mainland."

"But does the Islander have the range to get to the coastline?"

"As I said, you're the pilot so that's your problem. I've flown in it around the islands. It carries life vests and a dinghy but you know better than I about your survival chances if you ditch. Whichever way it goes, you'll be better off braving the South Atlantic than throwing yourself at the mercy of the High Court in London. Personally, I'd say your chances of avoiding a life sentence are quite slim if you choose the latter option. What do you think?"

The tone was harsh and accusatory.

"I've never flown an Islander before," replied Carmendez but his words were wasted. There was no reply. He risked a peek over his shoulder but as he turned around, the man had gone and the corridor was once again empty, the door to his cell ajar. Although taken aback at the turn of events, he wasted no time in accepting the opportunity and there might not be another one. He had not even heard the lock to his cell being opened but questioning the offer was far from his thoughts. Pushing against the heavy metal rungs of the door, a throwback to traditional cells, he made his way from the cell turning towards the rear of the building as he'd been instructed. The mysterious visitor had vanished and all was quiet. He risked a look back down the corridor but there was no movement from the duty desk at the front of the jail. As he moved silently towards the door he glanced around for signs of an alarm system. A fire alarm, or even worse, an intruder alarm going off at this time of night would end his escape before it was even underway. Nothing was immediately obvious and with nothing to lose he pushed the door latch on the outside door and it swung outwards into the large parking area adjacent to the building.

Outside the door sat the dark green Land Rover, exactly as his benefactor had promised. He moved quickly to the driver's side; damn these Brits for driving on the wrong side of the road. Sure enough, the keys were in the ignition and he hauled himself up into the cab looking around at the unfamiliar controls. With everything located he turned the key and the engine burst into life. He realised that he had flinched, involuntarily, as he turned the key, half expecting an explosion. So far this was all too good to be true but who the hell was his mystery patron? Reassured for the minute, he flipped on the headlights and gunned the throttle making sure to ease over to the left hand side of the road. That would be an instant give away if he drove on the wrong side, even in the darkened streets of the Capital. It would be an instant reason for someone to report him or, even worse, to be pulled over. Although the local policeman cum jailer was tucked up for the night, he had no idea how many military patrols would be on the streets looking for errant soldiers or airmen who might have over indulged in the local pub or decided to liberate a ride home. He looked across the car park towards the harbour and could see that the exit road to the sea front was jammed with vehicles. Although it was quiet around town at this late hour he wanted to avoid Ross Road. The coastal route was far too public so he steered towards the rear exit from the car park and made his way uphill out of town picking up Davies Road and heading east towards the airfield. As the truck made its way up the steep incline the diesel engine rattled in protest and heavy smoke poured from the cold exhaust pipe. The diesel fumes filtered into the cab competing with the fetid air from the heater which was just starting to blow warmer air across his legs. His unexpected departure meant he was ill-equipped for the cold and his clothes more suitable for a night in bed than the cold Falklands countryside. He had no idea at this stage how he would steal the aircraft but it was his only realistic option. There were unlikely to be any boats small enough for him to handle which could survive the 400 mile journey across the rough and treacherous waters of the South Atlantic and the oceans were no respecter of fools. He would have to be ready to fly before first light because there would be too much activity once the day shift clocked on at Stanley. The chances of getting to the aircraft unchallenged once the working day began would be negligible. He could get airborne safely and start the trip in the dark but he would need to take it carefully around those hills to the west. In the dark his chances over the flat terrain would be better but he would need a fallback in case the QRA Phantom was launched after him. With the massive difference in speeds it would not take long for it to run him down and if that happened his only option would be to duck and run. Maybe the northerly route, despite the hilly terrain, offered better odds of evading a pursuer. At least the moon was up. Once across the sea, if he made it that far, the passage would be easier. An islander would not show on primary radar once he coasted-out and he had no intention of helping by squawking on IFF. It would be a miracle if the Phantoms could find him in the open expanse of ocean if he could stay below the ground radar coverage and operate without lights. It would be good to make landfall on the mainland in the daylight. He vaguely remembered that the Islander had a range of about 800 miles, if it was fully fuelled and that should be more than enough to get to Rio Gallegos. Let's hope that figure was right or he might be taking an early dip in the sea and he was not too sure that the simple gear in an island hopper would be up to the job. The navigation equipment would be crude because the local pilots used mainly a map and stopwatch but he could hit the coast and head either north or south. He would quickly recognise a feature and be able to make his way to his home airfield. The islander could land in a field if it came to it; and it regularly did around here so that made it perfect for his purposes. He just hoped the keys to the aircraft were in the cockpit. If it was like any other small operation, hopefully they would. He wasn't sure he was up to the challenge of stealing a C-130, if not. He wasn't even sure if he would be able to start it up.

As he joined Airport Road he turned left and began the long drop back down towards Boxer Bridge which crossed the neck of the inlet in Stanley Harbour and on to the airfield. The dull streetlights barely illuminated the street and his headlights picked out the rough edge of the concrete road as he unconsciously eased towards the middle, uncomfortable with driving on the left. Putting a wheel off the side would probably mean that his walk to the Air Terminal would take quite a bit longer and he couldn't spare the time. Already faint signs of light were tingeing the horizon signalling an approaching dawn. Beyond the bridge he could see the lights of the airfield glinting in the darkness and he decided to dump the vehicle on the other side of the bridge and walk the remaining distance to the Airport Terminal bypassing the security post. He hoped he could avoid the minefields which still littered the area or that would be truly ironic if he detonated a mine inadvertently. That was one headline he was keen to avoid.

The Land Rover picked up speed as it ran down the incline back towards the harbour bypassing the town. He pressed the brakes to slow it down.

Nothing!

The large brake pedal pushed straight to the floor with a loud clash, hitting the unyielding metal of the floor beneath. What the hell was going on? The brakes had been fine as he had negotiated his way through the outskirts of the town. Please, not now! He looked ahead down the incline where the sharp 90 degree turn in the harbour road was picked out by the lights from a dockside gantry. Beyond, the road snaked off to the right towards the iron bridge and disappeared into the darkness. Slightly right of the bend along the edge of the harbour were the two commercial jetties belonging to FIPASS. Moored alongside were a few small ships ready to unload in the morning picked out clearly by the bright arc lights. There would be no refuge there with the jetties littered with equipment. It would be impassable at speed and the Land Rover was accelerating rapidly making a collision even more likely. He needed boggy ground to slow the crazy progress of the vehicle and his head swivelled on gimbals looking for solutions. There was no joy either side of the road as the truck would accelerate just as easily across the hard packed earth as it would over the pitted surface of the road. He didn't fancy his chances if he collided with any of the buildings which edged the narrow highway and any attempt to roll the truck guaranteed oblivion and, without doubt, he would be crushed by the framework of the cab. His indecision, unusual for a fighter pilot, sealed his fate. He decided to take his chances in the water which glowed dully in the reflected glare of the arc lights and hoped that the banks didn't drop off too steeply along the edge of the harbour. As the truck hit the water he would make his escape through the window if necessary. Pushing forward on the window panel it slid open, allowing the cold night air to rush into the cab giving an even greater sense of the unsustainable momentum. Why he did not consider using the large handbrake that would have given him at least a small amount of mechanical braking would remain an unsolved mystery. As he prepared himself for the onslaught, anticipating the rush of cold water through the window, he picked a point and aimed the steering. The thought of a cold swim back to shore didn't fill him with enthusiasm.

With his plan decided he reached down with his left hand to release the seatbelt which locked him securely into the seat. He cursed, frustrated with his vain fumbling and switched hands trying to free the stubborn fastener. It refused to move and, as he pressed the red button ever more urgently, he could see the bend approaching rapidly in the darkness. The buckle stayed doggedly attached. He switched hands yet again and struck the fastener hard, more in annoyance than with any hope of success. It still would not yield as he put his hands back on the wheel. Looking ahead, the bend in the road was rapidly approaching and the turn was impossible to negotiate at this speed. A short track disappeared from sight down a stretch of rough ground to the water's edge but it was off to the left. In desperation, he made yet another mistake as he yanked the wheel hard over, his vain attempt to negotiate the bend in the road upsetting the vehicle's equilibrium even further. The Land Rover bucked viciously, the front wheel digging in causing an instantaneous roll. The truck turned over rapidly a number of times, the iron fenders buckling under the strain and grinding against the concrete before plunging noisily into the dark cold waters of the harbour throwing up walls of water in its wake.

He would never know, but the brake lines had been cut as the truck had sat in the car park and the precious brake fluid had slowly leaked away as Carmendez had made his way eastwards. The seat belt buckle had been similarly neutered and it had been a professional job. The distance from the jail to the inlet had been calculated precisely and he was never intended to reach Boxer Bridge because his route away from the jail had been meticulously orchestrated and the potential exits had been sealed to make his choice predictable. The run back down to the harbour was always intended to be his nemesis.

In Stanley Harbour the ripples quickly disappeared as the water closed over the open sided vehicle before the natural swell of the waves, lapping ashore, took over once again. Beneath the surface there was no sign of an attempt to escape from the crushed cab and a solitary stream of bubbles was the only indication that the surface had been disturbed so recently. Only a single rubber skid mark would identify the scene but the insignificant smudge was lost on the occupants of a military Land Rover which minutes later passed over the bridge heading into town, its blue light flashing urgently. The military policemen inside had been called out to assist the local police with finding the fugitive who had already been missed. No one thought to question why the break out had been discovered so quickly given that the jail had been secured for the night. The mystery caller was not about to offer up why he thought the fugitive was armed and dangerous. As the Land Rover sped past the jetty the driver could have no idea that he had just passed as close to their quarry as they ever would.

CHAPTER 53

THE COASTEL ACCOMMODATION BARGE, PORT STANLEY HARBOUR

A group of aircrew clustered around the bar in the Coastel engaged in animated conversation. What should have been a raucous celebration was somewhat muted even though the Squadron had just achieved its first kill in a live air-to-air engagement. The stories had been flowing since the jets landed and some had already been embellished to enhance kudos. With more beer came less inhibitions and, inevitably, as the hands flashed in mock combat, replaying the engagement for the benefit of the eager onlookers, the stories were amplified.

Later, when the bravado was over, there would be quiet regrets. The Argentinian Skyhawk pilot had, in spite of everything, penetrated the defensive screen and had been able to release his bombs without being engaged by the fighters. Innocent people had died unnecessarily and the crews who had been involved somehow felt responsible. They hadn't squeezed the trigger that had released the bombs nor had they been lax in prosecuting their attacks. Everyone had done their best but, even so, they hadn't prevented the carnage. The Rapier engagement that had prevented the attacker making his escape, had come post-target when the damage was already done. A sense of failure was lurking just beneath the surface and there would be some heart-searching debriefings over the coming days in an attempt to work out why the Skyhawk had made it all the way through each layer of defence unscathed. It had been detected by the picquet ship but the missiles which might have brought it down had not been launched.

It had flown close by the air defence radar unit at Mount Alice without being engaged by the shoulder-launched missiles that were positioned at the site for that very eventuality. For their own part, If the Phantoms had been able to press home the attack over East Falkland, the Skyhawk might have been downed before it reached its target rather than after it had wreaked havoc. Why hadn't the Phantom crews operated in closer harmony with the Rapiers as the Skyhawk further penetrated the defensive screen? The Mirage had been an unwelcome confusion factor and, that it had been dispatched by the Argentinians for a common purpose, was a bitter-sweet irony. Both the Mirage pilot and his British counterparts had been tasked to destroy the Skyhawk but neither of the adversaries had been aware. That they had fallen over each other in their attempts to engage had worked in the Skyhawk pilot's favour. While they fought, he had sneaked past and hit his target at Heritage Hall. So far, there was no public sympathy for the fate of Lt Hernandez the Mirage pilot and his body which had washed ashore that morning would be repatriated quietly and without fuss or protest. Although chivalry in the air was long gone, there would be quiet contemplation later from his fellow aviators on both sides of the divide and empathy in crewrooms in both countries saddened by a common loss. In the meantime he had been a pawn in a costly show of force. There were so many questions but the debrief would take months and the lessons were for others to decide and act upon.

One pilot was withdrawn and reluctant to join in the boisterous celebrations. Razor swilled his beer around his glass, aimlessly, having learned of Karen's fate in the attack on the bus. His debrief with the Boss had been tense. No amount of platitudes from his mates could make him feel better and, above all, he had let down his navigator. The criticism had been unvoiced but, under these circumstances, the Squadron's first air-to-air kill should not have been the Electrone. His ham-fisted overstress had taken them out of the fight at a critical moment and the Skyhawk had avoided engagement. But for the intervention of the Rapier it might have made it back to the mainland and the outcome would have been a lot different. The conversation with the winchman had been unexpected and had stunned him. Unaware of his personal connection, the descriptions had been graphic and frank leaving nothing to his imagination. His impromptu decision to visit the site of the attack had, on reflection, been ill advised. The scene of devastation had been truly horrific and frantic attempts to bring order from the chaos were thwarted by the fact that it was a crime scene. The effect of high explosive incendiary rounds on the thin skin of the bus had been deeply shocking and he knew, instantly, why he never revelled in the effects of his trade. The crime scene tape stretching around the perimeter of the crash site had prevented him seeing the true carnage inside the shattered hulk and, for that, he suspected that he should be grateful. He was not sure what he had expected to achieve wandering around the perimeter. Was it closure of sorts? Karen had died and there was nothing that he could do to change that inevitable outcome. Stumbling across her notebook lost in the peat bog at the site had been the last thing he had expected and its contents had proved disturbing. Leafing through the tightly packed notes, the memories had been raw and he could still see her face. Mostly, the notes captured the routine trivia of a visit cut short, violently, but there was one section which piqued his interest. Who was Sullivan and, more importantly, where was he? The cryptic notes about a telephone conversation in Government House hinted at more than routine. One particular note was truly chilling:

"back-handers?"

He was not sure how to follow it up, with whom, or whether it was even a good idea. Karen obviously intended to do so but she was trained as an investigative journalist. Maybe she deserved his help? It was after all her only legacy; certainly from this fateful trip. Maybe her editor would know how to follow the cryptic leads? He tucked the charred book safely back in his flying suit pocket and swilled the beer around in his glass, contemplating.

With his bachelor's lifestyle that he had protected for so many years he had almost resigned himself to remaining single with its obvious charms. The brief and unexpected encounter had stirred longings which were not only a surprise but had been welcome. With momentous events consigning any such thoughts to the bin, he would park his emotions where they needed to stay and get back to flying. Any such ideas would have to remain unrequited for some time to come.

As another taunt from the Rapier squadron commander was launched at a hapless Phantom pilot, and a quick-fire retort was returned, Razor could only wonder what might have been.

CHAPTER 54

GOVERNMENT HOUSE, PORT STANLEY

In his office in Government House, the new Governor looked down at the headline in The Penguin News:

"Maverick pilot missing after break-out from Port Stanley jail."

And another:

"Vehicle crashes into Stanley Harbour, driver missing."

What had he inherited? Recent events had been extraordinary by any standards. Admittedly, in his time in the Diplomatic Corps he had witnessed some peculiar situations but the reality of this case was astounding. A Government Minister had been attacked by a combat aircraft of a foreign Nation on home soil. The former Governor's aide was missing in an area barely the size of an English county and a goodwill visit had been brutally disrupted with the perpetrator now missing. His staffer Warren Baird was an odd character even by MI6 standards and he was still not sure he had fully understood his parting shot as he had made his way to the car waiting to take him to the airport terminal. The shadowy First Secretary seemed careful with his words and his remark that "at least the loose ends are tied up" needed more thought. He would demand a full briefing on his return. He wanted to know everything that went on in this small Dependency if he was to exercise proper control. He threw the newspaper down onto the desk wondering whether the headlines were somehow connected. Only time would tell.

The call he had made earlier to the Argentinian Defence Minister had not gone well and that should have been the easiest aspect of the whole sorry mess. The pompous man had begun by expressing outrage at the loss of life on the tourist bus when it had been meted out by his own countryman. The counter argument which the Governor had patiently delivered had, initially, barely calmed the irate politician but the suggestion that contrition might be a more appropriate response than outrage had been eventually, albeit grudgingly, acknowledged. As Carmendez's involvement and his disappearance had been teased out, the conversation had become almost conspiratorial. He suspected that an accommodation would be forthcoming. What made him smile was that Argentina was about to receive a diplomatic protest via the United Nations that would prove far more effective than his own entreaty.

"Heather, get me the British Ambassador in Buenos Aires please."

He turned to page three of the Penguin Times and idly leafed through the sparse details of the attack as he waited for the call to be connected. The pictures really were horrific. His new aide had briefed him on events and he would monitor the progress carefully. One of his first priorities would be to visit the sites of the attacks to show his solidarity. Hopefully, that would offer a few photo opportunities to lift the grim mood. The search for the missing aide was going slowly and little had been learned. His whereabouts were still unknown and his abandoned vehicle had raised more questions than answers. He could envisage the local reporter who would be, frantically, digging for more information to pad out the stories, keen to feed the frenzy whipped up by countless international journalists who had kept her phone off the hook for the last few hours. It was a change for her to be so popular. After last night's freak accident, the recovery operation to lift the vehicle from the harbour was underway made easier by the fact that the huge cranes alongside jetty were located very close to the site of the crash. Luckily a security guard at the FIPASS dock had seen the Land Rover go into the water and had sounded the alarm. Attempts to locate the driver had so far failed and there was confusion amongst the hierarchy at RAF Stanley as to how the vehicle had found its way into town or who was driving. No one had so far been reported as absent. He was not surprised, nor he suspected were they in reality. One of his first warnings had been to guard his keys carefully even though his own distinctive form of transport should be safe. It was never a good idea to leave the keys in the ignition as vehicles were too easily "liberated" by troops eager to make use of any available transport and avoid the long walk into town. Divers were going down to inspect the wreck this morning and he was hopeful that the mystery would be quickly resolved. He wondered if, somehow, these events might be linked? He suspected the local newspaper would return to quiet obscurity quite soon once things died down.

The ring of the phone broke his chain of thought as he picked up the handset from the cradle and waited for the connection.

"Sir John, it's Julian Soames in Port Stanley . . . . . Yes thank you, I'm settling in very well. It's a little different to Vienna but charming in its own way . . . . . You will want to know, I've just spoken to the Chief Executive of the Islands Legislative Council. They have taken a ballot and it's unequivocal. Absolutely no interest in any type of accommodation over Sovereignty. None at all."

He paused again.

"No, no, you're right of course and I know the former Governor had a different view but recent events have polarised opinion over here. I think we can be assured that poor Sir Ronald will take some time to recover from his injuries. I'm afraid we must assume that he will not be back to the islands in the foreseeable future so we must move ahead. I've been warned I'm here for the duration. Yes, yes, London are completely onboard."

There was a further pause as he listened keenly to the other diplomat shaking his head, imperceptibly.

"They have already agreed to a new Constitution for the Islands which will be published by the Legislative Council very soon. It's quite clear, and this attack by the Argentinian aircraft has brought it to a head. The Islands stay British while ever there are Kelpers on this soil."

He nodded in response to another comment.

"No, I've told The Foreign Office. I'm sure they'll contact you with a line to take. I just wanted you to hear the decision first hand. Your task will be hard enough without having to second guess. Best wishes from here and I hope the meeting with the Argentinian Foreign Minister isn't too bloody!"

He replaced the telephone in its cradle and smiled. There was a new imperative to Island politics and he was very happy to be the champion.

AUTHOR'S NOTE

After a bloody conflict and regrettable loss of life, Argentinian forces surrendered at dawn on 14 June 1982 and 2 Para were the first unit to march into Stanley to the rapturous cheers of the islanders. Peace returned, although with nearly 1500 troops stationed on the islands, normality would never be quite the same. The first garrison at the airfield at Port Stanley was replaced by newly built facilities at Mount Pleasant and Mare Harbour. Once the service personnel moved out, the islands settled down to a new routine. The islanders had their say on their future when they answered a question set in a referendum, delivering their verdict on 12 March 2013. They were asked *"Do you wish the Falkland Islands to retain their current political status as an Overseas Territory of the United Kingdom? YES or NO?"* The answer was an unequivocal yes with an incredible 91% turnout of those qualified to vote exercising their right. Of the 1517 votes cast only 3 voted No. Hopefully politicians will heed the will of the inhabitants.

The events and characters described in the book are entirely fictional. No attack against Port Stanley occurred after the Falklands War nor is there any suggestion that it was mooted. The description of the way the Phantom operated is as accurate as I can recall, although time may have dulled a few details. The action in the Prologue and the descriptions of the action in South Georgia are, however, based on real events. Other places and incidents are not historically accurate. Heritage Hall in Port Stanley did not exist although the Town Hall did act as a courtroom. The first visit by Argentinian families to the cemetery in East Falklands was not until 1991 and took place many years after the fictional events in the book were set. Clearly, the attack on the bus is fiction as history also attests. The Electrone probed the islands defences for many years listening carefully to all the transmissions of the British forces and recording the information for later analysis back in Argentina. It went about its business largely unmolested until it was retired from service and is now on display at the Argentinian Navy Museum of Aviation at Bahia Blanca in Buenos Aires province.

Thousands of personnel from all three services have made the islands their temporary home over the years since Liberation. They have been welcomed by the islanders and have added to the rich history of the community in their own way despite their sometimes rowdy presence. What must never be forgotten is that, during the war, some local civilians also made the ultimate sacrifice defending that way of life. They were laid to rest alongside military colleagues in the ground they fought bravely to liberate.

Lest We Forget.

GLOSSARY

AGI. An intelligence gathering ship which monitors exercises and operations.

Anchor. Establish a combat air patrol in the nominated position.

Avtur. Aviation jet fuel.

Beta lights. The small iridescent marker lights set into the canvas rim of an air-to-air refuelling basket.

Blue-on-blue. An engagement against a friendly target.

Bonedome. Slang for flying helmet.

Bullseye. A reference point nominated by a control agency to give a reporting datum from which contacts can be called.

Cara Cara. The callsign of the air defence radar unit on Mount Alice.

CRT. Cathode Ray Tube usually used as a display for a radar warning receiver.

Charlie 4, 4 Plus, 8, Tiger Fast 60. A code used to indicate weapon state for a Phantom. Charlie denotes 2 external wing tanks, 4 Skyflash missiles, 4 Sidewinders and a gun. With the advent of AIM-9L an additional number was added after "plus" to indicate how many missiles were all-aspect capable. In this case, the Phantom would be carrying AIM-9Ls.

Chicken. A fuel call meaning I am down to diversion fuel.

Dark Area. The area called the height hole, close to a radar site within which the radar operator cannot see an airborne target.

DOF. Duty Officer Flying. An aircrew supervisor available to offer specialist advice to ATC controllers and to set the recovery state.

ELINT. Electronic intelligence.

Fat Albert. A nickname for the C-130 Hercules sometimes shortened to Albert.

FIGAS. Falkland Islands General Aviation Service.

FIPASS. Floating Interim Port and Storage System.

FIPZ. Falkland Islands Protection Zone. A 200 mile ring around the islands declared as protected airspace.

Fox. To take a weapon shot. Fox 1 denotes a Skyflash, Fox 2 a Sidewinder and Fox 3 a gun shot.

GCI. Ground Controlled Interception.

HAS. Hardened aircraft shelter.

Heads up. I am unable to prosecute the intercept.

HEI. High explosive incendiary cannon shells.

IFF Identification friend or foe. An electronic identification system.

ILS. The Instrument Landing System. An onboard electronic runway approach aid.

INAS. Inertial Navigation and Attack System.

Initials. A visual entry point on the runway extended centreline at 5 miles. Most visual approaches begin at initials.

ISO containers. Standard metal shipping containers.

Lindholme gear. Multi seat life rafts which can be air-dropped by transport or maritime patrol aircraft.

"Loadie." Air Loadmaster responsible for the cargo and passengers in the hold of a transport aircraft.

MANPAD. Man portable air defence system. A lightweight surface-to-air missile such as a Stinger.

Max Mil. Abbreviation for maximum military power. Full dry power without selecting reheat.

Measles or Exercise Measles. Tracking exercise for missile operators. Fast jets fly simulated attacks against the radar sites for training purposes.

MEZ. Missile engagement zone.

MPA. Mount Pleasant Airfield.

NCO. Non commissioned officer.

NOTAM. Notices to Airmen which publish exercises and items of interest to aircrew which might affect navigation.

On speed. The calculated final approach speed taking into account the remaining fuel.

Orbat. Order of Battle.

Pickle weapons. To pull the trigger releasing the weapons.

Pipper. The gunsight aiming marker used for weapon aiming.

Poster. The officer responsible for an officer's career and allocating the next tour of duty.

Puffin. The callsign for the air defence radar unit on Mount Kent.

QFE. A pressure setting for the altimeter which, when set, reads height above the runway threshold.

QFI. Qualified Flying Instructor. The specialist instructor on a squadron adept at teaching flying skills specific to the operational aircraft.

QNH. A pressure setting for the altimeter which, when set, reads height above sea level.

QRA. Quick Reaction Alert.

Rackets. A codeword for a radar warning receiver alert.

Radalt. Radio Altimeter which uses radio waves to measure height rather than barometric pressure.

R and R. Rest and rehabilitation (or relaxation).

RPG. Rocket propelled grenade launcher.

Rubs. Temporary hangars made from a rubberised material drawn over a steel frame.

RWR. Radar warning receiver.

RTB. Return to base.

SAROPS. Search and rescue operations.

Sitrep. Situation report. A verbal summary of the tactical situation.

Squawk. To transmit a code on the Identification Friend or Foe system.

Stud. A preset frequency on the radio box

TACEVAL. Tactical Evaluation Exercise. A NATO-sponsored operational evaluation of a unit's capability.

TAD. Tactical Air Direction frequency.

"Tally." Short for "Tally Ho" a codeword for visual contact with a hostile target.

UHF. Ultra High Frequency. A frequency band used by military aircraft for communications.

USAFE. United States Air Force in Europe.

Visident. A visual identification. A radar controlled procedure to join in close formation on a target in bad weather or at night.

Weapons free. Authority to engage delegated to lower levels of command. Hostile targets could be engaged.

Zulu. A code for use on the radio signifying that the aircraft is unserviceable.

ABOUT THE AUTHOR

David Gledhill is an aviation enthusiast and aviator. Already holding a private pilot's licence at the age of 17, he was commissioned in the RAF in 1974, and after training as an air navigator, converted to the F4 Phantom in the Air Defence role. After tours in the UK and Germany, he went on to be a radar tactics instructor on the Operational Conversion Unit. After transferring to the new Tornado F2 as one of the first instructors, he eventually became the Executive Officer on the OCU. His flying career finished in the Falkland Islands where he commanded No 1435 Flight flying the Tornado F3. During his later career he served as a staff officer in the UK Ministry of Defence and the Air Warfare Centre. He also served on exchange duties at the Joint Command and Control Center and the US. Air Force Warfare Center in the United States of America and as the Senior Operations Officer at the Balkans Combined Air Operations Centre.

OTHER BOOKS BY THE AUTHOR

"The Phantom in Focus: A Navigator's Eye on Britain's Cold War Warrior" - ISBN 978-178155-048-9 (print) and 978-178155-204-9 (e-book) published by Fonthill Media.

"Fighters Over The Falklands – Defending the islanders Way of Life" - ISBN 978-178155-222-3 (print), also in e-book format published by Fonthill Media.

"Tornado F3 – A Navigator's Eye on Britain's Last Interceptor" - ISBN 978-178155-307-7 (print) published by Fonthill Media.

"Tornado In Pictures - The Multi Role Legend" (print) published by Fonthill Media.

"Deception" will be released in 2015 on Amazon Kindle.

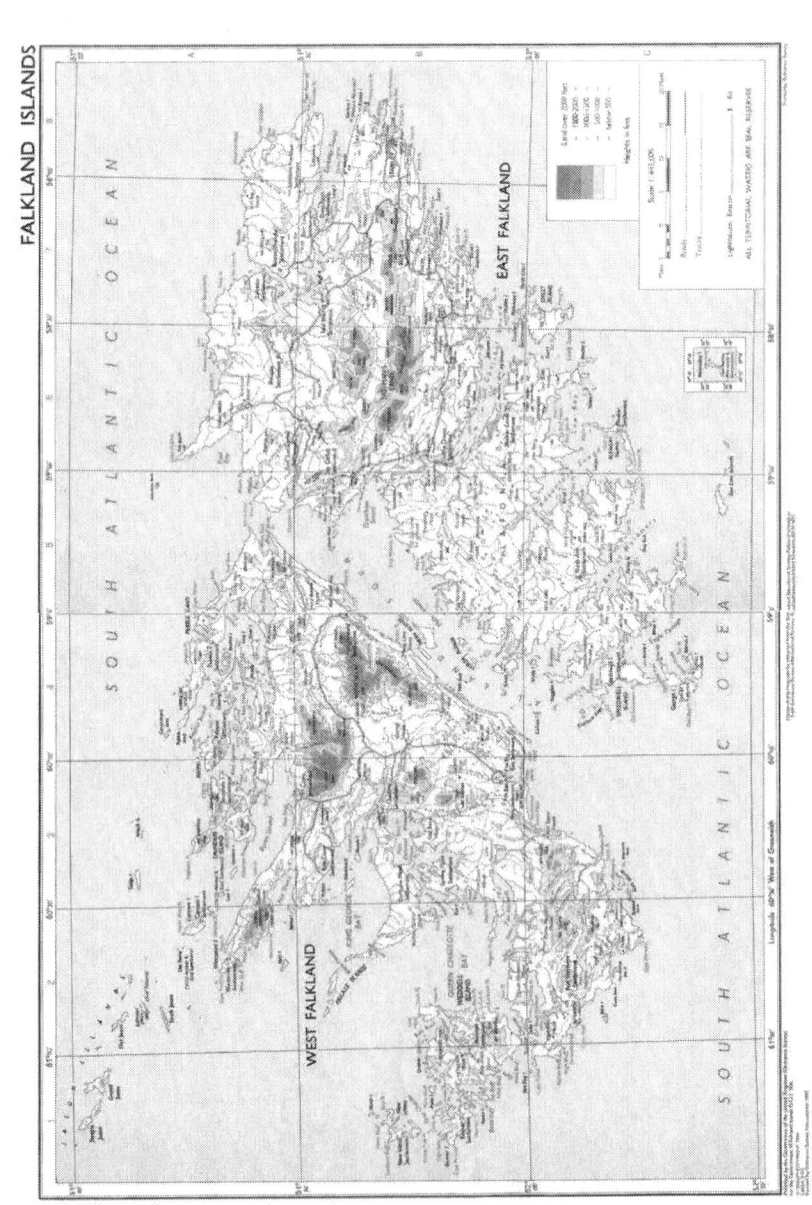

© Crown Copyright 1995

MAVERICK

Stanley Airfield

Printed in Great Britain
by Amazon